CROWN
OF
CRIMSON

UNDERWORLD GODS #2

KARINA HALLE
NEW YORK TIMES BESTSELLING AUTHOR

Copyright © 2022 by Karina Halle
All rights reserved.
No part of this book may be reproduced in any form or by any electronic or mechanical means, including information storage and retrieval systems, without written permission from the author, except for the use of brief quotations in a book review.
Edited by: Laura Helseth
Proofed by: Chanpreet Singh
Cover design: Hang Le
Cover model & photographer: Renee Carlino
Mask by: Xanti at Tuahadedana
Formatting by: Books & Moods

CONTENT WARNING

Crown of Crimson is the sequel to River of Shadows and book #2 in the Underworld Gods series. It can't be read as a standalone and must be read in order.

This book contains some scenes which might be triggering, including death of a creature, sexual assault, violence, MMF, and of course graphic sex scenes and coarse language.

PLAYLIST

Scan the code

You can find the spotify playlist to Crown of Crimson on Spotify.
Otherwise, here are a few songs that kept me writing:

"Stockholm Syndrome" - Muse
"Lost" - Rezz
"I am not a woman, I'm a God" - Halsey
"Goddess" - Banks
"Welcome Oblivion" - How to Destroy Angels
"This is a Trick" - +++ (Crosses)
"Knife Party" - Deftones
"Castle" - Halsey
"Loverman" -- Nick Cave & The Bad Seeds
"Find My Way" - Nine Inch Nails
"Born to Die" - Lana Del Rey
"So Below" - Bone
"How Long?" - How to Destroy Angels
"Parenthesis" - Tricky
"Mercy in You" - Depeche Mode
"In this Twilight" - Nine Inch Nails
"Apocalypse Please" - Muse
"Phantom Bride" - Deftones
"The Hand That Feeds" - Nine Inch Nails
"Edge" - Rezz

"Stripsearch" - Faith No More
"Heathen Child" - Grinderman
"In Chains" - Depeche Mode
"Bitches Brew" - +++ (Crosses)
"Various Methods of Escape" - Nine Inch Nails
"Do You Love Me?" - Nick Cave & The Bad Seeds
"Nothing Matters" - Tricky
"Sour Times" - Portishead
"Life & Death" - Rezz
"Corrupt" - Depeche Mode
"Violent Little Things" - Purple Hearse
"All the Good Girls Go to Hell" - Billie Eilish
"Dark Paradise" - Lana Del Rey
"World in Your Eyes" - Depeche Mode
"Blood in the Cut" - K. Flay
"Witching Hour" - Rezz
"Wish" - Nine Inch Nails
"Oxytocin" - Billie Eilish
"Passenger" - Deftones
"Gatekeeper" - Torri Wolf
"The Line Begins to Blur" - Nine Inch Nails
"Young God" - Halsey
"Angel" - Massive Attack
"Hostage" - Billie Eilish
"Gods & Monsters" - Lana Del Rey
"Butterflies and Hurricanes" - Muse
"The Space In Between" - How to Destroy Angels
"Beside You in Time" - Nine Inch Nails

GLOSSARY AND PRONOUNCIATION

Tuonela (too-oh-nella)
Realm or Land of the Dead. It is a large island that floats between worlds, with varied geography and terrain. The recently deceased travel via the River of Shadows to the City of Death where they are divided into factions (Amaranthus, the Golden Mean, and Inmost) and admitted into the afterlife. Outside the City of Death, Gods, Goddesses, spirits, shamans, and the dead who have escaped the city can be found.

Tuoni (too-oh-nee)
The God of Death, otherwise called Death, and King of Tuonela who rules over the realm from his castle at Shadow's End.

Louhi (low-hee)
Ex-wife of Death's, former Goddess, half-demon daughter of Rangaista.

Loviatar (low-vee-ah-tar)
The Lesser Goddess of Death and Death's Daughter. Her job is to ferry the dead down the River of Shadows to the City of Death, a role she shares with her brother Tuonen.

Tuonen (too-oh-nen)
The Lesser God of Death and Death's Son. He shares ferrying duties with his sister Loviatar. Tuonen is also a lord in the City of

Death and helps oversee things in the afterlife.

Sarvi (sar-vih)
Short for Yksisarvinen, Sarvi is a relic from the times of the Old Gods and originally from another world. Sarvi is a unicorn with bat-like wings that died a long time ago and is composed of skin and bone. Sentient, Sarvi is able to communicate telepathically. While he is a loyal and refined servant to Death, he is also vicious, violent and bloodthirsty by nature, as all unicorns are.

Ilmarinen (ill-mar-ee-nen)
Louhi's consort, the demigod shaman whom she left Death for. He lives with Louhi in their castle by the Star Swamps.

Eero (ay-ro)
A powerful shaman from Northern Finland.

Väinämöinen (vah-ee-nah-moy-nen)
Death's past adversary and legendary shaman who became a Finnish folk-hero. Väinämöinen has supposedly been dead for centuries.

Ukko (oo-koh)
A supreme God and the father of Tuoni, Ahto, Ilmatar, husband to Akka.

Akka (ah-ka)
A supreme Goddess, wife to Ukko, and the mother of Tuoni, Ahto, Ilmatar.

Ilmatar (ill-mah-tar)
Goddess of the Air, sister to Tuoni and Ahto.

Vellamo (vell-ah-mo)
Goddess of the Deep, wife of Ahto. Protector of mermaids. Vellamo

can be found in the Great Inland Sea.

Ahto (ah-to)
God of the Oceans and Seas, husband of Vellamo, brother of Tuoni & Ilmatar.

Kuutar (koo-tar)
Goddess of the Moon, Mother of Stars, protector of sea creatures.

Päivätär (pah-ee-vah-tar)
Goddess of the Sun, protector of birds.

Kalma (kahl-ma)
God of Graves and Tuoni's right-hand man and advisor.

Surma (soor-mah)
A relic from the days of the Old Gods and the personification of killing.

Raila (ray-lah)
Hanna's personal Deadmaiden.

Pyry (pee-ree)
Deadmaiden. Head cook and gardener of Shadow's End.

Harma (har-mah)
Deadmaiden. Head of the Shadow's End servants.

Tapio (tah-pee-oh)
God of the Forest.

Tellervo (tell-air-voh)
Lesser Goddess of the Forest and daughter of Tapio.

Hiisi (hee-si)
Demons and goblins of Tuonela, spawns of Rangaista.

Rangaista (ran-gais-tah)
A powerful demon and Old God, father of Louhi.

Liekkiö (lehk-kio)
The spirits of murdered children who haunt the Leikkio Plains. They are made of bones and burn eternally.

Vipunen (vee-pooh-nen)
An unseen giant who lives in the Caves of Vipunen near Shadow's End. The most ancient and wise being in Tuonela from before the time of the Old Gods.

*For my brother Kristian—
until we meet again*

PROLOGUE

DEATH
THE CAVES OF VIPUNEN

"Have you gotten cold feet?" the deep voice of reckoning booms across the walls of the cave.

"That's a rather modern phrase for someone so old," I respond, adjusting the blind mask. I wish I didn't have to wear this ridiculous thing every time I sought out the giant, but because I can see in the dark, Antero Vipunen takes no chances. They say there's no way to kill the God of Death, but there is and he's in the cave with me. Sometimes I think that Vipunen's power rivals that of the Creator, and he could destroy this whole world if he wanted to.

As such, I wear the blind mask so I don't piss him off. Part of me feels bad that both my children had to train in combat with him, wearing this heavy bronze and iron mask the entire time while wielding the sword. But at least they're the finest warriors now.

I also used to think that there would be no day where their

training would be put to use, but I feel that day creeping ever closer, like the snakes do if you stay too long in the crypt.

"Then what is it that has you seeking my counsel again?" Vipunen asks, louder now. In the background I can hear stalactites falling from the ceiling and crashing onto the cave floor, splashing into the underground lake. As it always happens when I'm in the caves, I'm brought back in my mind, eons past, to when I was just a young little shit, thrown here on my first day on the job as God of Death. I felt so vulnerable—naked and helpless then—and I despise the fact that today I feel the same.

It's a most unbecoming feeling.

"It's the girl," I tell him.

"The mortal, Hanna," Vipunen says. "Is there a problem?"

I let out a breath. Fuck. I hate how uneasy I feel. "I have some fears about the marriage."

Vipunen lets out a low, rumbling laugh. More stalactites fall to the ground, one sounding too close for comfort. "Fears about marriage? Did you not learn your lesson the last time?"

He can't see the *fuck you* smile on my face, but I hope he hears it in my tone. "Apparently not. I'm concerned that she may not be the one you prophesied about. Any chance you could, you know, clear that up a little bit? Give me something a little more to go on?"

Instead of being so fucking annoyingly vague from day one?

"To give you more information would be to interfere with your life and the natural order of things, and that I cannot do," he says.

"Cannot or will not?" I ask.

A cold blast of air comes rushing at me. I'm not the only one who can influence the weather and temperature with my moods. "You dare have contempt for me?" he bellows.

"No contempt, Antero, only frustration."

"Is it not your wedding day?" he asks after a moment.

"Yes, in fact she might be at the altar right now."

"Then you're cutting things a little close, don't you think?"

I sigh, adjusting the mask again. "I'm not asking if she's the one, or the chosen one, I just need to know if I'm making a mistake. What if I marry Hanna and the one I'm supposed to be with, the one that is supposed to save my kingdom, comes along?"

Another laugh. "You think that another mortal girl will come strolling along into Tuonela like that?"

"So then Hanna is the one…" I surmise, trying to bait him.

"I will tell you no such thing. This has nothing to do with me. This is your future, Tuoni, laid out in front of you. You either take it or you don't." He pauses. "You really do have cold feet, don't you? You want a way out. An easy way out. Well, no one told you to propose."

He's right. That was all my own doing.

I just couldn't help it.

After what happened with Surma, everything changed. Hearing his intentions, him working for the Old Gods, it made me realize that the uprising wasn't just a rumor. It was real and at our doorstep. I needed to do something about it, and quickly. I needed to marry Hanna in hopes that an alliance somewhere would form. Perhaps just the act of marriage itself, signaling to Louhi that I have moved on, that she is no longer the Goddess of Death, would do it, or telling the realm that I am part of a unit again would make them fall in line. Either way, it was time to act.

But then there was the surprising thing with Hanna herself.

I'd been so impressed by her, in awe of her, yet I did all I could to keep distance between us. The less distance, the less control I had. The more distance, the more my power remained firmly in check.

But when I saw Surma put his skeleton hands on her, I felt a protective beast rise up inside me, one I'd rarely felt before. I wanted to kill Surma more for that than for him being a traitor to the kingdom. I realized the lengths I would go to for her, and that scared me. Moved me.

As was the way she looked when I fucked her, when she was able to look at me, all of me, just as myself. No mask. No hiding behind anything. Just me, as I am. It's not that I didn't think she'd be enthralled, it's that I didn't think I'd feel so much warmth from her. Like she was baring herself to me at the same time, like she finally fucking trusted me.

And so, after spending all night thinking about her, about my future, about strategies, I realized the time was now. We had to get married, and maybe, if we were lucky, it would be something we both wanted.

CRASH

Suddenly a loud muffled noise comes from outside the cave, parts of the ceiling crashing down.

"What was that?" I yell, nearly falling over.

"Your keep is under attack," Vipunen says simply.

Another loud explosion rocks the ground beneath me and I press my gloved hands against my mask to hold it on.

"By who? Do you know?"

"By Louhi's son," he says.

My son? Tuonen? That doesn't make any sense, the boy's ambitions are ridiculously low. All he wants in life is to watch porn, ferry the dead, and be the referee for the Bone Matches.

"The shaman," Vipunen adds. "Rasmus."

My fist clenches. Fucking redheaded weasel. How the fuck is he attacking Shadow's End right now?

I turn to run out of the cave but the giant calls after me. "There is no use in hurrying," he says. "By the time you get there, it will be over. The attack can't do any major damage, it is only a diversion."

I come to a stop, my blood going cold. "A diversion for what?" I ask, even though I know the answer.

"Rasmus is here for Hanna," he says. "He is taking her with him."

It's like all the rage in the world starts to build inside my veins, growing tight and molten hot, ready for implosion. "Kidnapping *my* bride on *my* wedding day?" I grind out.

A pause hangs in the air, followed by a distant boom.

"She has not been kidnapped," Vipunen says after a moment. "She was given a choice. She chose to go willingly. She chose to leave you. On your wedding day." He adds that last part as if he has spite for me.

I still. My heart lurches against my ribs. The rage inside me ebbs and flows, changing and morphing. The anger goes from Rasmus, to myself, and then to Hanna.

Hanna.

"She left me," I say, practically stuttering. "She can't. That shouldn't be possible." Now my rage is directed to Vipunen. "If you knew this was going to happen, why didn't you tell me?"

"I can't affect what is already in motion."

"So what the fuck do I do now?"

My bride. My ex-wife's son has my fucking *bride*.

"I believe you know what to do, Tuoni. You do not need my counsel on that."

He is right. Hanna is mine, no one else's, whether she likes it or not. She entered into this bargain with me, and it was a fair trade. She offered herself up to me in countless ways, and I was a gentleman enough to not take her up on all of them. She is supposed to be with me, as my bride, for eternity, and she's gone back on her fucking word.

"I'm going to kill her," I seethe. "I'm going to cut her fucking wings right off."

"And if she doesn't die, it might mean she's the one," Vipunen says. "And you'll have to rule alongside her for the rest of your life, or face the end of your reign."

Fuck.

"Fuck!" I roar, throwing my head back, my yell echoing throughout the cave. I'm breathing hard, feeling my heartbeat in my head, and I just want to rage, rip this mask right off and break everything in this cave. But Vipunen would no doubt break me first.

So I have to live with the rage for a few moments. I have

to make friends with it. I have to let the red turn to black, let it settle in my bones.

And there, hidden underneath all the molten hot torment, is the source of my rage.

It's pain.

It's a dull ache in my ribs, right around my heart.

The same kind of ache I would get when I looked at her beautiful face as she came.

Oh, I ached for her. Craved her, possessed her, relished her when my cock was deep inside, when I felt she was no longer mortal but instead part of my skin and bones.

I ached for my little bird.

Now I break for her.

I swallow it down, welcoming the anger again. The anger I can deal with, the rage I can use. I just have to learn to control it so it doesn't get the better of me. I need to wield it like a weapon against the one who spurned me.

I need to make her suffer too.

"I'm getting her back," I growl, and start storming out of the darkness of the cave, using all my senses to find my way back to the light. "I'm getting her back and I'm making her pay. No one escapes Death, not even her."

Especially not her.

CHAPTER ONE

HANNA

"THE ESCAPE"

When I first got that phone call that my father was dead, my relationship with death suddenly materialized. Before, I hadn't given death much thought. I mean, who *really* does? Most of us go through life believing—hoping—that the one truth of life will never touch us. We bury that impending reality deep inside and live as if we, and the ones that we love, will live on forever. Death becomes something that happens to other people, but never to us.

For me, the news about my father snatched the ground out from under my feet. I felt betrayed by the world, like my reality shifted into something new, something horrible and unsure, and my place in it was no longer a given. I just couldn't trust life anymore. Leading up to the funeral, it was like walking on a tightrope, as if a single deviation would send betrayal to life itself, and if I wasn't careful, it would come for me too.

I started to hate death. With a passion. That unfairness and cruelty of it all. How dare he come for my father? How dare he come for any of us? All any of us want is to live, why can't that be enough?

Then I met Death.

Face-to-face.

No longer this impersonal, nebulous dark thing, but a physical being with thoughts and feelings and emotions.

A God.

And this God of Death? He made me fucking *laugh*.

He made my body feel things it's never felt before.

He awakened something inside of me, something I didn't know existed, something deep and primal, and to be honest, fucking terrifying. Like there's another version of myself that's been living in a parallel world, a thin veil between us, and for the first time she made herself known. She only gave me hints at what I might be capable of, who I really am, but it was enough to let me know I am so much more than what I've given myself credit for.

She made me feel *whole* for the first time in my life.

And now I feel like I'm leaving her behind, this better, more powerful version of myself that I didn't even have a chance to get to know.

And I'm leaving Death behind too.

I should be happy about this.

I know I'm doing the right thing.

The whole reason I ended up in Tuonela in the first place

was to rescue my father from death and I did that. I took his place, and while there was a chance I would never see him again, I still made plans to escape. I just expected it would take time. The last thing I expected was for Rasmus to get me on my wedding day—*today*—and set me free.

And now I've been given everything I wanted. I can see my father again, go back to my old life, my *real* life, in the Upper World, and return to the reality I belong in, not this land of death and decay.

Yet why do I feel like I'm doing something wrong?

Like this is some sort of mistake?

"Hold on!" Rasmus yells, his voice swallowed by the wind, seconds before we almost collide with a mountain.

Right. Perhaps it's natural to think everything is a mistake when you're riding a flying skeleton unicorn, high above the Realm of the Dead, during a supernatural magic storm.

I pinch my eyes shut, my arms around Rasmus gripping him tighter as the unicorn jerks upward seconds before we become a bloody pancake on the mountainside. I let out a scream that feels like it lasts forever, until suddenly we're leveling out again.

Sorry about that, a gruff voice says from inside my head, though it doesn't sound very sorry at all.

I open my eyes but I only see the dark purple mane of the unicorn flowing behind it like kelp, and the charcoal gray of the storm punctuated by the occasional flash of lightning. It feels like we've been flying for a long time, but perhaps it's only been minutes.

Who said that? I project inside my head, knowing my voice

wouldn't carry anyway.

"Hanna?" Rasmus asks, his voice faint despite being so close. "Are you talking to me?"

I forget that Rasmus can hear my thoughts sometimes. I think I've forgotten a lot of things about him since I've been held captive at Shadow's End.

So you can hear me? the gruff voice says again. *Been some time since any human could.*

Oh hell. I'm speaking with the unicorn, aren't I? It wasn't just Sarvi I was able to communicate with telepathically. Apparently, I can communicate with all of them.

My mind goes blank. I can't really think of a response, either to Rasmus or the unicorn as another mountain peak comes rushing toward us through the clouds, changing from a vague shadow to a solid threat. The unicorn veers up just in time, flapping its wings furiously, and I'm hanging onto Rasmus's jacket for dear life.

Sorry again, the unicorn says. *I'm not used to flying over the Mountains of Vipunen. If you could get your shaman to quell the storm, that would help immensely. Otherwise, the lot of us are going straight to Oblivion.*

"Rasmus!" I lean forward and yell in his ear. "Turn off the fucking storm! The unicorn is having problems."

Navigating, the unicorn fills in. *I'm having problems navigating. And the name is Alku.*

Hanna, I introduce myself, just before Alku nearly flattens us into yet another dark mountain peak and I scream again.

"I'm getting so fucking confused," Rasmus mumbles.

"The unicorn is talking to me!" I yell at him. "Inside my

head. Just like I'm able to communicate with Sarvi."

"You can talk to *Sarvi*?" Rasmus says with a hint of jealousy.

You know Sarvi? Alku asks, its gruff voice growing lighter this time.

"Yes," I say hastily. "Look, Rasmus, you said you created this storm as a diversion in order to get me out of Shadow's End, but I think we're far enough away."

"Fine," Rasmus says after a moment. Suddenly his body goes stiff under my grip and my scalp prickles as a buzzing field of energy seems to envelop us, making me vibrate from the inside out. The feeling is so similar to one I had when I picked up Lovia's sword.

It's magic.

Suddenly the winds die down to a gentle breeze, the lightning stops flashing, the thunder fades. Even the ever-present clouds start to dissipate, just enough to lighten the sky to a dove gray.

In the sudden calm, I'm not thinking about the ragged black peaks of the mountains appearing mere meters below us like gnashing teeth, nor the telepathically talking unicorn, or the fact that I have my arms wrapped around a person that I can only hope is still trustworthy.

I'm thinking about Tuoni.

Death.

The God himself.

I'm wondering what this weather means, the fact that the clouds are thinning enough for the sun to come through. His moods control the weather, and the land had been cloaked in relative darkness since he first started his reign.

Until the two of us grew closer.

It may have been only physical for the both of us, but it brought in a visible change to the kingdom—sunshine. Brightness and light.

Which means at this exact moment in time, Death is in a good mood.

Does Death still think I'm waiting for him at the altar? Is that why there's relative peace in the sky underneath Rasmus' spell?

My stomach twists at the thought. It shouldn't. I didn't want to marry Death. I didn't want to become his bride. And yet, part of me feels guilty for leaving this way. I wonder if he'll feel betrayed. If it will be more than a matter of defeat, of losing, if he cares that it's *me* that he lost.

You think too much, Alku's voice pops in my head. *It's distracting.*

"Sorry," I mutter.

Rasmus flinches, trying to crane his head around to look at me. "Mind filling me in what you're talking to my unicorn about?"

Alku snorts in protest. *His unicorn?* It asks in disgust. *I'm merely doing the shaman a favor. Starting to regret it, mind you.*

I press my lips together, holding back a smile. I'm so relieved that only Alku is picking up on my thoughts and Rasmus isn't anymore. The more he knew what I was thinking, the less he'd understand. I'm not even sure I understand it myself.

"I'm trying to figure out where we're going and what

your plan is," I say to Rasmus. "If you haven't noticed, I'm still wearing my wedding dress. You haven't filled me in on anything and we've nearly died twice over since you took me."

"Took you?" Rasmus repeats in annoyance. "I *saved* you, Hanna. You know, part of me is starting to think you'd rather have stayed Death's prisoner in Shadow's End, forced to be his bride."

Something inside me prickles. "I could have saved myself. I had a plan."

"Oh really? And what was that exactly? You were literally seconds away from becoming Death's bride. You'd be married right now had I not come in right on time."

I purse my lips and think that over for a minute as Alku's giant leathery wings beat rhythmically behind me. "How did you plan it that way? How did you know to create a diversion at the last possible minute?"

Since I'm behind him I can't see Rasmus' face, but his tone is light. "News travels fast in Tuonela. Your wedding day has been the talk of the realm for weeks now. I've been planning this for some time."

"You mean you've been in Tuonela this whole time?" I ask incredulously. "I would have thought you would have run all the way back home."

"I don't run away from things," he says stiffly, even though he ran like hell after Death let him, leaving me behind in the dust. "I hid. Strategically. I made alliances. I bided my time."

He's starting to sound like he's roleplaying in a new season of *Survivor*. "So you never went back to see my father? How do you know he's okay then?" Panic starts to work its way through me. All this time I assumed Rasmus went back and was keeping an eye on my father. "What about Eero? Noora? If he doesn't remember what happened, then he's completely vulnerable."

"He's fine," Rasmus says quickly. "Believe me. I may not have left Tuonela, but there are ways of keeping tabs. Your father is back at his cottage, he's still hidden by the cloaking spell."

"Yeah, but if he doesn't remember anything, he'll be back at the resort working, right? He's going to think Eero and Noora are his colleagues, his friends!"

Oh god, now he's really in danger, I think. *I think I'm going to be sick*. I peer down at the forests and snowy patches on the mountains. It's a long way down if I'm going to vomit.

"He's fine," Rasmus says again, his tone sharper this time, and it does nothing to quell my fear. "But the sooner we get you back to him, the better it will be. You just have to trust me on this."

In this exact moment, I don't think I trust anyone. I close my eyes, my heart sinking. "Why didn't you go back? Why did you wait for me?"

"Because," Rasmus says after a moment. "I had to."

We fly in silence for a while, my feelings all over the place. We soar over the mountains, then around the walled tower of the City of Death that pierces the highest clouds like a spear, and while part of me is still enraptured by the fact that I'm seeing this view of the Land of the Dead from a flying skeletal unicorn that can speak telepathically to me, my emotions are complicated.

All this time I had worried about my father and I was assured he was okay. Most of the assurances were from myself, having the aurora stone earrings that shine with his life energy, and thinking that if Rasmus were with him, he'd take care of him. After all, he often said that he was like a father to him. How could he just let him wander back to reality alone with the two people that tried to kill me?

A lightning strike suddenly slices the space in front of us, a burning electrical smell filling the air. Rasmus and I scream in unison, just as Alku lets out a snort of alarm. All at once, the mild weather disappears and gigantic black clouds come rolling toward us as if we're witnessing a storm on a time-lapse film.

"Rasmus!" I yell. "What are you doing?"

"I'm not doing anything!" he yells back as the storm gets closer.

I don't think there's a way around it, Alku tells me. *But I'm going to try.*

Alku veers sharply to the left, toward a set of low mountains that seem miles and miles away, the dark billowing clouds spreading across the land as far as I can see. Below us the forest grows more and more sparse, the land flattening out into various steppes and plateaus. Lightning strikes the few trees strewn about, scorching them or setting them on fire.

If this isn't Rasmus' doing, then I know whose it is.

This is all Death.

He's just discovered that I've left.

So you're the cause of all of this? Alku muses, picking up on my thoughts. *Funny, you know I've noticed the weather turning for the better this last while. Guess that was you, too.*

I don't say anything. I don't need to. It doesn't really matter now, since Death is conjuring up a storm that could very well kill us.

Just as that thought crosses my mind, a bolt of lightning comes down so close that my bare arms feel singed.

"That was too close," Rasmus yells, his voice going high.

Tell the shaman that I'm doing all I can, Alku says. *Unless he wants to help out with his own magic, we're going to need a lot of luck until we can find some place to take cover.*

"Can we turn around and go back? Maybe hide in the City of Death?" I ask.

If you go in there as a mortal, the chances that you'll be found out are high. You won't come back out, Alku warns.

"Can you do anything, Rasmus?" I ask him.

He grows tense beneath my grip. "I'm trying. It takes a lot of concentration and…"

And I'm pretty sure his storm isn't a match for what Death can produce on sheer emotion alone. Then again, Rasmus has surprised me so far.

Hold on, Alku says.

I tighten my grip and we suddenly dive down toward the earth, until it looks like we're going to smash into the desert-like land. Then the unicorn veers suddenly and the ground gives way to a gaping gorge, a rushing black river hundreds of feet below.

"Oh fuck, the Gorge of Despair," Rasmus says. "We'll be sitting ducks in there."

Does he have a better idea? Alku asks snidely as we dive

deeper and deeper into the narrow canyon, leveling out just a few feet above the water. The rapids here are frothing, the water so dark that I get this awful feeling I'm staring into space, an abyss of nothing, or perhaps an entrance to an even worse world.

At least down here, we aren't lightning rods, Alku adds. It flaps its wings, causing the water to ripple as we soar over it.

I glance up at the sky, just a narrow slot of darkness now high above the canyon walls. We're going further into the storm but as long as we're flying along the bottom of the gorge, we should be okay.

I should hope so, Alku says. *If we can get as far as the Hiisi Forest without being hit by lightning, we can take shelter there. Wait it out.*

"Wait it out? For how long?"

Until the storm subsides.

"But Death is causing the storm. What if he's angry forever?"

Alku doesn't respond to that.

"This is because of Death," Rasmus comments gruffly. "Should have figured. Looks like you really did a number on him Hanna."

"You're the one who stole his bride right before his wedding!" I point out. "You think he wouldn't be pissed?"

"Again, I rescued you. I *saved* you. I didn't steal you. You came with me completely on your own accord. Perhaps it's your own fault that Death is that worked up. What did you do, make the God fall in love with you?"

I snort. "If by love, you mean go from wanting to kill and

torture me to not wanting to kill and torture me *as much*, then yes."

No way in hell am I mentioning anything else. Rasmus doesn't have to know just how close I willingly got to Death. My mind starts to go back to the last time we had sex, but I have to stop myself from getting too deep because the last thing I need is for Alku to pick up on that too.

"Look," I say to the both of them. "I'm all for hiding out from the storm, but I need to get back to my father. Each moment I'm here and he's in the Upper World, he's vulnerable. As am I."

You're going to have to take things as they come, dear, Alku says. *I'm not making any promises that we'll even get out of this alive.*

Great.

Even with Alku going insanely fast, it still feels like hours pass until the walls of the gorge begin to lower and trees appear in the distance, their crowns whipped by the wind. The river gets wider, the rapids calming, and then Alku is flying to the right, shooting into the forest. We go until its giant wings can't navigate around the cedars and narrow brush and we come to a sudden stop.

The movement throws both Rasmus and I off the unicorn's back and we go flying through the air, landing in a heap on the mossy ground.

I'm winded and barely able to catch my breath as Rasmus grabs my arm and tries to haul me to my feet. Though the trees are providing some protection from the storm, branches are falling down around us, the wind tearing through violently, and the air smells like an electrical burn.

"We need to take shelter," Rasmus yells over the din and leads me over to a fallen cedar that must be ten feet in diameter and a hundred feet long. The upturned roots curve over like an arch, providing some protection, and he pulls me down so we're sitting tucked away into the tree, as if we're sheltering at the mouth of a cave.

"Wait a minute," I cry out, searching the forest. "Where's Alku?"

One minute the unicorn was depositing us here, the next it's gone. We're completely alone in the forest.

"Maybe it was tired of doing me a favor," Rasmus mumbles. "At least it got us this far."

I glance at Rasmus, seeing his face for the first time since I left Shadow's End. He looks older somehow, his cheekbones more prominent, and there's something about his face that stirs something in me, some vague recognition, not of him but of someone else. He also looks wired, his eyes shining. The adrenaline must be pouring through him.

"Well, now what?" I ask him.

He shrugs and opens his mouth to say something.

But before he can say a word, I'm suddenly grabbed from behind by pairs of hard, skeleton hands, and yanked down a hole into total darkness.

CHAPTER TWO

DEATH

"THE BETRAYAL"

Shadow's End has seen better days.

Vipunen said the damage would be superficial, but it's not from where I'm standing, at the foot of the entrance to the cave with all of Shadow's End before me, the castle stacked on top of the rocky outcrop like a set of iron knives.

Parts of the castle roof have caved in on some of the turrets, and a block of stones along the east wall has crumbled away into the sea, which is thrashing violently against the rocky shore. The wind here is sharp, the clouds unnatural. This isn't real weather and it's not of my doing.

This is all Rasmus.

How the fuck is that even possible? How could that redheaded skinny shit conjure up the power and the magic to do *this* to my castle?

And why the fuck did it take me this long to realize that he's Louhi's son?

I don't know how long I stand there for, like a fucking idiot, staring at my home, my castle, my land, and stewing in self-loathing and hindered by inaction, but suddenly there's a black blot in the sky and in moments Sarvi is landing before me.

Sir, Sarvi says, flapping its wings as its cloven hooves reach the ground. The unicorn sounds panicked for once. *I've been looking all over for you.*

"I was seeking counsel," I grumble.

The unicorn looks over its shoulder at the castle and then back to me. *I was afraid of the worst when I couldn't find you. I haven't had any time to figure out what's happening, though the attack seems to have stopped.*

"You were worried about me? How thoughtful," I say dryly. "I was filled in by the giant, only a little too late. Hanna is gone."

Gone? Sarvi's eye widens in its socket. *How?*

"I don't know exactly, other than Rasmus came back for her and she left willingly. He created this storm as well."

Oh. Sarvi says. *She left willingly?*

I grunt, feeling the humiliation inside me turning into anger, molten and waiting. "When was the last time you saw her?"

We were in the crypt. She was at the altar, waiting for you.

My throat feels dry and I attempt to swallow. "How did she look?"

She looked... Sarvi trails off, watching my face with

caution. *Beautiful. Like a queen.*

I thought as much.

"She wasn't crying in protest?"

Sarvi shakes its head. *No, sir. She seemed to accept her fate. So to hear that she's left willingly…can you be sure about that?*

"I can't be sure of anything, but the giant doesn't lie."

No, but perhaps Rasmus is the liar here. Who knows what he told her in order to get her to leave.

"Are you trying to make me feel better?"

I'm trying to make sure you retain your control, sir. I've seen what happens when you lose it.

He's referring to Surma. How quickly I killed one of my oldest advisors when I found him harassing Hanna. I don't regret it for a moment, but I was operating on pure violence and impulse. Perhaps a bit of pleasure too—the feeling as I snapped Surma's fragile bones between my fingers was indescribable. Almost as good as coming inside Hanna. But not quite.

I flex and unflex my hands, the leather of my gloves creaking, trying to dissipate the tension running through my veins. "Did you know that Rasmus is the son of the she-devil?"

If Sarvi had an eyebrow to raise, it would. *I beg your pardon?*

"Louhi," I practically growl. "Rasmus. That walking carrot stick is the son of Louhi."

How is that possible? I heard her consort was infertile.

I frown. "Where did you hear that?"

Around, Sarvi says carefully as it paws its black hoof against the ground. *I'm not one for gossip, but I do hear a lot. In the castle and outside of it.*

I ignore the unhelpful fact that my position as ruler of the realm has kept me out of the loop, so to speak. "So then, what did you hear about my ex-wife's lover?"

That Louhi had been trying for a long time to conceive a child with the shaman and wasn't able to. But that was a long time ago. It's hard to say when exactly, but perhaps they found success through a spell.

"And why was I never made aware of this?" I grumble.

Forgive me sir, I thought you knew. And I know you well enough to not bring up something like that unless I want my week to be ruined. Anything to do with Louhi is a, well, a rather delicate subject.

That brings out a growl from me. I knew that part of the reason why Louhi left me was because she wanted to gain magic from a shaman, and Ilmarinen, as useless as he is, fit the bill. I always assumed he would teach her spells or give magic to her. I also didn't think that she wanted anymore children after Lovia and Tuonen, especially as she shows zero interest in them.

But if Rasmus truly is the son of Louhi, then perhaps magic came into play in his creation, and if that's the case, then we might be in for a world of trouble. I've dabbled with shadow magic before—The Book of Runes inside the Library of the Veils contains a spell for a Shadow Self that I created—but many safeguards and precautions must be taken when invoking the magic and using the shadows, or else the shadows can become…difficult. It's one thing to create a double of yourself or a shadow twin, it's another if you're using shadows to impregnate yourself. A child born from that magic has the capacity to not only have a lot of power, but to do a world of harm in unpredictable ways.

I have to wonder if Rasmus even knows the truth about his mother.

If he does know the truth though, then that's the end of Hanna.

There's a sudden, sharp burst of pain in my chest at the thought that wars with the building rage inside me. As fantastically angry as I am at her for leaving, Sarvi is right in that Rasmus might have told her anything to get her to leave. And if he knows he's Louhi's son, then I have a feeling he's leading Hanna straight to her. My imagination is certainly depraved, but it isn't big enough to think of all the things Louhi might have planned for her.

"We have to find Hanna," I tell Sarvi.

The unicorn lowers its wings in gesture. *I'll take you to Shadow's End first. Lovia was with Hanna last, she might have more information on what happened.*

I quickly get on Sarvi's back and we take off. The storm is waning, which means Rasmus must be confident that he's in the clear but, until I find Hanna, I only have one way in which to stop them.

I let myself go to a dark place. A place darker than the Caves of Vipunen, where I first woke up in this realm, stepping into this role as the God of Death through pain and pure horror. I go to that dark place, a place where abhorrent monsters of anger and decay live, and I let it sink into my bones and consume me, just as long as it gets the job done.

In my bones, I feel a storm forming in the rest of the land beyond the mountains, something terrible and menacing and hungry. Something that should stop Rasmus and Hanna dead in their tracks.

It should buy us enough time.

Sarvi takes me right to his tower, and I'm already jumping off the winged beast and landing on the lookout, the stones shaking beneath my feet. I head straight down the stairs, Sarvi hurrying behind me. I'm grateful that Vipunen told me to build the passageways and stairways in the castle large enough to accommodate bigger creatures, knowing that Sarvi would be a loyal advisor and servant after that.

Sometimes I wonder just how much Antero Vipunen knows. As a child, all I heard were fantastical stories about him and that no one who ever laid eyes on the giant lived. I used to wonder if Vipunen was even a giant at all. How would anyone know unless they saw him? But I never dared to voice that growing up. Being a child of Gods meant you had rules to follow and roles to play and to never question the order of things. Order needed to be kept so that all the worlds beyond the worlds could function.

But now that eons have passed, now that there are dangers popping up that threaten to undo all this order, I'm second-guessing everyone and everything. Perhaps that's my failing as king and lord and God. Perhaps I should have been second-guessing everything from the very beginning.

I would have started with Vipunen. I would have figured out why no one can see him, why his cryptic remarks and prophecies only seem to add chaos to my life. He has told me that he is impartial to the world and yet he's been a part of my world since I first become ruler, taking on the role of a father figure, since my own father pretty much fucked off. Turns out Gods don't make the best dads.

Speaking of being a father...

"Lovia!" I call out as we reach the top landing. I can sense my daughter's frantic energy nearby.

She comes bursting out of my study, eyes round, blonde hair flowing behind her, wringing her hands together

"Father!" she cries out, borderline hysterical. "Where were you? We were waiting for you in the crypt, and then something started attacking the castle and I brought Hanna up to your room to keep her safe and now she's gone!"

"So I've been told," I tell her, marching past her, toward my chambers. The door is open and the room looks as I left it this morning, neat and tidy. You can't expect to rule over the dead if your bed is unmade.

"I'm so sorry, I'm so so sorry," Lovia goes on. "I told her to stay, I don't know what happened."

"It's all right," I tell her gruffly. "I'm not mad at you."

I go over to the window and note that one of the horns of the gargoyle outside has been broken off, as if someone had been perching on it. "I'm not a detective, but I'm confident Rasmus brought her out through here. I just don't know how." I lean out and stare at the straight drop to the sea below.

"Rasmus?" Lovia cries out. "How do you know it was him?"

I sigh and straighten up, looking at my daughter and Sarvi. "Because Vipunen told me as much. He also said Hanna went willingly with him. But Rasmus might have said anything to get her to leave." I study Lovia carefully. "Unless you knew Hanna was already plotting an escape."

She shakes her head, looking innocent. That's the problem with Lovia. She makes you want to underestimate her. While her mother outright looks like a demon (except when she shapeshifts into other women for short periods of time), Lovia's demon blood is hidden inside her. She looks angelic, though I know she's anything but. This daughter of mine has a world of secrets, and I don't even want to know half of them.

"Are you sure?" I coax her. "Is it possible that Hanna and Rasmus were planning this for some time, organizing her escape when all our guards were down?"

"I really don't think so…" Lovia says. She looks at Sarvi. "You saw her this morning, it's not like we had to drag her to the altar or anything."

"Yes," I answer for the unicorn. "Sarvi mentioned something about her accepting her fate, which isn't exactly the compliment you think it is."

"Listen, she wanted to marry you. Believe me, I could tell. She even said 'well who doesn't want to be queen?'"

I frown. "Hanna said that?"

"Uh-huh," Lovia says, nodding frantically. "If she's gone, it's not because she wanted to go. And there's no way anyone could take her from the room, the wards were up, I made sure of it."

"Some shamans can undo wards," I say quietly, making a fist. "The same shamans who might control the weather."

"Phhff," Lovia says. "Rasmus is just a kid. A shaman-in-training."

"Rasmus is your brother," I tell her, the truth coming out like a weapon.

She blinks at me and shakes her head, confusion etched on her face. "What…what are you talking about?"

"Rasmus is Louhi's son," I say plainly. "Vipunen said so."

She crosses her arms. "Yeah, well maybe Vipunen lies."

"You know he doesn't. This takes you by surprise, doesn't it?"

She stares at me for a few moments, and while there's no doubt that Lovia is shocked by this, there's something else going on in her head. "It does. So, he's Ilmarinen's son then. Rasmus is my half brother."

"That's what we assume," I say, my attention going back to my room. When I woke up this morning, I was certain I'd be bringing Hanna back here. I had made this bed imagining that I'd be throwing her on it later. I had dreamed of this moment, not because there was something binding about being husband and wife, but the opposite. It was freeing to me, knowing I could fully be myself with her.

I shake the thought away, a strange burning in my chest. Something bitter, like humiliation coupled with regret.

"I guess…being the son of a shaman would explain why his magic is stronger than I thought," Lovia says. "Then *we* thought." A strange sort of darkness comes across her pale face, making her look strangely unbalanced.

"Are you all right?" I ask.

She stares at me blankly for a few moments, then pastes on a smile and nods. "Yes. I'm fine. Sorry father, it's just kind of a shock when you're told you have a half brother, especially one that seems at odds with your family. That's all."

I nod. "I guess you're feeling your mother's betrayal too. That she kept him a secret."

She licks her lips and shrugs. "You know how it is with her. I'm used to being betrayed. It never even crossed my mind to be upset about it."

Some days I feel for my children. That things had to sour between their mother and I. I don't know what life is really like in the other worlds, other than the time I spend in the library, studying the Book of Souls, but I don't imagine most divorces end with one of the parents becoming a harbinger of doom intent on destroying the afterlife.

Sir, Sarvi speaks up. *Just in case Rasmus wasn't acting alone, we should question Hanna's Deadmaiden.*

"Good point."

"What?" Lovia asks me, unable to hear Sarvi's voice.

"Sarvi wants us to question Raila, see what she knows."

She swallows. "Oh. Kalma took Raila right away. He assumed she was behind the attacks. I don't know what he's done with her."

Oh for fuck's sake. Can't anything go right today?

I rub the heel of my palm over my forehead and groan. Kalma does things the way I do things, which is to usually torture those we consider to be usurpers. There might not be any of her left. "Where did he take her?" I ask with a heavy sigh.

"I don't know," she says helplessly.

I walk over to the nearest mask, propped up on the dresser

beside the bed—this one a silver skull with fox ears—and place it over my face. I should have been wearing my mask outside but in my haste I forgot it in the caves. Seems more important than ever to keep up the illusion of terror and power, even when I feel it slipping through my fingers like sand.

Then I stride out of the room and head down the hall and grand staircase, with Sarvi and Lovia trailing behind. I go all the way down to the main level and then outside to the stables. The skeleton horses are already on edge, their broombrush manes bristled. I don't know if it's because they always get this way around Sarvi, or because of what they've just gone through.

"Easy there," I say to them in a voice I pull up from the base of my chest.

The horses immediately relax, nickering softly.

I would spend more time with them if I could. The animals and creatures of Tuonela may be half-dead in many cases, but they're still my creatures and in my care. It pains me to know if any of them are suffering or treated unfairly. It's one of the reasons why I've always made sure Sarvi has had full autonomy. Well, Sarvi would have insisted upon it anyway.

I continue down past the stalls until I get to the paddock where pigs were once kept before Pyry decided to cook them up for a few feasts. I should have stopped her and regret that I didn't.

There is Kalma, the old man, half bones, half human, holding Raila down on the ground, in the shit and hay, a sickle raised in the air ready to slice through her.

"Kalma," I say loudly, his name reverberating through the stall.

Just in time, too. Kalma pauses, the sickle shaking slightly, catching the light from the nearby lanterns and making it quiver.

"Raila has nothing to do with what happened," I quickly inform him. "It was Rasmus who started the attack on Shadow's End. He has Hanna now."

Kalma straightens up, slowly lowering the sickle. Is it strange that even though he's been a decaying half-skeleton since I met him, I can see the age in him and it disturbs me? There shouldn't be such a thing as age in the Land of the Dead, and yet the proof is right in front of me. The proof is everywhere. The pigs that were slaughtered for our feasts were plump and whole, but given enough time in this land, they would eventually rot, their muscles wasting away, leaving them half-skeletons like so many other ancient things.

Does that mean that I one day will age and die? That Lovia and Tuonen will as well? Will they one day have to bury me? We are supposed to be immortal as Gods, but I know that's not the case. Every God's reign eventually comes to an end. It might take decades or centuries or eons—all the weak, mortal grasps of time—but it eventually ends.

Everything ends.

I shake that thought from my head. Philosophical thinking like that will never get me anywhere.

"Are you certain?" he asks.

I stare at Raila. With her black veil and headdress, I can't get a feel for her, I can't even sense the way she might be looking back at me. I've never been able to really know my Deadmaiden's and Deadhand's intentions, for better or for worse. But it does look like she was seconds from losing at least one of her limbs, and I know that if she had, she'd be useless as a Deadmaiden or servant. Believe it or not, good help here is hard to find.

"I'm certain," I say, though I mentally shoot a thought to Sarvi to keep her under watch. Even though it seems this time it was all Rasmus' doing, there's a reason why my advisor quickly assumed she was behind it. We all believe there is a traitor in our midst, most likely one of the help, who acts as a spy for the uprising, but all we have to go on is gut feeling and nothing else.

Kalma lifts one shoulder in a shrug and then leans over, grabbing Raila by the neck and hauling her up to her feet. "Death has spared you this time. I think this means you ought to be on your best behavior from now on."

Raila nods, her thoughts telepathic. *I never give anything less than the best for my master. Nor for my master's wife.*

My lip curls in a snarl. "She is not my wife yet."

Of course. I cry your pardon. In all the chaos, I forgot that the wedding was interrupted. Now that things have calmed, shall we pick up where we left off?

"She's gone," Lovia says to her.

"Hanna is gone?" Kalma says in surprise.

I narrow my eyes, trying to bite back the anger. The chain I have around it is getting shorter and shorter. Not long before it snaps. "She is gone," I say gruffly. "Rasmus took her. I have created a storm to the north which should stop them."

"You have to go after her," Kalma says, his hands together as if in prayer as he walks toward me, his robes flowing behind. "You have to bring her back and marry her. You need to do this for the prophecy."

The fucking prophecy.

I grunt. "I know what I have to do."

"Are you planning on saving her?" Lovia questions, folding her arms across her chest. "Or punishing her?"

"Depends on how I feel when I see her," I admit.

"Don't do anything you'll regret," Lovia warns me. A flash of worry comes over her bright eyes. "Maybe...maybe you should just let her go."

I balk at that, defiance flaring inside me. "Let her go? She made a promise to me. I am making sure she upholds her promise. Let her go? What is wrong with you daughter? You're the one who was wanting this."

"Don't forget about the prophecy," Kalma interjects.

"If, *when*, I find her, I will find out what her intentions were," I add, making a fist. "If she meant to leave, I will not let her go. I will drag her back here, make her marry me, force her to uphold her end of the bargain. She will not be rewarded for being disloyal to me, for being a liar, a fucking traitor who goes back on their word. She will be punished. Severely. Don't think I don't know how."

"And if she was coerced by Rasmus?" she asks.

"Then I will kill Rasmus," I tell her. "Sorry to have to do that to a brother of yours, but I will have no mercy."

"Brother?" Kalma asks, brows raised.

I wave at him dismissively. "It's a long story." I nod at

Sarvi. "It's time to go."

I grab hold of Sarvi's mane and pull myself up on its back. I adjust my mask, looking down at Lovia, Kalma, and Raila.

"In the event that they haven't gone far, keep the Deadhands on alert and the castle surrounded. I'm taking no chances."

And at that, Sarvi flaps its wings, the force blowing back the hay, and we fly off into the sky.

Not a hint of sunshine to be seen.

CHAPTER THREE

HANNA

"THE BONE STRAGGLERS"

I scream as my world goes black.

The sound is immediately muffled by a boney hand that stretches across my mouth. The fingers that grabbed me are slimy, cold, and smell like decay, the fumes going up my nose like gasoline, making me want to retch. More hands are wrapped around my wrists, my elbows, my waist, my ankles, and others pull at the lengths of my wedding dress, ripping it, and I'm absently trying to figure out just how many creatures have hold of me as they pull me under into the darkness, further and further into a dank hole.

Fight back, I think to myself, even though I don't know where I am except probably underground, and I don't know who has me. *Fight back*.

I try to conjure up the will, the power, that side of myself that lays just beneath the surface, the one buzzing with electricity and sunshine. But the skeletal hands are wrapping in my hair now, and pain is coursing through my body, and I can't concentrate on anything much except trying to scream for Rasmus to help me.

Finally I feel air on my face, like the space around me has opened up, and all the hands let go at once. I fall on to hard-packed earth, the wind knocked out of me.

Whispers fill the void. Male voices, ragged and harsh, punctuated by the occasional clack of bones.

Jaw bones.

I immediately picture the Deadhands that served Death and wonder if he's sent his army out after me. For a moment there's a touch of relief, that it's Death that has come for me and not something else. Better the devil you know and all that.

But then a match is struck and in the flickering flame skeletal bodies come into view. There must be a dozen of them, all wearing ragged clothing that hangs off them in shreds. Literally living dead people. Most of them have swords or axes that are pointed my way, crystals or stones tied around their neck, and they're in various stages of decay. Some have flesh sticking to parts of their face or hands, hanging off them like their clothes, others are just smooth bone.

Their eyes are fathomless dark holes, save for the occasional eyeball rolling around in the socket.

Bone Stragglers, I think to myself, trying not to shudder at the thought. *These must be the Bone Stragglers I've heard so much about.*

Slowly lanterns along the dirt wall are lit and I push

myself back on my elbows to get a quick look. I'm on my ass in a cavern carved into the dirt. There are roots of trees and other plants reaching down through the ceiling, damp cobwebs strung here and there, and beyond the skeleton people, tunnels disappear into darkness in all directions.

"So it is you," the nearest skeleton says to me with those disturbing clacks of its jaw. It reaches into a worn leather strap at its waist and pulls out a rusty knife which he brandishes at me. "We have been waiting for you."

I stare at him, then the rest of them hovering in the background. My heart is still going a mile a minute but, despite the weapons pointed my way, I don't think I'm in any immediate danger. And by immediate, I mean in this exact moment. I might be sliced and diced in the next.

"You've been waiting for me?" I ask carefully. "Why?"

"You're Louhi's daughter," the skeleton says. "Salainen. The prophesized one."

I blink. Though part of me is aware that if I play along I'll have a better chance of surviving this, it's not enough to hide my surprise. "I'm sorry, what? Louhi's daughter? Lovia?"

The skeleton shakes its head. "Not Loviatar. Salainen. I have met you before, *Sala.*"

Holy fuck. What does that mean? How is that even possible? Do I have a twin out there or something?

Suddenly Rasmus' voice echoes throughout the tunnels. "Hanna! Hanna!"

The sea of skeletons part as Rasmus is led toward me, two large skeleton men on either side of him, daggers pressing into his throat, close to drawing blood.

"You're alive," Rasmus gasps, his blue eyes wide as he looks me over. "Did they hurt you?"

The lead skeleton looks over at Rasmus, but keeps his blade pointed at me. "And you call her Hanna. Has she not told you her real name?"

Rasmus looks to me, brows raised. *What is he talking about?* his voice suddenly cuts into my head.

I have no idea, I answer back, hoping he can hear me now.

"Go on, tell him," the skeleton says to me. "You are Louhi's daughter, Salainen, part of the Prophecy of Three, as told by Rangaista. The child of a shaman, born from the shadows, who will defeat Death. End his rule. Usher in the new age, open the portals to Kaaos so that Kaaos can rule again."

I look back at Rasmus. *Can you shed some light on this?*

Rasmus presses his lips together and shakes his head, a line between his brows. He clears his throat. "Tell me about this prophecy," he says to the skeletons.

Even though the skeleton's eyes are just empty black holes, I swear I see anger in them. "I only know what Louhi has told us. We have spent eons waiting for the signs and they are starting to appear. I met her, not long ago, when Louhi sent Sala to have a meeting with us, to tell us to wait, that our time was coming soon."

I manage to swallow. Even though it's cold underground, my skin feels tight and hot, my confusion building. It's like I'm suddenly second-guessing everything. I've never met these skeletons before, but now I'm wondering if I have some secret other life that I'm not even conscious of. Is that even possible?

You're in the Land of the Dead, anything is possible.

"Please, indulge me," Rasmus says, talking carefully as he eyes the daggers that are still pressed into both sides of his throat, right below the jaw. "Treat me like an idiot that's been lied to by their friend. I only know of one prophecy, that there is a mortal girl out there that can touch Death, and that their union has the ability to unite the land. Right?"

"It is all part of the Prophecy of Three," the skeleton says in annoyance. He looks back to me and waves his weapon, puncturing the air as he talks. "A shaman will have three children. One will raise the Old Gods. One can touch Death and together will destroy the Old Gods and the uprising. And one, born from shadows, will defeat Death, leaving the kingdom to Kaaos. She," the skeleton says, stabbing his blade near my face, "is the one born from the shadows. She will destroy Death and bring Kaaos back to this world. And once again, all of us will be equal."

I project my voice toward Rasmus. *Might be in our best interest to at least pretend that I'm the* Kaaos-*bringer.*

He frowns at that, having heard me, but there's a wariness to his expression, as if maybe he's second-guessing how well he knows me.

I swear, I add quickly, *I am not this shadow-born whatever the hell. I don't even know if I'm the one to touch Death. And I'm certainly not the one who will raise the Old Gods. The whole lot of them omniscient creeps can stay buried.*

You were able to use Lovia's sword, he muses, eyes narrowing. *That does seem like someone the daughter of Louhi would be able to do.*

I'm not the daughter of Louhi! I yell inside my head. *I'm just a fucking social media manager, not the daughter of a demon!*

I mean, my mother has been pretty awful at times and sometimes I wonder if we're even related, but she's not a literal demon.

Maybe I should have left you at Shadow's End, he says snidely.

Yeah, well maybe you should have!

"What is going on here?" the skeleton man says sharply, looking between the two of us. "Are you communicating in your heads?"

Rasmus clears his throat again and looks at the skeleton man. "I am merely trying to get answers from her. Seems she's been lying to me since the day I met her."

Well fuck, now I can't tell if Rasmus is being serious or not.

"Michael," one of the skeletons says, coming forward. "How can we be sure this is Salainen?"

Michael? The head skeleton's name is Michael? Not Skeletor or Bone Thugs?

"Because it is her," Michael says adamantly, gesturing to me. "I've met Sala. We all have. This is her." He pauses and looks around the cavern, all the skulls turned his way. "Is it not?"

A few of the skeletons come closer to me. I scramble backward until my shoulders hit the earth wall, their sinister fingers outstretched toward me.

"There's only one way to find out," one of the skeletons says, holding up a sword. "The real Salainen should turn to shadow when the blade goes in. Should pass right through her."

Oh fuck!

"Rasmus!" I scream for help, managing to roll out of the way just seconds before the sword stabbed the dirt where I was.

Suddenly the ground starts shaking, several of the skeletons knocking into each other, and Rasmus takes advantage of the distraction to fight off the ones who were holding him. He runs toward me, lifting me up from the ground, then places me behind him, shielding me from the rest of the Bone Stragglers. They stagger toward us, ready to fight, but then rocks start to fall from the ceiling of the cavern, along with clumps of dirt, knocking many of them out. Weapons fall from their hands, and bones separate from the bodies.

"What's happening!" I yell, holding onto Rasmus' jacket and peering around him as dirt falls into my hair.

"I'm not sure," he says, just as the middle of the cavern caves in. The skeletons scream, jaws clacking, bones splintering, as they're buried by earth and rock, then I'm screaming once again as suddenly hundreds of skinny tendrils come out from the hole in the ceiling and start sliding down the walls. They look like impossibly long thin white worms, and they move as if they all operate as one.

"Oh my god, what are *those*!?" I screech but then my words die on my lips as the tendrils come for us, snapping around me and Rasmus impossibly fast, binding us together until my chest is smashed against his back.

"Don't panic," Rasmus says, though he sounds on the

verge of panicking himself. "I think I—"

All of a sudden we're snatched off the ground and yanked out of the cavern and up through the collapsed-in ceiling. We're flung through the air, the tendrils releasing us until we land on a patch of moss, back in the forest again.

"Rasmus," a raspy female voice says that makes the hair on my neck stand up, "back so soon?"

CHAPTER FOUR

HANNA

"THE MYCELIA"

At first, I don't know what I'm looking at. Rasmus and I are on top of fuzzy green moss that stretches out into the forest, the pines and cedars being whipped violently by the wind, branches and needles raining down. It's darker than it should be, and I have to wonder if the clouds have gotten darker and lower, or if a lot of time had passed since we were underground with the Bone Stragglers.

Then I realize it's dark because there's something giant hovering over us, blotting out the sky. The same giant thing that's talking to Rasmus.

I blink rapidly, trying to get my eyes to adjust. It's like… it's like the moss has started to grow up the side of a wide tree, except instead of bark there's flesh. Pale white skin. And the moss continues up, curving in around a waist, then up to breasts, shoulders, neck…

I expect to see the moss-covered face of a giant woman on top but instead it's a mushroom cap. It's a giant fucking moss woman growing out of the ground with a mushroom for a head.

What the actual fuck?

"I wasn't planning on making a stop," Rasmus says to the mushroom lady, getting to his feet. He reaches down and pulls me up, noting the bewildered expression on my face. "Hanna, this is a dear friend of mine. Sammalta."

I stare up at the mushy lady, feeling painfully normal and mortal. "Pleased to meet you?"

She has no eyes or mouth in that mushroom cap head of hers, and yet I can sense her expression all the same. She's not amused.

"You should be pleased," she says haughtily. "I just saved your life."

I look over to where the ground caved in right beside her. A few of the white tendrils are retreating underneath the moss.

Holy shit. Those tendrils are actually mycelia belonging to the mushy lady. I try to think back to my biology classes in high school. Or is it that the mushroom lady belongs to the mycelia? Either way, even though she did save our lives, and Rasmus seems to know her, I'm not trusting anyone anymore, especially not talking mushrooms.

"My apologies," I say to her. "It's been a whirlwind since I left the castle."

She doesn't say anything for a moment and the pause feels weighty. There's no feeling like you're being scrutinized by a twenty-foot-tall naked mossy mushroom lady.

Then she says to Rasmus, "So you did it. She's here. I suppose congratulations are in order. Or at least a thanks."

"I didn't want to bring her here," Rasmus says quickly. "You know my aim was Death's Landing and then home."

"So I'm guessing this weather isn't because of you," she muses, thunder crashing nearby as if on cue. "Then Death has discovered your plan. You're lucky you even made it this far."

"It was all thanks to Alku," Rasmus says, looking around the wind-whipped forest. "Have you seen the unicorn?"

"Alku is taking shelter," she says. "Which is something I advise you do as well until this passes."

"What if it never passes?" I ask, trying not to sound panicked.

"Never is a strong word," the mushy lady says. "It doesn't apply in place like this. Come on. Let's get you out of this weather."

The mushy lady starts to sink straight into the ground until all that's left is moss and a tiny mushroom.

"Remember when I told you to not eat the mushrooms here," Rasmus says to me as I stare wildly at the place where the mushy lady was. "That's part of the reason."

Suddenly the white strands of mycelia come shooting out of the ground right for us.

I scream, more out of surprise than terror this time, and the tendrils wrap around both Rasmus and I, lifting us a few feet off the ground, then start moving us at a rapid rate over the moss and through the trees. Falling branches nearly flatten us a few times, the ones from the iron pines landing like bombs.

"What's happening!?" I manage to cry out. Can't I have a moment of peace where I'm not being groped by skeletons or dragged around by mushrooms?

"She's taking us to her home," Rasmus says. I look over at him and with his red hair blown back by the wind and the sparkle in his eyes, he looks like he's having a hell of a good time. "It's where I was hiding out, planning to free you."

We zip through the forest until we start to slow, a clearing opening up in front of us. The most god-awful smell fills the air and I grimace, my stomach turning sour.

"Oh god," I say, scrunching up my nose. "What the hell is that smell? The Bog of Everlasting Stench?"

"Not quite," Rasmus says. "It's decay. The Pile of Decay to be exact. You'll get used to it."

"Pile of Decay? Sounds like they should be opening up for Corrosion of Conformity."

"Didn't figure you'd listen to metal," Rasmus comments, grinning at me. "You might be a true Finn after all."

The mycelia come to a sudden stop. In front of us, in the middle of a clearing surrounded by what look like birch or poplar trees, is a massive pile of bones, fur, skin, and other things I don't want to get too close of a look at. At the front of the pile is a ribcage that looks like it belongs to a blue whale, big enough to walk under.

The mycelia yank us back to the ground and disappear under the earth until I'm on my feet beside Rasmus. He reaches out and grabs my elbow to steady me before looking me over.

"I have to admit, you must have looked like a beautiful

bride."

I'm pinching my nose shut, trying not to inhale the disgusting fumes from the Pile of Decay. "*Looked* like?" I say in a nasally voice.

He smirks and looks me over with a shrug.

I glance down at myself. The wind is whipping my dress around, or what's left of it. The long train is now torn to mid-calf, and the once pristine fabric is wet in places and black and brown with dirt. I can only imagine what my face looks like.

A cymbal crash of thunder makes me jump and Rasmus tugs me in through the giant awning of the rib cage. "Come on, the storm isn't going anywhere."

I stare up at the ribs as I pass underneath them, at the moss growing on them and the tiny mushrooms cropping up in places.

"Uh, whose ribs are these?"

"T-Rex or something like that," he says.

"A T-Rex?" I repeat. "Are you sure?" I mean, the dinosaur was big, but a T-Rex didn't have a ribcage large enough that you could walk through it.

"Don't worry, this one died a long time ago," he says. "Whatever it was."

My worry about a bigger than normal T-Rex appearing and snatching me up in its jaws is quickly replaced by the smell getting even stronger as we step into darkness. It's hard to tell if we're inside dead creatures or going into a cave.

Rasmus keeps leading me forward until we come across stairs made of bone that spiral down into the earth. The further down we go the darker it gets until I'm blindly following

Rasmus through the black.

Finally, we reach solid ground and stop.

"Where are we?" I whisper to him. Thankfully the smell seems to have dissipated, but the fact that I'm in the pitch-black underground somewhere has me feeling off-kilter again.

"Where Sammalta lives," he whispers back. "Mushrooms feed on decay. And darkness. Hold on."

I hear Rasmus rustling for something when suddenly my eyes focus on a spot of light right beside me. Slowly I see the outline of Rasmus' fingers and realize that there's a light emanating from inside his clenched fist.

"Mind your eyes," he says to me and then he opens his hand.

There's a glowing sphere on his palm that's growing brighter and brighter, enough to make Rasmus wince but it doesn't hurt my eyes at all.

"What is that?" I ask in wonder. It's like he has the sun in his hand.

"It's a sunmoonstone," he says. Then he takes the sphere and winds up, pitching it forward like a baseball. I watch as the glowing stone flies straight through the air, illuminating the space it travels through, the light sticking around long after the sphere has sailed past.

I don't even know where the sphere lands because I'm looking around me in awe as its soft light reveals the mushy lady's home. Unlike the dirty, creepy underground tunnels and caverns of the Bone Stragglers, this place looks absolutely magical. The walls are made of bone and agate, dirt and moss, and there's a network of mycelia stretching from floor to ceiling. They seem to glow and sparkle in the light, giving the illusion of being amongst sparkling lightning strikes.

The thought gives my heart a twist. They also remind me of the runes etched across Death's body, the silver lines that pulsed when souls passed over. I had always thought that if I touched his runes that I would feel the energy pass through to me, but the truth is, all of Death felt like that. Every inch of him. I'm not sure I'd ever felt so alive than when my skin was pressed up against his.

The memory feels so vivid, so real, that my body grows hot, and it takes me a moment to realize I'm being spoken to.

"What?" I ask dumbly, bringing my head back to the present.

"I said you're not what I had imagined." It's the mushy lady's voice, but the cavern remains empty. Only the mycelia glows when she speaks, once again reminding me of Death.

"Oh," I say, glancing at Rasmus. "What did you tell her?"

"He said that you're beautiful," she answers for him.

"Oh…" I'm vaguely flattered that Rasmus would have said that about me, though I feel like she means this as an insult.

"And you are quite beautiful, for a mortal, I suppose," she says reluctantly. "It's just that you have another quality that he didn't even mention. A quality which makes sense as to why he would go to such lengths to save you from Death."

I want to point out that I didn't need saving but I swallow down my pride. I eye Rasmus. He looks perplexed, gnawing on his bottom lip. "And what quality might that be?" I ask.

"Magic," she says to my surprise. "It's in every cell of your blood. It shines like the sun."

"I told you, she is the daughter of a powerful shaman," Rasmus says. "Torben Heikkinen."

"I know Torben," mushy lady says cautiously. "He is not a stranger to this land. Our paths have crossed many times, Hanna. To my surprise though, he has never mentioned you. I didn't quite believe it when Rasmus had said you were his daughter, but now that you are here, I feel it so clearly."

"He was probably trying to protect me," I tell her, hoping that was the case and not that he was ashamed at having a very unmagical mortal for a daughter.

"He probably was," she says. "Or protect himself."

I frown. "What does that mean?"

Though I can't see the mushy lady, I feel her hesitation. "Who is your mother?"

"My mother? She's…I don't know. Normal. Too normal. And mortal. Human. She lives in Seattle. Left my father when I was young, brought me to the States. Remarried this guy, George. Thinks I'm a perpetual disappointment."

"Hmmmm," mushy lady says.

"Why?" I ask.

"What do you know about the Prophecy of Three?" Rasmus speaks up. I glare at him, even though he's asking a more important question. "The Bone Stragglers took us because they thought Hanna was someone called Salainen. Said they look exactly alike. Is that shadow magic or…?"

"What's shadow magic?" I ask.

"So many questions," mushy lady notes dryly.

"Can you blame me?" I ask, defensively throwing my arms out. "This isn't my world, and I don't even know my own world that well."

"Sometimes the answers to our questions come from deep within," she says.

"Yeah, thanks, I already tried yoga," I tell her. "The only thing I learned was that it's boring as hell."

"Perhaps you learned that you're boring as hell," she remarks.

I gasp loudly, almost laughing at her audacity. "What the fuck?"

Did this talking fungus just call me *boring*?

"Look," Rasmus says quickly, giving me a tense look, "the Bone Stragglers mentioned shadows when it came to Salainen. They said she was part of the prophecy and that she would destroy Death and bring Kaaos back to the land. That's obviously not Hanna though. She's never met them before."

"You know that for sure?" mushy lady says.

"Uh, *I* know that for sure," I say, raising my hand. "I'm not some shadowy chaos bringer. I'm boring, remember?"

"Hmmm," she says again. The mycelia on the walls dim a little as silence fills the cavern.

I look at Rasmus expectantly. "So this is where you spent your time? In here? With her?"

He runs his long fingers along his jaw. "She's a bit prickly...but she knows a lot. She taught me a lot."

"Such as?"

"She gave me Alku. She taught me magic. I couldn't have learned it otherwise."

"So mushy lady knows magic?"

He gives me a pointed look. "You know she can hear you

right?"

I gesture to the empty cavern. "She ain't saying anything."

"She's checking the network."

"What network?"

"You know how fungi communicate, don't you? In our world, they use electrical impulses to deliver messages along the pathways, the mycelia. Some say they have a language similar to us. Well, down here, it's literal. She's just one part of a larger network that stretches all across Tuonela. She knows a lot, because she's everywhere, and she can pop up in any place."

The mycelia threads start to glow again, signaling her presence back in the cavern.

"Rasmus," the mushy lady's voice booms, making my bones vibrate. "You are the son of a shaman, are you not?"

"I'm not," he says impatiently, as if she should know this. "I've just been trained to be a shaman. By Torben. Remember?"

"Yes. You told me this before, I know, but there is a reason I ask again, because I don't think you've been truthful with me."

Rasmus gives me a nervous glance as he says, "What do you mean?"

"I may know all, but I don't profess to know the truth. If you lie, I might just believe it. But perhaps you might not know it's a lie."

"Honestly, I have no idea what you're talking about," Rasmus says with exasperation.

"You are the child of a shaman, Rasmus," she says.

I watch Rasmus closely. Death told me that Rasmus'

mother was a Lapp Witch, that he was raised by his grandmother, that his parents died when he was young. But if his parents died young, it wouldn't surprise me if his father was a shaman and he didn't know it.

His eyes flutter in surprise. "I'm…what? I'm not."

"You were adopted," she points out.

"Yes," he says hesitantly. "By my grandmother."

"You never knew your birth parents."

He swallows thickly. "No. They died when I was a baby. So I was raised by my grandmother. She legally adopted me."

"Do you know for sure that was your real grandmother? Or did you just accept it because you were young and didn't know any better?"

He stares into the cavern with a blank expression, and I can tell his brain is sifting through the past.

"Does it seem unbelievable then to know you come from a shaman?" she adds.

He presses his lips together, frowning in thought. I'm starting to think he doesn't know his mother is a Lapp Witch.

After a moment, mushy lady goes on. "When you look inside, you find the answers. Power and magic, it runs through the blood, just as it does through Hanna's. It's passed on from generation to generation. It's a giant, unseen network, not unlike the one that I belong to. It stretches across time and, even though you can't see it, you know it exists. This thread connecting all of us. A mortal can only learn so much. A mortal with shaman's blood can learn so much more."

Rasmus seems to be deep in thought.

"Do you know who his father is then?" I ask her.

"Rasmus was never born in your world," she says after a moment. "He was born in this one."

"What are you talking about?" Rasmus says quietly, looking frightened for once.

"You were born in a pool of black blood," she says to him. "Screaming like any mortal child would. Your mother held you close, her hands around your little neck, and thought about killing you then. But she hesitated. Your birth wasn't an accident, you were wanted, oh yes, all she wanted was the son of a shaman. But she couldn't be sure which prophecy you would fulfill. Was it the one that she wanted? The one to raise the Old Gods? The one to destroy Death? Or the one that would make Death stronger in the end? The prophecy was a secret at that time, but your mother feared Antero Vipunen, who knows all, and creatures like me, who find things out in time. She was fearful that if anyone else knew the power the child had, they would destroy it before she could figure it out first. Before she could kill the boy herself."

I'm studying Rasmus' face this whole time, trying to see if any of this makes sense to him. She had said that he had been lying to her. Was that true? Or is this news to him as well?

"In the end," she continues, "his mother decided the best thing for her would be to wait and see what would become of him. So she had her daughter take the baby out of Tuonela. Left him at a hospital, where mortals would eventually adopt him, take care of him. But even though the shaman never knew he had a child born in another realm, the baby found its way to the shaman anyway. When he was old enough. When he was ready to be trained. When the shaman needed an apprentice."

The last sentence makes my blood run cold.

Rasmus was my father's apprentice.

My father, the shaman.

"What exactly are you saying here?" I ask her, my voice echoing in the room. I'm staring at Rasmus with wild eyes now, and his expression matches mine.

It matches mine a little too well.

Oh my god.

"The both of you know the truth. You've always known it. But maybe only one of you is finding out right now."

"Are you saying I'm Torben's *son!*?" Rasmus exclaims.

At the same time I'm pointing at him and crying out, "I'm his *sister!*?"

Mushy lady goes silent. I stare at Rasmus, dumbfounded. Suddenly I'm looking for every single similarity we have. Our height, our athletic build, the cut of our jaw, our cheekbones. His hair may be red, and mine is mahogany, his eyes blue, mine brown, but I see it.

I see my father in him.

Because he's my father's son.

Rasmus is my brother.

"If Torben is my father…then who is my mother?" Rasmus manages to eke out, staring at me in the same way I'm staring at him.

Silence fills the underground.

"Who is my mother?!" Rasmus screams, a vein popping on his forehead.

"I have a hard time believing that you don't know," she eventually says. "Her blood would be unmistakable." She pauses. "You're Louhi's son."

CHAPTER FIVE

HANNA

"THE TRUTH"

I take a step away from Rasmus, all those reasons to distrust him coming to a head.

"Louhi?" I sputter out. "The ex-wife of Death? The horned demon woman? The one that wants to raise the Old Gods? That's your mother?"

Rasmus shakes his head, his face paling. "She isn't. She can't be."

"You knew all this time…"

"I didn't know!" he yells at me, hands going to his red hair and tugging. His red hair.

Never trust a redhead.

"Fuck," I swear, remembering Death's motto. "And I just left with you. I believed you."

"Hanna," he practically growls, grabbing my shoulders, his fingers digging in as his wild eyes search my face. "I didn't know who my real parents are, but it's sure as hell not her. I would know, I would know it."

"You do know it," mushy lady says, seeming more like an omniscient god now.

"I don't!" he yells at her, looking around the cave in a panic. He brings his gaze back to me and I can tell he's being earnest. "Please believe me. I didn't know Torben was my father, I didn't know Louhi was my mother. I don't even know how it's possible. Think about it. Think about it for a second, okay Hanna? We both know Torben well. Would he ever be involved with someone like Louhi?"

"No," I say automatically. "He would never. My father is a good man, he wouldn't…and he would have been with my mother…" I trail off at that. My mother never talked about her relationship with my dad. Every time I asked, she would brush me off and get mad at me, so I learned to stop asking. I don't know how long they dated. I don't even know how long they were married. Rasmus is six years older than me, it's more than possible that my father wasn't with my mom when Rasmus was born.

But that doesn't even matter because my father would never sleep with a freaking demon.

"Death told me that your mother was a Lapp Witch," I say. "Not a demon."

"Louhi is both of those things," mushy lady says. "And while she may no longer be the Goddess of Death, she is still a Goddess in her own right."

"Well, fuck," Rasmus says. He absently walks to the

middle of the cavern and sits down on the ground, his head buried in his hands.

I can't blame him. I don't know how to feel about any of this. On one hand, I feel an affinity for him knowing that we share the same father. No wonder he looked up to him the way he did, that he went through all those lengths to rescue him from Death. His father figure was literal, and we know now we share the same blood.

On the other hand, he is the son of Louhi. Which means that her blood is running through him. That he's part demon and can't be trusted and that there's a chance he's still lying through his teeth about all of this.

But it just doesn't make sense. There is no way my father would sleep with some she-devil.

"So now what do we do?" I ask, though I don't expect either of them to have an answer.

"You take your truth," the mushy lady's voice says, now coming from all corners of the glowing cavern, "and you learn to make it your reality."

"Right," I mumble, just as my stomach starts to twist. This time in hunger. I barely ate this morning, I was so nervous about the wedding and…

I look down at my dress, dirty and torn. How the hell was the wedding today? It feels like weeks have passed but I'm not even sure if night has fallen yet. It's impossible to tell with the storm raging above ground, and the isolation of the cavern.

A shiver runs through me, the cold and damp of being underground and the sheer exhaustion of the day making me feel like I'm getting sick. How the hell did Rasmus live down here like this? I don't think I'd last a day.

He's the son of a devil woman, maybe he can put up with anything.

I look over at Rasmus. Sitting on the dirt floor, his head in his hands, knees drawn up, his lanky body looks small, like he's a little boy sent to his room for punishment. My heart softens in my ribcage and I'm starting to feel sorry for him. I really don't think he knew about Louhi and I'm certain he didn't know about my dad. He's given me some looks before that a brother would never knowingly give his sister. No, the fact that we're half brother and sister is as a surprise to him as it is to me.

I don't know how I'd react if I found out my mother wasn't my real mother. I suppose part of me would feel a sense of relief. It would explain so much, how my mother always treated me like I was a burden, a chore, something I never really understood because, if she really disliked me so much, why didn't she leave me in Finland with my father?

But, despite how strained and unfair our relationship seems, how I spent all of my youth trying to please her to no avail, how jealous I was of my friends who had mothers that actually loved them and cared about them, at least, *at least* my mother isn't related to the devil.

Right?

"Mushy lady?" I ask, my voice echoing.

The mycelia pulses out a sharp burst of light. I've insulted her. Well, serves her right for calling me boring.

"Sorry, *Sammalta*," I say, trying not to smile. "Can I call you Sam?"

A pause, the mycelia flickering. Then a deep, "No."

"Just checking. Listen, I still have some questions."

"I'm sure you do," she says. "But perhaps it's time to rest."

I gesture to the empty space. "I'm not sure it matters much to you, but there is nothing to rest on. I hope you at least had like a toadstool seat for Rasmus to sit on while he was here."

A deep sigh reverberates through the air.

"I offer you shelter from the storm, nothing more," she says.

"You also dropped a bunch of truth bombs on us. Speaking of which, you asked me who my mother is. Why? She's not… she's not Louhi too, is she?"

I tense up, not knowing what her answer is going to be.

The mycelia glows and then goes dark. Perhaps she's checking the network. I look over at Rasmus, who lifts his head out of his hand to glance at me.

"I don't believe so," Sammalta says eventually.

I exhale loudly in relief. "Well there's that." Then I wince and give Rasmus an apologetic smile. "Sorry."

He just shrugs and lies back on the dirt. "It's fine. It's all fine."

But we both know he's anything but fine.

Something cold and wet splashes on my forehead, rousing me from my sleep.

I quickly sit up, my heart getting into gear. For a moment I don't know where I am, I just know that I'm somewhere I shouldn't be, someplace unnatural, and it's so dark I can't see a thing.

Then my eyes adjust. There is a faint pale-white glow coming from the corner of the cavern. The sunmoonstone sphere is still emitting light, except it's changed from the light of the sun to the soft glow of the moon. In front of it is Rasmus, his long limbs stretched out on the patch of moss.

When mushy lady decided that question time was over, Rasmus made her provide a little more for us while we rode out Death's storm. Her mycelium arms went to work, collecting moss from the forest floor and bringing them into the cavern to make us beds. Then she brought some tart apples the size of grapes, and chalices and bowls carved from agate and onyx, filled with filtered water that comes from a nearby aquifer. Lucky for us mortals, the aquifer is around a darkened corner at the end of the cavern and drips down into an underground stream—the privacy makes for a makeshift bathroom and place to get clean. I rinsed off in the cool water, using a bunch of dried moss as a sponge, while Rasmus lit a fire to dry out our clothes.

That same aquifer is now dripping onto my forehead. I stare up at the ceiling at the moisture gathered there and inch out of the way before the next drop falls. I let out a low groan. Every single muscle hurts. Makes me realize just how cloistered and pampered I was at Shadow's End. The only exercise I got was from doing naked gymnastics with Death. Which, even though it got my heart rate up, was a far cry from the thrice weekly workouts I would do back home.

Home. Los Angeles. The idea that I'm so close to being

back there feels unreal. In fact, so unreal that in my mind and memory, LA feels more like a fantasy land than Tuonela does. It's like I've lost all connection to the life I once had, to the person I once was, and I'm not sure I can ever really go back. The heat and sun and grimy glitter of the city is going to feel horribly boring after my time down here.

Yeah, but boring is safe, my inner self reminds me. *Boring keeps you alive.*

But there's a difference between *being* alive and *feeling* alive. In my boring, safe life back in LA, I was kept alive, I was safe and surviving. But I never felt alive. I never felt connected to the earth and the sun and the moon and all that is magical and possible. I never felt the power of being alive pumping through my veins, invigorating my cells.

Funny how it took a trip to the Land of the Dead to realize my capacity for living.

I sigh, stretching out my arms, looking down at my clothes. I only have my wedding dress to wear, and I ended up using a knife made of white, luminescent selenite to cut away the ripped parts. Now the dress is up to my knees in rags, and with my boots, I look like some kind of dirty steampunk heroine.

I reach over and grab the knife, feeling it between my hands. It's cold to the touch and glows ever so slightly under my grasp. The carved ridges of the blade don't seem sharp enough to make a dent in butter and yet they were able to slice through layers and layers of material no problem. The mycelia had brought me the knife when I asked, but I'm wondering if they'll notice if I take it. Though I'm pretty sure we'll make a run for Death's Landing once the weather allows, it can't hurt to have a weapon on hand. Not just against all the things in this land that want to kill you, but with Rasmus being Louhi's child, it wouldn't hurt to keep my guard up.

So, I take the knife and slide it into my boot which is nice and dry from the fire that Rasmus had made earlier. Then I lie back, out of the way of the dripping water, and attempt to get back asleep.

I've just entered that weird twilight land between waking and dreaming when I hear Rasmus say, "Hanna? Are you awake?"

"Mmmmphf," I groan, rolling over to look at him. He's backlit by the sphere and I can't make out his face but for a moment he looks foreboding, ominous, as if it's not him at all. That it's someone else that is watching me. That if he turned his head toward the light, it would expose sharp jagged teeth in a leering grin, empty eyes that promise nothing but pain and horror.

"What is it?" he asks. "You look like you've seen a ghost."

My breath catches in my chest as I stare at him, until the illusion of something terrifying slowly fades away and I see that it's only Rasmus in front of me, no one else. "I couldn't tell where I was for a moment," I manage to say, trying to brush off the disturbing feeling.

He nods. "I'm not sure what time it is but I've got enough rest. I think I'd like us to get moving." He clears his throat. "Sammalta?" he says, projecting his voice. "Are you there?"

The mycelia glows.

"I am always here, just as I am always there," she answers.

All right then, Cheshire Cat.

"How is the storm doing? Do you think we can chance it?" Rasmus asks.

The white strands around the cavern pulse. "I cannot predict the future."

I roll my eyes at her non-answer while Rasmus presses her. "Would you be able to find Alku for us?"

"The storm is no better than it was yesterday," she says.

"Well that's exactly what I wanted to know," Rasmus says, sounding annoyed. He reaches over and picks up the sunmoonstone sphere, holding it in his fist until the light grows brighter and illuminates the cavern with the shine of the sun.

He gives me a curious glance, frowning. "What do you think? Stay down here for a few more days, hoping that Death's storm dies down?"

I shake my head. "I want to chance it," I tell him. I think I'd go mad if I had to stay here any longer. Besides, I don't like to wait things out, I'd rather face them head on if I can. "We don't know how long Death will stay angry at me for. Might be for eternity. The God knows how to hold a grudge."

"Fair enough," Rasmus says, getting to his feet and dusting off his pants. He reaches down and pulls me to my feet. "We better get going then." He pauses, giving me a shy smile. "Sister."

I laugh nervously. "Sounds weird doesn't it?"

He shrugs. "I could get used to it. I have to admit, it's actually kind of nice to have someone you're related to." A dark look comes over his eyes. "Growing up, that's really all I wished for."

"Rasmus," mushy lady's voice comes through. "If you're going for it, I don't want Alku's life at risk. You better go to the portal at the Shaman's Way. It's closer than Death's Landing."

"Sounds good," Rasmus says. "Probably best I don't go near the Great Inland Sea anyway."

"Why not?" I ask, since it was the way we came in to Tuonela. "Sea monsters? Typhoons?"

"Well, yeah, all of that. And the fact that I never did Vellamo that favor of bringing her a dress made of moonsilk from Kuutar. Remember she said she'd feed my bones to the mermaids? I mean, I love being devoured by mermaids, but not in the literal sense."

"You know I saw Kuutar," I tell him, "when I freed my mermaid friend, Bell."

"You know Bell?" he asks, licking his lips.

I grimace. "Oh god. Please don't tell me you know Bell in a personal way."

He rolls his eyes. "I haven't fucked every mermaid, if that's what you're wondering."

I raise my hand to get him to shut up. "That's not what I'm wondering and I don't want to hear it either way."

"Of course, there's a reason why the Shaman's Way was never your destination to begin with," mushy lady interrupts our conversation from getting into even weirder territory. "You'll have to pass over the Star Swamp to get there and it's far more dangerous. Even more so during a storm where there is no shelter. Except for Louhi's castle."

"Wait a minute," I protest, eyeing Rasmus. "We're going near your mother?"

I don't like this. Not when we've just discovered their relationship to each other. What if she can tell her son is near?

"I don't like it either," he says. "But I think it's our best shot."

Well, I don't feel bad about taking the knife now. Looks like I might need it after all.

CHAPTER SIX

HANNA

"THE STAR SWAMP"

We leave the cavern, going up the winding stairs made of bone and agate, the sphere lighting the way. I know we're near the surface because that ghastly smell comes wafting through with the wind and I almost gag.

"Oh god," I cry out, covering my nose with my hand.

Rasmus grunts in disgust as we push through a wall of dead and rotting leaves that have been blown up against the entrance to the underground. Once out, we pass under the rib cage of the dinosaur, wind whipping my hair in all directions. My kingdom for a hair-tie!

The storm hasn't weakened at all. The ground is littered with leaves and branches and patches of ice. Flakes of snow are blown about with each gust of wind, a kind of cold that cuts you to the bone.

his hair. "Where is Alku?"

"Are you sure the unicorn is going to show? Mushy lady didn't exactly answer you."

Before Ramus can answer, I hear a snort above the roar of the wind and Alku appears in all its winged, decaying glory. The unicorn lands in front of us, lowering its head.

At your service, Alku says.

"Are you sure you're up to this?" I ask it. Even though it's pretty much our only way out of Tuonela, I also don't want to put the creature's life at risk.

I promised a favor, Alku says with a shake of its purple kelp-like mane. *And favors are followed through to the end. Come now. If we're lucky there might be a lull in the storm.*

I look to Rasmus. "Perhaps we should have traveled at night, when Death was asleep."

Alku snorts. *Death has not been sleeping. There has been no break in the storm.*

Part of me is flattered that I have the power to cause the God of Death to lose sleep over me. The other part is a tad scared. Let's hope that Death's vengeance is relegated to this storm and I won't have to see him in person, because I'm starting to think he might not be so nice to me. In fact, I wouldn't be surprised if he'd try to kill me out of pure rage, much like he did to Surma.

I push that thought out of my head. Rasmus swings onto the unicorn's back and reaches down for me, pulling me up so that this time I'm between Alku's neck and Rasmus. I make a fist in the mane just in time as Alku flaps its wide leathery bat wings and takes off into the sky.

It's not the easiest lift-off. With the wind whipping the trees around, Alku has to stay just above the treeline, or we'll be caught in the swaying limbs or knocked out by falling branches. But if Alku ventures too high above the forest, the winds get more violent and the lightning strikes get closer. I've never seen lightning and snow together like this, and it's both beautiful and terrifying. It feels like we're in a snow globe that someone has dropped and is just bouncing around.

Despite the turbulent weather, Alku keeps flying, and by the time I'm practically covered in a layer of ice, the forest below us becomes more and more sparse. The firs and cedars fade away to birch and aspen, then orchard trees, then bushes and ragged brush before finally all that's before us is a great expanse of white.

"Is this The Frozen Void?" I ask, trying to get my geography straight.

The Void is to the northwest of the Sea. This is Star Swamp, Alku tells me. *If it wasn't covered in snow right now, you'd be able to see the pockets of nothing.*

"Pockets of nothing?"

The swamp is comprised of narrow strips of grass and solid ground. In between those strips is the swamp. When you look down into the pools, it's so black it's like looking into space on a clear night. Because you are looking into space. You're looking into the black nothingness, the void which is Oblivion. If you fall into that water, you fall into space, into Oblivion, to float for eternity.

"Right," I say slowly, scared shitless. "So, avoid the swamp at all costs. Got it."

Luckily, we're not too far from the portal at Shaman's Way. Just a little bit more. Hold tight.

I hold its mane tighter and its bat wings flap at a faster rate, matching my racing heart.

"Having a good chat?" Rasmus asks, his voice behind me sounding vacant.

"Sorry, I forget that you can't hear the unicorn," I tell him, craning my neck to give him a half-smile. "Alku was just giving me a geography lesson."

"Oh," he says.

"Must be frustrating when you can't hear everything," I say, picking up on a strange vibe from him.

He doesn't say anything to that. In fact, his energy seems to change, like his body is growing tense.

Frowning, I twist around fully at the waist to get a better look at him.

His eyes are completely black.

I gasp. "Fucking hell! Rasmus?"

He just stares out at nothing, a blank expression on his face, except for those horrible black eyes, like they were plucked from a great white shark and stuffed in his skull.

Alku! I yell inside my head. *Rasmus doesn't look like he's doing too good! His eyes are all black!*

Have his eyes done that before?

No! And he looks like he's in a trance of some sort.

I see. I'll try and fly faster if I can. Hopefully he remains in a trance before we can touch down to safety.

I look back at Rasmus again. Fucking hell, he's creepy. With his pale skin and red hair, the black eyes look positively demonic, which makes me wonder if the demon side of him is coming through. Maybe because we're closer to Louhi out this way?

Uh, Alku, I say to the unicorn, *just how close are we to Louhi's castle?*

Castle Synti? Alku asks, a tremor to its voice. *Don't tell me you want to go there.*

No! No, I just, well, I don't know if Sammalta filled you in on what's happening with Rasmus, but it turns out he's Louhi's son.

What?! the unicorn exclaims, its wings slowing. *The son of Louhi? You should have told me that before we took off.*

Would it have made a difference?

Yes! I most definitely wouldn't have flown so close.

It's then that my focus goes to the tip of the unicorn's black iron horn and the space beyond it. At the blurry white horizon, a dark shimmery structure emerges, like something from a twisted fairytale. It looks like Shadow's End in one way, yet there's something inhuman about it, like it wasn't built by Gods at all but something else, something of another world, some place worse than this one. The sight of it makes me feel like I'm going to throw up, a physical aversion.

That's it, I think grimly. *That's her castle.*

Castle Synti, Alku says. *They say it was built by Old Gods whom she conjured through the veils, came straight from* Kaaos *and enforced the castle with pure evil.*

Enforced with pure evil? Probably not up to code.

Suddenly the energy behind me changes as if Rasmus is glowing with the same sort of energy that's coming from Louhi's castle. Before I can turn around, his hands are around my neck, squeezing *hard*.

Holy FUCK!

Alku! I scream in my head, my hands going to his and trying to pry his fingers off. They're holding me like a vice, they're that strong, my windpipe bursting with pain. *He's choking me!*

Hold on! Alku yells.

I'm about to tell him I can't hold on, I'm trying to pull Rasmus' hands away from my throat, unable to take a breath, but the unicorn suddenly veers to left.

My scream is choked. Instead of trying to knock Rasmus off-balance, I'm falling to the right along with him, my hands shooting out to grab hold of Alku's mane but it's too late.

We're falling through the sky, right down toward the Star Swamp.

I'm going to die, I think, and not because we might land on a snow-covered patch of Oblivion, but because, despite the fact that we're free-falling, black-eyed Rasmus is still holding onto me.

With the little energy I have, I manage to twist around mid-air, separating myself from Rasmus moments before we crash, gasping for breath.

I hit the ground hard, snow flying up all around me, and I sink for just long enough that I know I must have gone into the water, into the swamp, and that it's all over for me for eternity.

But then I realize I was just sinking through the snowdrift and after a couple of seconds, I do a quick internal check of my body. I'm not in too much pain, just sore and cold and my neck is bruised, but I think I'm all intact.

Remembering where I am, I quickly get to my feet, trying to be as careful as possible because if I'm not dead yet, one wrong step might fix that.

The snow falls off my clothes and I frantically look around. Alku is hovering above me, relief in its eyes, but Rasmus is nowhere to be seen.

Oh fuck. He didn't…he didn't fall into the swamp, did he?

On one hand I would be relieved because he was just trying to kill me but…fucking hell, Rasmus is my brother now. And that sharked-eyed psycho wasn't Rasmus at all. He'd been possessed.

Stay still, Alku commands, coming closer to me, the wings beating hard enough to blow my hair back. It's like standing under a helicopter. *I don't want to land in case there isn't ground beneath me.*

I glance around anxiously. In the distance, the shiny black façade of Synti Castle stands like a sentinel guard. Between us is nothing but sheets of white snow and ice. No sign of Rasmus. No patch of land Alku can trust.

Alku comes closer now, lowering its horn. *Grab hold of my horn.*

"Are you kidding me?" I cry out. "Then what? You'll fly across the swamp with me holding on? I'll let go. I won't make it."

I'm starting to panic. I can already feel the sensation of trying to hold on and my hands slipping. Falling a second time I know I won't be so lucky.

You don't have a choice, Hanna, Alku says. *We're closer to Shaman's Way than you think and I know you're strong, stronger than you give yourself credit for. You can do this.*

I glance down at my arms, arms that I was once self-conscious of because of how muscular they naturally are. All those years of fighting and lifting weights and going to the gym might finally come in handy. Maybe Alku is right. Maybe I have to view the unicorn horn as doing chin-ups. I've spent a hell of a lot of time hanging from those bars. I just have to hold on.

I just have to hold on.

"Okay," I tell Alku, trying to sound strong. I hold my hands out, ready to reach as the horn comes closer.

But then Alku's eyes widen in their sockets.

Behind you! Alku yells.

I whirl around to see Rasmus emerging from the snow like a bear after hibernation, coming for me with this dumb kind of rage.

His eyes are still black as sin.

I scream and Alku flies forward, knocking me to the ground as it lunges at Rasmus, attempting to spear him in the chest with its horn.

But Rasmus is fast, faster than he's ever been, and he's ducking to the side and out of the way, disappearing in the snow again.

Meanwhile Alku can't correct in time and his horn sinks into the snow and the giant unicorn is propelled into a summersault, its wings furiously flapping as it tries to right itself.

"Alku!" I scream helplessly as the unicorn goes flying over, landing in the snow with a thud until it nearly disappears.

Rasmus is still out of sight, but I don't have time to worry about him. I try to run over to Alku to make sure the unicorn is okay, praying I don't take the wrong step.

Its horn is sticking straight out of the snow, not moving. Then it inches forward and Alku's massive head rises out of the snow, mouth open in a cry, showing a row of fanged teeth, which would be most unexpected and frightening if I weren't in such shock. It shakes its neck and withers, mane flying, and tries to get the snow off.

I'm all right, Alku says, struggling to get up. *I'm just…I'm just…*

I can't see the unicorn's wings, but the snow moves up and down like its trying to flap them. *I think I'm sinking…* Alku says, its voice straining as it tries to lift its leg and pull itself up.

Oh hell no.

"No, you're not," I say, trudging through the snow even closer.

Don't come any closer! The unicorn yells, pure terror in its voice. *I'm sinking into Oblivion.*

I shake my head, swallowing hard. "You're just sinking through the snow, keep trying, you'll make your way out."

The unicorn's eyes widen. *No. I can't feel my legs. I can't…*

"You're frozen!" I cry out, trying not to panic. "You need to get out of the snow. Let me help you."

I'm in the Star Swamp, Alku says hopelessly. *Please, please don't come any closer or you will fall in.*

I shake my head, tears springing to my eyes. I don't even know Alku very well, but the unicorn has only been a help to me, and I refuse to give up on it. *The Never-Ending Story* did a number on me when I saw it as a child, I don't want to go through that in real life.

"Please, Alku, just try. If I could just get your horn, maybe I could pull you out." I come forward an inch.

Alku just shakes its head. It doesn't say anything else.

"Alku," I say again, holding out my hands. "Let me try to save you."

It blinks. It stops struggling. For a moment I think it's sinking further but instead there's a blackness rising up from the white canvas of the snow, a blackness that feels just as empty and soulless and horrible. It slides up the unicorn's neck like an oil spill, erasing Alku as it goes.

"Alku!" I scream.

But it's too late.

The blackness takes over its head and then suddenly it just ceases to exist. Like the blackness was just an illusion in the air, a moving shadow that's suddenly gone.

Alku has been taken by Oblivion.

"Oh god," I cry out, collapsing to my knees. I know I don't have time to be sad or to be in shock, that an evil Rasmus is still around and I'm still surrounded by a hidden swamp that will quite literally kill me. And yet the loss of Alku stabs me right in the heart.

We were so close to escaping this world. And this is all my fault.

All my fault.

"So we finally meet," a deep voice says from behind me.

I jolt, startled, my eyes glued to where Alku was, too scared to turn around. It's a voice I've never heard before. Low, raspy, dripping with malice. It's a voice that sinks deep into my marrow, threatening to rewrite the blood inside me.

I know it's Louhi before I even turn around. Every cell inside me tells me so. They tell me to run, far far away.

I try to swallow the fear lodged in my throat, but even breathing feels impossible. I'm afraid I might turn to stone if I don't move.

I turn around and look.

Standing about twenty-feet away from me is the most terrifying and powerful-looking being I've ever seen.

She's tall. Maybe as tall as Death. Seven feet? Eight feet? She's wearing a long black robe that's cut down in a V-neck to her navel, iron armor plates at her shoulders and elbows. Giant wings come out from either side of her back, held in a V-shape, but they don't seem like wings that would let her fly, they're too thin and ragged for that, the color black and transparent enough that I can see through them.

Her skin is pale, bordering on a greenish-gray color, her breasts are large and high, creating some impressive cleavage, and she seems to have scales in some places. Her neck is long with a face that rivals Angeline Jolie, with razor-sharp bone structure, cheeks that could cut glass, full lips, and bright, pale green eyes that hold malevolence as she stares at me. Her brows are made of a dark boney growth and she doesn't have any hair on her head—instead, she has six pairs of black rams horns growing right out of her skull.

If I wasn't so dehydrated, I would definitely pee my pants.

She's not alone either. Beside her, kneeling in the snow, is Rasmus.

Rasmus has a collar around his neck, an iron one that looks no different from the one Death used on me. Rasmus's hands are curled around the metal and he's staring at me with his old blue eyes, free from demonic possession for now.

A demon that was obviously Louhi. If she was able to get into Rasmus' head, there's a chance she might get into mine.

"You know, I've heard so much about you, Hanna," Louhi says, her lips pursing in amusement as she looks me over. "About how selfless you are. Frankly, I didn't believe it, that you would go through all this shit to get to your father, to take his place at Shadow's End, but then you went and did it, didn't you? And now I got to see you in action right here. You nearly risked your life to save that unicorn. But that to me doesn't scream *good* or *selfless*. It just tells me that you're purely stupid."

"What are you doing with Rasmus?" I ask her, surprised I've found my voice. She's invoking such fear in me that I don't think I can function enough to survive. "You know he's your son, don't you?"

She laughs, throwing her head back. It's a cackle. Of course she would cackle.

"Oh. You really are that stupid. To think I wouldn't know my own son. You're the one who never clued in that he was your brother."

I blink at her, going still. "How did you know that?"

She raises her razor-sharp chin. "You think your little

mushroom friend's network is private? That fungus is all over the land. Doesn't take much magic to learn how to tap in. I knew you were coming. Might have even put the idea in her rotting brain to have you come this way."

I clench my jaw, giving Rasmus a look of disappointment. From the way he is though, looking scared and weak next to his mother, I know that he feels it. I don't think he knew that mushy lady was leading us astray.

But hell. Maybe on some level he did.

"And to think you were to become the next Goddess of Death," she says, slowly pacing back and forth, her black robe gliding over the snow like silken tar, her pale eyes flicking over me. She laughs again. "Wispy little thing, aren't you?"

I bristle, surprised at my reaction. I spent my teenage years counting calories and exercising so I could be a "wispy little thing" but my height and body would never allow it. Now that I've embraced who I am, someone tall, someone strong, I'm taking that as an insult.

"I'm not little and I'm not wispy," I sneer at her.

"Hmmm. Full of bravado though," she says, looking down at me. "You would have kept Tuoni on his toes, that's for sure. You should be glad that Rasmus did us all a favor by taking you when he did."

My mouth drops as I look to Rasmus. "This was all part of it? You tricked me!"

Rasmus shakes his head violently. "No!" he protests, blue eyes flashing. "I didn't, I swear I didn't!"

"Oh, shut up," Louhi says, and she swiftly yanks the leash, practically snapping Rasmus' neck in half. He yelps in pain and falls over in the snow, his hands at the collar, gasping for breath. "It's my fault really," she goes on with a sigh, showing her son zero concern. "I should have intervened in his life earlier. I waited thirty years to see what he'd become, and it's almost too late to undo what's been done to him." She gives me a sharp look. "What *your father* has done to him. Made him weak."

I hate that she's mentioning my father. A fierce protectiveness comes over me, making me feel feral. "Don't you dare talk about him. My father—our father—made Rasmus into a good man, a powerful shaman."

Okay, considering I don't really trust Rasmus and I don't know him all that well, I'm talking out of my ass. But still, my father did train him, and it's obvious that he believed in him. Rasmus has enough power to create a storm and launch an attack on Shadow's End, which must have not been an easy feat or else all the shamans would do it. And Rasmus cared enough about my father, without even knowing their true relationship, to go to Tuonela to get him...even if I was what was sacrificed.

"A good man?" Louhi repeats with a curl of her upper lip. God she's so ugly and beautiful at the same time. "What does that have to do with anything? Good means nothing. Do you know how easy it is to poison good? To corrupt it? It takes but a moment to cross over. In the end, darkness prevails."

I shouldn't laugh at that, but I do. "Darkness prevails? How original. No wonder Death was happy to see you go."

I don't see it coming.

Louhi opens her mouth and a long, forked gray tongue

shoots out, wrapping around my throat like a python and picking me off the ground, twenty, thirty feet in the air.

For the second time today I'm being choked to death, a scream dying inside me.

Louhi's slimy tongue swings me out in front of her, dangling me high above a patch of seemingly innocent snow.

"In your world you have such a thing as Russian Roulette," she says, sounding sinister despite her tongue being in use. "Let's play my version of the game, shall we? If I drop you, there's a chance you'll land in snow. There's an even greater chance you'll land in the void of Oblivion, just as your unicorn friend did."

I curl my fingers over the tongue to loosen the pressure on my throat, but she's far too strong and her tongue is too slippery, coated with a fine black sludge that makes it hard to get a grip. I don't want her to drop me into Oblivion, but if I don't take my chances, she's going to strangle me to death, and that's a one-way ticket to Oblivion, too.

"Rasmus," Louhi says to her son, puffing up her chest. "In my world, you're just a bottom feeder with an empty brain. If you're going to get anywhere, then you must watch and you must learn and you must *do*. In order to have power, you must let power corrupt you. Then everything is limitless."

Rasmus is still lying in the snow, breathing hard. He lifts head to see me.

Fight her, his broken voice projects into my brain. *She's going to kill you.*

I can barely form thoughts enough to answer Rasmus, but I know he's right.

A little magic would be nice, I think to him, the corners of my vision going blurry and gray as I lose oxygen.

I can't, he says painfully. *The collar, I think it's draining me. But you're the daughter of Torben, too.*

Too bad I don't know any magic to draw upon.

But I do have a knife in my boot.

Using what little strength I have left, I bring my legs up and reach into my boot, pulling out the selenite blade. Before Louhi can act, I swipe the glowing white knife at her tongue, severing it. Black blood splashes everywhere.

She screams in agony.

I scream in fear.

And then I'm falling.

Falling fast.

About to smash into the waiting snow that rushes up at me.

Suddenly the air vibrates with energy. Out of the corner of my eye I see something large and black flying toward me at breakneck speed.

Seconds from crashing into the snow, a hand reaches out and grabs my arm, jerking me upward.

A hand I know too well.

A metal hand.

CHAPTER SEVEN

DEATH

"THE EX-WIFE"

We were almost too late.

After a day and night of flying and searching the land for Hanna, we finally came across some intel this morning. According to Tapio, God of the Forest and a fairly good ally at times, Hanna and Rasmus had been spotted at the Pile of Decay and had recently taken flight on a unicorn.

Tapio's daughter, Tellervo, then said that she overheard the fungi talking, and that they were heading toward the portal to the Upper World at Shaman's Way. Thank fuck for that, otherwise we wouldn't have been there in time. Sarvi took off in that direction, maybe twenty minutes after they left, and all the while I was preparing for the worst. There may have been a grain of guilt in thinking that my storm may have caused them to take the shorter route out of this world, knowing that Louhi's lair was close by, and knowing now that Rasmus is Louhi's son, my guilt was replaced by suspicion.

The unicorn, which Sarvi said was named Alku, was just a speck in the sky when I saw it fly down toward the ground. By then I had to say a few spells with help of the shungite key around my neck to conjure up some favorable winds to get us there faster.

I felt Louhi before I even saw her. She feels like a freshly drawn bath at first, something you can slip into and let your inhibitions down. That's what makes her so lethal, so poisonous, so insidious. There's something about how pure and honest her evil is that pulls you in and makes you want to stay. Then the water gradually gets hotter, and hotter, until your skin is burning off and if you don't act fast, you'll just be another bag of bones for her to claim.

Do you feel that? I asked Sarvi.

Before Sarvi could answer, there she was. She appeared in the white line of the horizon like a blackened scar. The closer we got, the more the scar separated into three.

Louhi in her formidable glory, Rasmus in the snow beside her, and Hanna.

Hanna dangling high above the snow, Louhi's tongue wrapped around her neck, squeezing the life out of her. I can sense when someone is near death, part of my *gift* I suppose, and Hanna was.

I didn't need to tell Sarvi to fly faster.

From the excited look on my ex-wife's face, I could tell she was close to snapping Hanna's neck, ending her life for good.

I knew we might not reach her in time.

But because Louhi was so focused on killing Hanna, she wasn't aware of her surroundings. Didn't see Sarvi coming.

And Hanna, she surprised me. She surprised Louhi too.

When it looked like all was lost, she reached into her boot and pulled out a selenite knife, a knife that only works as a weapon depending on who is wielding it. For a mere mortal, selenite is a weak salt-based crystal that can't cut through anything and is prone to breakage.

But when Hanna used it, she was able to slice Louhi's formidable tongue in half.

Louhi's scream made me smile.

And I was still smiling as we flew between Hanna and the ground and I was able to grab hold of her arm, pulling her onto Sarvi's back as the unicorn flew upwards and away from the swamp.

Louhi is still screaming at us. We're taking a few victory laps above her head, Hanna safely wedged between me and the unicorn's neck.

"You!" Louhi screams up at me as we fly in circles, blood pouring out of her mouth as what's left of her tongue retracts in a messy splatter.

"Yes, me," I say, lifting up my mask to give her a dashing grin. "Long time no see, she-devil."

She screams again like a caged animal, knowing that if she attempted to speak, she'd sound like an idiot.

"I'll save you the trouble of what you want to say," I tell her. "Would be the kindest thing to do, considering your new impairment. You're going to tell me that I'm a dead God, that my time as ruler is over, that Hanna will never be as good of a Goddess as you, that I'll rue the day I crossed you. To which I will counter all of that as being a lie. You're in a position of weakness, Devil Woman, which is why you think your son Rasmus will help you, since your other children will not. Rasmus might be coerced, or perhaps he already has been, but you will remain nothing but a weakness in this land. Whatever uprising you hope to have a hand in, you will merely watch from the sidelines as the Old Gods fail to rise, wishing you could have helped, while knowing deep down your contribution would have been worthless anyway."

Louhi screams louder. She throws the chain attached to Rasmus to the snow and flaps her ugly wings, shooting up to us, her hands outstretched, fingernails growing into claws. Always forgot that part of her anatomy; she tried in vain to leave scars on my back. She was never able to leave her mark on me.

I'm about to tell Sarvi to puncture her wing with its horn but before I can, Hanna takes the selenite knife and whips it through the air toward Louhi. The knife goes right through the thin membrane of her right wing, creating a hole which causes Louhi to lose flight, spinning out of control.

I hate how fucking impressed I am. How fucking *hard* I am. Hanna can probably feel it too, because of how her ass is pressed right up against me.

My god, this woman might eat me alive. I should probably just end her here. Toss her off Sarvi's back and feed her to my ex. I'm still furious at her for leaving and yet I'm starting to doubt I have the balls to truly punish her and make her suffer for what she did.

"Shit," Hanna says under her breath. "I liked that knife."

"I'll get you a new one," I tell her. "Come on Sarvi, let's head home before she regenerates."

Sarvi nods and its wings beat furiously away from a screaming Louhi, writhing in a black blotch on the snow.

"Won't she follow us?" Hanna asks, looking over her shoulder, trying to see them in the background. I catch her eyes for a moment—even with my mask on it's like she sees me for what I am underneath—and I pour cement over my heart to prevent it from cracking. I'd forgotten how beautiful she is, her fairy eyes that act like pathways to another world.

I avoid her stare. "She doesn't have the means," I tell her gruffly, finding my composure, refusing to let myself feel anything, not even her beauty. "No unicorn will obey her. Not many other creatures that can match their speed in flight. Of course, there are rumors of flying lizards that live in the cliffs of the Iron Mountains but I have yet to see them. At least not the large ones."

"You said she can regenerate though?"

"Louhi may no longer be the Goddess of Death, but she is still a Goddess, thanks to her father. Rangaista is what you mortals may think of as Satan, though perhaps he is not the end-all and be-all of all that is evil. Just one devil among others. An Old God. And since she is his daughter, she is a Goddess. As such, she is immortal until killed, and she's very hard to kill. Seems the more evil someone is, the harder they are to get rid of. You have to wonder why that is."

"You think being good gets you killed?"

"It doesn't get you much, does it little bird?" I ask her. "Look at you. All these selfless sacrifices you made, and yet here you are. Still stuck with me, still being forced into a marriage that you don't want, still unable to leave this land and see your father again."

I hear her swallow, her body tensing in front of me. It's only now that I realize she must be wearing the dress she was to be married in, of course now it's dirty and torn to shreds, her long dark hair in knots and harboring moss and twigs.

"There is a lot I need to talk to you about," she says quietly.

"And who says I want to talk to you at all?" I say, leaning in until my lips graze her earlobe.

She sucks in her breath, trying to hide a shiver from me, but I can feel everything her body is doing, how hard she tries to shut things down. That's another thing about me. I can sense when someone is close to death, but I can also sense when someone is truly feeling alive. I know when Hanna's body is ripe and ready for me, more than she knows herself.

"I know you're mad," she says after a moment, her muscles tensing. "I've seen the weather."

I slip my hands around her waist, squeezing her. "You don't know the half of it, fairy girl. You've never really seen me mad."

Her head dips. "I saw what you did to Surma," she says in a low voice.

"That was a thoughtless rage," I admit, squeezing her until she gasps. "I don't regret it, Surma deserved it, but there's a certain madness I'm fond of that takes a lot of deliberation and thought. It's a calculated anger and believe me, you don't want to be on the receiving end of it. On second thought, perhaps you will be."

I lick up the back of her ear until she shivers. That was a mistake. One taste of her honey skin and I feel my dick get harder. "I'm already furious at you and what you did," I manage to say. "The fact that I just saved you from Louhi may have tempered that a bit, but I have no doubt you're going to do or say something that will provoke me again. You thought I was a monster before…"

"Maybe I liked it when you were a monster."

I can't help but chuckle. I slip a hand into her hair and make a fist, tugging on it until she lets out a soft gasp. "Careful what you wish for, Hanna dear, especially in this land. Wishes have ways of coming true, and yet never in your favor."

"Is that a threat?"

"I'm full of threats, little bird."

Sarvi clears its throat. *Pardon the interruption, sir, but do you mind toning down the weather? I'm getting tired.*

I thought I made the storm disperse when I found out where Hanna was, but I suppose my own volatile emotions at the moment are still influencing things. The lightning and thunder have stopped, but the wind is still fierce and I can sense the fatigue in Sarvi as the unicorn flaps its wings.

"My apologies," I tell Sarvi. "I need to keep myself in check. Perhaps it would be best if we spend the night somewhere, if you need the sleep?"

It's not ideal—I want Hanna back at Shadow's End as soon as possible—but I don't want to cause any harm to my loyal companion either.

We shall see, Sarvi says. *We'll make it past the gorge at least and see how I feel.*

The three of us fly in silence for a few minutes and I do what I must to concentrate on the task at hand—getting home and what to do with Hanna once we get there. I do what I can to not smell her or feel her or think about her in any pleasurable way.

Hanna breaks the peaceful silence. "Okay, so say Louhi does scrounge up some flying lizards. Or a giant eagle. Or say she decides to come after us on foot, then what?"

"You're really worried about her?" I ask.

"Uh, yeah!" she exclaims, craning her neck around to give me the most incredulous look. "She has Rasmus, and he isn't with her by choice, that much I can tell."

I narrow my eyes at the sound of his name. "Can you really tell though?"

"We'll come back to that in a minute," she says, and I'm amused at the way she's trying to command me already. "Your ex-wife is insane. And powerful. And I don't know what's stopping her from getting a convoy together and going after Shadow's End. Especially if she has magic on her side."

"She has magic but it's not always on her side," I tell her. "Her magic is merely borrowed from Ilmarinen, her consort. I've heard the rumors about him, that she keeps him in a cage, barely keeping him alive, using special tools to drain the poor bastard's blood and use that for magic. But that's black magic and black magic sometimes has a mind of its own. It can turn on you." A worry line forms between her brows. "There are wards up to keep Louhi out of Shadow's End, if that's your concern," I go on. "If she was on her way to us, we would know it. Even if she shapeshifts."

"She can shapeshift?" she says with widened eyes.

"Only for short periods of time."

Her frown deepens and she sucks on her lower lip for a moment, which causes my blood to run hot again. "Hmmm. That might explain a lot."

I'm not sure what she's talking about, but I don't press. I have a lot of questions for her as it is.

Eventually, once we pass over the Gorge of Despair, Sarvi tells me that it needs to rest. I don't argue, though I want nothing more than to return to Shadow's End, put my feet-up, and get one moment of rest and some good coffee before figuring out what to do with Hanna. Coffee seems like it would fix everything, the stronger, the better.

We land on the top of a rolling hill, brown grass waving in a wind I no longer control. In front of us, the tan hills undulate like a velvet snake all the way to the base of the Iron Mountains, where dark forests flank the base. Looking to where we've come from, the hills level out into the barren steppes of the Liekkiö Plains, the River of Shadows cutting a sharp swath through it.

I have an affection for this part of Tuonela, so much that I had my Deadhands build a secondary, smaller castle into the sides of the mountain. With the river passing in front, the black water dark yet calming in contrast to the smooth brown hills, it's a home away from home. Which sounds mundane, but sometimes I want a little mundane. All my life I've been attracted to the darkness and chaos—there's a reason why

Shadow's End is a gothic dream surrounded by the wildest seas—and yet there's a small part of me that yearns for the light. That *needs* it. This land here is about as tranquil and bucolic as Tuonela gets. If I were ever to be happy again, I suppose the wide sky would be the clearest, brightest blue.

"Where are we?" Hanna asks as I dismount Sarvi, then reach for her waist and pull her off, placing her on the grass beside me. The breeze whips her hair across her face and I have to fight the urge to tuck it behind her ears.

"A resting place," I tell her, flexing my hands at my side. "It's not as spacious as Shadow's End, nor does it have any of the amenities you're used to. But it will give us shelter while Sarvi rests."

It is a peaceful spot, Sarvi says wearily, giving its mane a good shake. *You will be safe here, Hanna.*

"Safe from who?" she says under her breath, giving me a loaded look. My fairy girl is still as feisty as ever, which makes me want to fight with her all day.

Safe from whom, Sarvi corrects her.

I'm about to grab Hanna's elbow and guide her down the hill toward the castle—which is hidden in the mountainside—when her attention goes past me towards the river, a wash of fear on her brow.

"Looks like we have company," she says grimly.

CHAPTER EIGHT

HANNA

"THE SON"

Death stares at me for a moment, his gray eyes curious under his mask, then finally turns his head. Oh to be a freaking God and not be afraid of anything. I mean, he literally just saw his demon ex-wife strangling me with her psycho-long tongue and he's as cool as a cucumber, enough so that he was totally fine with stopping in the middle of nowhere without any protection.

And now someone else has shown up, probably to raise some sort of hell. At first, I can't get a good look at them from where we are, just that it's a tall figure in black with a bone-white skull face.

A freaking Bone Straggler? I think, immediately tensing, my body remembering the feel of their skeleton hands. Then I notice the boat in the wide river, tethered to the shore. There's three tanned women on the boat, wearing bikinis, as if they're on some influencer trip of the Underworld. The sight is so out of place and jarring, especially with the swimsuits' neon colors, that all fear fades away.

"What the hell is this?" I find myself saying out loud.

Death grumbles something under his breath, folding his arms across his broad chest. In the short amount of time we were apart, I had forgotten just how massive this God is.

But the approaching person is also tall, almost equally so.

"What are you doing here?!" the skull man yells at us. His voice is low yet playful, and I realize he's not a Bone Straggler, just wearing a mask like Death.

"What are you doing with *them*?" Death asks the masked man, nodding stiffly at the boat.

The guy strides closer in a casual jaunt and that's when it dawns on me. His skin isn't as dark as Death's, his hair is short, flopping over on his masked forehead, and while he's super buff, with the broadest shoulders, he's not as massive as Death. Yet I can see he's very much like his father.

This must be the Son of Death.

"What do you mean what am I doing with them?" he asks Death, coming right up to us. "I'm ferrying the dead to the city."

Death looks at the girls on the boat. "Are you sure they're dead and it's not a shaman's trick?"

"I'm not my sister, I don't fall for just any magic," his son says. Then he looks to me, and through his mask I see the twinkle of his eyes. Somehow I don't need to see his face to know that he's a looker.

"I'm going to guess you're Hanna, the one with the magic

tricks," he says with a wink. He extends his hand and I stare at it. Unlike his father, he's not wearing gloves. "I'm Tuonen, if you couldn't tell."

"I figured," I tell him, placing my hand in his. His palm is large, grip is strong. "I've heard a lot about you."

"All good things I presume?" Tuonen says, taking his hand back and waving it in an exaggerated manner, like I'd just crushed it.

I let out a small laugh and gesture to the bikini gals on the boat, immediately feeling an easy rapport with him. "Enough that I'm not surprised to see you ferrying a bunch of hot babes around."

He shrugs, glancing back at them. "Just a lucky day, I guess. Apparently they all drowned together. Had too many shots of tequila in Mexico then tried to do a dive into a cave. All for that Instagram that you mortals are all hung up about. Can't tell you how many people I've had come across because of that thing."

I glance over at the girls. They're all chatting to each other as if they're back at the bar in Cabo or wherever they were before they died. Having come into Tuonela as someone alive, I briefly wonder what it feels like to be dead here. Judging by these girls, it seems like a pretty seamless transition.

"You better be on your way," Death says gruffly, placing a metal hand on his son's shoulder. "Just make sure you're taking them to the city."

"Where else would I be taking them?" Tuonen asks with a scoff.

Meanwhile I'm staring at Death's hand, struck by the fact

that he can't even touch his own son with his bare skin. My heart pinches at the thought, with the sudden realization of how lonely that might be, how isolating. I'd seen him with Lovia before, and he'd told me how it was as a child, different from the rest of his siblings and his parents, and yet it's never really hit home at how powerful it is to be without true touch for those you love.

Death catches me staring at his hand and I feel a bristle of cold wind, perhaps his discomfort with my pity, and he abruptly takes his hand off Tuonen's shoulder.

"Wouldn't be the first time you've fucked with the newly dead," Death says to him, clearing his throat.

I blink at them for a second, my mind tripping over what he just said. "Sorry, did you just say fucking the dead or fucking *with* the dead?"

Tuonen looks rebuked. "Fucking the dead? What kind of God do you think I am?"

"Your reputation precedes you," Death tells him.

I can tell Tuonen is scowling at him under his mask. "There's no rush," he says, sounding like a teenager who's putting off doing the dishes. "The girls will get to the city, the Golden Mean probably. It's up to the Magician to decide where they go. Until then, I can take a break." He tilts his head at me. "Besides, I've been waiting to meet my future stepmother."

"Who is the Magician?" I ask, even though I'm feeling weirded out at the fact that I'm going to be Tuonen's stepmom. Under the mask, I'm assuming he looks about my age, but the reality is that he's eons older.

Hell, I'm weirded out that I'm going to be a stepmother at all. It must have been hours ago that it looked like I was escaping the Land of the Dead for good. Instead, I nearly died at the hands (well, tongue) of Louhi, Rasmus was captured, poor Alku died, and now I'm back in Death's possession, who seems just as intent on making me his bride as he was before. I haven't even had a moment to try and figure out how I feel about all of this, not that my feelings seem to have much weight when it comes to it.

"He's the gatekeeper at the entrance to the city," Death explains with a hint of impatience. "He decides what faction the dead are put in."

"I thought that was your decision," I say.

"It is the Book of Souls' decision," he says. "I merely facilitate the process. The fate of everyone is decided the moment they take their last breath. The second I feel my runes pulse with their passing, their chapter in the infinity of time is finished, the end is written."

"The Magician pulls a card," Tuonen explains. "He shows the card to the newly dead. The card tells them where they're going, and I escort them there."

"He pulls a card?" I repeat.

"It is direct correspondence from the Book of Souls," Death says, sounding impatient again. "They either draw Inmost, the Golden Mean, or Amaranthus. Whatever the book decides for them, the card decides the same."

"Technically it's not really the book that decides," Tuonen interjects. He jerks his thumb at the girls who are still gabbing away on the riverboat. "Perhaps these ladies had plans later in life to run a few puppy shelters or donate their money to the homeless, but they know they've been living a benign life so far. Their souls aren't awful, they aren't altruistic either. It's how people decide to live their lives that influences what the book chooses."

"Wait, how do you know that they don't have altruistic souls?" I ask. "Just because someone got drunk on vacation and died and happens to look banging in a bikini doesn't mean that they're not good or even great people. Judgmental much?"

Death lets out an amused huff, fixing his eyes on me. "You're not even a Goddess yet, fairy girl, and yet you're questioning a God."

"He's a lesser God, isn't he?" I point out.

"Ouch," Tuonen says, grabbing his heart in mock pain. "She knows how to get me where it hurts. You might make a good stepmother after all."

He turns his attention to Sarvi, who is grazing on the grass nearby, like a normal horse would, though the longer I look at the skeleton unicorn, I realize Sarvi isn't actually eating the grass, but instead sucking up insects from the ground. "So, what brings you and your steed out this way anyway?" Tuonen asks us. "Thought you'd be in a hurry to get married since your wedding was…interrupted."

A low guttural rumble comes from Death. "Sarvi needed to rest," he says gruffly, another cold breeze coming through and ruffling Tuonen's thick black hair.

"I see," he says. He turns to me. "Now, tell me, future mom, are you actually planning on going through with the wedding this time or are you running away again?"

I'm immediately defensive. "I didn't run away."

Another deep grumble from Death.

"Is that so?" Tuonen asks. He leans back slightly on one heel, folding his arms across his chest as he looks at me. I'm very aware that there are two very similar Gods of Death with skull masks on about to interrogate me. It's a little intimidating, to say the least.

"See, I had heard otherwise," Tuonen goes on, and from the tone of his voice I'm realizing he's more like his father than I had thought. "Rumors fly all over this land, the Gods don't have much else to do than gossip. One rumor said that Rasmus had stolen you, the other said you went along willingly, and had been plotting your escape with him all the time you were in Shadow's End. And yet another rumor, this is probably the most chaotic of all, is that you were in cahoots with Louhi to infiltrate my father's kingdom and bring about his demise."

"That's ridiculous," I tell him. "Louhi just tried to kill me with her tongue. Did the rumors tell you that?"

I look at Death for him to corroborate the story, but he doesn't say anything. His eyes remain cold under the mask.

"So then, which rumor is true?" Tuonen asks, a slight edge to his voice.

I have a feeling that neither of them will like the truth. Either way, I'm not sure I want to discuss this in front of him. This should be between Death and I, not a family affair.

"Don't you have some dead bikini babes to take to the afterlife city?" I say, gesturing with my head toward the boat.

Tuonen bristles at that and I swear two black horns protrude a couple of inches out of his hair on the top of his head. I try to focus my eyes, wondering if it's the wind messing with his strands or a trick of the low light.

"You better get on your way," Death says gruffly to him.

Tuonen pats at the top of his head in haste and that's when I realize, yes, he actually has two small horns there that seem to have come from nowhere. He gives me a curt nod, followed by a grunt, then turns on his heel and stalks off toward the waiting boat.

Part of me wants to go with him. Though he's definitely on his father's side when it comes to things, I think I'd rather be with him than Death right now. I also wouldn't mind interacting with the bikini girls. Even though they're dead, I'm craving some interactions with normal people from my world, just so I can feel like I have a handle on things for a moment. It's like everything has been happening and coming at me non-stop for a while and I haven't had time to just breathe and figure out what to do next, and the more situations and Gods I come across in Tuonela, the more confused I get.

"He doesn't like me, does he?" I say under my breath, watching as the Son of Death gets in his boat.

"Frankly, I don't think I like you either," Death says.

My mouth opens and I look over at him in surprise.

He lifts his chin, his gaze growing intense. "It would depend, of course, on what you're about to tell me," he adds.

Then he reaches out and grabs me rather harshly by the elbow, the metal of his gauntlet pinching my skin. "Come along. It looks like rain."

I look up to the sky as he pulls me across the waving grass, heading toward the forested mountain slope. The clouds are lower, darker, which isn't a surprise thanks to Death's worsening mood. I glance helplessly at Sarvi, feeling like the unicorn is my only ally in this, but Sarvi is in the midst of lying down, long half-skeletal legs tucked under its hefty body and isn't paying me any attention.

Death leads me into the forest and I struggle to keep up with his long strides. Here the trees are iron pines with thin trunks, low brush and berry bushes growing in the shadows. I don't see any mushrooms, which is probably for the best because I would definitely crush them under my boot. Traitor fungi.

"Can I ask you a question?" I ask as we follow a narrow pebble path between the pines. The rocks under my feet feel like marbles and it's hard to keep my balance.

"I'm the one asking questions here."

I ignore that. "Am I going crazy or did your son just start growing horns out of his head?"

Death lets out a huff of air. "You aren't going crazy. He has horns. Inherited them from his mother. Lucky for him they only emerge when his emotions are heightened. Anger works like a charm."

"Wow. Do they…get bigger than that?"

"Quite a bit," he says, a touch of awe in his voice. "I assume it's why Tuonen has such an emotionless and lazy approach to life, though I wish he'd just accept his horns and let himself care about things a little more."

"Things like what?"

He glances down at me. "Taking a sudden interest in my family?"

"Shouldn't I? If it's going to be my family now, too."

He suddenly stops and I crash into his back. He turns around, the air around us growing colder, and presses himself up against me until he's just this wall of muscle. I swallow hard, refusing to take a step back, not letting him intimidate me even though that's exactly what he's doing.

"I don't understand you, fairy girl," he says to me, voice deepening. It makes shivers run down my neck and shoulders. "Not even a little. Why did you leave me?"

The blatancy of his questions startles me.

"I didn't leave *you*," I tell him. "It wasn't…personal."

He studies me for a moment and his eyes feel like they're probing around deep inside my soul, as if he'll distrust every word I say. I guess I can't blame him.

"Don't tell me not to take things personally," he says, voice gruffer now. He reaches out and grabs me by the back of my neck, his grip cold and tight. I gasp, so aware of his power. "I won't ask you again. Why did you leave me?"

I swallow uneasily, caught in his grasp with no way out. "Because I don't belong here. You know I don't."

He shakes his head ever so subtly, his fingers bruising my skin. "After all you've seen, all you've done, all you've felt, and you're still blind to the world around you. This is your world, Hanna. You know it is. You know you belong here more than you've ever belonged in your other life, and more than that, you belong here with me."

My jaw tightens as I try to ignore the way my heart is

skipping in my chest. "You're sounding sentimental."

"You're mistaking sentiment with facts," he says, lowering his masked face toward mine. "A mistake I'm sure you won't make again. You belong with me, because that is the bargain we made. There is no escape for you. Not now, not ever. You made a promise to me, and your promise will be held to the very end."

There's a finality in his words that makes my blood run cold. For a moment he loosens his grip and sighs deeply. "I know you don't like being told what to do, but you could have had it all," he says, almost wistfully. "You could have had my trust. Now you will become my wife and there won't be an ounce of trust or love between us."

My heart skips again. "Who said anything about love?"

"Hmmph." He tilts his head, examining me. "I could have loved you, you know."

Oh. That I didn't know. And for reasons I can't explain, it feels like he's pulled a pin out from my heart and I'm slowly deflating.

"Don't look so surprised," he says, noting my fallen expression. "You had me all lined up. But that's what you wanted, isn't it?"

I shake my head. "I didn't...Tuoni," I say his name carefully, "please. I didn't leave you on purpose. It wasn't to hurt you."

"You didn't hurt me!" he snaps, eyes flashing silver. "You wounded my pride. Sometimes that's all a God has for himself."

"Rasmus was taking me out of here, he was taking me to

see my father," I try to explain. "Can't you understand that I did all of this for him? I agreed to marry you for him. So that he could live and be free. I love my father, how could you expect me not to run to him the first chance I get?"

Silence falls between us for a few beats, tension thickening. His metal fingers massage the back of my neck and somewhere in the distance a bird whistles from the trees.

"In time, I would have brought your father back here," he says after a moment. "In time, I would have given you everything you asked for. But that privilege has been revoked. You betrayed me when you left with Rasmus, and I won't ever forgive you for that. You will still marry me, because we made a deal and in the event that you can fulfill the prophecy, but there will be no love lost between us. You will spend your life at Shadows End until I one day touch you…and die."

I swallow the brick in my throat. "And if I don't die?"

"Then we will rule together, uniting the land. I will be a fair husband to you, little bird. A powerful king." He brings his face close again, as if to kiss me, even though the mask is in the way. "But I will never love you. Not after this. Do you understand?"

My hands move on instinct. I reach up and place my fingers on the sides of his mask and slowly pull it off, revealing his face.

A gasp catches in my throat as I'm struck dumb by his otherworldly beauty. It wasn't long ago that this face was gazing at me with something kinder than it is now, and yet it feels like I'm seeing him again for the first time. His smooth, perfect bronzed skin and high cheekbones, broad nose, the strong cut of his jaw, the shiny thickness of his ebony beard. His black low-set brows over intelligent gray eyes smudged with kohl, the kind of eyes that tease you with the secrets of the universe, eyes that used to make me feel like a goddess when I wasn't.

Then there are his lips. Full, supple lips that my skin knows intimately, a mouth that has whispered secrets that only my body has understood.

He's not just beautiful—he's powerful. It radiates off of him, entangling you in its dominance until you're caught in a web, too dazed and submissive to even plot your escape.

Somehow, though, I manage to stay on solid ground.

"I want you to say that to me without hiding behind a mask," I tell him bravely.

His eyes flicker over my features, as if reading a map, and then his gaze steels, a cold wind that wraps around me. "I will never love you, Hanna."

"And if I happen to fall in love with you?" I whisper, knowing that will never happen now.

His mouth curls into a contemptuous smile. "Then you have all my pity."

Ouch. My stomach twists into a million knots as his cold words cut into me, the way he really seems to mean it. He finally lets go of my neck and turns away, sliding his mask back down on his face. I don't protest. I'd rather not see his face now, see how little he cares for me.

A loveless marriage for eternity?

I never should have left with my brother.

CHAPTER NINE

HANNA

"THE WEDDING"

With Death giving me the coldest of shoulders, I force myself to pay more attention to my surroundings than to him. We continue up the path toward his mountain castle, the stones slipping under the tread of my boots, and when I get a better look at them I notice they aren't stones at all, but some type of crystal.

"What is this, hematite?" I ask, bending over to pick one up. To my surprise, the metallic pewter sphere quickly jumps off of me, rolling back along the path on its own accord. "Don't tell me those are sentient too."

"Shadow stones," Death says without glancing at me. "They are linked to my blood, as well as Lovia's and Tuonen's. They operate on intentions. In this case they provide a path to the castle. When I'm not here, they will purposely lead others astray. That, along with the wards in place and a couple rockhounds, means the mountain lair remains a secret in the land."

"I'm sorry, but *mountain lair*?" I repeat.

"You got a better name?"

"Castle Grayskull?" I offer. "I mean, that was the first thing off the top of my head."

He doesn't react to that. He may have a fondness for the classic movies of my world, but I'm going to assume he's never watched Saturday morning cartoons. Suddenly an image of Death as a child fills my head, him sitting on a couch in skull and crossbones pajamas, slurping from a bowl of cheerios and watching *He-Man*. Inexplicably, he also has facial hair. I have to bite back a smile.

We follow the slippery shadow-stone path for a few more minutes, leading us through the dark forest and up to the sheer cliff of the mountainside where it disappears into the mossy earth. There's nowhere else to go except up, and while I've been known to rock it at a climbing gym, I'm not about to scale something of this magnitude.

Then Death waves his hand in the air, a pewter key dangling from his fist. It catches the light as if the sun is shining on us and suddenly the air in front of us shimmers, then parts like a curtain, revealing a narrow staircase of slick black steps that lead up the mountain side, which is further back than it first looked.

Now *that* was magic.

Death looks at me over his shoulder. "It's a steep hike to the entrance. Do you need a hand?"

How gentlemanly of him to ask, I think grimly. Out of

stubbornness I shake my head. "I can handle it."

He studies me for a moment, then nods before heading up the steps.

They're even steeper than they looked, and made of a glassy rock, like obsidian. I go up a couple, trying to keep my balance as my boots slide back and forth, and I'm just about to eat shit when Death is suddenly beside me, moving faster than my eyes can see, wrapping his arms around my waist and pulling me up against him.

For a moment I forget that the man seems to hate me, and that I'm being forced to marry him. For a moment I forget about everything except how natural it feels to have his body against mine. Despite his armor, I can feel his heart beating, which in turn makes my chest grow warm, for heat to flare through me. I'm not sure how I'm going to survive marriage with him if my body is always going to react this way around him.

"This is the second time today I've saved you from falling to your demise," he says roughly. "You can thank me, you know. You're already in my debt as it is."

He hasn't let go of me, thank god, because I'm pretty sure I'd fall backward.

"Thank you," I say. It sounds weak even though I mean it.

"You know, part of me wonders what would happen if I let go," he muses darkly.

Uh, no thanks.

"I'm being serious when I say thank you," I say quickly, my fingers gripping his coat. "You've saved my life. Twice in the same day."

"What I mean is that I have a feeling you'd save yourself," he goes on. A look of quiet awe comes through his eyes. "You don't quite realize how you shine when push comes to shove. I saw what you did with that selenite knife. That blade doesn't cut for any mortal, and yet you were able to sever Louhi's tongue like it was a sheet of paper. You threw the knife and it pierced her wing like a leaf. You shouldn't have been able to do that, Hanna, not to anyone, but especially not to her. But, when it came down to it, you did." He shakes his head. "And yet you still don't believe you belong in this world."

Then he turns, his hand firmly at my waist, and pulls me up the rest of the stairs, my feet barely touching the steps, until we reach a large metal door. Still holding onto me, he slips the key into the iron lock and turns it. The door opens with a threatening moan.

I'm not sure what I was expecting with his *mountain lair*, but it's a lot smaller than I expected. From what I can see there is just a narrow hall with impossibly high ceilings, giving the feeling of walking through a keyhole itself. The faint light from outside the open door does little to illuminate where the hall leads.

"We need a sunmoonstone," I say, looking around the darkness.

"Where did you learn about those?" Death asks suspiciously.

"Rasmus," I say, though I feel like saying his name is risky territory now. "He had a few." I pause. "The mushroom place was dark, too."

He mutters something under his breath then goes still for

a moment before waving the key in the air.

Suddenly scones are lit one-by-one down the long hall, illuminating narrow walls the same shiny black as the steps outside.

"How did you do that?" I ask. "You have ghosts powering the lights in here too?" I think back to what he said about how he lights the Library of the Veils.

"No ghosts here," he says. "Just magic."

He tucks his key beneath his shirt, the collar open enough for me to get a glimpse of his chest and the silver lines cutting across his tanned skin. The lines glow for a moment before fading.

"Someone just died, didn't they?" I ask.

"Someone is always dying," he says wearily. Then he sighs, and lifts his mask off his face, cradling it in his hands, his attention down the hall. "Come on, we might as well rest if Sarvi is."

I follow him down the hall, his heavy boots echoing, passing by small dark shapes that move along the walls. I peer at them curiously, realizing they're actually snails the size of my fist, but instead of a shell for a back, they carry the small skulls of some unknown creatures.

"I think you have a snail problem," I tell Death as we near the end of the hall.

"Skull snails," he says. "They're useful to have around. They suck up pests and bad energy." He pauses. "They're also poisonous, so don't touch them."

Of course they are.

We come into a square room. There is a large fireplace

with two chairs in front covered with layers of pelts and fur, and an iron table between them. Two doorways are on opposite sides of the room, the doors closed. There's nothing else here.

"Is this it?"

"Not up to your standards, is it?" he comments.

"I just spent the night underground with fungus," I remind him. "I don't think this place is up to *your* standards. You don't exactly like roughing it."

He grumbles at that and places his mask on the table. "Sit down."

I exhale and sit down on the unknown animal furs. At least the chair is comfortable.

"This is the receiving room," he says as he eases his big frame down across from me, making the chair look tiny. "If I ever had visitors here—or intruders—this is as far as they would get. The rest of it is further back into the mountain. There are even passages that lead from here to the City of Death, though it would take days in the dark to get there."

"Will you take me to the city one day?" I ask. "Before the shit hit the fan, you said you were going to put on a Bone Match."

He watches me for a moment with careful precision. It's like being observed by a giant panther. Then he leans further back in his chair, his eyes gleaming, and taps his metal fingers against the end of the chair arms.

"Hanna," he says patiently. "You have to understand that I don't trust you. However you thought things were going to go before, they aren't going to go that way now. I don't know what you went through from the moment you left Shadow's End. Who you saw, who you talked to. What you told them."

"I didn't tell anyone anything," I protest. "Rasmus came on Alku, he took me—"

"You went willingly," he says sharply.

"Yes. I went willingly. He said he was going to bring me to my father in the Upper World, my father who is there alone, with no protection against Eero and Noora. With his memory wiped, he won't even know that they were trying to kill me. Can't you see why I wanted to get back?"

He wiggles his jaw slowly. "And you believed him."

"I had to believe him. And you know what, I still do. Despite him being Louhi's son, I don't think he ever meant to put me in harm's way. He wanted me out of this world." I pause. "He's my *brother*."

Death stares blankly at me for a moment. "*Your* brother?" he finally says.

"Louhi and my father…" I start, unable to shake the disgust. "I don't know how it's even possible. But you mentioned that she can shapeshift and perhaps she tricked him. This could have been quite some time before he met my mother. I'm sure she never even knew that my father had another child."

Or…maybe she did.

"Fucking Torben," Death says quietly, staring at the wall, shaking his head slightly. "All this time he had me fooled that he was some hapless old shaman when he'd been screwing my ex-wife." He looks back to me, brow furrowed. "Are you sure he's Rasmus' father and not Ilmarinen?"

"You mean her current lover boy?" I shrug. "Believe me, I would love that if that were true. But according to the mushy lady, Rasmus is my half-brother. He got the information the same time as I did. Not only that, but he found out that Louhi is his mother as well…" I trail off, thinking of how scared and weak Rasmus looked under Louhi's collar. I wonder where he is now, if his mother is treating him right or corrupting him with demonic abuse. I pray it's not the latter.

He gives me a look of disbelief. "And you really believe Rasmus didn't know? Hanna, he led you right to her."

"We didn't have a choice," I point out. "It was your weather that made us take the shortcut."

If that makes him feel guilty, he doesn't show it. "And the she-devil conveniently appeared in the middle of the Star Swamp, where your unicorn conveniently went down."

"It wasn't like that. Rasmus was possessed. He was trying to strangle me. We fell off. Alku died trying to save me."

Things grow quiet, the sound of my quickening breath filling the room. Death is deep in thought, running his fingers over his jaw. "This changes everything."

"How so?"

He gives me a sharp look. "Louhi has Rasmus, her son who happens to also have the blood of a shaman. What do you think she's going to do with him?"

"I've been trying not to think about it," I admit uneasily.

"She's either going to bleed him dry like she does to Ilmarinen, or…"

"Or?"

"Or he's going to be on her side very soon. Learning her

magic. Corrupted by the Old Gods. She'll use him like a puppet on a string." Suddenly Death gets to his feet, his chair toppling over. "We need to get back to Shadow's End. Now."

He reaches down and yanks me up to my feet and we're storming down the hall before I even get a chance to think.

Sarvi didn't seem all too pleased at having to fly back to Shadow's End so soon but, being a dutiful servant, it didn't argue with Death. The short rest seemed to have been enough to get us to the castle at a fast pace and it wasn't long before we were landing in the gardens.

My mind immediately leapt back to the last time I was here. Unlike the rain that's starting to come down, it was a sunny day, the sky the bluest hue I'd ever seen. I was…I think I might have even been happy. Especially when Death ending up fucking me against the garden wall.

This time though, there is no happiness between us. He lifts me off Sarvi's back and then takes a firm hold of my hand, pulling me along until we enter the castle through the kitchen doors.

The two Deadmaidens, Harma and Pyry, look up in haste from the counter where they're chopping vegetables.

Master, Harma says in surprise through her red veil, her face eternally hidden like the rest of them. *You're back so soon.*

So nice to see you again, Hanna, Pyry says in a careful voice, communicating in my head just as Harma does. *I hope you're staying this time around.*

"She's staying," Death grumbles, pulling me along. "We'll be in the crypt getting married. If anyone asks for us, they aren't invited."

Oh! Harma exclaims. *Shall we cook up a big feast in celebration!?*

"There's nothing to celebrate," he says grimly over his shoulder as he takes me out of the kitchen and into the castle, then over to the steps that lead down to the crypt.

"We're doing this now?" I exclaim, trying to keep up without falling down the stone stairs that descend into darkness.

"No time like the present," he says. "Sarvi!" he yells as if the unicorn is right beside us and not out in the garden still. "Get Kalma."

"You think Sarvi can hear you?"

"Sarvi hears everything," he says, adjusting his grip to be on my wrist, as if he's afraid I'll try to bolt the closer we get to the Sect of the Undead.

Truth is, I'd run if I could. I was creeped out here on our wedding day and I'm creeped out now. We walk past the cellars where Death keeps his wines and other fermented drinks, past the dungeons and torture chambers which make my blood crawl, and then finally to the crypt where a row of candles burn, outlining a path to the door.

Seeing it again makes me feel sick, like it's been coated in pure poison.

"You could at least let me change for the wedding," I tell him.

He tilts his head toward me. He slipped his mask back

on the moment we left his mountain castle, and with the dim shadowy light down here, I can't see his eyes in the mask at all. "You're still in your wedding dress. I'll have to take your word for it that you looked better than this before."

As much as I didn't want to get married, it was a really pretty dress. A rich red gown like one a deviant Disney princess would wear, with a red veil to match, all to compliment my crimson crown. Now my dress is nothing more than dirty tatters. As much as I don't want to get married to Death, it doesn't feel right rushing like this.

But he doesn't seem to care. He takes out his key from beneath his shirt and slips into the iron lock, turning it with a loud *click*.

A shudder runs through me.

Death glances at me, though I still can't see his eyes. "You're afraid," he comments.

"Not of you," I tell him quickly. "Of this place."

He nods slowly. "That I understand. I'm not fond of it either. But it is the way things are done."

"Is this where you married Louhi?" I ask.

He nods again. "Yes. I suppose tradition doesn't always promise the best, does it?"

He then places his metal gauntlet on the marble door and pushes it open with a creak I feel in my bones.

The crypt is already lit up, candles burning everywhere, fueled by some invisible source that never runs out. Perhaps powered by the Old Gods who want to keep their influence alive, though my Deadmaiden Raila told me they were lit by those who still worshipped them in secret.

Either way, the glowing light illuminates all the horrors.

Giant, black snakes slither away from the door and toward the darkened corners of the room, past the six statues that flank the aisle. Like before, it's the statues that make my blood run cold, even more so than the snakes.

The statues are all turned toward us when I swear—I swear to God—when I was here last they weren't facing the door. They're all standing there with hands outstretched or closed in prayer, their eyes gouged out and bleeding red and gold tears. Gilded antlers, spikes, or bones protrude from their heads in the form of rudimentary crowns while their shoulders and arms are covered in melting candles.

"Fuck," Death swears under his breath, and his hand goes to my waist, pulling my toward him as if to protect me. "It's been awhile. I'd forgotten how fucked up this place is."

I swallow hard, leaning into his frame. "Can't you get rid of it?"

He scoffs. "Don't think I haven't thought about it. Vipunen is adamant about keeping the Saints and the Sect intact."

"Why?"

He lifts a shoulder. "I don't know why. Truthfully, I don't know the reason behind most of the things he says. I may be the God of Death, but he's been around longer than me, longer than my father even. He was here before Tuonela, before the Kaaos. Sometimes I wonder if he's the Creator himself, watching the future he planned unfold from inside the caves."

"I would like to meet him," I say simply. I want to figure

out what his damn deal is.

"Is that so?" he asks in mild amusement. "You will. Once you're queen, you will be training with him. I'm taking no chances when it comes to you or the prophecy. You'll learn to defend yourself, just as Lovia and Tuonen have."

"You think I'll be in danger, even cooped up inside this castle for eternity?" I say, though my humor feels flat at the moment.

"I'm not taking any chances with you," he says. "Not anymore."

I expect him to take me toward the altar, but he doesn't move. Instead he stares at it. If I could see his eyes, I think they would be transfixed.

The altar itself is morbid, created out of large bones, and placed on top of it is the crown of crimson. It's just as I saw it last, made of shimmering gold and silver that seems to shift under the flickering lights, red jewels along the base.

More than anything, I get the creepy impression that the crown is sitting there, watching and waiting for me.

Perhaps always has been.

And somewhere, far in the distance, I hear a song. I hear singing, chanting, something senseless and melodic and compelling and not unlike what I heard when I approached the Book of Runes in the Library of the Veils.

"What is it?" Death asks me.

I frown. "I hear the singing again."

He watches me for a moment before turning his attention back to the altar. "Is it the crown?" he asks in a low voice, as if he doesn't want it to hear him.

"I don't know," I say and, just like that, the chanting fades. Shit, I hope it was coming from the crown and not these creepy candle fuckers.

The ground shakes slightly under our feet and we both turn around to see Kalma and Sarvi coming toward the crypt.

"This is a bit of a rush, don't you think?" Kalma asks as he enters the crypt. He nods at me, giving me a kind smile. "Hanna, nice to see you again."

"We need to get this over with before something else goes wrong," Death says, putting distance between us as his hand slides to my elbow, cold air slipping between us. "We're doing this now."

"Very well," Kalma says, walking past us toward the altar, his Jedi-type robes flowing behind him. "Let's get started then." He stops and picks up the crown. "Since there are no formalities, or other witnesses, Sarvi, you will have to be the witness here."

Sarvi nods, its iron horn catching the candlelight. *I will*, it says, even though only Death and I can hear the unicorn's verbal response.

Kalma gingerly picks up the crown in his skinny hands and holds it out in front of us. The energy coming off it is indescribable. Not threatening, but not benign either. "Then Tuoni, Hanna, please approach the altar, walking side by side but not touching."

That's easier said than done considering how wide Death's frame is. I keep to the side of the aisle, brushing past the statues instead as I walk forward.

You'll regret it, an inhuman, echoing voice says.

I stop and turn to look at the sightless statue I just walked past, one with spikes sticking out of her crown, her eyes gone, just sockets filled with tears of waxy blood.

We'll make you regret it, the voice says again, and I swear it's coming from the statue.

"Hanna," Kalma says patiently. "Don't mind the statues, please. Keep walking."

I'm barely unable to take my eyes off the figure, the way it seems to be staring at me without any eyes. I can feel it reaching into the depths of my brain, slithering around like snakes. The more I stare at it, the more I realize that its face is made up of dozens of other, smaller, screaming faces, as if countless souls are trapped under the marble skin.

You will make her rise, the statue hisses as I start to walk away, nearly tripping as I go.

By now Death is standing at the altar, his mask pushed up on his forehead. He's frowning at me, confused. Maybe a little fearful. I have to admit, I like it when I see fear in him, even if I'm currently feeling it myself.

"What is it?" he asks me.

I could keep it to myself and pretend nothing happened because it would be easier that way. But I don't. "Uh, that statue just threatened me. I think."

"What did it say?" Kalma asks.

"It said I'll regret it, they'll make me regret it, and that I will make her rise. I don't know who *she* is."

Death and Kalma exchange a look. "Have the saints ever spoken to you?" Death asks him.

Kalma shakes his head. "No. But that doesn't mean

they don't speak to others." He dips his chin, eyes on me. "I understand how disconcerting that must be, but you must come forward, Hanna, to take the crown."

I nod. "Okay," I say, my voice coming out small. I mean, I already had cold feet about this whole thing, what's a little threat from a statue that may or may not house a dead saint?

I continue walking down the aisle until I'm at Death's side. I keep glancing over my shoulder at the statue, expecting it to move but it doesn't. Behind me, Sarvi stops in the middle of the crypt and watches us. The patches of hair it has are stiff, reminding me of the way my old neighbor's dog would get whenever you walked past the fence. Something has Sarvi spooked too.

"Hanna Heikkinen, of the country of Finland of the Upper World," Kalma says, bringing my attention back to him. I'm about to tell him that technically my country of residence was the United States but then he says, "Hold out your hand, palm up."

"Why?" I ask as my scalp prickles with alarm. I make a fist in response.

"It is part of the ceremony," Kalma says. His old eyes squint in a smile. "It won't hurt much, I promise."

"*Much?*" I repeat, my brows raising.

"I'll go first." Death lets out a huff of impatience and takes off his gauntlet, undoing multiple straps, the metal clinking as he reaches over and places it on the altar. I rarely see his hand and watch in awe as he holds it out to Kalma.

Kalma flinches. I know he can't help it. He gives Death a quick, sheepish smile and Death flips his hand over so his palm is facing up. His skin looks so soft and pure, as pale as the moon.

"What's happening?" I ask.

They don't answer me. Kalma takes the crown and pulls one of the bleeding spikes off the top of it, like he's plucking a porcupine. He holds it out and with a swift motion cuts a line down the middle of Death's palm.

"Jesus!" I swear, watching as the bright-red blood rushes up out of his skin, coating the spike.

Death doesn't move a muscle, his face impassive as Kalma withdraws the spike and places it back on the crown. The blood runs down toward the base of the crown and freezes, hardening into a jewel-like crystal.

"Bloodstone," Kalma says with a nod. "Now, Hanna, it's your turn."

My eyes go wide. "Can't we just exchange rings or something?"

Death doesn't smile at that. In fact, I think he's close to calling me a chicken.

So I suck up my fear and hold out my hand, palm up.

Kalma plucks out another spike, the one beside the one that cut Death, and then holds it out above my skin. Wasting no time, he brings the spike down against my skin. The pain erupts, my blood rushing from the cut and I bite my lip to keep from crying out.

"Good girl," Death says appreciatively under his breath.

I relax slightly at his praise and Kalma takes the blade away, placing it back in the crown. I watch as my blood does the same as Death's did. It runs down the metal length of the spike and then hardens into a crimson jewel.

"Now what?" I ask, mesmerized by it.

"We keep going," Kalma says, pulling out another spike.

"What?!" I exclaim.

Death holds out his bare palm again and, to my surprise, the wound has totally healed itself, leaving no trace that he was ever cut. Kalma makes another quick incision in the same place and puts the bloody spear back in the crown.

"Wait a minute," I tell them, panicking. "I'm not Death. I haven't healed."

Kalma gives me a stiff smile. "I suppose that's a bit of a problem when a mortal marries a God. Normally we can make you bleed a million times. Sorry, Hanna. This may hurt more than I promised."

Oh my god.

He grabs my wrist and holds my hand out this time, knowing I'd probably fight back, and makes another cut alongside the other one, the blood still fresh.

"Fuck," I grind out, the pain sharp and searing. I look up at Death, because this whole damn thing is his fault. To his credit he does look apologetic.

And so the rest of the crown gets its crimson jewels this way, Kalma taking turns slicing me and Death open again and again, making us bleed.

I'm near fainting when it finally ends, feeling woozy on my feet.

"Now that the crown is complete," Kalma announces with reverence, "it is time for the blood pact."

More blood? Holy fuck, I'm not going survive this.

Kalma reaches out and grabs my wrist again, turning my hand palm up, my hand positively screaming in pain, my skin bright red and bloody with five different cuts that pulse with my heartbeat.

Death then takes his hand, and for a moment I think he's going to touch me, but instead he holds it inches above mine. Kalma pulls out an actual blade from his pocket and slices upward into Death's hand once more until his blood spills out of his palm and down into mine. Some blood splatters onto my dress (and I'm now getting why the brides here don't wear white), some on the stone floor, but most gathers in my open hand like a crimson pond.

This is very unsafe, I can't help but think to myself, as if Death was a normal mortal human full of diseases. But while I'm watching his blood pool on my palm—his a shade lighter and brighter, almost metallic compared to mine—it seems to take on a life of its own. His blood swirls and moves of its own accord, pushing itself and my blood back down into my wound until it's all gone.

"Tuoni of Tuonela," Kalma says in a deep voice, "your blood is now a part of hers. Hanna Heikkinen, your blood is now mixed with his. This formalizes your blood pact, creating a bond that shall not be broken. Tuoni, God of the Dead, King of Tuonela, you now have a wife. Hanna, Goddess of the Dead, Queen of Tuonela, you now have a husband. May your blood run together as you rule together, forever and ever. And ever."

He gives us both a smile of encouragement. "Well, this should be the part where you're happy."

I look at Death. Tuoni. My *husband*. He's staring at me with such an odd expression that I can't get a read on him. Then again, I may look the same.

I don't think either of us know how to feel.

"I know in your world, Hanna, it's customary for the bride and groom to kiss to commemorate the moment," Kalma goes on, clearing his throat. He looks to Death. "But, it's not customary here. Neither is the physical consummation of your union. If that makes you feel any better," he adds under his breath.

"Thank you, Kalma," Death says stiffly. "But there's still the matter of the crown."

"Oh, that's right," Kalma says, clapping his hands together. He twists to grab the crown from the altar and holds it above my head.

She will rise and you will lose everything, the statue's voice comes into my head.

I look over at the creepy statue just as Kalma lowers the crown on my head. It feels hot, like the metal is melting onto my head, and I swear the statue smiles at me.

"There we go," Death says quickly as he slips his gauntlet back on. "Now it's done."

Then he grabs me by the elbow. "Come along, wife," he says, pulling me down the aisle. "There's the matter of the honeymoon."

The what?

Sarvi steps out of the way as Death brings me out of the crypt and past the candles, over to the cellars and dungeons, taking me down a wide, dark hall. This doesn't seem like honeymoon material *at all*.

We come to a sudden stop in front of a wide gaping hole in the floor, a blackness that seems to go down forever. Definitely not honeymoon material.

"What are you doing?" Kalma asks from behind us.

Death pulls me close to him, leering down at me. "You think that just because you're officially a queen now, I'm going to treat you like one? After what you've done? You can't be trusted, Hanna. I can't risk you getting loose again, because I know now that you'll never come back."

Sir, Sarvi's concerned voice cuts through from behind us. *Pardon me, but I don't think this is fair. You should take a moment and think again.*

"What is he doing?" I ask Sarvi, my voice shaking.

But Death answers the unicorn for me. He brings me over to the edge of the hole until my feet are dangling over it.

"This is the oubliette," he says scornfully. "It's where I put people to forget about them. I don't think it will help me with you, but at least you'll learn your lesson this way. I said I was going to tear your wings right off, little bird. Now you have no way to fly."

Then he lets go of me, snatching the crown off my head at the last minute.

I scream.

And I fall into the darkness.

CHAPTER TEN

DEATH

"THE CONJURING"

"I feel like you're judging me," I say, leaning back in my chair and swallowing a gulp of sweetvine wine. I know it's too early to be drinking, but frankly I need it.

Sarvi stares at me from the other end of the table. We're in the war room, waiting for Kalma before I start our meeting. I haven't seen either of them since the wedding yesterday and I have a feeling they're a tad upset at the way I treated Hanna.

I am not judging you, Sarvi eventually says in a careful tone. *I just don't understand how throwing Hanna in the oubliette immediately after making her queen was the right thing to do.*

I let out a bitter laugh. "I never said it was the right thing to do. You know I don't always do the right thing, try as I may."

I am very aware of that, Sarvi says with a swish of its tail and I feel my loyal steed's judgement double.

"Sorry I'm late," Kalma says, coming into the room with a few books under his arm. "I was up in the library, damn ghosts had hidden what I was looking for."

He takes a seat at the middle of the long wood table and places the books on top. "What did I miss?"

"Nothing," I say, having another swig of wine. "Just Sarvi judging me."

Kalma and the unicorn exchange a glance. Even though Kalma can't verbally communicate with the equine, they seem to understand each other anyway.

"I take it this is about Hanna?" Kalma asks with a raise of his gray brow.

"Naturally. And so, what are your thoughts on the matter, since we're all talking about it." I lay out my gloved palm and gesture with my fingers. "Come on, come on, let's get it out of the way."

Kalma exhales, staring down as he moves the books around on the table. "I think she is the Goddess of Death now, and the Queen of Tuonela. What you do in your relationship with your wife is none of my business." He pauses, shooting me a dark glance. "However, as someone who now answers to this queen as much as I answer to you, I will request that you treat her with a little more dignity."

Hot anger flares through me and I grip the wine glass until the stem nearly shatters. "She's a traitor, Kalma."

"Then why did you marry her?"

"You know why," I grumble.

"You believe she might fulfil the prophecy," Kalma says.

"And if that's the case, the prophecy speaks as not only the one you will be able to touch, but the one whom you will love and marry and unite the land against the uprising. Pardon me for saving this, Tuoni, but though you may have just married her, this is not how you treat someone you might possibly love in the future."

I give him a loaded look. Why the fuck are they piling on me this morning? I shouldn't have to put up with their tyranny. They shouldn't even be questioning a single thing I do.

"And what do you know about love, old man?" I ask him.

"I would ask you the same thing," he retorts calmly. "Considering how your first marriage went."

"Hanna betrayed me," I say through gritted teeth. "She was set to marry me and she ran. She went off with Rasmus, someone she barely knew. He broke through the wards and all the protections she had, and she went with him willingly. Didn't even try to say goodbye. How do you know she won't do it again? How do you know she hasn't already sold our secrets?"

Kalma gives me a steady look. "I don't know Hanna well, but she didn't set out to betray you, nor did she give any secrets. What could she possibly say, and to whom? She's just a mortal woman trying to survive, who only wanted to see her father again."

"She's a traitor," I repeat. "And she's in the oubliette because she cannot be trusted. She got what she deserved. End of story."

Oh, come on, Sarvi says with a scoff. *This isn't about trust.*

This is about her humiliating you, so you in turn must humiliate her. Eye for an eye. I know how you operate.

I glare at the unicorn. "Careful there Sarvi, or you'll end up as glue."

"What?" Kalma asks. "What did Sarvi say?"

"Nothing," I say quickly. "Let's talk about the bigger issue at hand, shall we? I called you to this meeting because we need to talk about Rasmus and Louhi, not Hanna." I pause. "Although, I did find a bit of information that might make you sympathize with my position a little."

Sarvi rolls an eye. I ignore that.

"Hanna says that Rasmus is her brother. Half-brother. His father is Torben, not Ilmarinen."

They both stare at me blankly.

"Torben and Louhi?" Kalma says in disbelief. He runs his hand over his face. "The sneaky devil. I would never have thought."

"Whether this is true or not, the fact remains that this is the first I'm hearing of it, and it rankles me that Hanna found it out before I did. I need to know what else I'm missing. What else don't I know." I look at Sarvi. "You have your ear to the ground, so you say. Rumors, outlandish or not—I need to know about them in the event they end up being true."

Regretfully, I had heard nothing of the sort, Sarvi says. *Everything that Louhi does is done in secret. It is the way of a demon.*

"Not much of a secret if Hanna found out from the mycelium network," I point out.

The mycelium network will always favor those that bring the most decay, Sarvi says grimly. *They need death to survive. In your rule, those which are dead cannot die again once inside the City of Death. In the rule of the Old Gods, death can happen again to all in the afterlife. The city will collapse, offering no protection. That is the meaning of Kaaos and thus brings more decay. The mycelia claim to be impartial in politics, but they will always favor the ruler who brings the most death and destruction.*

"Another reason not to trust Hanna." I clench and unclench my fists. "Rasmus took her right there to the mushrooms."

"Hanna wouldn't have known," Kalma interjects. "And I doubt Rasmus would either. The fact that Hanna and Rasmus are related shouldn't change anything, regardless."

"No? She just found out she has a brother. That would only make her trust him more."

Except we both saw what happened, Sarvi says. *Louhi tried to kill Hanna. Rasmus was completely captured and under Louhi's control. I don't doubt that Rasmus is compromised from here on out, but he broke Hanna's trust in the end, whether he meant to or not. That was a shock to her, and it looked like a shock to him too.*

"I can tell by the look on your face that Sarvi made a good point," Kalma says. He slides a book towards me. "In any rate, Rasmus is a threat and Louhi's power may be growing exponentially with him in her clutches. With Illmarinen's shaman blood-magic harnessed, and Rasmus' half-demon, half-shaman blood, we can all agree that she will be coming for us with more power than we've seen before. Maybe not today, maybe not tomorrow, but she will come. Rasmus broke through your wards with ease, Tuoni. Louhi will be able to do that and more."

"Don't remind me," I mutter. I take the book, turning it over. There are strange symbols etched into the peeling snakeskin hardcover. "What is this?"

"I thought that desperate times called for desperate actions," Kalma says solemnly. "Desperate spells, so to speak."

I flip open the book, my eyes taking a moment to adjust to the language. It's all symbols, symbols which I know since all the languages of the worlds have been imbedded in me since birth, but it still takes a moment to nestle in my brain.

"These are in Dharcascian," I say to Kalma, shutting the book closed. "These won't do anything. I've worked with them before. Their magic is no match for a shaman from the Upper World, let alone Louhi."

Not that I'm suggesting this, Sarvi speaks up. *But Louhi has the upper hand because of shaman blood…*

"Yes?" I reply testily. "And?"

You have access to shaman blood, too, Sarvi says.

"What shaman blood do I have?"

"Hanna?" Kalma says in surprise. "If she has any magic, she doesn't know about it."

I narrow my eyes at Sarvi. "What exactly are you suggesting here? Louhi has blood magic from Ilmarinen because she bleeds him. I may be cruel but I'm not about to do that to my wife."

I most definitely wasn't suggesting that, sir, Sarvi quickly goes on. *What I meant by that was that you shouldn't discount her. Torben's blood is in her, just as it is in Rasmus. Just because Rasmus was trained by Torben, doesn't mean Hanna can't learn a thing or two.*

"And who is going to train her?" I ask. "Do I look like a fucking shaman to you?"

She might not need any training, not in the shaman sense. The longer she's here in Tuonela, the more it will come out. I see it, and I know you see it, too. The changes in her. How less…mortal she becomes. I'd be careful if I were you. One day you may be on the receiving end of her ire.

I laugh. "Oh Sarvi. Don't you know that her ire is what turns me on?"

The room grows silent. Seems I have a way of making my disciples uncomfortable.

Kalma gets to his feet, sighing heavily, and reaches over to take the book back. "I'll go back to the drawing board."

"Forget it," I tell him. "I know what I need to do. At least for now. And it doesn't involve relying on Hanna." They don't seem to understand that none of us should be relying on her, not when I can't trust her.

Then what's your plan? Sarvi asks with another tail swish.

I get to my feet and brace my arms against the table. "It's time to invoke my Shadow Self."

"Now?" Kalma cries out softly. "This is the worst time to start playing with shadows, Tuoni."

"According to you, there is no right time. Look, I understand the risk, especially with Louhi growing more powerful. But if I can conjure my Shadow Self, that will create a decoy. We can draw out the usurpers, we can draw out Louhi, Rasmus, the Bone Stragglers, whoever the fuck else is in favor of the uprising. I'll call for a Bone Match, get

Tuonen to referee, and show off the new queen. My Shadow Self will be with her, and I'll be in the background watching. That's just one example of many where my Shadow Self will come in handy."

"I don't like this," Kalma says, shaking his head.

Neither do I, Sarvi says.

"Desperate times call for desperate magic," I say, straightening up. "An old man told me that once." I pass by them as I walk toward the door. "Now, if you'll excuse me, I'm going to need to do this alone."

I stride out of the room and up several levels of stairs before I get to the Library of the Veils. The door is shut, as always, guarded by wards. I run my gloves over the skeleton carvings along the middle of it and a familiar hiss comes out, the sound of a giant lock unlatching.

I step inside and the darkness fades as the lights come on, illuminating the massive space. Energy rushes at me as it always does, making the runes tickle across my body. The Library of the Veils has always held so many spirits, imprints of every living soul across the ages, and the air is thick with them, like dust motes. So many veils overlapping, creating an intersection which entangles so many of the dead who don't want to be dead. They are restless spirits and they are forever angry at me, thinking that because I am the God of Death, I am responsible for their demise. Arguing with them is pointless.

I wave the dust away with my hands, ignoring their indignant cries.

Rauta, my iron dog who is lying on the carpeted floor, raises its head. It looks at me with an enthusiastic whimper, it's tail wagging with a heavy thud. Even when I feel unappreciated by my family or the entire fucking world around me, Rauta is always happy to see me.

The dog has one important job and that's to guard the Book of Runes, which floats mid-air above it. Even if Rauta weren't here, the book would be impossible to take, but you can never be too careful. The Book of Runes has all the magic in all the worlds, a lot of which I don't even understand, but if it were to fall into the wrong hands, I'm inclined to think the entire fabric of the universe would be ripped to shreds.

"You're a good dog, aren't you Rauta?" I say to it, crouching beside the hound and petting it.

The dog's black tongue rolls happily out of its mouth and then licks my hand.

"Such a good dog," I say again and then straighten up. The Book of Runes is floating right in front of me. I pluck the book out of the air. It's deceptively heavy and I turn it over in my hands, immediately feeling the words as they leak off the pages and make their way up my arms, nestling into the pulsing silver lines. All Gods are predisposed for magic, but we are not shamans. We must learn the magic, but we can't always ask for it. The Book of Runes feeds us what we need to know.

In this case, I need to relearn the spell of the Shadow Self. If the book doesn't think I'm worthy of relearning this, then I won't be granted access. It's a dicey move. I last brought out my Shadow Self when I was still with Louhi, centuries ago. We were on the verge of the breakdown that would splinter us for good. I conjured him as a last-ditch effort to save us because I thought that she could be happy with him, that I could live in Shadow's End and she could live in her ice palace in the Frozen Void with my double. With the way the magic is done, it's still *me*. But it didn't turn out like that.

Since then, my Shadow Self has been contained inside a glass bottle in the eastern wing, waiting for my return, if I were to ever return. Opening the bottle won't be enough to let the shadow out, not if I want to use it as I have before. I have to perform the right ritual to fully infiltrate it, otherwise the shadow will be loose and won't be bonded to me anymore. A shadow without a host is one of the most dangerous things. A being that can be harnessed by anyone who knows the right magic. Especially dark magic. It may even be able to kill a God.

But, before I even take the book to the bottle in the east wing, I'm tempted to pay a visit to the Book of Souls, the volumes that take up the majority of the library, stacked in huge hardcovers from floor to ceiling, forty feet high.

I want to look at Hanna's entry.

I've perused it before. I've done my research on my little bird, the moment that she infiltrated my world. I know her life, have seen it unfold in the pages. I probably recall more of what she's seen and gone through than she does. That's the funny thing about mortals, they don't retain as much as they think they do, and as they age the memories slip away like sand. Half the time they don't realize why they're acting or feeling the way they are because they don't remember the moment that burned them, that scarred their subconscious and shaped them.

But I do. I can see it all on the pages, films that play just for me. It is perhaps the most important and sacred privilege I have as a God, this insight into every soul.

I find the stack which has her birth year and open the volume Hanna is in, and flip to her entry—which I've already marked with a white swan feather.

I start at the very beginning, a part I normally skip over because I don't care much to see a baby being born. I am the God of Death, not the God of Life—whoever that is. I am used to being there for all ends, not for many beginnings.

Frankly, they make me uncomfortable.

At the start of Hanna's life, I see Torben handing her to her mother. It looks like it's in a bedroom, which means she had a home birth. Her mother is lying in bed, dazed. She has dark hair, similar to Hanna's, and pale skin, freckles. Her eyes are closed and she shifts uncomfortably.

Torben holds Hanna. She is wrapped in a blanket, sleeping, just as her mother is sleeping. Torben, looking like an old man with his gray hair and beard even back then, brings Hanna over to the foot of the bed and he stares at Hanna's mother.

He stares at her for a long time.

Then down at Hanna.

I focus in on Torben's face.

It is not the face of a man with a newborn daughter. There is no joy, but there is pride and there is worry.

There is fear. Fear above all else, and not the usual fear of "oh fuck I'm a father now" because I know what that fear feels like.

It's the fear laced with guilt, like he's doing something he shouldn't.

Curious, I think. I watch as he eventually taps his wife on the shoulder. She wakes up. I've never really looked at her before, but aside from her dark hair and general prettiness, she doesn't look much like Hanna, her features too bulky. Hanna's features are all soft lines and ethereal beauty, like the rare times I've woken in the night to glimpse pure moonlight on the ocean, before my mood would cause a tempest to roll in.

The mother stares at Hanna. She doesn't move. Her eyes widen. Torben tries to get her to take the baby but she shakes her head. She doesn't want anything to do with her, looks at Hanna as if she's afraid of her own child.

Then baby Hanna starts to cry.

I watch the page but the story gives me no more. I flip it over and see Hanna being spoon-fed baby food by Torben. She's maybe half a year old. Hanna's mother watches from a distance, distrustful.

I turn through the rest of the pages I have looked through before and I can't find out anything else except that Hanna's mother disliked her from the start. I ache a little, knowing all too well what that feels like. My own mother was more Goddess than nurturer to me and my siblings, but because she could never touch me, I felt the isolation more than my siblings did.

We are the same, I think, running my fingers over Hanna's face.

But the thought is foolish. We are nothing alike. She is a mortal and I am a God.

And yet, I doubt she really is mortal after all. That's the reason I'm looking in her book to begin with. It's more than her being Torben's daughter and for her shaman bloodline to come through.

I think she has the blood of a Goddess in her as well.

But, after looking at her book, the only thing I'm convinced of is that her mother is not her mother at all. Torben had brought Hanna to her, but Hanna came from someone else…

Or somewhere else.

I close the book and exhale. I know I have eternity to figure this out. With Hanna as my wife now, she's not going anywhere, not if I can keep her under lock and key this time. I will get to the bottom of her lineage, and if not me, then Vipunen may eventually lay his cards down.

Until then, there are bigger, more pressing things to worry about. Louhi. The uprising. I need to stop thinking I have two different enemies out there and start thinking of them as one. Louhi and the uprising may have different motives, but the goal is the same—me out of the picture.

I put Hanna's book back on the shelf and then walk down the aisles toward the eastern wing. It's different here, quiet. The ghosts that haunt the library don't come down this way. I think the eons of magic scares them away. Some spells can conjure the spirits forward, pulled into this world in a corporal form. If dark magic is practiced, the spirits can be enslaved, much in the same way that my Shadow Self can. The very possibility of that happening must keep the ghosts at bay. No one wants to be a slave for eternity.

I pass by the rows of dried herbs, crystals, salts, and tinctures, past the bone altars and terrariums and small statues of various creatures, Gods, and Goddesses carved into obsidian, death wood, and empathic glass. At the very end of the hall is a small ceremonial room, shielded by tall velvet curtains. I draw them back, step inside, close them behind me.

It smells musty in here, like old smoke and frankincense. I haven't been here in ages. I should come more often just to make sure everything is in its place. Even though no one except me, Sarvi, and Kalma have access to the library in general, sometimes magic itself can become sentient under the right conditions.

The room is small, shelves on either side with books, jars, and bottles. There is one window, tall and curved, as if the eye of a giant dragon is peering inside the castle. Unlike the stained glass or cathedral windows of the rest of the library, the window here doesn't look onto the wild sea or the sharp mountains beyond Shadow's End. It looks out into the *etetteri*, the very fabric of the veils itself. A glimpse, a portal, to the dimensions of the universe.

Truth be told, it's fucking creepy. It's like the ominous dark void of Oblivion, but with galaxies, planets, stars, black holes, crystals, rainbows, all stretching into an infinity that even my own brain can't comprehend. There are shapes and colors that shimmer past the window that I know aren't visible to any mortals, there are worlds that exist on the smallest of atoms, universes in which this one is just a grain of sand. It's everything all at once and it's what I, what anyone, really, must tap into when accessing magic.

Below the window to the veils lies another altar, this one carved from the ametrine that grows in the tunnels to Vipunen. Right now, the color is the purple of snowdrop flowers but will turn yellow when the magic is activated. On top of the altar is almost everything I need: a long knife with a tourmaline skull at the handle, a thin unlit black candle, and a quartz bowl.

I grab my shadow bottle off the shelf. It's clear glass, with a stopper at the top, a stopper that seems too weak and insignificant to keep what's inside the bottle—a swirling dark storm made from the very essence of who I am.

I get on my knees and place the Book of Runes in front of me. The book opens by itself and flips to the page of the Shadow Spells, letting me in.

I let out an exhale of relief.

I unbutton my shirt.

Take the knife.

"*Luojan nimessa kutsun varjominan,*" I say quietly under my breath, closing my eyes. I don't read the words, the book already put the words inside me. "*Kutsun varjominan jonka estan tassa maailmassa ja kaikiaa maailmoissa.*"

I take in a deep breath, steeling myself for what is never not gruesome and painful as fuck. It's enough that I hesitate, having second thoughts if I want to go through with this.

But the book is in me now, and it wants to finish what I have asked it to do.

It takes control of my hand and plunges the knife into my heart.

I roar with pain, the knife stabbing deep. I can feel my heart beating with the blade it in, a stubborn son of a bitch that won't die, definitely not by my hand.

Blood spills from the wound and I grab the bowl. It fills, splashing onto my shirt, and I put it back onto the altar.

"*Minun verestani tulee sinun vertasi*," I grind out through the pain. "*Sinun varjosi minun kontrollini.*"

I heal fast. The cut is closing, blood already drying up.

With another bellow that shakes the room, I rip the knife out of my heart.

Breathing hard, I put the bloody bowl on the altar, the knife beside it, then take the candle and dip the wick in the blood. When I pull it out, the candle is lit, a bloody red flame. The altar starts to change from purple to yellow.

With great care, I pick up the bottle. The shadow inside swirls faster and faster, as if hurling itself against the glass, trying to break free.

"*Olet vapaa, mutta olet minna,*" I say with the greatest reverence, popping the top off while blowing the candle out at the same.

The shadow from the bottle escapes. It mixes with the smoke from the candle, creating a cloud that dances in front of me. I close my eyes and inhale, deep and long, sucking in the shadow smoke until it fills my lungs, until it fills every crevice in every cell, and I can feel my own blood imprinting on it.

Then I twist around so I am facing the rest of the room and I exhale.

The smoke flows out of my chest like a black serpent,

swirling around the room until it finally clears and, when it does, it reveals another man in the room.

Another God.

Naked, he is seven feet tall, all muscle, no fat. Dark brows over pewter eyes, long black hair flowing over his shoulders.

A snarl on the lips.

Silver lines etched over smooth brown skin.

I'm staring at myself.

CHAPTER ELEVEN

HANNA

"THE OUBLIETTE"

Pain.

All I feel is pain, completely taking over my body, filling me from head to toe. The kind of pain that makes you break into pieces on the inside, the shards cutting fast and deep as they go.

But it's not a physical pain. My body does hurt. My side is sore, probably bruised, from how I fell down the oubliette. My stomach is gnawing at itself, having not been fed in days, and my mouth is so dry that I can't even swallow.

Instead it's the pain in my heart, this heavy, aching feeling in my chest that has me gasping for breath, wishing I could reach in through my ribs and quell the bleeding.

I open my eyes, my face pressed against the old, musty hay that lies on the floor of the oubliette, and see only darkness. I don't know how long I've been down here in this deep hole in the ground. It seems like the moment Death pushed me over the edge I've been lost in nightmares. Like my body finally gave up and decided to rest, perhaps for infinity. Maybe that's the point of a place like this. It's not so that others forget you, it's so that you forget yourself.

I wish I could. I'm fully awake now, and the pain is so strong that I want to disappear into my dreams again, even though those brought me agony as well. In my dream I was with my father, flying on Alku above the Star Swamp. The two of us were making a run for the portal, to escape from Tuonela for good. We were almost there…and suddenly Louhi was below us. She waved my selenite knife at me, mocking me, taunting me, then threw it up where it speared the unicorn in the throat. Alku went down and my father and I were hanging onto each other, falling toward the swamp of darkness and stars that opened wider and wider, a mouth with teeth made of bones.

When we hit the surface, all that remained was pain. The loss of Alku, the loss of my father yet again.

And the loss of what could have been.

Dreams are funny in that they often slip past your subconscious and into your soul, until it feels real. What's the difference of whether something really happened or not if it feels like it did? Lying here, the pain seems to root in all realitics.

Alku did die. I didn't know the creature, but if it wasn't for me, it would be alive still. All it was trying to do was help us, help me, and I got it killed. Sometimes when I close my eyes, I see the pain and horror on its face as the Oblivion stole its body, I feel the pure helplessness as I stood there unable to save it. I'm not sure when the images will stop replaying.

My father is alive according to the aurora stone earrings on my ears that glow with his life energy, but only so long as Eero and Noora are on their best behaviour. But it feels like he's dead all the same. Unless he comes into Tuonela once more, I'll probably never see him again. Never hug him, never talk to him, never feel that unconditional love that has kept me going, one foot in front of the other, for as long as I can remember. I have so many questions to ask him.

I want to know why he never told me about Rasmus. I want to know how that even happened, how could he have slept with Louhi, knowing full-well the monster that she is. I want to know the truth of why I was taken to America.

Did my mother discover who he really was? Did she learn he was a shaman, or did she learn about Rasmus? Did she take me away from him because she was afraid of what would become of me? Was she protecting me?

Did she ever love me or…did she fear me? Because I grew up believing the latter, even if I didn't realize it at the time. My mother, who never had the time of day for me unless she was able to mold me into something of her choosing. And of course, try as I might, I was never able to do that, never able to become what she wanted.

And yet, throughout the years I thought my mother wanted me to be like her. To be a version of her, following in her footsteps, which is why I bent over backwards trying to please her, trying to shuck off my own identity, as unknown and evolving as it was. Every day I would get home from school and rehearse what I was going to say to her over dinner, what I could talk about that would make her like me. Whether it was a good grade on a test, or a compliment a popular girl gave me, or how well I did in gym class, I held onto everything in hopes it would make her be proud of me. Give me *something*.

But it was never about that. She didn't care if I was like her or not, she just didn't want me to be like my father. She didn't want me as myself. And when I finally broke under the pressure, when I couldn't dance anymore, couldn't be skinny anymore, and stopped trying to become what I wasn't, she fully pulled away. The minute I was eighteen, she was gone and I was homeless. She discarded me like old jewelry she didn't want to wear anymore.

Slowly, my family disappeared.

I was fine with that, or so I told myself.

Then…family reappeared.

In the form of Rasmus, a brother I never knew I had, one that I want to trust despite what happened to us. And if I do trust him, then I mourn for him, because he's caught in Louhi's snare and all the good that was in him, the adoration and devotion to my father—*our* father—and his concern for me, that will never surface again, not when his mother will corrupt him. She'll drain him so that there's nothing good left in him. The demoness will win.

And then there is Death.

The one person that I believed maybe, *maybe*, could become my family one day…well, fuck. Scratch that. He *is* my family now. We're married. As insane as that wedding ceremony was, it happened. I'm now married to Death. I'm his wife, his Goddess, his queen.

A queen at the bottom of the hole, soon to be forgotten by him.

A spark of anger flames inside me, but I don't have the energy to keep it going. Death wants to punish me for what I did. He thinks me leaving him was a crime of the highest order, and the God wants me to pay. Sometimes I don't even think he believes in the stupid prophecy, I just think he wants to torture me for eternity because he's bored.

Bored and lonely. And my pain gives him pleasure.

Well, your pleasure gave him pleasure too, I remind myself, remembering the weeks before, how he treated my body like I was a queen already. I can still see the look in his eyes as I came in front of him, the way he looked at me as if I was the sun itself, rare and precious and powerful.

The memory makes my heart beat a little faster. It's not enough to bury the pain in my chest, but it's distracting enough. How could we have gone from that to *this* so quickly?

Wait.

What's that?

I squint.

The dark shadowed wall of the oubliette that I've been staring at absently is…moving. The more I try to focus on it, I realize I'm not staring at the stones but *something* in-between me and the stones.

Not good.

I gasp and sit up, my head spinning painfully as I do so.

Don't be alarmed, my queen, a voice in the darkness says. *I've come to tend to you.*

I blink, my pulse slowing as a familiar shape steps forward. *Snap.*

A match is struck, first illuminating satin gloved fingers and a black lace sleeve until I see my Deadmaiden, Raila, standing before me, her face shrouded by her black veil.

"Raila," I say, though my voice cracks.

Don't try to talk, she says, crouching down at my level, the match still burning steadily in her hand. *You've been down here for too long without any water. Hold fast.*

She takes out a wad of curled ferns from beside her and sets them on fire. The flame ferns immediately light up the oubliette.

There's nothing down here except the hay on the cold ground. But, beside Raila, is a woven bag and on the other side of her a large bucket of water.

I brought this for bathing, she says nodding at the water. She reaches into her bag and pulls out a cask made of leather and holds it out to me. *But this is for drinking. It's the same water, I just added some dried hot poppies and chestnut fir needles to give you energy.*

I gingerly take the cask between my hands and tip it back into my mouth. The water is cool and warm at the same time, the poppies and tree needles giving a kick that feels good on my throat.

I drink fast, unable to quench my thirst until the cask is empty.

I will get you more, Raila says.

I nod and wipe my mouth, feeling brighter already. "Thank you. How did you get all this down here?" I look up through the oubliette at the surface, dimly lit by candles in the dungeon area. There's no rope. "How did *you* get down here?"

I can be agile when I want to be, she says rather mysteriously. Then she opens her bag and brings out a mesh bag of dried fruit, handing it to me, then a simple cotton dress with lace trim. *I brought you food and a change of clothes as well.*

I clutch the dress to my chest, feeling the smooth, clean material. I haven't had a change of clothes in a disgustingly long time. "Did Death give these to you?" I ask, part of me hoping he's had a change of heart.

She shakes her head and I hate the pang of disappointment in my chest. *No. I did this on my own. I heard what happened after the wedding. I couldn't let him treat my queen this way.*

"Even though he's your king?" I ask.

She shakes her head. *I am in his debt, I know, but I answer to you, as well. You are my priority at this moment and all moments, for I am your Deadmaiden, not his.*

I can't help but smile, even though my dry lips crack as I do so. I'm touched that she actually cares for me. Perhaps it's more out of duty, but it still counts. Seems like she might be the only one that does.

"Won't you get in trouble if he finds out?" I remember the way that Kalma immediately removed Raila from the castle the moment Rasmus started his attack. Seems she was on rocky ground with Death already.

She stares at me for a moment. Naturally I can't see her eyes, but I feel them.

Whatever will be, will be, she finally says. *I can handle a little trouble. I almost lost my hand earlier, but it was the master who saved me in the end.*

That surprises me. "What happened?"

Let me tend to you and I will tell you what I can. She gestures to the bucket of water. *The water is warm, I just heated it in the kitchen, and it's been infused with summer sprigs.*

The Hanna of California would have never let someone else bathe her from a bucket, but since I've been at Shadow's End, it's become part of my life. Now that I'm a filthy mess at the bottom of an oubliette, I feel zero shame.

I get up and strip, my dress practically disintegrating as I take it off. Good riddance. And to think I got married in it. Then I walk over to Raila, my naked body glowing under the light of the flame ferns. I don't feel subconscious at all. Instead, I feel like the light is giving me life and energy and power. My skin glows as if lit from within. I don't look dirty, I just look strong, my muscles more defined than ever.

You look like a queen, Raila says with a nod. *The Queen of Tuonela.*

I give her an appreciative smile and she reaches down for the sponge in the bucket.

"So, tell me what happened," I say to her as she starts running the sponge over my shoulders, the warm water sluicing over me. The smell of the summer sprigs fills my nose, like a mix of lavender and mint, and my skin feels instantly refreshed. Man, if I could bottle this stuff up and lug it back to California, I could be a millionaire.

She lets out a small sigh. *As you know, the moment Shadow's End came under attack, Kalma pulled me aside. Took me all the way to the stables to interrogate me. Seems he thought I had something to do with the attack.*

"And why would he think that?"

I told you that they think one of the Deadhands or Deadmaidens is a spy for Louhi or a recruit for the uprising. Perhaps even more than one. Kalma automatically assumed it was me because I'm your Deadmaiden. She runs the sponge over my arms and I hold them out. *Had Master Tuoni not come back in time, Kalma would have cut off my hand. He may have cut off even more pieces of me. I can't lose any more of my limbs.*

"Kalma?" I question, trying to picture it. "But he's so... grandfatherly. He doesn't seem like he could hurt a fly."

My queen, everyone here could hurt a fly. Myself included.

She's got a point there. Death rescued Raila from Inmost, so she's basically an escapee from Hell. She's done some *stuff*.

"Why did Death stop Kalma?"

I suppose he found out the truth. That it was Rasmus. Which brings me around to you, my queen. If you don't mind me asking, what exactly happened?

I haven't even had the chance to talk about everything with Death, so I lay it all out on Raila as she washes me. By the time I finish talking, I'm completely clean, my hair wet from being rinsed and pulled back into a braid, and I'm dressed in the new gown. It's simple, like a sundress, and pale yellow. There's no need for undergarments so I'm both physically comfortable and emotionally comfortable from purging everything that happened to me over the last few days.

Bringing it back to what the Bone Stragglers said, Raila says as I sit on the overturned bucket, munching on small dried apples. *They believe you are part of the prophecy of three?*

"Yes," I say between bites. "Have you heard of that before? Death never mentioned there being three prophecies before. Just the one."

Raila grows silent for a moment. *Death doesn't know there are three.*

I nearly choke on my apple. "Are you kidding? How do you know that?"

It's…something that wouldn't reach his ears.

"Don't you think he should know?"

If he should know, Antero Vipunen would have let him know by now. If I were you, I wouldn't tell him.

I blink at her. "He's my husband."

It still feels foreign to say and yet it's starting to feel real.

Your husband who threw you down here.

Good point. But still.

It will throw off the natural order of things, she goes on. *It should be up to Vipunen to decide.*

"Well then, I'll ask him when I meet him," I tell her.

That would be the wise decision. You must start thinking wisely now that you are queen. There is still so much for you to learn.

"So then how come you know about the prophecy of three if Death doesn't?"

Don't forget where I came from, she says knowingly.

Right. Inmost. "Then tell me about it. What does it mean?"

She shrugs lightly, her veil flowing as she does so. *No one really knows anything beyond what is said. Rangaista, like all the Old Gods, wasn't very specific in telling Louhi. But Louhi believes it and that's what counts. Those in favor of the uprising, they believe it too. Perhaps that counts for more.*

"But why did they mistake me for that other girl? Is there someone else in Tuonela that looks just like me?" I try not to shudder. The thought gives me the creeps.

I can't say. Perhaps that's something else to ask Vipunen.

I'm going to have a shit ton of questions for this giant. Assuming that I'll be let out of here to actually meet him.

Suddenly a rope comes down from above and slaps against the stone wall. Both Raila and I gasp and look up to see blonde hair flowing over the opening of the oubliette.

"Raila!" Lovia yells over the side. "What on earth are you doing down there?"

"Lovia!" I yell up at her. I can't help but grin at the sight of her again. Along with Raila, I feel like she's one of the few allies in this place that I have. "Is this a rescue mission?"

"It was supposed to be!" she says. Then with the grace of a Goddess, she leaps over the side of the hole, grabbing the rope at the last minute and swinging down until she lands beside us, her blonde hair whipping around her like cornsilk.

She smiles at me, looking as gorgeous as ever. I can't help but throw my arms around her and give her a tight hug, whether she likes it or not. I've never been much of a hugger so it startles the both of us.

"Hey," she says to me, sounding surprised. She pats me on the back, apparently not much of a hugger either. "Nice to see you, too," she says with a melodic laugh.

"Sorry," I say, pulling back. "Just nice to see a familiar face."

"Can't say I blame you," she says, then gestures to Raila. "Especially when this one doesn't even have much of a face." Her gaze sharpens. "What are you doing down here Raila? And *how* did you get down here?"

My Queen needed attention, she says. *I am here to serve her.*

Lovia lets out an exaggerated sigh and shakes her head as she looks at me. "The utter devotion in your Deadmaiden. I swear mine can't be bothered to even make small talk. I mean, she's been mute since my father put that spell on her, but still. The effort would be nice." She looks me over. "Least she got you cleaned up. Wasn't looking forward to hauling you out of here in the state you were in. Sarvi told me *everything*."

"Wait, *Sarvi* told you? I thought only Death and I could understand the unicorn."

"I manifested it," she says with a shrug. "I've spent some time in the Crystal Caves, it really opens your brain in new places. You'll understand when you go there. Anyway. Have to say I was a bit insulted I wasn't invited to the wedding this time around."

"You didn't miss much," I assure her, and I automatically make a fist with the palm that had been cut and bled. Luckily it seems to be healing. "I'm going to guess your dad doesn't know you're down here with me?"

"My father?" She laughs again. "Hell no. But you're family now, so I'm not about to let you stay in the oubliette, no matter how cranky he is."

I look between the two of them. "You're both going to get in trouble for doing this."

Lovia waves dismissively. "Phhfff. Look, he won't say shit

to Raila because I won't even mention it was her. I'll take it all on. I don't care." Her expression grows solemn as she looks at me. "I told him to let you go, Hanna. When I learned that you had left, I told him he should just let you go. He wouldn't."

"So you're not mad that I left to begin with?"

She shakes her head. "Once I learned it was Rasmus who took you, I understood why you left. You had to see your father again."

Finally, someone who gets it. I feel my shoulders loosen with relief.

"Did you know that I'm related to Rasmus?" she asks me, her lip curled in disgust.

"I know now," I inform her. "I was there when he found out. I also was there when he found out that *I'm* related to him too."

Lovia looks stunned. "Excuse me?"

I nod. "Turns out your mother and my father…"

Her brows shoot up. "You have got to be kidding me. And he didn't know either?"

I shrug. "Seems like he didn't. I know it sounds crazy, but I trust him."

"Sarvi told me he's with Louhi now," she says grimly. "I think whatever trust you had in Rasmus should be gone now."

I look at Lovia for a moment. After seeing Louhi, it's almost impossible to imagine that Lovia is related to her. I never saw Tuonen's face under his mask, but he did have horns growing out of his head. But Lovia, with her long blonde hair and perfect face and bright personality, she seems as far removed from her mother as possible. I have to wonder the last time Lovia spoke to her. She talks about her from time to time, but it's like she's talking about a villain, not the person who gave birth to her.

And I thought my relationship with my own mother was complicated.

"Well, no matter now that you're here," Lovia says to me. "Might take some time for my father to trust you again, but that can't happen until I get you out of here. You strong enough to climb the rope, or do you need me to carry you?"

She asks that so sincerely that I have to laugh. "I'll be fine. Raila fixed me up right."

I give Raila an appreciative nod and then place my hands on the rope hanging from above. I'm still quite weak so it takes me longer than I thought it would to pull myself up, especially with my sore palm. By the time I get to the top, pulling myself over onto the stone floor of the dungeon, my hand is rubbed raw and my muscles are shaking. But I made it.

Lovia quickly follows, her movements like a dance, and I'm envious. Even though I'm a Goddess in name, I'm still a basic mortal and I'll never have the preternatural grace that she does. I know she learned a lot in training with Vipunen, but there's no way I'll be at her level. Gods always have the advantage.

"You coming up?" Lovia yells at Raila over the side.

I get to my feet and look over the edge beside her. Raila stomps out the flame fern fire with her shoe, then throws the bag over her shoulder and picks up the empty bucket.

Instead of grabbing the robe, however, she crawls up the side of the oubliette like she's a fucking spider monkey, her satin gloved hands disappearing into the cracks of the rocks, moving so fast that she emerges out of the hole in seconds.

"What the fuck was that?" Lovia exclaims.

As I said, I'm agile, Raila says and there's a small hint of pride in her voice as she places the bag and the bucket down on the dungeon floor.

I look to Lovia, my eyes wide. She looks just as shocked as me. Okay, so that's something new—and slightly horrifying—to know about my loyal Deadmaiden from Hell. She puts Peter Parker to shame.

As impressed as I am though, I have a mission ahead of me. A God I need to fight with. Anger that needs a place to go.

A place in this castle to rightfully claim.

"So, now that I'm free," I say, dusting off my dress, "where's my husband?"

Though Raila's face is hidden by her veil, she exchanges a look with Lovia.

The master is in his solar room, at the very top of the castle, Raila says.

That's all I need to know.

I turn to go.

CHAPTER TWELVE

HANNA

"THE SNOWBIRD"

"Do you really want to start a war right now?" Lovia says, reaching out and grabbing my arm to stop me. "I must admit, my father is fun to fight with, but he's also never tossed me into the oubliette to rot."

"I can handle myself," I tell her.

She swallows and glances at Raila with a helpless look. "Alright then." Then she shoots me a quick smile. "Guess I have to listen to my stepmother now."

I shake my head and roll my eyes. It's going to take eons before that term means anything to me.

Lovia lets me go. I turn and go up the steps out of the dungeon, my bare feet slapping against the cold stone. From behind me, Raila protests that she should accompany me, but Lovia tells her to stay back.

I hurry, just in case. I make my way up to the main floor, then up the numerous winding staircases lit by flickering candelabras, passing Deadhands on the way. Their empty socket eyes under iron helmets stare straight ahead, their swords and armor encased over their bones clanking as they go. I hold my breath as I go past each one, afraid that they might stop me, remembering the way skeleton hands feel against my flesh, but all of them pass by me like I'm not even here at all.

By the time I get to the very top floor of the castle, I'm not even out of breath. I should be, since stairs are always a killer for me no matter how hard I work out, but I feel like I could go all day. In fact, I feel better—stronger—than ever. Strange, considering how little I've had to eat and drink.

I've never been to Death's solar room, though I know where it is. I follow the long hall toward the south wall of the castle and don't even pause when I see the iron doors closed shut.

I put my hand on the knob and turn it as if willing it not to be locked and barge right in. I'm met with a darkly furnished office and library hybrid with floor to ceiling windows that makes you feel like you're in the middle of the rainstorm currently lashing at the windows and blurring the glass.

Death, sitting in a throne-style chair, immediately jumps to his feet, a move that makes the room shake, an old leather-bound book falls from his lap to the floor, a cup of coffee spills onto an iron side table.

"What the fuck are you doing here!?" he bellows, staring at me in a mix of fury and confusion. He's the most casually dressed I've ever seen him, almost disheveled. He's wearing black pants with boots, same as usual, but his charcoal shirt is unbuttoned and untucked with darkened patches on it, as if wet. His beautiful face is free from the mask, his long black hair loose around his shoulders.

The sight of him is a threat to my senses. I'm so fucking angry at him, and yet all my body wants to do is fuck him.

Thankfully my anger wins over.

"How dare you!" I yell at him, storming forward, pointing at him with unrefined rage. "You're a fucking monster!"

He reaches out and grabs my wrist, holding me in place, eyes blazing as he looks me over. "You've bathed. You've been dressed. Who the hell let you out?" His eyes narrow into silver slits. "What did you do to them?"

"Do to them?" I say, trying to rip myself out of his grasp but his grip tightens, the thick leather of his gloves creaking. "I haven't done anything. Your daughter knew that a queen's place isn't thrown into an oubliette."

"Now you're calling yourself a queen?" he practically sneers.

"You know I am!" I yell. "I might not be getting anything out of this marriage, but I married a king, a God. I have the crown of crimson, even if you took it away from me, it's still mine. I am the queen now, the Goddess of Death. And I know exactly how a queen should be treated."

"Is that so?" he says unkindly, his other hand going to my other wrist, holding me in place. "Is that how you think it works here, in this world you know nothing about, a world you insist you don't belong in? I married you to uphold a deal and hopefully fulfil a prophecy. Never did I say we would be equals, never did I say I would give you any special treatment."

"I don't want special treatment!" I'm practically shaking with anger. "I just want to be treated as a human being, because that's what I am. I know I am just a Goddess in name, I know I will never be equal to a God like you, but I am not the dead either. I am real and I am alive and I am breathing and I am here!"

His nostrils flare, lip curling slightly. He looks like an animal about to go feral.

"You will learn your place," he says through gritted teeth.

"Or what?" I threaten. "What will you do to me? Throw me back in the oubliette, wait for me to rot? Bring me out as queen only when it suits your agenda? You know what we're both waiting for, why not get it over with?"

His brows snap together. "Waiting for what?"

I quickly twist my wrist and wrap my fingers along his leather glove, and before he can react I'm yanking it off, leaving his hand bare and exposed. With speed that surprises me, I grab his forearm on the sleeve, an inch from his bare skin, and bring his hand toward my face.

"What are you doing!?" he cries out, fear distorting his features. He snaps his hand back, trying to keep it far away from me. I toss his glove over my shoulder, out of reach.

"Touch me," I goad him. "Do it. Touch me and see what happens. Get it fucking over with."

"I'm not doing that," he says, breathing heavily now as he clutches his bare hand tight against his chest.

I come toward him, trying to grab him, but he reaches out

with his gloved hand placing his fingers around my throat as a way to hold me in place.

"Hanna," he whispers harshly. "You don't know what you're asking for."

"I'm asking for the truth!" I growl, my throat pressing against his gloved palm as I speak. "I am sick and tired of these prophecies, of not knowing which one I'm going to fulfill. I need to know. You do too."

He looks confused for a moment, then shakes his head, his grip around my throat loosening enough to let me breathe better but still keeping me from reaching his bare hand.

"You have a death wish," he says, voice lowering as he looks me over in disbelief. "You're even more reckless than I thought."

"You're the one making me this way, trying to keep me under lock and key," I tell him. "What did you think was going to happen? That I was going to be a doormat, a submissive? If I'm the one you can touch, then I know I'll be your equal."

"And if you're not the one you'll die," he snarls with a violent shake of his head.

"What does that matter? Then all that's left is the fucking deal we made. Is it really that important to you to uphold some pointless bargain to the very end? What do you even want me for?"

His nostrils flare again as he breathes in and out, his chest heaving. He swallows, his muscle ticking along his clenched jaw as he does. Heat rises up between us, invisible flames that seem to bind us.

"You won't even—" I start.

But, before I can finish the sentence, he does what I almost told him he wouldn't.

He kisses me.

Oh, how he kisses me.

It's not a sweet kiss, nor is it a wedding worthy kiss. It's a fervent action full of venom and fire. His lips are strong and punishing, my mouth opening helplessly to his, his tongue sinking in deep. His mouth takes from me and it demands and it dominates and only here, only now, do I want nothing more than to submit.

Holy fuck.

His grip on my throat loosens, then slides up to my chin, holding me steady as the kiss intensifies, a whimpering sound escaping my lips. It ignites an inferno far down inside me, bringing forth this insatiable shaking need that cuts deep, surprising me. It claws through me like a ravenous beast and I'm trying to grab him in every way that I can to pull him closer to me.

I nearly forget about his bare hand and he growls at me in warning to stop, the low rumble running through me and undoing every last knot that was holding me together.

Suddenly I'm being pushed backward, my legs tripping over themselves, until my ass hits the edge of a desk. Then Death lets go of me, goes over to the glove that I threw to the floor and snatches it up.

He turns to face me, making a show of putting the glove back on, his fiery eyes never leaving mine. "As exciting as it would be to fuck you one-handed," he says, wriggling his fingers, "I'm not taking that risk today."

And with preternatural swiftness, he's at me again, his frame looming over me. He reaches down and grabs my ass, effortlessly hoisting me up onto the edge of the desk, then yanks down my neckline until my breasts are exposed. My nipples are already stiff and aching for his touch and he wastes no time, covering my skin with thick tongue, nipping at me until I'm gasping with pain and pleasure.

My fingers sink into his hair, making fists that grow tighter each time he sucks at my nipple, an intense heat building between my legs that feels too wild to restrain.

I know this man, this God, my husband, can make me come just by playing with my breasts alone, and as if sensing that, he suddenly pulls his head back, his mouth wet. Darkness comes over his eyes as his focus leaves trails over my breasts, to my neck, my mouth, then meeting my gaze. Every inch of me burns under his watch.

"You fucked up a good thing, you know that?" he whispers hoarsely, a hand going to the hem of my dress and pulling it up slowly. He doesn't break eye contact.

"What?" I manage to say, my heart beating so fast I can feel it in my throat.

"You had it all with me," he goes on, voice even rougher now, a hint of malice in his eyes. "My big, hard cock giving that sweet little cunt of yours everything it wanted. I spoiled you, little bird, spoiled you rotten by making you come every night. But I'm not going to spoil you anymore. Because you don't deserve it. You only deserve punishment."

I try to swallow but my mouth feels like sawdust. "You did punish me. You threw me in the oubliette for our honeymoon."

"You should have stayed down there," he warns. "Instead, you're here. And your punishment will continue." He lowers his mouth to my neck, gently brushing his lips up along my skin until I shiver. "I'm going to fuck you with everything I've got, right here, right now, but I'm not going to let you come. You don't deserve it."

I stare at him for a moment, taking in the sincerity in his eyes. Shit. I think he actually means it.

"I'm a hair trigger with you," I manage to say, my version of a threat.

"I know," he says with a villainous smile. "Which will make things more difficult. And more fun. For me, anyway."

He closes his eyes and breathes in deep through his nose as his hands slowly work up my inner thighs. "I don't even have to touch you to know how wet you are. I can smell it, like the finest perfume. I always know when you want me, which is more or less all the time, isn't it? You greedy little thing."

He reaches down and undoes his pants, pulling out his dick so that it slaps hard into his palm. Though it hasn't been more than a week since I last laid my eyes on it, the sight of it still shocks and intimidates me. Only a God would be blessed with such a perfect cock and I'm fairly certain that if I were fucking Death back in the real world, there's absolutely no way he'd be able to fit inside me, not with a dick of his size. Here, he makes it work, pushing me to the brink of pain but never quite over.

Must be magic.

"You should see yourself," he says, deriding me with a sneer. "After all I've put you through and you still want it that badly. You're practically panting."

I can't help but give him a mean grin in return, reaching for his cock until its hot thickness is in my hand. I can't even make a fist, but it's enough for his eyes to momentarily roll back in his head, his wicked mouth dropping open. "I could say the same thing to you. I left you on our wedding day and yet here you are, unable to get enough of me."

His eyes spring open in anger and a low rumble comes from his chest. He swiftly parts my thighs wider, his movements rough, then places a hand at the small of my back as he shoves himself into me.

I cry out, the sound echoing throughout the solar as the air is pushed out of my lungs and he seems to fill every cell of my existence.

"Fuck!" I say through a gasp, grabbing hold of his shirt, trying to keep myself from falling apart. I'd forgotten how brutal he could be and, even when I'm as wet as I am, it's still a lot to take at once.

"You feel that?" he murmurs as he leans forward and licks up the rim of my ear. "You feel how hard I'm going to work you?" He pulls out slowly, so slowly, the rigid length of him passing over every sensitive groove inside me. "You'll be begging to come in no time."

He thrusts in again with a loud grunt and I gasp. I reach down, wanting to give myself a hand, to help release the pressure that's building inside me to uncontrollable levels, but he grabs both my wrists with one hand.

"Not allowed," he says, continuing to pump his cock into me, his breathing raspy with exertion. "That would be cheating."

"Fuck you." I scowl, trying to get my hands free.

"Fairy girl, I'm the one that's fucking *you*." He punctuates his words by kissing me savagely on the mouth, his tongue lashing against mine, making the heat inside me build even more until I feel like I'm drowning in a pressure cooker.

"When are you going to start calling me your queen?" I gasp against his lips, feeling so trapped in the way he's holding my wrists together, the punishing way his hips won't stop slamming into mine. With each thrust I feel like I'm being pushed over the edge, but the freefall never comes.

"When you start acting like one," he answers gruffly. He bites at my neck, sucking my skin between his teeth until I cry out in sharp pain. "When you want to be one." He pulls back and stares at me, his eyes an inch away. I can barely focus, my heart galloping in my chest, and yet I'm already swept away in his eyes. They're gray like the rain clouds outside the windows, with flashes of silver that shift around. It's like staring into a lightning storm.

"You say you're a queen," he says in a low voice, as if it's a secret, "and if you are, it's because you married a king. But you don't want to be a queen, Hanna. You don't know what you want." His eyes close and I feel a sense of relief, the intensity of his gaze was becoming too much to handle. With a shaking breath he pulls out then pushes himself back inside me, deep as he can go, until I feel like I'm one spark away from explosion.

"I want to come," I tell him, trying not to sound desperate, even though that's what I am and he knows it. He *wants* that.

He eyes me and grins, the kind of smile that would kill you on the spot.

"Beg for it, little bird, and maybe I'll change my mind."

Apparently I have no shame, not when his dick keeps pushing me to the edge, when every nerve inside me is so tightly coiled it physically hurts that I haven't come yet. "Please make me come," I whimper. "I need to come."

He thrusts in hard with a deep grunt and then lets out a most wicked laugh. "I don't think so."

Then he pulls his dick out of me and lets go of my hands. He grabs me by the waist and brings me off the desk and before I can get my footing, he flips me around. He pushes me down so that my breasts are flattened on the desk, the edge pressed into my hips and my ass facing him, then he pins my wrists together at the small of my back.

"Asshole," I swear at him, my cheek against the desk.

"If that's what you want," he says, and with his other hand he spreads my ass. I tense up, wondering if he's actually going *there*, then I hear him spit. Something wet lands on my cheeks, trails down the crack and he's rubbing the soaked tip of his cock up from my cunt to my ass.

Holy shit. Death just spat on me.

He keeps running his cock back and forth, the sound so slick and so lewd. Then he pushes in slightly, testing me, perhaps wondering if I'll object to this.

But I don't. I try to make myself relax instead, curious as to what this will feel like, wanting him everywhere he can go.

"Oh, you're trying to be a good girl now," he says, keeping my wrists in place. "Hoping it will win you some favors?"

He doesn't give me a chance to answer before he squeezes himself inside me.

Oh. My. God.

"Fuck, Hanna," he says through a moan, his fingers squeezing my wrists together even harder. "And I thought you couldn't get any tighter."

His words trail off into a gasp. I can't even breathe. Can't even think. I feel so impossibly full and entwined with him that I'm not sure where he ends and I begin.

Before, Death was moving with precision, controlling every single movement. Now I feel the control melt away. His breath is thickening, his pace is picking up. The way he slams his hips into my ass, making the desk move, diving deeper inside me, the primal, guttural sounds coming from his lips, I know he's getting closer to losing all control.

So am I. He keeps pounding me, in and out, faster, deeper, bringing me to the edge, wires inside me stretching and stretching and ready to snap, and yet I can't come.

It's pure torture.

But not for him.

I'm trapped where I am. I can't move but I wish I could just to see the expression on his face, a look I'll never get tired of. To see this mighty God of Death succumb to pure pleasure is my new religious experience, my body his altar.

He's unraveling faster now. There's pain where the desk cuts into my hips, from how my arms are yanked back behind me, and yet that pain is all worth it when I hear those quick little breaths and the slap of his balls as he drives into me, feel the sweat from his body dropping on my skin.

He sounds so wild and beautiful and *raw*.

When Death comes, he comes hard. His hips stutter against my body and a low, animalistic groan fills the air, a cry that reverberates in my bones. I feel him pump and spill into me, the once frantic thrusts now growing slow and lazy as he finishes.

He lets out a shaking exhale and lets go of my hands. My shoulders burn from arms being held back like that and I flop against the desk. He places a large, hot palm at my lower back, then carefully pulls himself out of me, his breathing heavy.

I hear him clear his throat, swallow. Maybe he's speechless.

"Well," I say, inhaling deeply, "I guess most wedding nights end with the groom not able to make the bride come."

I pause. Wait.

"I can make you come with a single lick of my tongue, a touch of my fucking fingertip," he rumbles at me, his defenses up. "I wasn't *letting* you come, there's a fucking difference."

I'm glad he can't see the knowing smile on my face. "Whatever you say."

He lets out a growl of determination, just as I thought he would, and in seconds he buries his face behind me, mouth on my cunt.

I yelp at the assault, his tongue passing hard over my clit. He's no liar. One lick and I'm coming in an instant.

"Oh my god!" I scream, my back arching sharply as the orgasm tears through me, my entire upper body lifting off the desk like I've been possessed. I'm seeing stars, my vision blurring, the world spinning, and I'm writhing and bucking beneath his relentless mouth, coming again and again and again. It's like I've had a million orgasms stored inside and they're all coming out at once.

My fingernails have dug circles into the desk by the time my body finally starts to still. I feel completely wiped, like I'm a clean slate now, like I've slipped back into the past, back into those nights with Death when I'd dream all day about him. About how he can make me feel this way.

And that's when it hits me. I've been protesting and kicking against the idea of being his wife, of marrying him, of having to hole up in Shadow's End as the Goddess of Death. I've been clinging to my past life, to a past version of myself. But, taking my father out of the picture, my love for him and the need to make sure he's okay, I actually like being here with Death. Not at the bottom of the oubliette, not as the subject of his distrust and scorn. But as his queen.

It doesn't make any sense and yet…I think it's meant to be.

Or maybe that's the orgasms talking.

Death straightens up behind me, running his hand over my ass.

"Don't say I never do you any favors," he says gruffly before lightly spanking my pussy.

I let out a gasp, then grin to myself. I try to push up off the desk. My limbs feel like jelly, and my muscles are still shaking from coming so many times.

He reaches out and helps me up, spinning me around until I'm pressed up against him, this big hard beautiful wall of a man. His cock is still rock hard, sticking straight up between us, ready to go again.

Dear lord. I can't believe I actually married him.

I can't believe I married a fucking *God*.

"I missed this look," he says after a moment, his gaze softening. I'm startled as he reaches out and rubs his thumb across my lips before gently tucking a strand of hair behind my ears. Gives me a smile so fleeting that it feels like a secret.

A sudden loud chirp comes from the back of the room, making me jolt, interrupting this rare, quiet moment.

The spell is broken.

"What was that?" I cry out.

Death reaches down and pulls up his pants. "The snowbird."

"Snowbird?" I repeat.

He nods, doing up the buttons on his shirt and jerks his head toward the corner where a few old, yellowing globes and darkened bookshelves are lined with ancient texts. There's what looks like a birdcage in the corner, covered by an animal pelt.

I tug down at my dress to make sure I'm properly covered, then walk over to the cage. I pull off the pelt and gasp.

In between the iron bars is a bird…I think. It's about the size of a chicken, stark white with red eyes, but instead of feathers it is covered in lizard-like scales. The only feathers are on its bat-like wings.

"Oh my god," I gasp, unable to believe my eyes. "Is this… is this a dinosaur?"

"Is it?" Death says, coming up behind me.

"Yes! It's like a pterodactyl or pterosaur or something. Maybe it's a baby, but it might even be full grown."

Death shrugs, as if he doesn't have something extremely rare and fascinating in his study. "I don't know what it is. Sarvi found it on the mountain. Thought I might like to keep it, or at the very least, I can catalogue it."

"You sure like to lock things up and throw away the key," I mutter.

"I took my chances with you, didn't I? One day the snowbird will be tame enough to be free and I won't fear it leaving. Can't say the same for you."

I glance at him sharply. "You're a real control freak."

He glowers at me. Then he looks back to the dinosaur and a look of realization comes across his brow. "That reminds me. You never happened to come across a mermaid in your chambers, did you?"

CHAPTER THIRTEEN

HANNA

"THE MASK"

It's so nice to have you back in the castle, Raila's voice wakes me up. *Already the weather is improving.*

I blink and roll over in bed so that I'm facing the window. Outside it's still gray and overcast, but the rain has stopped and the light is different, as if the clouds have thinned a little.

Figures. All Death needed to lighten his mood was to fuck me up the ass. I don't say this to Raila, of course.

After our angry tryst in the solarium, he made me leave the room. Said he had some important work he needed to do. Naturally I asked what the work was, bringing up the point that if I'm going to be his queen, that I should know what's happening.

But the only thing he'd concede was that I was to take my old room back. Not his room, mind you, which should be where I belong. But, since the alternative was the oubliette, I decided beggars couldn't be choosers.

And after the way he fucked me yesterday, it's apparent I have no problems being a beggar. Part of me is annoyed that I played into his little game so easily, that all my resolve disappeared the moment he kissed me. As if he wasn't a major asshole who literally tossed me into a freaking oubliette. Once again, he has my libido wrapped around his gloved finger.

Of course, the other part of me is fucking delighted that he took me the way he did. Death shows so much restraint and control sometimes that I want nothing more than to watch him unravel. I love the way my body undoes those carefully wound threads.

To be honest, lying here in my room, even though I'm not sharing a bed with him, I feel like a queen. I feel strong. It's like…even if it's just something physical, the way our bodies come together gives me power. Perhaps I can't win my husband over with my wits or my heart (not that I've given him the latter) but I know I can bring him to his knees if I want to.

And I want to. I need to. The more I exercise that power, the more he'll realize that I am his equal in the end, someone that deserves to rule at his side.

Of course, I'm just a freaking girl from California so I don't know shit about how to rule anything, let alone a kingdom of the dead, but I can learn.

I will learn.

Starting today.

I'm going to have my first training session with Vipunen.

Come now, Raila says, pouring more fragrant sea salts in the bath she has running for me. *The day is underway.*

I groan, my muscles stiff from yesterday's antics, and take a sip of the coffee she put beside my bedside. There's some poached loon eggs and strips of wild turkey bacon, mountain rye bread with frostberry jam, but I'm too nervous (or excited) to eat.

I gulp down the rest of the coffee—it tastes like the best brew I have ever had, no surprise since Death puts so much pride in his coffee selection—and then get out of bed and go over to the toilet.

Raila gives me privacy while I do my business (I'm okay with being bathed and dressed but that's where I draw the line), then I step out of my nightgown and into the bath. It's the perfect temperature and I sink right into the scented water.

You'll need another bath after you finish your training, Raila says to me, rubbing a black sea sponge over my arms. *You'll have worked up a sweat. This bath will help relax your muscles, making it easier to wield the weapons.*

Death had stopped by my room late last night. I assumed he was here for sex, like our night-time dalliances used to be, but to my disappointment, he kept his distance and instead told me that I would have my first session with Vipunen in the morning and that Lovia would take me there. He didn't tell me much else and that's probably for the best because I think I'd psych myself out.

But now that I'm up and it's happening, I want to know everything.

Unfortunately Raila can't answer any of my questions

because she's never been in Vipunen's presence at all. It isn't until I'm almost done with my bath that Lovia shows up with answers—and an outfit.

"Good morning," she says cheerfully, sashaying into the room with clothes in her hands. Today she's wearing a peach-colored Grecian gown that makes her cheeks look extra rosy and her tits look perfect. Ah, to be immortal. She stops in front of the bath and holds out a metallic jumpsuit. "I'm here with your new wardrobe."

I eye the clothes while making a vain attempt to cover up my nudity. "What is that, a catsuit?"

"A catsuit?" She frowns at it. "It wasn't made by a cat, if that's what you're thinking. In fact, this was made by the seamstress here. She's a Deadmaiden too, but she's responsible for clothing us, you know, when I don't feel like going to the Upper World to go shopping. She has your measurements and is willing to make you whatever clothes you want, in fact she's already made you a ton. They're in the closet." She nods at my wardrobe then grins proudly at me, shaking the suit again. "And this is your custom-made training suit."

Having worked in fashion, the idea that I have custom-made clothes ready and can get more of them anytime I want, in whatever style I want, is an absolute dream, but I'm distracted by the training suit. It's all one piece, from toes to hands and fastening at the neck, but while some parts, like at the feet and crotch, are of a slinky black material, the rest is like a combination of chainmail and spandex. It looks tight and uncomfortable and I have no idea if it's supposed to be some sort of armor.

"Is this supposed to protect me?" I ask. "And what exactly do I need protection from?"

"You'll see," she says brightly and then jiggles the outfit again. "We're on a schedule this morning, so let's get you into it. You ate already, right? You're going to need your strength."

She hasn't touched her food, Raila admonishes me.

I give her a put-upon look and ease myself out of the bath and while Raila dries me off, Lovia goes over to get my breakfast. The two work in tandem feeding me and dressing me, and I don't think I've ever felt more like a child.

Yet when they're done, I sure don't look like a child. The jumpsuit leaves nothing to the imagination and you can even see my muscle definition under the chain mail. To my surprise, it's not uncomfortable at all, in fact, it feels like I'm barely wearing anything.

"Again," I say, inspecting my body. My ass looks especially perky. "How is this supposed to protect me?"

Lovia laughs. "This is just your first layer," she says. "More will be added as the sessions progress. Iron pieces on your shoulders, your chest. Today you'll probably be fighting with wooden sticks. Then again, I've seen the way you handle a sword—even though it happened to be my sword—he may bump you up a level."

"So do I actually fight the giant?" I whisper, suddenly terrified. I'm picturing Mickey Mouse and the giant from *Jack and the Beanstalk* but Mickey is wearing a ridiculous catsuit instead. It doesn't end well for Mickey in my brain's version.

She nods, pulling my hair back into a braid while Raila pours me more coffee from a carafe. "You do, but it's not what you think. You're fighting something, you just don't know what, or who, it is. You never see Vipunen, of course. No one ever has. Apparently you die if you do. So you wear the blind mask. But fighting with the mask on is great training regardless because it teaches you to rely on your senses."

"Maybe it's great training for you, but you're a Goddess," I tell her. "You're, like, perfect. I'm just a basic bitch human being who has zero training in swordplay or fencing. I can dance and I can take a hit and I can kick, but I don't know my way around a weapon."

She chuckles, turning me around and putting her hands on my shoulders. "Hanna," she says kindly. "Sarvi told me what you did with a selenite knife. And I saw what you did to those swans with my sword. You are not a mere mortal, not in this world anyway. You can handle this, I promise you."

I swallow, my mouth feeling suddenly dry. My stomach twists with unease. "But—"

"No buts. You're going to do fine."

I don't believe her, but it doesn't matter. In no time, Lovia is taking me out of my room and down all the stairs of the castle.

"Isn't your father coming?" I ask, looking down the empty corridors. He could at least see me off before I go and fight a giant. What if I don't come back?

She shakes her head. "His training with Vipunen was when he was a young boy and it was very different from what Tuonen and I went through. He lived in that cave with the giant for a very, very long time."

"And he never saw him once?"

"Not once. To hear him tell it, he was blind after he emerged from the cave, he had gotten so used to not using his eyes it didn't matter. Of course, his sight came back."

Jeez. Hell of a childhood Death has had.

We exit the castle and head to the stables, the air smelling of manure and hay, a scent I actually love. Lovia brings out a big draft horse from a stall. It's white with a dark mane and tail, dappled with blue-gray. Not a visible bone or hint of decay on him. He looks healthy more than anything.

"This is your horse now," Lovia says. "He came to us recently, hasn't had the chance to rot. It's not sentient as far as I know and I've been trying to communicate. But either way, he's yours. Give him a name. Or not."

The horse looks at me with big black eyes that have translucent crescent shapes in them, like looking at a waxing moon in the night sky. "Frost Moon," I say. I reach over and give him a stroke down his neck. "Frosty for short. You better not fucking die on me."

"Whoa," Lovia says, grasping the bridle. "Morbid, much?"

"If you haven't seen *The Neverending Story*, then you don't know," I tell her, grabbing Frosty's long mane and hoisting myself on his back like it's second nature. I'm riding bareback but it's comfortable on a horse of his size.

"Seems so," she says. Then she goes and brings another horse out of the stable, this one thin with wild eyes and a metallic black coat. She gets on her horse, her dress flowing under her, and we head out of the stables and then through the gates of Shadow's End, passing under the giant iron gargoyles that perch over the arched tunnel.

"It's a long walk to the caves," Lovia says over her shoulder. "Easier to ride there. Even easier to fly, but Sarvi already said he was busy."

"Now that you guys can talk, you sound like best friends."

She laughs. "I have to admit, it's nice to have someone else to talk to in this place. Someone I can confide in, you know?"

"Well, there's always me," I point out, feeling a little forgotten.

"Of course," she says, giving me a quick smile. "Right now there's you. But in time, you'll be one with my father. Once you start to feel like the queen, once the two of you start getting along, you won't have time for me. At any rate, I'm leaving, remember? Soon as you get someone else to take over the ferrying duties for my brother and I, I'm going back to the Upper World. I'm not letting that dream go."

"You should never let your dreams go," I tell her adamantly. She has a point, as much as I hate to think of Lovia and I not being friends. As she called me the other day, I am technically her stepmom. I don't think I'm meant to be her friend. I married into her family and even though it doesn't feel like it right now, at some point Death and I should be ruling together. That's what I want, after all.

And in that ascension, I will probably lose her friendship. Look at Death. Look at how being a king has caused him to be isolated from everyone else, including his own family. It's lonely at the top. Even though I lied yesterday when Death asked me about Bell, and I told him I'd never seen a mermaid in the fish tank, in hindsight I wish I hadn't helped to yeet her into the sea. She might have been my only friend in the end.

There's always your husband, I remind myself. *One day, maybe eons from now, Death might end up being both your lover and a friend.*

My heart warms at the thought, a few butterflies in my belly. That's what I really want. It's just too scary to ask for it, let alone admit it to myself. I'm just a little too proud at times.

We ride for a while until we eventually come to where the craggy mountains rise from the earth. There, in the dark rock, is a deep cavern—a slash that runs at least fifty feet high.

Lovia dismounts first and tethers her horse to a stone hook outside the entrance to the cave, then does the same to my horse. I get off and give Frosty an appreciative pat before following Lovia inside.

Though the entrance to the cave is incredibly wide, I can see that the ceiling slopes dramatically as it disappears into near darkness. It should be pitch-black but I think I see a tinge of green glowing light at the end of the cave, though it could just be my eyes.

"Don't mind the bats," Lovia says, walking over to the cavern wall just as hundreds of bats suddenly drop from the ceiling, taking flight in a flurry of wingbeats and squeaks.

I yelp, covering my head. I'm an animal lover through and through but I've never been a fan of bats, especially ones that are basically little flying skeletons with fangs.

"They'll settle down," she assures me. "They're basically to scare stupid people away."

"I thought this place would have a lot more defenses," I say, still trying to avoid the bats, though they seem to be going back to their places on the darkened ceiling.

"Vipunen can protect himself when it counts," she says. "Here. Choose your weapon, then choose your mask."

I look over to see her gesturing to a row of swords and axes hanging from grooves in the rock wall. Above the weapons is a stone shelf of elaborate masks in various metals, decorated with jewels, all the eyes covered so you can't see out.

I glance at her, not sure where to start. "How about you pick?"

She gives her head a firm shake. "No. You must pick what is calling to you. While your weapon may change, your mask will be yours for all time."

I go for the easiest pick first. There are a few wooden swords among the silver and iron ones, each done up with a carving or skull insignia of some kind, some with red or citrine jewels. But even though I'm reaching for a wooden one, my hand is going to another sword. It's long and thin, the blade shining brightly as if it's being lit by the sun, gold toned silver.

I pick it up, my hand closing over the hilt, which is adorned with red stones that would match my crown.

"Interesting choice," Lovia remarks in a low voice.

I look at her in alarm. "Why? The wrong choice?"

"There is no wrong choice," she assures me. "But it's interesting all the same. I thought you would have gone for a wooden stick. After all, whatever you choose, Vipunen will fight you with the same."

"You could have told me that before!" I cry out, wanting to put the sword back but it won't leave my hand.

"It's better to let your mind be open, not fearful," Lovia

says, then nods to the shelf above. "Now pick your mask."

My eyes graze over each one, beautiful and unique in their own different ways. "Please tell me there's one that I should stay away from…"

She laughs but doesn't say anything.

I sigh, adjusting my grip around the sword. Fuck, it feels good in my hand. Too good, just like the selenite knife did. With my other hand I reach up and touch the masks. They're all surprisingly light, all beautiful, but only one is really calling to me. I have always had a deep need inside me to have everything in my life be matchy-matchy, and so I go for the one that most compliments my sword.

It's made of bronze and comes in two parts: the mask and a halo-type crown, because apparently I want to be a little extra. Both the mask and the halo crown are covered in intricately carved deadhead moths, wings splayed, and appliqued with shimmering red jewels. It's macabre and gorgeous and I know it needs to be mine.

"Great choice," Lovia says. "I would have said you'd go for that one or this one with the little agate mushrooms."

I shudder. No freaking mushrooms ever again.

"Alright, now what?" I ask, feeling nervous now that the fun part is over.

"This is where I leave you," she says.

"What?" I exclaim. She's leaving me now?

"Mmmhmm," she says. She takes the crown from my hand and puts it on me, the headband part first, followed by the blind mask, until my whole world goes dark. Then she reaches down and presses my hand into the sword. "Don't let go of this whatever you do. I'm going to put you in the right direction and you're going to walk straight ahead. You'll know when you have to stop."

Oh my god!

"I can't just walk into a cave blind, I'm going to collide with the wall!"

"You won't," she says adamantly. A heavy pause as if she remembers I'm a bumbling mortal. "Well, if you do, just don't drop the sword cuz you'll probably never find it again. And keep walking."

"But then what?"

I don't like this at all.

"You'll know when you come across Vipunen. I'll come back in a few hours with the horses to pick you up, assuming he doesn't send you back way of the Crystal Caves. If he does, don't drink the water. You'll never get out."

I blink, too much information being thrown at me at once. "What?"

"Okay time to go," she says, grabbing hold of my shoulders and then turning me around. "Walk forward. I'll see you in a bit."

I don't move but I hear her walk away.

"Oh!" she says, sounding far off. "And don't remove your mask or you'll die! Okay, bye!"

"Lovia!" I yell at her. My voice bounces off the walls of the cave and I hear the bats begin to stir, but she doesn't respond.

Something tells me she's gone.

Chapter Fourteen

Hanna

"The Training Session"

"Well, fuck," I swear. I'm standing here in the cave like a total idiot, completely in the dark, shaking in a stupid cat suit, wearing a mask and crown and holding a sword and I'm supposed to just walk forward without knowing where I'm going.

This sucks.

I take in a deep breath. I wanted to meet Vipunen. The training I could take or leave either way—on one hand, I love to fight, love bettering myself, feeling powerful and pushing my body. On the other hand, all of this shit terrifies me.

Yet the thing I cling to the most is the fact that I can finally meet the giant and ask him questions. I'm not sure he'll answer anything, but this is as close to an omniscient God that I'm ever going to get. I mean, that's pretty cool.

I exhale, my breath shaking as I do.

Okay, woman up, I tell myself. *Queen up. Goddess up. You can do this.*

I start walking forward, gripping the sword tight, my steps unsteady as I do. The stone ground beneath my feet is uneven and I don't know if I'm going to walk right into a cave wall. At least the mask should protect my face if I do.

I wince as I go, then after a few steps, stop. Try to hear beyond my thundering heart and raspy breath. I need to rely on all my senses now and I have to trust that my body knows what to do. Throughout my years of dance and martial arts, I let my body take the lead. I think I need to do the same now.

So, even though I only see darkness, I see in my head that I'm on stage. I'm walking, dancing, I don't see the audience, I don't see anything and I just let my body do what it wants to do, what it was born to do.

In this half-dancing, half-walking way I keep going forward into the darkness. I can feel the cave walls are close, that the echoes of my feet are duller, it's getting colder, and I'm going faster, the ground sloping downward.

Down and down I go until I feel the space around me open up and I'm met with a sudden burst of energy that stops me in my tracks. I know my eyes are open because the edges of the mask glow a green color and then turn to a white light. Oh, man, please tell me I didn't just die.

"Hanna Heikkinen," a voice booms. It is a voice unlike any I have ever heard. It's multi-layered, deeper than this cave, older than the dawn of time. "Queen of Tuonela, Goddess of the Dead."

Gulp.

I go still. I can't help it. My body completely freezes. A mix of fire and ice flows toward me, like someone's turned on a heater and an air conditioner at the same time.

"I would tell you not to be afraid," Vipunen says. "But that would be foolish. You can't stop the fear you feel, not yet. You will learn in time to live with the fear and let it feed you, fuel you. For now, be afraid Hanna. Be very afraid."

Well, fuck.

"Hello." I clear my throat. "It's nice to finally meet you."

Even when you're shitting your pants, it's good to keep your manners.

Vipunen chuckles, causing the cave to rumble. "I suppose you've heard a lot about me."

"Just that you're the all-knowing God who taught Death everything he knows."

"I'm not a God," he says, and from the way he trails off I feel like he wants to say *I am the God of all Gods*.

"Well, you're definitely a big somebody," I tell him.

Silence falls. In the distance I hear the *plunk* of water, like something is dripping into a puddle or pond.

"Do you know why you're here, Hanna?"

"You're going to train me how to fight?"

"I'm not going to train you. I'm going to uncover what you already know."

I shuffle on my feet, moving my sword from one hand to the other. "I appreciate your faith in me, but I've never fought with a sword before. I can fight with fists and feet. I practice—"

"I'm aware of your life, Hanna. I know what you have

accomplished in your meager years. You don't need to explain any of yourself to me. I know it as I know everything else."

I have to admit, it's comforting when someone knows what you've gone through. You cut out all the small talk, the getting to know each other stage. Then again, I don't know shit about him.

"Are you psychic?" I ask, eager for information. "Do you see the future?"

"I see many futures, yes. However, I rarely know which one will come true, which one will come forward. The wills of those in this life create different futures for themselves."

"Come forward?"

He sighs with a touch of impatience. His breath is warm and cool and damp. It smells vaguely like rain on pavement. "Mortals have the mistaken belief that they move into the future," he explains. "That is not true at all. The future moves into you. That is how manifesting works. There are an infinite number of futures and possibilities out there for you. Time passes through you, it moves past you. You stay still. Whatever energy you put forward is what will align with a future with that same energy, and that is the future you will attract."

"This is sounding like a bunch of woo-woo," I say.

He laughs again and somewhere something heavy, like a rock, splashes into water. "Says the Goddess of Death as she faces an unseen giant."

He has a point. "So you can't see my future?" I ask.

"I can see infinite versions of it. No doubt you can see the same."

Hmmm. I guess I can see the many different ways my life

will turn out.

"Can you tell me if I end up being part of the Prophecy of Three?"

Silence. More dripping.

"I told Raila about the prophecy," I tell him, going on. "She's my Deadmaiden. I guess you already know that. I'd heard about the prophecy when I was captured by the Bone Stragglers. Guess you already knew that too. But she had said that I shouldn't tell Death. Why is that? Shouldn't he know?"

"I admire your devotion to him," he finally says. "I didn't think you would choose that future for yourself so soon."

"What do you mean?"

"I know what has happened between you both, there are no secrets where I am concerned. I expected you to hold your ground a little longer around him, let that anger fuel you. It has fueled you in life so far."

My cheeks burn in a flash of shame. I'm glad he can't see them beneath the mask. "I didn't expect to be grilled about my feelings today. And I am holding my ground," I add quickly. "I just believe that if I'm going to be married to him, if he's my husband and king, I should know why I can't tell him certain things. We're supposed to be equals."

"Ah," he says. "So that's the path you're choosing."

He says this as if it's the wrong one.

"Look, I came here trying to find my father. I did. I saved him, or at least I got him out of Tuonela. I didn't expect to be eternally stuck here. I had a life in LA, you know, and I know you know this. That's all gone now. All I have now is to live a whole new reality in a whole new world, and so far nothing is happening to me by my choice."

"You are wrong," he says simply. "You chose to give up your life in exchange for your father. You chose to come to Tuonela in the first place. You didn't have to listen to Rasmus, you could have turned and gone home but you didn't. You aren't passive. You have been making choices this whole time. It's time to own those choices, Hanna."

I throw my arms out in exasperation, stabbing the air with my sword. "What do you think I'm doing? I am owning my choice in that if I'm going to be queen, then I'm going to be the best freaking queen there ever was. If I have to spend the rest of my life married to a man who might not ever be able to touch me with his bare hands, who might not ever be able to love me, I am going to do everything I damn well can to make sure I am his equal. And that begins with not keeping any secrets from him, regardless of how complicated our relationship is. So, please, if you may, tell me why I can't tell Tuoni about the prophecy."

More silence. I'm breathing hard and the sword is shaking slightly. I lower it.

"You can," he says. "It's only fair that he knows."

I growl. All that song and dance for nothing.

"Fine," I say and then throw out my sword. "I think I'm ready to fight."

With a loud metallic *clang* something strikes my sword, knocking it right out of my hand where it clatters to the stone.

"You aren't," he booms. "But you will be."

"Ow," I cry out, shaking out my hand. My wrist feels like it's been holding onto a jackhammer.

"Pick it up," Vipunen says. "Try again."

"I don't know where it is," I say helplessly.

"You do," he says. "Stop relying on your eyes. They'll give you nothing and you don't need them. First lesson in shucking your mortality."

I sigh and carefully get down on my hands and knees, the ground cold and damp. "I'm not sure I want to *shuck my mortality*," I tell him, moving my hands around, trying to feel for the sword. "That would mean death, wouldn't it?"

"For some," he says simply.

Finally my hands touch metal and I pick the sword up, getting to my feet.

The sword is immediately knocked from my hands again.

"Stop that!" I cry out, feeling frustrated. For a giant, I definitely get the feeling that there's someone closer to my size standing not far from me, also with a sword. I wonder if it's Vipunen, part of Vipunen, or someone else entirely. Guess I'll never know since I can't remove the mask.

"Pick up the sword, try again," he says.

I sigh and get on my hands and knees again, searching for the sword. This time it meets my hand, as if it's been drawn to me.

"Interesting," Vipunen says.

"What?" I say, grasping the sword. I take a moment before I get to my feet, trying to visualize what will happen. I will get up and he will try to knock the sword away from me. I need to think ahead.

I get up and I immediately step back and feel a swoosh of air where something swings in front of me.

"That you're learning fast," he says. "Faster than I anticipated."

I'm anticipating he's going to take another swipe at me, so I dodge to the side, and I feel the air where I was being stabbed. I also know he's going to get faster with his strikes, so I move my sword out, my grip strong.

THWACK!

A metal sword strikes mine, sending rattling shockwaves through my wrists and arms, making my bones feel like a xylophone. But I manage to not let go.

I feel he's about to make a move from my other side, so I quickly adjust my stance and hold out my sword again.

THWACK! THWACK! THWACK!

I'm moving, my wrist switching back and forth, the sword feeling light, the movement effortless. With each turn, I meet Vipunen again and again, until I feel I can't keep up anymore.

I jump back, wanting a moment of reprieve, and my sword is knocked away again.

This time I'm not frustrated. Instead, I'm freaking proud of myself. I don't know who the hell that was, wielding a sword like it was second nature, if it's always been in me as Vipunen says or if in fact I'm just a fast learner, my body enhanced by this land. Either way, I held my own.

Vipunen says, "Pick up the sword, try again."

"Can we take a break?" I ask, hand on my hip, breathing hard. "I don't know if you've noticed, but that was pretty impressive for a mortal, let alone a beginner."

"If you've come expecting praise, you've come to the wrong place."

I laugh. "Wow. I can definitely see where Death picked up some of his most winning personality traits."

"Pick up the sword, try again," he says.

"You need to put that on a bumper sticker," I grumble, reaching down and finding the sword. Like before, it seems as if it comes to me. I grasp it, trying to gather the energy.

And we spar like this for what feels like hours. My hands are rubbed raw, my muscles ache, my lungs burn. I was hoping I could spend the session firing questions at him, but I'm too tired and way too focused to talk.

"You've had enough for the day," he announces. "We will pick up tomorrow."

Sweat has pooled beneath my mask, but I don't dare wipe it away. I blink as it stings my eyes. "How long do these sessions go on for? What exactly are you training me against?"

"At the moment, you are vulnerable," he says. "You must be able to defend yourself, especially if the uprising were to happen. You have seen the Deadhands and the Bone Stragglers. Imagine an army of millions swarming the land, coming after you and your family."

I gulp. "Well, I think in that case I'd be screwed no matter what happens."

"That is defeatist talk," he says with an admonishing tone. "You are not here to cower in defeat. You are here to—"

"Pick up the sword and try again," I finish dryly.

"Yes," he says tersely. "At any rate, the queen must learn to protect herself, whether from attackers, kidnappers, or all-out war."

"And Tuoni?" I swallow uneasily. "Will he not protect

me?"

"He is not sworn to," he says. "But if you are the one, then he will."

"And if I'm not the one?"

"Without knowing the circumstances, you could be asking the God of Death to risk all to save your life. He is the God of Death and he did not marry you out of love. You are a new introduction to a carefully constructed world that he has been running for eons. You can never assume Tuoni will save your life when it comes to it. He most likely will choose his world and his role over you."

I can't help but flinch at Vipunen's words. Freaking *ice cold*. I mean, I kind of figured that, but it really hurts when it's coming from the mouth of an ancient giant.

"Gee, tell me how he really feels," I mutter, gripping my sword.

"It is time for you to go back," he says. "But through the way of the Crystal Caves. Only there may you take off the mask. There is a path that will lead along the water, all the way back to the castle. It is much faster that way."

"How do I get there?"

"Just walk straight ahead for seventy steps. I will guide you."

Oh god, now I have to count? I do as he says, walking straight, my legs feeling like jelly. At seventy steps, he tells me to go to the right for ten steps, then straight for twenty, then turn right for three and keep walking.

"Okay, well bye I guess," I say to the giant as I walk blindly forward, still ever so conscious of walking into a wall.

He doesn't answer. I feel nothing but cold dead air at my back and I feel he has retreated to wherever he goes.

What the hell does he do down here all day? If I was some wise old giant I'd be out and about, stomping around, not kept underground. Though maybe he doesn't want to flatten the world around him. Maybe he keeps himself here out of safety.

I ponder the life of Vipunen, of how old he really is, if he can shrink himself or perhaps split himself into many forms and what those forms could look like (I could have been having a sword fight with a pig for all I know), when suddenly the space around me changes.

Underneath my mask, light glows lavender and I feel a warm, healing energy press down on me from all sides. There's this feeling of the space opening up, and in turn it feels like my brain is opening up, and I can hear the lap of calm waves and a magical tinkling sound.

I know I'm in the fabled Crystal Caves.

I take off my mask, prepared to wince at the light, but I'm already adjusting.

Holy shit, I'm in heaven. The cave is glowing with thousands of crystals, pink and purple amethyst, clear quartz, rose quartz, and pale citrine, all of it covering nearly every inch of the cave except for the sandy-looking ground. They emit a soft light, as if lit from within, making the water of the underground lake look like it's a shimmering pool of Lisa Frank stickers. I feel like I'm standing inside a gigantic geode.

I wipe my brow, my skin instantly cooled, and then place the mask on a shelf of amethyst teeth, followed by the halo crown. I place the sword beside it and before I know what I'm doing, I'm undoing the buttons of the catsuit at my neck and peeling it off. I don't wear underwear anymore (luckily the catsuit had a built-in bra for support and protection), so I strip down until I'm totally naked.

The tinkling sound of the crystals gets louder and a hum comes from the base of my brain, making my muscles immediately relax. It feels like I'm getting a scalp massage.

Instinctively my feet move toward the water. The ground looks like sand but when I step on it, it doesn't shift. On closer inspection, it's like a type of extra soft white moss that my feet sink lightly into.

The lake is wide and continues around corners and bends, the crystals rising out of the surface like towers. I want to go swimming. I don't know if it's safe but suddenly it's all I want to do, this pressing need to get my body wet. I step into the lake, bathwater warm, and when I get into my waist, I realize that the water isn't just reflecting the crystal cave ceiling, it's actually glittering. It's as if someone dumped a million tons of glitter into the water and it twinkles and shimmers around me in a pale lavender that shifts to milky white, depending on the light.

Soooo pretty.

I dive in, feeling the water caress me like a lover's hands, then come to the surface. I'm smiling. I'm laughing. I'm happy. What a magical place.

I do some slow laps, marveling at the beauty around me. I feel like I'm being drugged in a very good way, how one feels with a cold beer on a hot sunny day.

I lazily swim back to the shore and then sit in the shallows, watching my hands create patterns in the swirling sparkles.

There was something that Lovia told me about these caves, but I can't remember now. Something about how it helped her communicate with Sarvi. Is that what's happening here? Is being around the crystals making my mind expand with their energy? Is this like some giant meditation den? I don't mind the idea of that. I doubt I could get any kind of private self-care or meditating done at Shadow's End.

She had also said something about the water. That I should drink it?

Yes, it seems to say to me. *You need a nice drink after sweating so much. You must replenish yourself.*

I cup my hands and bring the water to my hands, drinking it down. It feels cool on my throat and I swear I feel it sink all the way down through my body, like I can actually feel each cell being hydrated.

Freaking trippy.

I sigh, leaning back on my elbows. The crystals chime and twinkle, the slabs of amethyst above me shine like iridescent purple teeth. The hum at the base of my neck intensifies.

I feel good.

More than good.

I am high as a fucking kite.

Shit, I think, but then I laugh, because who cares?

Then I notice the water rippling, moving, a wave coming toward me.

Faint panic moves me to my knees, ready to get up.

Just as a dark head breaks the surface, black hair flowing

around it.

Tuoni rises from the depths like the God he is. I see him in slow-motion, his large hard body sparkling with milky lavender, the rivers running down every carved plane of muscles, over his massive chest, his grooved abs, the tight Vs that run along his hips. His cock is sticking right up already, as if he's come here to fuck me and I automatically find myself getting wet with the urge to lie back and just spread my legs.

What is happening to me?

"Here you are," he says to me gruffly. His shadowed eyes seem to glow silver under the light of the crystals, and his runes burn white. He is completely naked aside from brown leather gloves that go up to his elbows, and somehow that makes him look even hotter. Definitely didn't know I had a glove fetish until I met Death.

"What are you doing here?" I ask, my voice sounding far off, like it doesn't belong to me. Heat presses inside me, a gnawing feeling between my legs, a hunger that I know won't be going away.

It's *very* distracting.

"I was worried," he says.

I raise my brow. "Were you worried that I was hurt, or worried that I'd run?"

"Both," he says.

I try to give him a look of disdain, but it turns out I can't. I'm feeling all disdain slip away. All emotions seem to still. All I feel is…feeling.

My body, wanting his in a most desperate, visceral way.

It wouldn't be so bad, a voice inside tells me. *Just to let your thoughts slip away, just succumb, just be. It's how the Gods do it. They feel. They don't overthink. They don't let their emotions dictate what they do or don't do, they just feel. Let that part of you take over. Become the Goddess you are.*

All my resolve disappears.

My body turns to fire.

I give him a salacious grin as I bend over and scoop the glittering water into my hands, about to take another drink.

"Don't drink the water," Death says quickly, holding out a palm to stop me.

Oops.

CHAPTER FIFTEEN

DEATH

"THE CRYSTAL CAVES"

There's a lot of things that you need to worry about when you're ruling over the land of the dead, but the one thing I haven't worried about for centuries is my wife. I haven't had a damn wife to be concerned over.

But now I do, and fuck if that's not a total shame that she's starting to occupy my thoughts at all hours of the day.

I was visiting my Shadow Self in the eastern wing of the library. I don't know how long I'd been in there with it, getting to know the ropes again. It takes time to fully infiltrate the Shadow Self and learn how to operate it. It's about splitting yourself in half, learning how to be two people instead of one, and there's some trial and error along with the magic. It's why my Shadow Self is bound to that wing for now, kept in place by wards, because I still don't have perfect control over it yet.

Apparently I'd been in there all day, though, because I'd

suddenly remembered Hanna, and when I left my Shadow Self and went to find Sarvi, the unicorn told me that Hanna hadn't returned from Vipunen yet.

It's not that unusual. Lovia would train all day, so did Tuonen. But I'm paranoid about Hanna and I couldn't help but conjure up two scenarios.

One was that she'd done something stupid, like take off her mask, and Vipunen killed her. The other was that she somehow bested Vipunen or Lovia and took off again.

Sarvi immediately took flight at my command, scouring the land on the way to the cave entrance, but only found Lovia waiting outside with the horses. Apparently Hanna was still inside.

So I decided to go by the other entrance to the cavern, the tunnels that lead from Shadow's End and follow the water way deep into the land underground until they reached the Crystal Caves. The further in you go, the harder it is to walk, until the most natural thing to do is swim.

For me, swimming is second nature. I spent as much of my youth as possible in the Great Inland Sea, swimming among the mermaids and sea monsters and with my brother Ahto, as he learned to be the God of the Oceans and Seas. For someone whose touch was considered so lethal that I was always sheathed in layers in the event that any part of my skin could kill, swimming afforded me freedom I couldn't have on land. To be naked, to feel the water over every part of me, including my hands, it made me feel something close to happiness.

So I took off my clothes—keeping my gauntlets on,

leather wrapped to my elbow—and jumped into the cold sea water. I swim faster than I can walk, and I followed the underground waterway until it came to a close in a warm, wide-open glittering pool surrounded by glowing crystals.

That's where I found Hanna.

Naked.

On her knees.

A most spectacular sight.

Unfortunately, I realized too late that she had already had some of the water to drink. The white and amethyst crystal mica sparkled on her mouth, smeared across her chin.

"What happens if I drink the water?" she asks, only sounding mildly concerned. The lids on her eyes are heavy, her breasts seem to be getting larger, nipples hard as flint and pink as snowberries.

"You lose your inhibitions," I say, walking slowly through the water toward her. "It's not a bad thing."

From the way her eyes are locked on my now very hard, very potent dick, it's definitely not a bad thing.

"But you told me to not to drink it," she says with a coy smile. She wets her lips with her pink tongue and my balls ache with a stab of feverish need. "Like I made the wrong choice."

"You made a choice, but it doesn't have to be the wrong one," I tell her.

She gives me that sweet smile again, a game in her eyes. I'm not about to stop playing it with her.

"So I take it that your session with Vipunen was a success if you're here," I note. She starts shuffling toward me on her knees, deeper into the water. "He finds the caves a reward of sorts." But from the way she's eying my cock, I think I'm the one who will be getting the reward.

Hanna stops right below my dick, staring up at me, her big brown eyes holding a faux innocence. There is nothing innocent about her right now. The lust that's wafting off her is building with each second.

"Can I lick it?" she asks sweetly, wetting her lips again.

Fuck me.

I am speechless. I am rarely speechless.

I make a noise that gets stuck in my throat.

"Can I suck it?" she asks, reaching for me with her small, delicate hands. I tense as she wraps her fingers around me. I'm so thick, so hard, so long that she can't even hold me properly, and yet she handles me with ease, like she does this all the time.

She grins, wetting her lips once more until her mouth is glistening, then slides my cock inside.

I hiss in a breath, my eyes pinching shut as the sensation overwhelms me, but no, no, I can't close my eyes to this, even if watching her will make me come far sooner than I want to.

My eyes snap open and I stare down at her. She pops my head out of her mouth, a trail of spit connecting us, and starts licking up my shaft with cat-like delicacy.

"What are you doing, little bird?" I whisper to her, my hands sinking into her hair at the top of her head. "Do you want me defenseless?"

She grins. Yes. She does. She may be lost to the inhibition right now, no deep thoughts or feelings, only the strong urge to fuck and give pleasure and revel in God-like behaviour, but she wants that from me. Wants to undo me, to get in my head and under my skin.

I'll let her. Just for today, just for now.

She wants me to defile her. I will defile every inch.

And she can do the same to me.

She goes at me and I am leveled. It takes all my strength to stay on my damn feet, she's sucking me off like she's been starved for weeks, famished, ravenous, unable to get her needs met.

The whole time she does this, her teeth grazing the top in an expert way, her tongue as it strokes up the underside, she keeps her eyes on me. Even when she's taking me so deep—*fuck*—how is she not choking? I'm literally crammed inside her mouth, down her throat—I can feel her tonsils.

This isn't natural. I don't know how she's able to do this the way she is, I'll chalk it up to a side effect of the crystal water, but I'm not able to think about it too much because with each savage suck of her mouth I feel less like a God, more like I'm operating on a lizard brain. All feeling, no thought.

Luckily, she seems to be feeling the same way, too.

I watch her, feeling crazed. I need to fucking come so bad it makes my bones hurt.

She pulls my dick out of her mouth for a moment, then tilts her head, her fingers digging into the skin of my backside. She tugs herself forward, placing my balls in her mouth.

Fuck! I nearly stagger, weak at the knees.

She works them with the right combination of rough hands and soft mouth, cupping them, licking them, sucking them. Her lips feel like velvet. Then she pulls back and smiles up at me with her perfectly wet mouth and it takes my damn breath away.

I married her.

I am actually married to this woman, this mortal, this little bird, this fairy girl.

My Hanna.

How did I not know she could do this?

That's it. I need to move my bedroom to these caves. I'm not leaving this place. This will become our new home.

"I'm going to come, fairy girl," I tell her, my fist tightening in her hair. I've messed up her braid into a wild mane of tangles that reminds me of sex.

"Then come," she says in a throaty voice before sliding my cock back between her lips.

I'll be hard again in a moment anyway, hard enough to fuck her into infinity, so I let myself go. Relinquish all control. Give it to her.

My body gets warmer, tighter, then I come with a deep moan that makes the crystals around the cave chime, pouring down her throat.

She swallows, takes all of me in with gusto, even when I keep coming and coming.

Finally, my hips still against her head and I release her hair, hoping I didn't hurt her. For as soft as she is, she seems to like her fucking rough and hard, but even so I don't want to cause her pain unless she wants it.

But from the way she pulls me out of her mouth and gives me a wicked smile, delicately wiping some cum from the corners of her lips, I know she probably didn't feel a thing.

"My turn," she says, settling back in the water, on her hands and knees. It's shallow enough that the water only covers her wrists.

A low rumble comes from my chest at the sight of her, waving her perky perfect ass at me. I had her like this the other day, something that surprised me. I enjoyed punishing her as I did, even though she still won in the end when I let her come.

But I don't want to play that game today, not here, not when she's so open and vulnerable and willing. I feel like I could take her in any way I wanted and she would be grateful, I feel like I could ask her any question, and she would be honest.

I get down to my knees, the water splashing around me, getting behind her ass, then spread her legs with my hands. I dip my head, my mouth watering already. I waste no time in licking her. Tasting her. She moves back into my hands, wanting more already.

"Starving, aren't you?" I murmur against her wetness. I'm practically drowning in her and it makes me feel godly to know that this is all because of me.

She makes a tight little noise and I thrust my stiff, long tongue deep inside her. She stiffens, that little noise evolving into a deep and primitive moan as she squeezes and milks my tongue. Her inhibitions left her a long time ago.

The orgasm tears through her, seeming to take her by surprise. One moment she's pushing her ass into my face, eager for more, the next she's convulsing, bucking like a wild horse.

I keep at her, relentless till the end. I don't stop at one orgasm, I go the distance. She comes again and again as I suck at her, lap her up, until she finally collapses into the water, the shimmering purple and white splashing up her sides. She looks more like a fairy girl now than ever.

I watch her lying there, her back rising and falling rapidly, her fingers splayed in the white moss.

Then I become the greedy one.

I reach down and flip her over, lifting her up a few inches so she's just out of the glittering water. I spread her legs, her cunt looking extra pink now in the glow of the cave, still wet from my mouth, and I loom over her, covering her with my body.

"Hello," she says to me in this soft voice, running her hands over my shoulders with a tenderness that moves me. Her big eyes look deep into mine.

"Hello," I answer. I'm not one for sweet talk, bed talk, anything soft. But it would feel rude not to answer her. "I'm going to fuck you senseless now."

She grins, biting her lip as she pops her hips up and wraps her legs around my waist. "Okay."

I push myself into her with a low moan. She's *so* warm. So soft. She's velvet inside. She squeezes and holds my cock with a greedy sort of hunger, like she'll never let go, and I hope she never does. Then she rolls her hips under me, wanting me to go in deeper. She's so small and tight and I know my size pushes her to the limit, but even so she acts like she can't get enough. Whatever I give her, she takes and takes and takes.

This queen.
My queen.

I shove inside her as far as I can go, kiss her neck, breathe in deeply. She smells like a woman. Sweet, mortal. Like pears grown overripe on the tree, ready to be picked. Soft inside, so soft, so tender. Fragrant. Smooth. Curved. Beautiful. In my hands, on my cock, getting messier by the second.

I pull back and notice she's staring past my shoulder with a look of awe on her face. I crane my neck to look up. There's a giant crystal above us on the ceiling of the cavern, reflecting the image of us from below. She's staring at the two of us fucking; my body big and dark, hers pale and small, my ass clenching as I drive myself into her, her dark hair spilling back on the white moss, the pastel water lapping at our skin.

Fucking paradise.

"Do you like what you see?" I murmur to her, turning my attention back to the kissable skin of her neck. "Do you like watching me fuck you like this? See how tiny you are underneath me, how wild you look? How well you take me, like this was what you were destined for?"

She lets out a strangled cry and I drive up into her even harder.

"My queen takes my cock like she lives for it," I whisper, tongue around her ear, causing her to tremble beneath me.

Her grip on me tightens and she moves her head back to look me in the eyes, both want and determination warring in them. She licks my upper lip in a kiss that brings out a hot spike of need. Feverish. Wild.

I want to lose myself in this. I want to lose myself in ways

I've never let myself be lost to. My life, my world, is controlled by me but here, inside her, I just want to be free.

Fuck. Guess these crystals still have an influence on me, too. My thoughts are getting away from me. I need to just fuck, need to let loose this beast.

I grind into her, deeper, deeper now, wanting to unleash myself but managing to calm the surge in my dick. Barely. I can't think anymore anyway, nothing is making sense except the movement of my body against hers.

I suck her nipple through my mouth and feel it stiffen against my tongue, before giving sharp nips with my teeth. From the way that it makes her cry out, abdomen stiffening, her hips bucking up, I know she feels it in her clit. I can make her come this way if I want to, but there's so much more to explore.

I lift up my head, licking a path over her full, sweet breasts as I knead them with my fingers, feeling a stab of rage inside me at how fucking unfair it is that I can't feel her tender flesh with my bare hands. But she doesn't seem to mind. In fact, her focus is up above me, staring at our reflection again. Her eyes go glazed and fiery, sharp and greedy, and I know the sight of me fucking her is pushing her to the edge.

I can feel the tension building inside her now, the way she's moving her hips, the shortened rasp of her breath. She's close to coming. I want to draw it out as much as possible, but I also know we have all the time in the world.

I push up inside her, a hard, deep thrust that sucks the air from my lungs.

She gasps, her nails scratch down my back, holding on

tight. I hope she draws blood. I hope the marks she leaves will stick around for a while.

"You are in my soul," she whispers in a breathless kind of awe, and her words strike me, a sharp blow. It hurts, this special kind of pain, and I don't know why. Is it because I want it to be true? Is it because I'm afraid?

"Tell me again," I say to her, closing my eyes as my lips go to her neck. "Tell me that again. Make me believe it."

I want to believe every word you say.

"You are in my soul," she says again, and then lets out a throaty giggle that both makes me harder and makes me realize this could all be an act, a false reality, one that the crystals are influencing.

"I am in your cunt," I answer with a harsh grunt, grabbing her throat and pressing down on her windpipe for leverage as I thrust in deeper.

She takes that well, so well. Everything I do to her she embraces it, succumbs to it. I could fuck her here for the rest of my life, and if we're not careful, we might end up doing that. The Crystal Caves have a way of warping both your senses and time itself. I could end up fucking her to death if I'm not careful.

Sooner or later, release comes for me. I may be a God, but even I have limits, especially when it comes to her.

I slide my gloved fingers over her clit, knowing the rough texture of the ostrich leather will act as a flame to a wick, and she immediately comes. Her garbled cry echoes throughout the cave, making the crystals chime and sing, her hips slam up against me in violence. She clenches me as she does so, milking me to within an inch of my sanity. Wet. Hot. Tighter than tight.

My release rips through me.

It feels like she's rerouted the circuits in my brain and I've been reduced to jellyfish-like intelligence, all nerves and cells and desire. I know I'm loud, so loud that the ground shakes and crystals crash down into the lake, but I can't help it. I'm fucking *roaring*. More an animal than a God. Back arched, head back, my body staked over hers, dick in deep, spilling inside of her.

"Oh," she says through a hoarse gasp. "Oh…Oh." She's still writing beneath me, eyes rolled back, mouth open wide and wet and I'm struck by an abstract need to fuck her mouth again. But that would be ridiculous.

I lower myself onto her, keeping most of my weight on my elbows, my heart hammering in my chest. It's hard to swallow. I'm unfocused, off-balance. Need a few more moments to right myself and feel in control again.

"I love being your queen," she says, exhaling shakily.

I freeze. Pull back. Stare at her.

Her lips are swollen from sucking, from kissing, sweat beads her forehead. Her mahogany eyes are sated from the orgasms and they gaze at me with such sincerity that I know she's telling the truth.

She loves being *my* queen.

I feel a thread in my chest being pulled and, for a moment I want to say fuck it, and just let her yank my heart loose.

But I can't. I can't let her do that. I can lose myself inside her, in her body, in the heat of our fucking, but I can't lose my heart to her. I don't even trust her.

I can't trust her.

I want to, though.

CHAPTER SIXTEEN

HANNA

"THE KNIFE"

I wake up in the softest silk sheets, my body sinking in a bed so welcoming it's like my limbs have been encased in a marshmallow. My eyes flutter open briefly before closing again, the smell of a bonfire on the beach filling my nose. Woodsy, smoky, crisp ocean air. I inhale deeply, loving that smell and not knowing why. It's like it triggers a memory, and in that memory is one emotion.

Desire.

My eyes fly open, focusing now. I see a huge window with a soft shaft of sunlight coming in. The sunlight is so beautiful and jarring that I'm fascinated by it, then I look past the windowpanes to see a gargoyle outside. A familiar looking one.

I don't have gargoyles outside my room.

I blink and suddenly sit straight up. The black silk sheets

fall away from me and I'm totally naked. I pull them to my chest, my nipples aching as the sheet rubs against them.

Oh my god.

I know where I am.

A low chuckle sounds from the corner of the large, dark, beautifully decorated room. I watch as Tuoni gets to his feet and walks over to me. He has that strut again, the walk of a great beast of prey. I'm the prey, he's the beast.

"So much modesty," Death says dryly, stopping at the foot of his four-poster bed. It's bigger than King-sized. It would have to be, for a man of his stature. "After all we've been through."

I swallow and the act alone triggers a flashback.

Me, naked and on my knees in a glittering lavender pool, surrounded by crystals. Him with his dick in my mouth. I'm not just giving him a blow job, I am giving him an *experience* and I've committed myself one hundred and ten percent to his pleasure.

Another image slams into my brain, my nails digging into the tight muscles of his ass as I hold him close, my lips wrapped around his balls, and holy fuck, what the hell happened to me?

"So you remember," he says, running his hands over his jaw as he stares at me. "I was a little worried you wouldn't. Thought I would have to tell you and you'd not believe me."

I blink, more images sliding into my skull. The training session with Vipunen. How proud I felt. How hard I worked. The journey through darkness to the Crystal Caves. The utter beauty of the gems. The way I wanted to just let every emotion and thought go, be one with the center of the earth, with the energy of the land, and that was even before I drank the water.

"The water," I say slowly, licking my lips. Another image slams into my head. Holy hell. "I drank the water. Lovia told me not to and I did anyway."

"Don't blame yourself," he says, walking around the bed and sitting on the edge of it next to me. "The caves make even the Gods feel hedonistic. I can't imagine the effect on a mortal."

I have a hard time meeting his eyes. I feel like I can see my soul in them, and I don't know if I like that. I look out the window, watching the shaft of sunlight as it starts to fade from sight, like a cloud is coming overhead. I frown. Does his mood change so quickly?

"Why do you look ashamed?" he asks in a low voice. Cautious. "It's not like we haven't had sex before."

I give my head a shake and look back at him. "I'm not ashamed."

"You feel violated?"

Not exactly.

Actually, the more I remember what we did, the more it doesn't bother me. I've done drugs before. I know what it's like to have sex on them. This was about a thousand times more potent than that and I was a thousand times more unrestrained.

No doubt I had the best sex of my life, and that says a lot considering who I've been screwing of late.

It's that I worry about what I said to him. What I told him. To have crazy monkey sex in a crystal cave is one thing. I'm not ashamed of that in the slightest. But to let my words and feelings flow as openly as my legs were spread…that's something else.

I try to flip through the memories on hand, and yet I can't remember anything I said. It's possible I didn't say anything.

Possible, but not likely.

"You are my wife," he says, and the softness of his voice surprises me.

"I know I am," I say and I reach over to touch his hand for reassurance. I rarely reach for his hands. Not because I'm afraid of them, but because such a simple action speaks of an intimacy the two of us don't share. Except when we're naked, it seems.

He clears his throat, pulling his hand away from me. His attention goes to the window. Seems like a safe place to stare. It's only now I notice part of the gargoyle perched outside is missing a horn.

"So, what happened?" I ask, keeping my tone light, aware that it's growing darker outside, the sunlight fading fast as his mood fades. "Crystal water makes you horny or something?"

He snorts at that, and I feel pleased for amusing him. "Something like that. More like it gives you a one-way look into what feeling like a God is like."

"No thoughts, only fucking? Don't take this the wrong way, but you seem to have a lot more substance than that."

Another quick smile, this one dry. "I'm glad you think that. I haven't always been this way. I'd like to think I'm still not in some ways."

I let my gaze coast over his body. He's so big and hard and broad, it's hard not to stare at him. He's wearing a black shirt, black pants, boots, gloves—all the same as usual. His hair is anchored back in a ponytail of sorts, his beautiful face on full display. His eyes are rimmed and smudged with kohl liner, something I find so incredibly sexy, especially the way it makes his gray eyes pop. I know he does it so that it fills in the empty socket space of the masks he wears, but it's a look I like. A lot.

"You took to the water well," he says after a moment. My cheeks burn and he glances at me thoughtfully. "I saw glimpses of you. What you are. What you could be. You're not…" he licks his lips, eyes narrowing in thought, "you're not who you think you are, fairy girl."

"You've said this before."

"But you must know it's true," he says, more urgency in his voice. "You know you belong here, with me, in this world. That there are parts of it that sing to you. That make it feel like home. You know it. Vipunen knows it."

"Vipunen knows what?" I question. "He wouldn't tell me anything."

"Maybe you ask the wrong questions," he counters. "While you were sleeping all this morning—recovering from me fucking your brains out—" he adds with a smirk, "I paid the giant a visit. I wanted to know how it went, in the event that you didn't remember. He said you surprised him. Of course, I tried to get more information out of him but he said anything else he had to say about you, he would tell to you alone."

I feel that flash of pride again. I've surprised the omniscient ancient giant. That can't be no small feat.

"When do I see him next?" I ask.

"Tomorrow morning," he says. "You need extra rest."

I raise my brow. "Because he worked me out too hard or because you did?"

His eyes glitter. "Both." Then a grave look flattens his brow. Something is weighing on him.

But there's something weighing on me too.

I inhale deeply.

"I have to tell you something," I say, at the exact same time that he does.

We look at each, eyes wide.

"You go first," he says.

"No, *you* go first," I say, making sure I sound more adamant.

He stares at me for a moment, eyes searching, then nods. "Fine. Hanna, don't let this news upset you in any way, because it's all based on gut feeling and not much else but…I have reason to believe your mother isn't your birth mother."

I swallow, blinking at him.

I knew this day would come. I knew it in the deepest trenches of my soul that my mother was not my birth mother and that one day I would find out. I knew it, and all the same…

It kills me.

How can something feel so right and wrong at the same time?

It makes so much sense. I never felt she was my mother. She never felt it either, because she wasn't. But I had gotten used to it. Used to her, to our awful, cold, never-evolving relationship.

On one hand, I feel relief in knowing my instincts were right, in knowing there was a reason why she couldn't love me like a mom should have.

But on the other hand…I've never felt more abandoned and alone.

Neither mother wanted me.

"If she's not my mother, who is?" I haven't realized I've spoken my thoughts out loud until Death sighs heavily.

"I don't know," he says. "But I will find out."

I frown at him. "But how did you find out?"

"I looked you up again in the Book of Souls," he admits. He doesn't look ashamed in the slightest. "I was curious. I went to your very beginning. Saw your father right after your birth, or so it seemed. But when he gave you to your mother, who was sleeping, who seemed to have given birth far earlier… she didn't look at you as if you were hers."

I suddenly throw the covers back and get out of bed, not caring that I'm nude.

"I have to go to the library, you have to show me," I tell him, going for the door, but he calmly reaches out and grabs my arm, pulling me toward him, then my other arm, anchoring me between his legs. I should know by now that trying to escape from his grasp is futile, but I try anyway.

"You just have to trust me on this," he says in a low voice.

"Why can't you just show me? I've been there before."

"You shouldn't show someone their own book."

"Who says?" I say through a squint. "You just made that rule up."

"Library is off-limits," he says, voice bordering on a growl now. His eyes are cagey. "For the next while. I'm, uh, doing a magic experiment."

My mouth drops open. "A magic experiment? What does that mean?"

"It means the library is off-limits," he says again, pulling me even closer to him. He's fully clothed and I'm entirely naked and somehow I'm in-between his legs. How am I not surprised? "You can't get in without me anyway. It will expel you."

He adjusts his grip on my wrists, tilts his head as he looks me over. Maybe he expects me to protest but I know when to choose my battles. I ain't getting into that library unless he wants me to.

"Now your turn," he says.

"My turn what?"

His gray gaze is steady, playing no games. "You had to tell me something. What is it?"

I can scarcely remember, I'm still so focused on everything else. I'm also focused on his scent, his body throwing off massive amounts of heat, the pressure building between my legs, how hard my nipples ache.

Damn it! Why does my body do this to me?

He lets go of one wrist and cups me hard between the legs, pulling me closer that way. I gasp and he starts rubbing me with his palm.

He is *not* helping.

"Tell me," he says. "Tell me what you were going to say. If you don't tell me, I'll stop."

"Then stop," I say, but I'm bluffing.

He doesn't stop because he knows it. He works his hand further between my thighs and I know I'm already drenching him.

He stills and then holds me there. "Tell me."

I sigh, breath shaky, and say, "There is a prophecy of three. The mushroom lady told me. So did a Bone Straggler named Michael. It's not just the one prophecy that you know, there are two others."

Now he's really still, a deep line etched between his arched black brows. "What are the other prophecies?" he asks quietly.

"A shaman will have three children," I recite. "One will raise the Old Gods. One can touch Death and together will destroy the Old Gods and the uprising. And one, born from shadows, will defeat Death, leaving the kingdom to *Kaaos*. Michael thought I was the one born from the shadows. He says that he's met her, that her name is Salainen, that she's with Louhi, and that she looks exactly like me."

He grabs me harder, an acidity in his eyes. "Why the fuck didn't you tell me this earlier?"

"I tried," I tell him. Despite myself, I move down into his palm, wanting the friction. Jesus, there must still be that damn glitter water in my veins.

"You didn't try hard enough," he snarls.

"You didn't give me a choice!" I snap. "You dragged me here, married me, then threw me down a glorified well!"

"Are you going to bring that up for the rest of our marriage?"

"Yes!"

He growls. "You've fucked me enough since then to talk

to me."

"Oh but wait, wait, I thought you were fucking *me*?" I say mockingly.

He reaches up and grabs me by the back of the neck, pulling me so that I'm pressed against him and his fingers thrust up inside me. I moan, mouth open, unsure what to do, feeling too many things at once.

"I am your king," he whispers harshly, his gaze so dark and dangerous. He thrusts another gloved finger inside me. "You kneel before me."

"I kneel before no one," I snarl at him.

He leans forward and kisses me, capturing my lip between his teeth. "Another reason why I can't fucking trust you," he murmurs, giving my lip a tug before covering my mouth with his, letting out a groan as he does so.

His tongue is strong and deep, bringing out a deep noise from the depths of me as he nearly has all four fingers far inside. His thumb roughly slides over my clit as long, leather-clad fingers curl over my g-spot, and then I'm coming on my feet.

Oh…oh god.

My neck arches and I let out an animalistic moan, my knees buckling as I'm taken by surprise so completely.

He grabs me by the waist just before I collapse to the floor. Then he lies back on the bed and effortlessly hoists me up and over until I'm straddling his face.

I stare down in shock and awe, still riding the wave of the last orgasm. My legs are quaking, held in place by his big gloved hands that wrap around my thighs and his eyes peer out from between my legs. Dark against pale. Rough stubble against the softest flesh.

"Tell me more," he says, lips brushing against my pussy as he speaks. His eyes are still dangerous and completely carnal in their desires.

Not gonna lie, this is an odd approach to getting me to talk, especially since I would have talked anyway, but I don't try and fight it. Instead, I press down on his face.

I feel his lips pull into a smile before his tongue assaults me, sliding up and down, his grip tightening as he pulls me against his mouth.

"Talk," he murmurs against my skin, sending shockwaves up through my spine.

I gasp, trying to control my breath. "I…I don't know much else. All I know is that Salainen…she…she is the… Kaaos bringer. The bad one…and she looks like me. But maybe it's Louhi pretending to be me? I don't know."

He sucks my clit in between his lips, then swirls his tongue around. I'm almost coming when he pulls his head back. I try to push down in desperation but he's holding me up.

"And you've never heard of her before? You've never heard of this prophecy?"

His beard is tickling me and I shift, wanting his tongue back in place. My abs are getting quite the workout, keeping me upright on him, trying to maneuver.

"No. No, not at all. I swear to you, I had never heard of the prophecies before this, and I wanted to tell you, but…"

"But?"

Shit. I don't want to rat Raila out, tell him that she said not to tell him. But I can't lie either. Not the way he's breathing on me. I'm so close to coming already, which means I'm close to losing my thought process. "I wanted to ask Vipunen first. I didn't want to worry you."

That was the truth.

He grunts and then pulls my hips back down until I'm crushing his face again. He licks up into me, exploring me with deft precision.

"Oh God!" I cry out, bucking against his mouth.

Your God. I can't hear what he says as he eats me out, but I know it all the same.

I come hard again, so hard that I fear I might be choking him. My hips pop against his jaw, grinding down, and he grips me so hard that I know I'll have bruises all around my thighs tomorrow. He is relentless.

I have relented.

I nearly collapse forward but my back arches and my head goes back, heart hammering in my chest, in my throat, in my jaw.

"Not. That. I'm. Complaining," I say, pausing between each word to catch my breath. "But. You sure have a way of getting me to talk."

"I know," he says, adjusting himself below me.

"I was going to tell you anyway."

"You can't lie when I'm making you come," he says, looking awfully proud of himself. "Think of it as a lie detector test. I found that out in the Crystal Caves. Thought maybe it was the water that made you so honest, but I think it's just you being a greedy little thing."

While I hate the idea that I did say something honest and vulnerable to him yesterday, I can't even be annoyed at him. At the moment, anyway. I'm sure I will later when the orgasms subside.

"I wouldn't lie to you," I tell him. I stare down at his mesmerizing eyes, eyes that still don't trust me. "You're right when you said that you are my king, just as I am your queen. We are in this together. I don't want these other two prophecies to come true. I want us to be as prepared for them as possible, though, to figure out what to do next, if anything. Maybe this changes nothing."

"You know it changes everything." He looks so grim between my legs, it's almost comical. "But we can't do anything about it until I get more information. I'll find out more."

"And you'll tell me what you find out," I demand. "I'm part of this, too."

He says nothing but somewhere in his expression I see him concede.

I exhale loudly, my muscles starting to cramp up from my position. Death, it seems, is perfectly comfortable with me on him like this.

I climb off his face then collapse fully on the bed. I make a feeble attempt to cover myself up with the sheets but fail. I'm *spent*.

Death wipes his mouth and gets up. I lie back and stare at the black canopy above the bed, waiting for my heart to slow down.

I almost drift off when I feel the bed sink from his weight.

"This is for you," he says gruffly.

I roll my head to the side and see him sitting beside me, a selenite knife in his hand.

Oh my god!

I sit right up, reaching for it.

He places it in my hand and I make a fist around the smooth, cool handle, holding it tight.

"Where did you find this?" I ask, turning it around.

"I didn't find it," he says. He clears his throat and averts his eyes. "I made it. For you."

My stomach flips with butterflies. I swallow hard, heart beating fast again. "You made it for me? How?"

He's still not looking at me, which I somehow find adorable. Adorable isn't a word I thought I would ever use to describe Death, but here I am. "It's from selenite," he says. "There were formations in the crystal cave. I took some and carved a dagger out of it. Thought you should have one since you're able to wield it so well." Finally he looks at me, a hint of pride in his expression. "Maybe Vipunen will let you train with it."

I grin happily at him and look down at the knife in my hands. It seems so soft and fragile, glowing as soft white as the moon, and yet I know the power it holds. The fact that many aren't supposed to be able to use it as a weapon means even more to me. I run my fingernail over the blade and even that scratches it. So fragile and yet so strong.

Clutching it to my chest, I say, "Thank you," and I hope he knows how much I mean it.

He smiles for a moment. It's like looking at the sun. "It was nothing." Then a shadow passes over his gaze, his smile falling. "But if you ever use that knife against me…"

I stare at him in surprise. "Are you saying this has the ability to hurt you?"

"You hurt Louhi with it. No doubt you could hurt me, too."

"Could it kill you?"

More darkness passes over him. "Are you planning on putting it to the test?"

I shake my head. "I can't kill you. Who else would spend eternity making me come?"

He watches me for a moment, his pupils dilating, then bursts out laughing.

It's the kind of sound that makes your soul sing.

"You're full of surprises, fairy girl," he says, getting up and walking toward the door. "Never stop surprising me."

CHAPTER SEVENTEEN

HANNA

"THE REVEAL"

"Pick up the sword, try again."

I scowl under my mask, tired of hearing that phrase. When this session is over, I want to ask Lovia and see if there's a Vipunen support club where we can bitch about this shit.

This is the fifth time I've trained with Vipunen. A week has passed since the first session, but it's been nothing but a blur. I've been up at dawn, riding to the caves with Lovia, then training with Vipunen until dinner time, sometimes after. I don't go back the way of the Crystal Caves because I'm too wary that I'll be sucked into them for ages, just rolling around in my own hedonism. I need to keep my eye on the prize, and that's excelling. I can't settle for anything less; it's too dangerous.

We need to make sure I can defend myself. I get better and

better every day. Lovia has told me that it takes years to fully train, but that Vipunen is putting me on the fast track because I'm apparently a natural, and the dangers are more pressing at the moment than they ever were for her or Tuonen.

Those dangers, of course—the uprising and Louhi—are made more complicated by the Prophecy of Three. I've talked to Death more about it, he's talked to Vipunen about it, and I've tried to talk to Vipunen about it, but the giant remains cagey and guarded over his words. Says that he doesn't know what is what when it comes to Louhi because Rangaista's devil magic blocks him.

Death doesn't seem to believe that. I'm not sure I do, either. I think Vipunen knows everything, but he wants to influence things in a certain way and so he withholds information whenever it suits him. He acts like he's an impartial God of sorts, but I get the feeling that he isn't. He's self-serving.

"Can I use my knife yet?" I ask.

"How can you use a knife if you can't wield a sword properly?" Vipunen answers.

I scoff. Can't wield a sword? What the hell does he think I've been doing?

"If you want to use your knife," he says after a moment, "then the combat will change. The distance will shrink. I will have to get very close to you and you may not like that. A blind mask can only do so much."

I run my tongue over my teeth, thinking about that. We've been battling with swords non-stop, and while I may not always win, I put up a good fight. In a battle I think (okay, I hope) I could hold my own, given that I'd be able to freaking *see* my opponent, on top of being able to anticipate their every move.

"My attacker may not have a sword," I tell him. "They may sneak into my chambers and attack me there as I sleep. I may only have my knife under my pillow. I need to know how to defend myself with it."

"Very well. Put down the sword, push it behind you. Take out your knife."

I had the seamstress of Shadow's End fasten me a leather holster for the knife. I want it with me everywhere and I don't plan on losing this one. I reach down to where it's strapped around my thigh and pull it out. I kick the sword behind with my foot. It seems to go reluctantly, clattering slowly across the stone ground.

I get into a powerful stance, and get a good, solid grip on the knife when I feel a rush of heat surge toward me, energy that rattles the fillings in my teeth.

Vipunen is at me, so close that I swear I could touch him. Instead, he touches me.

He presses something sharp into my stomach, which thankfully doesn't pierce the chain-mail armor.

"You have died," he says. His voice is now so close it feels like it's coming from inside my skull.

"Try again?" I ask hopefully, sucking in my belly until he removes the knife. I can barely think, everything is red like I've closed my eyes to the surface of the sun and it's trying to fight its way through.

Don't open your eyes, don't open your eyes, I chant to myself, on the off-chance that my mask is providing no protection.

He stabs me again, this time deeper, pressing into me with a pinch of discomfort. Any harder and I think the chain mail might tear.

"Stop it!" I cry out, hating how discombobulated I feel.

The knife withdraws and the energy swirls around me like I'm in a whirlwind, coming at my back now.

He presses the weapon into my spine.

I gasp and whirl, trying to face him.

"You're disappointing me, Hanna," he says.

I have to bite my tongue from swearing at him. I don't think he'd appreciate it.

"You're too fast," I manage to say, trying to stab him with my knife but only meeting air. Meanwhile he gets me on the side, on my arm, on my hip, in my chest, relentlessly. I'd be dead a million times over by now.

"You're too slow."

Stab. Stab. Stab.

"You wanted to play with your special knife," he adds. "Show me what you've got. Show me its power."

"It's not the same knife as I had," I say, twirling and twirling, swinging at the air. "Maybe it doesn't work the same way."

"It's still selenite, it should behave the same. You're just not ready. You don't want anyone getting close to you. You battle with swords because you can keep others at a distance."

"Yeah! People who are trying to kill me!"

"You have to let others in, Hanna," he says.

"So they can stab me? Got it."

"I know in your world they have a saying. Keep your

friends close and your enemies closer. Your most lethal blows should come when you're close. You can't understand your opponent from a distance."

He knocks the knife out right from my hand.

"Pick up the sword, try again," I grumble. My palm feels naked without it.

I bend down to pick it up and Vipunen stabs me in the back.

Hell!

"You're clumsy," he says.

"I'm. Trying. My. Best," I say through clenched teeth, getting to my feet with the knife in my hand and feeling winded.

"Not hard enough. Not with who you are and what you've learned. You talk about your past life as if it held some importance to you. Show me then who that person was. Who was this fighter you seem so proud to be?"

That did it.

This time I sense him coming. I let my body take the lead, just as I had when I first came into the cave.

I go into a roll, summersaulting over and over before pushing up to my feet and immediately jumping to the left, with my knife thrust out to right.

I hit him.

I didn't expect to, so it takes me by surprise. My knife sinks into something quasi-solid, like I'm stabbing a piece of Jell-O, and I feel energy surge up the knife into my hand until it knocks me flat on my back.

I let myself be stunned for half a second before I roll out

of the way, conscious of another stab.

"Very good," Vipunen says. "I have to say, that hurt."

"Sorry?" I tell him, getting to my feet. "Maybe you should be wearing armor."

I feel his force rush toward me again and I'm doing the *ginga* all over the place, dodging and moving as we do in capoeira, avoiding his weapon.

"Stop running," he says. "Stop avoiding. Start fighting."

"Fine," I say and, as I feel him come toward me, I go low into a *rasteira*, a leg sweep that should knock any human being off-balance.

My feet meet with that soft substance again and it makes it harder to follow through, like moving through quicksand, but I concentrate, keeping my legs swinging across before I press down on my hands and flip up, coming forward with the knife.

I stab him.

Once again I feel the energy surge into me and I'm blown backward. I manage to stay on my feet this time, though my mask is almost knocked off and my knife feels like it's fused into my palm.

I push my mask back down, breathing hard, muscles tense and primed, senses working overtime. I can hear the drip of water in the distance, smell the musky rain scent of the giant, feel his energy beaming. I'm waiting for him to strike.

"Throw the knife at me," he says. He sounds further away and everywhere all at once. I can't pinpoint him.

"Last time I threw a knife, I didn't get it back."

"You didn't have enough time with it," he says. "Throw

the knife at me."

I take in a shaking breath and imagine where he is. My mind creates a dark room, and in the dark room appears a tower of light. I rotate my body so I'm facing that light, then I take the knife and hurl it. I see it in my head flying through the air like a shooting star, hitting the target.

I'm about to actually throw the knife in the same fashion when I realize the knife is no longer in my hand and I'm being pushed back again by a gust of heat. I stumble, trying to figure out what happened, and before I even can—SLAM!

The handle of the knife slams back into my palm.

Like a freaking boomerang.

Vipunen lets out an appreciative grunt.

"What just happened?" I ask, making a fist around my precious weapon.

"What I thought might," he says.

"And what is that?"

Silence. More dripping from the corners of the cave.

I wait for him to speak. Keep waiting.

Finally, he says, "Take off your mask."

My breath catches in my chest. I swallow. "What?"

"Take off your mask, Hanna," he says again, deeper now, so that I feel his voice in my bones. "That is a command."

I shake my head vigorously. "But I'm going to die if I do."

"You have many tests in front of you. Tests in which death might be one of the answers. You have to start taking these tests, Hanna, or you'll never be what you need to be. You'll never advance."

I gulp.

"Take off your mask," he says. "Or I'll take it from you."

I don't want that, my mask ripped off like I'm a stubborn child. I place my hands on the side of the mask. My fingers are trembling.

I lift it off, but I keep my eyes pinched shut, hard enough you'll need a vice to pry them open. Immense light turns the flesh behind my eyelids bright red.

"Open your eyes and look at me, Hanna," Vipunen commands.

"I can't," I whisper, the mask shaking in my hands now. "I'm afraid."

"Remember what I told you about fear."

I can't fucking remember what he said about fear. The only thing I can remember now is pick up the sword and try again.

"Open your eyes. Or I can do that for you, too."

I picture stubby giant fingers poking me in the eyes. No thanks.

Without much of a choice, I take in a deep, steadying breath, say a little prayer that my death, if warranted, is quick and painless, and with any luck I don't end up floating in Oblivion for eternity.

I brace myself.

I open my eyes.

For a moment I'm not sure what I'm looking at. It's just this light. A big, impossibly huge white light that is hundreds of feet tall and wide. The cave itself is auditorium-sized in order to fit the light inside, though I swear all this time the cave has been a fraction of the size. In the corners of the cave, where the light doesn't fully reach, I can make out a glowing neon green lake with stalactites hanging above it. See, that's what I had been expecting.

"What the—?" I whisper, trying to take it all in. I can't really comprehend it because it's more than just a light. If this is Vipunen, he's definitely giant but, like…a being made of light beams. There's no physical form here. I feel like I'm staring right into the sun, or rather, the sun is staring right at me.

He chuckles. The sound fills the room as if it wasn't the size of a football stadium. "Just as I had thought."

"Thought what?" I ask, trying to peer at the light harder, *see* if I can see a shape of some sort. "I didn't even know you thought, I thought you always knew." I pause. "Wait a minute. Am I dead? Because I'm seeing a white light…"

"You are not dead," he says. "But many others have died by seeing me in my true form. They lose their minds. You, Hanna, you can gaze upon me and you're not even squinting. Your eyeballs should have melted by now."

Oh, great. But he's right. I should be wincing. I know that the light is impossibly bright, and yet I'm staring right at it with no problems at all. Could be my vision will be absolutely destroyed after this.

"So, what does this mean?" I ask him. "The fact that I can look at you and not go crazy. What does it signify? Has it answered the question about the prophecy?"

"It has not," he says. "We both know that you are part of the prophecy because you have the blood of a shaman. But the fact that you can see me? It means you also have the blood of a God."

Now I'm blinking. "I'm sorry…what?"

"*Goddess*," he corrects himself. "Your father is Torben, a mighty shaman. Your mother, she is a Goddess."

"Oh. Okaaaaay," I say slowly. I rub the heel of my palm along my forehead, trying to think. I mean, I always knew I wasn't normal but as soon as I discovered my father was a shaman, I figured that explained a lot. Even when Death told me my mother wasn't my birth mother, I didn't assume my birth mother would be a freaking Goddess. I mean, who makes that sort of leap? Shaman magic could have explained so much of what has been happening with me.

"You must have known that deep down?" he comments after a moment.

"I don't know what I know anymore," I say. "A Goddess? You say that because I can look at you?"

"Sometimes answers appear when you're looking for other answers," he says.

"A Goddess," I say to myself quietly. I shake my head. "I don't…I don't feel like I have those kinds of…powers."

"You're still only half a God. A lesser Goddess, just like Lovia."

"So then, who is my mother?" I pause, fear punching my heart. "Oh god, please don't tell me it's Louhi." Mushy lady told me it wasn't, but I don't trust her anymore.

"It's not Louhi," Vipunen assures me.

"Okay then, who is it?" I try to think about the Goddesses in these parts but I'm coming up short. "Oh, Vellamo? The intimidating one in charge of the mermaids?"

"I can't say."

My eyes widen at the glowing light. "You can't say? You mean you know?"

"It would take a few moments to figure it out. But this is something you must discover on your own. It is imperative that you do. It will save your life."

I throw my arms out. "Oh gee, it will save my life. No pressure."

"Take comfort in knowing that you already have all the answers. Have faith in that. It is a fatal human flaw to want everything now and all at once, and not realize everything is happening now and all at once. It is always now."

I'm having a hard enough time trying to come to terms with the Goddess stuff, my brain doesn't want to tackle the concept of time.

"Am I the one to unite the land?" I ask him, even though I've asked him this every day to no avail. "Because I can see you, am I…"

Don't say the chosen one, don't say the chosen one.

"…am I the chosen one?" I cringe at my cliched words.

"It depends on what happens next," Vipunen says.

"Okay. Then, who are the others? Who are the others in the prophecy?"

"One you have met already. And one you will meet. Under circumstances that will make you wish you trained a little harder."

"Oh, that's not fair."

Rasmus is obviously one of them. The Bone Stragglers are adamant that Salainen is the Kaaos-bringer, which means

Rasmus is the one to raise the Old Gods. Unless he's the one who can touch Death, and whoo boy, wouldn't *that* be a plot twist.

But what if the Bone Stragglers are wrong? What if everyone is wrong. What if…what if I'm the Kaaos-bringer and Salainen is the one to touch Death and unite the land? What if I'm the one to raise the Old Gods and Rasmus is the Kaaos-bringer?

"Your mind is too busy to fight anymore," Vipunen says, sounding resigned.

"Well I'm sorrrrrrry that you just dropped a bombshell on me that I'm half Goddess!"

Vipunen pulses, the light growing brighter and brighter until I feel it flow over me, into me, like a sun just went supernova. Then the light suddenly withdraws, going back to normal.

I look down. The selenite knife has turned hot in my hand, glowing like it has a light itself. My arms are doing the same. They shine with light, as if the sun has been poured into my blood and the rays are coming through my skin. I am positively glowing, beaming, shining, and heat begins to build between my shoulder blades, growing hotter and hotter.

"Interesting," Vipunen says again. "I'm curious to see how long that lasts."

My eyes go wide. "What did you do to me?"

"I did nothing to you. You are doing this."

"What the hell?" I run my hands over my body, the light splaying everywhere. "People are going to need sunglasses to look at me!"

But as soon as I say that, the light begins to fade, like someone put a dimmer switch on my body. My back cools.

Praise be.

"Time for you to go, Hanna," Vipunen says, sounding tired now. "I am sure you'll want to share your news with Tuoni."

I keep watching my skin until it looks normal again. "So, he really doesn't know?" I cock a brow at the light.

"He only suspected."

Hmmm. Well, it feels pretty damn good to have some good news to share for once. Not that me being the daughter of an unknown Goddess is great…

Oh, who am I kidding?

It's fucking fantastic.

CHAPTER EIGHTEEN

HANNA

"THE SHADOW SELF"

I come bounding out of the caves like a child hopped up on birthday cake, about to go on a pony ride. As usual, Lovia is waiting outside on her horse, holding onto Frost Moon's bridle. Sometimes I wonder what she does while waiting without having something like an iPhone to keep her occupied, but she seems quite content to just stare off into the distance, lost in her thoughts. The Gods are better at living than humans are, after all.

She looks over at me, her blond hair pulled high into perfect plaits today, and arches a perfectly groomed brow. "I take it training went well today?" she asks.

"It sure did," I say, mounting Frost Moon with ease and gathering the reins. While the sword stays behind in the cave, I take the blind mask with me and it hangs off my back. My selenite wonder knife is firmly tucked in its holster.

Lovia looks me over, pursing her lips as she scrutinizes me. "You seem different somehow."

I can't help but beam at her. "I just discovered a very important piece of the puzzle."

"I don't know what puzzle you mean, but do tell," she says, her eyes dancing as we take off toward the castle in an easy trot.

"I'm a Goddess," I say triumphantly, my hair flowing behind me. Heading toward the dramatic silhouette of my keep, I feel more like a Goddess than ever.

"That's only just occurring to you?" Lovia asks.

I laugh. "Yes. Because I'm not just a Goddess in name only. I'm a Goddess just as you are." I glance over at her perplexed face. "My mother isn't my mother at all. My mother is a Goddess."

Lovia pulls her horse to a walk and I do the same. "What are you talking about?"

"Vipunen just told me. My mother is a Goddess. Even your father knew that I wasn't fully mortal, he just couldn't prove it, but Vipunen just did."

Her frown deepens as she looks me over again. "Are we... sisters?"

I shake my head. "No, thank hell."

She raises her chin, her gaze turning to flint.

"Sorry," I go on. "I forget that you're Louhi's daughter sometimes. But no, she's not my mother. That's all we know, though. We don't know who my mother actually is."

Lovia seems to stew over the Louhi comment longer than I expected her to, enough that the air fills with a touch of frost, my breath coming out in a cloud. Hmmm. I'm starting to think that Lovia has some traits from her father.

"I have a hard time believing Vipunen doesn't know," she finally says. Her posture relaxes a little and the frosty air blows away. "He knows everything."

"I know. He says it's crucial that I find out on my own. Says it will save my life."

She rolls her eyes and gives me a half-smile. "Of course he'd say that. So, do you have any suspicions on who it is? Does my father?"

I shake my head. "I haven't told him yet. He doesn't even know I'm half Goddess, he just knows that my mother isn't really my mother."

"And how do you feel about that?"

I'm surprised at the intimacy of her questions. I shift in my seat. "I'm not sure yet. Part of me feels relief, because I'd always suspected, you know, and it's nice to have answers." I sigh, feeling the familiar knot in my chest that's been there ever since Death told me the news. "At the same time, I have more questions. Who was my birth mom? Why did she abandon me? Why did Torben raise me in the Upper World?"

"I hope you find those answers soon," she says with a sympathetic nod.

We ride for a while, Lovia talking about all the cities in Europe she wants to visit once she can get out of Tuonela. I promise her that I'll bring up her pending sabbatical with Death at some point—she thinks I'll have a better chance of convincing him. I told her that I have a hard time convincing him of anything.

Unless, you know, I'm convincing him of giving me an orgasm. But I'm not about to share that information with her.

We're almost at the castle when I give her another tidbit of good news.

"Oh, I forgot to tell you," I say, biting my lip. "Vipunen made me take off the mask."

She yanks her horse to a stop. "He *what*?"

I nod. "I had to take it off and look at him."

Her eyes turn to blue saucers. "Hanna! What the hell? You're not…no, *no one* has ever seen him without dying."

"I'm aware," I say, trying to not sound like I'm boasting. "But I saw him and I didn't die."

She blinks at me rapidly then gives her head a shake. "I can't believe it. You…out of everyone, *you*? Fuck, now I'm really wondering who the hell your mother is."

I don't take offense to any of that. I'm just as surprised as she is.

"That makes two of us," I admit.

"So, what did he look like? Or will I die if you tell me?"

I laugh. "He looked like light. Like a giant mass of light hundreds of feet tall and wide. That's it. Just light."

I can see her trying to picture it, her brow scrunched up comically. "Light? That's not what I expected. I knew he gave off light, I could tell around the edges of the mask, but I didn't think he would *be* just light."

"Obviously it seems he can change, maybe shrink or become solid when he's fighting us, but yeah. Big ol' giant lightbulb."

She laughs at that, but I still see the awe in her eyes as we ride into the castle. Like she still can't believe it. I can't either.

And I am *dying* to tell Death. I can't wait to see his reaction.

"Do you know where your father is?" I ask Lovia as I dismount in the stables, giving Frosty an affectionate pat and plant a kiss on his velvet muzzle.

"He's been in the library all day," she says. She gives me a warning look. "And he said that no one can disturb him."

Yeah. That's what he's been saying all week. I've been busy training all day and into the night, so I've barely been around anyway. I don't even see him at dinner. I usually eat it in my room alone, or with Lovia and Kalma in the dining hall.

Speaking of rooms, I've moved into his. Unofficially. I still have my room because it turns out, when push comes to shove, I actually enjoy having a place to myself where I can think and feel like I'm not getting in the way. There's not a lot of privacy in Shadow's End, or at least something that feels *mine*, so I cling to what I have. Plus, I've seen Death's closet. It's large, but in no way big enough to accommodate all the dresses I've been accumulating since I've been given access to the seamstress.

But I have been in his bed each night. We talk, just a little, his mind is preoccupied with whatever he's doing in the library, and my mind has been focused on my training. But where our words may fail us, our bodies never do. We come together each night in heat and desire, animalistic cries, gloved hands on soft skin and limbs sliding along silk sheets. He makes me come over and over again until the morning and yet, even with so little sleep, I wake up more refreshed and recharged than ever. I know that in time we may become something more than a physical need to each other, but for now it's how we connect. It's almost…necessary for our connection, for our evolution as a couple. I feel like the more he's inside me, the closer to him I get, and the more I understand him, and I can only hope it's the same for him. If we are to rule together as king and queen then we must be united, and there is no greater union than the one of our bodies in bed.

I head into the castle, wandering the halls, hoping to run into my husband somewhere. Though my training ended earlier today, it's still getting quite late and I'm hungry despite being so excited about everything.

I go to the kitchen and pester Pyry into cooking faster, then take my plate of mountain rye slabs (basically a flatbread with some tart tomatoes and melted slices of *renost*, or reindeer cheese) and a cup of lavender ale and go up to my room.

When I'm done, Raila runs me a bath and I have half a mind to tell her what I learned from Vipunen. But for some reason I don't. I guess because I already told Lovia and I feel bad Death doesn't even know yet.

Or maybe it's this small kernel of a feeling that I can't completely trust her.

"Where is Tuoni?" I ask Raila after I've dried off and she's slipping a soft, long-sleeved nightgown over me. "Still in the library?"

He is. He is not to be disturbed, she says.

Jeez. How many times can I be told that I can't go and bug him?

Naturally, the more I'm told not to do something, the

more I want to do it.

I go up to his room after and wait for him in bed.

Eventually I fall into a deep sleep, the exhaustion from the day hitting me all at once.

When I wake up, I'm still in the dark and I'm drooling, my face smashed up against the silk pillow. I have no idea what time it is, but the crescent moon has shifted positions in the sky. Some nights the moon moves faster than others so it's not the best indicator of time, but at any rate, it's late and Death isn't back yet.

Am I supposed to just sit on this information by myself? I'm a Goddess, damn it!

I get out of bed, deciding to pay Death a visit. I have no doubt that the Library of the Veils will repel me with all the wards it has going around it, but it doesn't hurt to try. Maybe I can stand outside it and yell, and he'll hear me and I can give him the news.

I leave the room and walk through the halls. The candles are flickering from the sconces on the stone walls, lighting up the corridors, and everything is dead quiet. I'd forgotten how eerie it is to wander around Shadow's End at night. The last time I did this was when I freed Bell, then got caught by Surma, who Death then killed in front of me. That whole thing felt like it happened in another life, and yet here I am in my nightgown, walking soundlessly through the creepy castle, up to no good. At least now I'm queen, and it's my castle. I belong here more than the old Hanna did.

I go all the way up the stairs to the level where the library is. Already I can feel the strange energy emanating from the room, the massive iron doors feeling especially foreboding without Death by my side.

I throw my shoulders back in mock confidence and walk over to the doors. There is no keyhole and no handle. There are only intricate designs carved down the middle. Last time Death ran his hands over them and the doors opened for him.

I reach out, wanting to do the same whilst also being scared that it might have some sort of protective mechanism, like it will burn my hands off or something.

Before I have a chance to touch the designs, the door hisses, making me step back. It slowly opens revealing Death on the other side.

He's shirtless, wearing only pants. No shoes.

No gloves.

I stare at his bare hands, the sight so foreign to me.

"Uh, what are you doing?" I ask him.

He clears his throat but doesn't say anything. There's an odd look in his eyes, like he's not all there.

I notice he's not letting me inside.

"Sorry to come up here like this," I go on. "I was warned repeatedly by everyone not to come and disturb you, but I was waiting for you in bed and you never showed and well, I need to talk to you about something."

He frowns at me. Then smiles. It's a strange smile, a bit empty. It makes him look ditzy. Then I realize he doesn't have his usual eye makeup on, so he looks innocent at the same time. Younger.

"Come on in," he says, his voice hoarse, like he lost it somewhere. He backs up and gestures for me to come in with those bare hands of his.

"You sure?" I ask. "I thought this was some big secret thing."

He smiles again. "Come on in."

Is he drunk? High? What's wrong with him?

I step inside the library, keeping a wide berth from him with his hands as unprotected as they are, and the doors slam shut with a howl of wind. White figures rush in the air toward me, over me, then rebound against the door, as if they were trying to escape and failed.

"Ghosts," Death says simply. He smiles again.

I smile back, though mine is unsure. "Did you want to put some gloves on? Or is this crucial to whatever magic experiment you're still doing?"

"Come with me," he says. His voice is so odd. Raspy, and yet it's like he's trying to sound upbeat or something. It does not gel.

He turns and starts walking toward a section of the library that I've never been to. I follow, still keeping a safe distance. His ass looks especially fine tonight and I find myself wondering why he doesn't walk around shirtless more often. His shoulders are a work of fucking art. I've always been a sucker for a broad, muscular back.

This wing of the library is so much cozier than the rest, and I can tell it's the place where the magic happens. There are tons of Turkish-style rugs, velvet tapestries on the walls, lots of candles, jars of herbs, bottles of green or black liquid, old books, bone carvings, crystal skulls. It smells like incense and a thin layer of smoke hangs above my head.

Death stops in front of the back of the room where tall curtains are drawn closed. He beckons me forward with a bare finger, the other hand going to the curtain as if to pull it back.

There's a prickle at the back of my neck, a feeling of unease creeping through me. I can't explain it, but something is off here and I don't know what it is. Maybe it's just the fact that Death has his gloves off and he's not giving me any explanation.

"I don't want to get too close," I tell him, inching forward until I'm as close as I want to go. "Maybe you should put some gloves on. Would make me worry a little less."

He tilts his head, seeming to think something over.

Then he reaches out for me with his hand.

I scream and try to move back, my heels tripping on the rugs, but he's fast.

Too fast.

He grabs my wrist, his grip strong, preventing me from falling backward onto the carpet. The feeling of his palm on my skin makes me scream again, expecting certain death, for me to disintegrate into Oblivion, just as it happened to Alku.

But as he pulls me toward him, his other bare hand going to my waist, and grins down at me, I realize I'm not dying.

I'm not dead.

Holy fucking shit.

I AM the chosen one!

I break into the biggest grin, my heart leaping in my chest.

"You just touched me!" I exclaim. "I'm the one! The prophesized one! The chosen one! I'm the one to unite the land."

He just smiles at me, and what little lucidity I saw in his eyes suddenly fades, like all the lights upstairs were just turned off.

"The chosen one," Death's voice booms, mocking me. It doesn't come from the man holding onto me, it comes from behind the curtain. The man who is holding me may look like Death, but with sudden clarity I know he isn't.

Suddenly the curtain parts open.

Death steps out.

My Tuoni.

The real God.

He's also shirtless, but he has his leather gauntlets on up to his elbows. The look on his handsome face is pure amusement, a wicked gleam in his shadowed eyes. Oh yes. This is my husband.

I stare at him and then eye the version of him holding onto me, gazing down at me with vacant eyes, a half-smile frozen on his face.

"Okay, before I have a total meltdown, will the real Slim Shady please stand up?" I ask.

"Who the fuck is Slim Shady?" Death asks, a snarl to his lips.

Yes, this is definitely him.

I give him a look and try to get out of the grip of the other Death but he's not moving. "Can you tell him to let go of me or do I need to knee him in the balls?" Part of me really, really wants to do it, too. Would serve him right for the whole oubliette thing.

I watch as Death's eyes go completely white, like they roll

back in his head.

Creeeeepy.

Suddenly the Death that's holding onto me lets go and then walks back, retreating to the corner of the room. He sits down on an ottoman and stares at the floor.

The real Death's eyes go back to normal and he gives me a twisted smile. "It's still not perfect, but I'm getting there," he says.

"Look, you're going to have to humor me because I have had no clue what you've been doing up here and I have no clue how this is possible." I gesture to the other Death. "Who the hell is that? Do you have a twin?"

He nods, running a hand over his jaw, making his beard bristle against his glove. "I do now. That's my Shadow Self. That's my experiment. I let him loose from his bottle, been trying to perfect him until I let him loose into the public."

I make a face, not understanding any of this. "Why do you need a twin?"

"So that I can be two places at once," he says. "It's not unusual for kings or queens to have them, especially in times of need. Doppelgängers, as you might call them. In my case, however, he is created from me, fused by magic. He doesn't have his own autonomy, he isn't his own person. He is me."

I glance at the Shadow Self, who is staring blankly at nothing. "So, he's like a stupider version of you?"

Death snorts, but when I look back he's glowering. "He is me. Through magic, I learned the art of splitting myself. I have to master the duality of mentally being two places at once. What he feels, I feel. He is me. I am him."

"So, when you touch my skin with his—your—bare hand…"

His face falters. "I wasn't able to feel you in that way," he says, quiet disappointment in his voice. "It's as if I were still wearing gloves."

"Oh," I say, feeling disappointed too. Then it dawns on me. My brows go up in horror. "Wait a minute. How did you know his touch wouldn't kill me, too?"

He looks a little sheepish. "I tried it out on Rauta. He didn't die, so…"

"Your iron dog? That's it?"

"Hey, Rauta means a lot to me," he snaps. Then his eyes soften. "What did I feel like?" he asks quietly. "What did my hands feel like to you?"

"It's hard to say, since I was screaming, thinking I was going to die," I admit. "Wasn't really paying attention to the details, you know?"

I turn and walk over to his other self. I reach down and take his big strong hand in mine, clasping my fingers around it, giving it a squeeze. Though the Shadow Self doesn't look up, he does squeeze back. I can almost feel Death inside him, making him move. "It feels nice," I say quietly. "You have very soft hands."

Suddenly I feel Death at my back and he places his gloved hands over my shoulders, holding me in place. He brushes my hair out of the way with his nose, puts his mouth at my neck.

I immediately sink into him.

"I've missed you," I find myself whispering.

"I'm with you every night," he murmurs, lips brushing

softly against my skin, making me shiver with delight.

"I know," I say, my eyes falling shut. "But tonight you weren't."

"I'm with you now."

I want to tell him about me being a Goddess. I want to tell him about seeing Vipunen in his true form. And yet all the urgency melts away. Thoughts fade, as they always do when he's kissing my neck, when my body starts responding to his.

He continues to gently suck at my neck, hand sliding down to my waist.

Need licks up my spine like a bonfire.

My hand is still in the hand of his Shadow Self and his grip is getting tighter. I look down at him to see his Shadow Self staring up at me. There's clarity in his eyes now.

"Are you…practicing?" I ask in a throaty voice, holding eye contact.

"Do you mind?" Death says. "It would be a great test to see what I can do. What I can feel." His hand slips over my breast, making me gasp. My nipple strains against the thin fabric. "What I can control."

The Shadow Self keeps a hold of my hand as he gets to his feet. I'm suddenly caught between two versions of Death; My husband and his Shadow Self, both looming over me in all their dark and Godly glory.

"Do you mind?" Death asks again. His grip on my shoulders tightens and he turns me around so that I'm facing him now, his Shadow Self at my back. "Do you mind if you become part of the magic?"

He's so damn beautiful it hurts.

I swallow hard, trying to tell him that I don't mind at all, but all I can make is this weak noise of want that gets caught in my throat. Death is pressed up against me, hard as a fucking rock, and he's pulling down my nightgown, exposing my breasts. He glances down at me through his dark lashes, his gray eyes simmering as he takes me in. There is so much want and desire in them that I find myself getting weak at the knees, weak in the soul.

Then the Shadow Self slips a bare hand over my shoulder, holding me in place. He's hard as hell too, his cock pressed up against my ass.

Oh my gods.

Plural.

CHAPTER NINETEEN

HANNA

"THE DUALITY"

My old roommate had a threesome once. She was dating a guy, very casually, and it turns out he was dating another girl. Also very casually. They all got drunk at his house one night and voila.

I asked her about it the next day, all ears, and she said it was fun but it definitely created some weirdness between them. They ended up breaking up, and the other girl broke up with him too. She said the dynamics changed, creating and breaking possessiveness. Things were easily complicated when three people are involved intimately.

I would have assumed the same under any other circumstances, as I am very much a one-man kind of woman when it comes down to it.

But here, with my husband—the God of Death—in front of me, pulling my nightgown off over my head, and his body double, his Shadow Self behind me and running his bare hands—bare hands!—over my shoulders in a sensual manner, I have to remind myself that this isn't two different people and there isn't someone else to have things get weird with after.

"Are you sure that he's still you?" I still ask. My voice is coming out breathy and quiet in the room. My pulse is beating rabbit-fast in my neck.

Death throws my nightgown to the floor and brings his molten gaze from my chest to meet my eyes. "Do I look like a man that would share?" he asks dryly.

I swallow thickly. No. He doesn't. He is possessive to the core.

"The man behind you is still me," he says in a low voice. "He feels what I feel, he thinks what I think. I see through his eyes. We are one, just as you are one."

He reaches out and brushes the hair off my neck with his gloved hands, places his lips below my ear, breathing in deep before sucking in my skin.

"I don't know how to do this," I say pathetically.

His *other* chuckles from behind me and, moments later, Death does too.

Whoa.

"You don't have to do anything," he murmurs against my neck. "You just have to *be*. I'll take care of everything, in every possible way that I can." He licks up to my ear and I shiver, the sensation shooting right through me, making me throb between my legs. "Just *relax*, little bird. Let me worship you like the queen you are."

Oh.

I can't argue with that.

His mouth comes over mine and he pulls me into a deep, long kiss. A kiss that I feel all the way to my toes. It immediately relaxes me, my body sinking against the other who is holding me in place, his cock pressed up against my ass, and stokes the flames inside me. I'm bracketed by Death on both sides.

Fucking *surreal*.

With his tongue searching my mouth, teasing in places, rough and fast in others, lips meeting mine with a soft hunger, I feel his Shadow Self run his hands down my arms, then down my waist, over my hips, my ass. It's such a strange feeling now to have bare hands moving over me that I have to keep reminding myself that it's not some stranger, that it's still Death. And even though he can't feel my skin the way he wants to, I can feel his.

It feels *good*.

Death lowers his head to my breasts, torturing my nipples with little flicks of his tongue. His Shadow Self digs his fingers into my hips and lowers himself to his knees, so that his face is at my ass.

Oh. My. God.

With Death sucking at my breasts, long hard pulls of his mouth that make my toes curl, the other him slides his large, smooth hand between my thighs and parts my legs. I widen my stance, already unsteady, and he holds me tighter.

His face buries between my cheeks from behind, running a long tongue along me before pushing it inside me.

"Oh god!" I cry out, the sensations already too much to

handle.

Death chuckles against my breast. He's sucking, licking, nipping, paying special attention to both of them, taking his time, but there are a lot of pauses between what he's doing with his tongue and what his Shadow Self is doing with his tongue. He alternates, and I realize he's not fully able to be in both bodies at the exact same time. His actions are a few seconds off from the other's.

Not that I'm critiquing. Not when he's eating me out from behind and also licking my breasts. It's blowing my mind.

And my body too, since my knees are buckling, legs shaking. Somehow I manage to rock my hips, bearing down, trying to get more purchase against his ravenous mouth, even though I know I'm pushing myself over the edge with each pass of his tongue.

I've barely had time to give myself over to this, to savor it, before I'm coming. The knot between my legs sizzles and snaps like a livewire and I'm crying out gibberish, my eyes rolling back, my body vibrating as the orgasm crashes down on me.

He is—they are—still going at me by the time I come back to reality from whatever far-off universe I was just flung into.

"No," I whisper, trying to find my voice. "Wait."

I drop to my knees right in front of Death, staring up at him with lust as I reach up and attempt to unbutton his pants.

He lets out a rough grunt, eyes flashing with want, and removes his pants, while his Shadow Self, already on his knees, grabs my hips with bruising strength and yanks me back. I feel the head of his cock press into me and then, before I can take in a breath, he's driving himself straight into me.

"Fuck!" I cry out. He feels even bigger than normal somehow, or maybe his Shadow Self is enhanced, and I can't remember how to function, like he's just pushed all the thoughts from my head.

He grunts with pleasure, from behind me and in front of me, almost in synch.

I watch as Death guides his cock toward my mouth and I take its heavy, soft length in my hands, sliding it into my mouth. It gets messy fast, me licking and sucking his cock with reckless abandon while his *other* rams into me from behind. His hand slides down and I feel his bare fingers on my clit for the first time, and while I've gotten used to the rough texture of his gloves, this feels so soft and slippery, it's like heaven.

Keep going, I think, staring up at Death and urging him with my eyes while I suck him off. I have a vague memory of doing this to him in the Crystal Caves. I was somehow able to deep-throat him then, and while I don't think that's possible now, I still try to take him in my mouth as far as I can.

I feel like I'm at a banquet filled with starved beasts and none of us can get our fill. I'm feasting on Death, he's feasting on me, and this primal hunger is driving us forward, lost to total lust and annihilation.

Death's focus is locked on me, glued to my lips, watching with glazed eyes as he thrusts into my mouth, both pairs of hips moving in near tandem from either end of me. I reach out and grab his muscular ass. He's so strong, so big, and I dig my nails into him as I start to shake with need.

It's enough for Death, anyway. He comes into my mouth, pumping into me and down my throat and I drink him down like I've been wandering around a desert, parched with thirst.

Then I'm coming again, his Shadow Self perfectly stroking my clit with his fingers, his dick hitting the sweet spot inside me with each rough thrust. A few pumps of his hips later and then he's coming inside me. I've been filled with him at each end.

Even though I'm already on my knees, I nearly fall when his Shadow Self pulls out of me. I push myself up off my elbows, trying to breathe in deep, wanting my heart to slow down. My legs are still shaking. Everything is trembling.

"Lie back," Death tells me, and gestures to the Shadow Self behind me. "Ride that cock."

I raise my head to look at him just as Death grabs me by the hair and pulls me roughly to my feet. The pain feels good, wakes me up. Oh, we're being rough now, are we?

"Feeling a little demanding?" I ask him.

He answers me by gripping me by the back of my neck with his big leather-covered hand and kissing me savagely. I whimper into his mouth, running my nails over his chest, scratching lightly. Even though I just came, I feel heavy between my legs, hot, molten pressure building again. I don't know how many times and different ways we're about to fuck, but I have a feeling I won't tire of this anytime soon. My body is already wanting more.

With an ache between my legs and feverish need clawing through me, I do as Death says. I pull apart from his lips and look behind me. His Shadow Self is lying back on the rugs, waiting for me, dick straight up. Thank God I'm flexible enough for this.

I go over him, reverse cowgirl style, then lie back so that my back is pressed against his chest, my legs spread, knees bent, the tips of my toes touching the floor on either side of his thick waist. I feel him reach down and try to guide his cock into my ass, which makes me freeze.

"Hold on," I say. "Just hold on a minute here."

Death looms over me and realizes the error of his ways.

"Give me a second," he says.

He drops to his knees and starts licking me out. I let out a warped cry, his tongue taking me by surprise and in no time I'm wet as sin and dripping between my thighs and onto his Shadow Self beneath me.

Death then reaches for his other's cock and starts sliding it over my wetness, again and again, guiding his Shadow Self back and forth, creating the most X-rated porn sounds I have *ever* heard, only stopping when his cock is slick enough.

He then pushes that cock inside my ass.

I gasp, grateful for the easy slide in, willing myself to relax as he slowly fills me.

This is insane.

Insane!

I have never felt more wonderfully debased or fantastically degraded, as animalistic and caveman human, than I do right now. This is the lushest, most decadent, primal experience I think I'll ever have. And from the look on Death's face, the way his features contort with mind-blowing pleasure, I know he's feeling the same way.

And so with that, I give myself to him, to all versions of him, completely and fully. His Shadow Self grabs me by the waist, bare fingers circling my waist, and pumps me up and down on his cock, while Death hovers over me, guiding his own dick inside my cunt.

HELL!

I'm so fucking full, I can't breathe. Two cocks inside me at once, but only one husband. One king. One God.

"Fuck me," I whisper. "Be a savage God."

With a low growl, Death lets loose.

He fucks me hard, both ways, and I am bracketed between his two large, hard bodies, captured between them, caught between two forms of Death until we are just a writhing mass of indulgence and desire. They both want the same thing. They want me. And I think they want each other.

My tits bounce, two pairs of hands roam my body, bare and gloved, and every inch of my body is touched, my skin feeling too tight and hot, the need to come taking over all of us.

Pleasure. The most hedonistic kind. It coats our bodies, fills the room, amplified by the wet sound of our fucking, the rough and raspy breaths as the three of us move together as one.

We come as one.

It happens like a pin being pulled from a grenade. Death's head goes back and he roars like an animal. He shoots inside of me, I'm bucking between them, my world moving like an earthquake. I see stars, something like Oblivion, but so much sweeter.

I haven't even come down to earth when they both pull out of me at the same time, and my god there is going to be such a mess on these rugs. I hope he can have them dry-cleaned, though knowing Death he probably has some magic to deal with it. If he can create a double of himself to pleasure me with, then surely he can get cum out of a carpet.

I take in a deep breath, about to sit up, when his Shadow Self reaches down and flips me over so I'm on my hands and knees.

"Again!?" I cry out. Holy shit, is he not exhausted? I am, and there's only one of me.

"One more time," Death says from behind me, his voice hoarse. "For me. You can take it."

"*I* can take it, what about you?"

"I'm almost ready," he says as his Shadow Self grabs my ass, presses his cock against me. "We're almost there. Almost in tune. I think *this* will work. This will be what does it."

This? What's so special about this time?

But when his Shadow Self drives himself into my aching pussy (I am going to be *sore* tomorrow), I look over my shoulder to see Death standing behind his Shadow Self, hands on his own fucking hips.

Oh my god.

Oh my god.

Death is going to fuck himself up the ass.

I have never been so intrigued, I can't not watch this. His Shadow Self meets my gaze, then Death himself does. Both of them are staring at me, smirking arrogantly.

I nearly roll my eyes. Figures. Every man's dream is to fuck himself, right? Removing a rib to give yourself a blow job seems like child's play when you can just create your own other to screw.

Death hisses in a deep breath, hands gripping hips, getting ready.

Lube! I almost shout but as I watch him push his cock into his ass, I remember he's a God and probably doesn't need it.

But as much as I love watching Death rail himself, the pleasure and strain contorting both their features as they fuck each other, the Shadow Self is also fucking me. Hard. I'm getting rugburn on my hands and knees trying not to slide across the carpet as the two massive Gods fuck on top of me. I can feel Death when he's deep inside himself, like it's being passed on to me.

I think I'm losing my mind.

And I am.

We fuck and grunt and it's wild and lewd and, and…

I go off like a bomb, the kind that scatters you.

I come apart, screaming as I do. The other orgasms blew my mind, but this one feels life-altering, like it's not just about the sex anymore but that something else has been unleashed into the air, like this moment has become bigger than any other.

I'm still crying out when I feel Death's pumping slow and I watch intently as he starts to come. The corded muscles in his neck stand out, his nostrils flare, his jaw clenches. I watch this happen to both versions of him and it's happening at the exact same time.

He did it.

He fused.

He is fully split between him and his Shadow Self.

They both howl, a loud guttural sound ripped from the depths of their lungs, mouths open, their eyes pinched shut, backs arched in pure ecstasy.

Fuck. This is the hottest thing I've ever seen in my life.

As if to punctuate the magic of the moment, wind suddenly howls through the library, causing loose feathers and herbs and torn pages to fly through the air. It all swirls above us like a small tornado, and the floor shakes until books fall off the shelves. The candles around the room all light at once, their flames flickering and the smell of brimstone fills my nose. Thunder and lightning crash, not from outside the castle but from inside the library, as if a storm is happening just down the hall. My hair stands on end, I feel the electricity in my teeth.

Then the wind suddenly stops and the feathers and papers fall to the floor, pieces of lavender and rosemary raining down into my hair.

Death's Shadow Self pulls out of me and I collapse onto the rug, my body pushed to the point of exhaustion. Death has always been one to convince me to keep fucking even when I've come so much that I'm too sensitive, but in this instance I feel exhausted to the very core. I want to slip into the deepest, darkest, dreamless sleep for a very long time.

His Shadow Self lies down beside me on his back, eyes closed.

Then Death does the same on the other side of me. He's

breathing hard and I can still hear thunder crashing in the distance.

Magic dances in the air.

"Are you okay?" I ask him, my words coming out in a slur.

He blinks slowly. His eyes are iridescent silver for a moment until they fade back to gray. "That was…an experience I have never had before," he says slowly, licking his lips.

I smile lazily at him. "I bet you thought you'd tried everything."

"I truly did. To know that life can offer you something new as a God…is something else."

Even though my body is completely wrecked from what we just did, excitement drums in my chest. "Want another surprise that will rock your world?"

The corner of his mouth quirks up. "Hanna, I never thought I would ever say this, but at the moment, I'm a little tired."

I laugh and reach out, using all my energy to smack him on the chest. "No," I tell him. "I have something to tell you. It's why I came up here to find you."

He frowns. "You weren't looking for sex?"

"Not exactly. Vipunen told me something."

Now I have his attention. "What?" he asks, eyeing me sharply.

"He told me who my mother is. Well, not specifically who. But that she's a Goddess. I'm half a Goddess, Tuoni."

He stares at me for a moment, taking it in, then cracks a smile so wide his dimples show. Dimples! Ugh, my heart is melting on the spot.

"Of course you are. Of course. I knew it." He sounds so validated and so happy at the same time. "My fucking Goddess of Death. I knew you weren't just a mortal, or half a shaman. You are a Goddess through and through. It is in your blood, and it is finally coming out."

"You're bringing it out of me," I tell him.

"It's the land," he says adamantly. "It's your land. Relish it, Hanna."

He takes my hand in his and holds it on his chest, pressing it above his heart. He looks so happy that it makes the fact that I don't know who my mother is a little easier to handle. Still…

"Do you have any idea who my mother could be?" I ask. "Vipunen wouldn't tell me, of course. He said I would find out and it would save my life when I did."

He scoffs. "That fucking giant. No. I have no idea." Then he frowns, a look of horror dawning on his features. "It's not—"

"No," I tell him quickly. "It's not Louhi. Vipunen confirmed that."

He closes his eyes and exhales with relief. "Thank the Creator." He stares up at the ceiling in thought. "Okay, so if it isn't Louhi…there're only so many others. I think maybe I'll call a meeting and get to the bottom of this."

"A meeting of the Gods?"

He nods.

My heart rate increases. Sounds like a big deal.

"Did Vipunen tell you anything else?"

I shake my head. Then stop. "Wait. Yes. He told me to

take off my mask and look at him."

Death goes still, then looks at me with widened eyes. "And did you?"

I flash him a boastful smile. "I did."

"You saw Vipunen and lived to tell about it?"

"The girl who lived," I say, though he doesn't get my Harry Potter reference. "He looked like a great big being of light, hundreds of feet tall," I add, knowing what his next question would be.

Death looks like his mind is blown. He gives a subtle shake of his head, mouth opening and closing as if trying to find the words. "All this time," he says quietly. "All those years, I was never allowed to lay eyes on him. Only that very first day that I appeared in the cave as the new God, when I swear I saw giant red eyes, but now I'm doubting it because I was never allowed to be without my blind mask after that. I was kept in the dark by the one who trained me, made me the God I am, and yet you…you were able to see him. More than that, he *asked* you to see him. Hanna…"

I wince. "Does it make you mad?" I figure I would be all sorts of jealous if I were a God, unable to see a father figure I'd had for eons, and then some mortal girl just waltzes into Tuonela and gets a look on one of her first visits.

"No," he says. He brings my hand up to his lips. "I'm not mad, little bird. I'm impressed. I'm more than impressed… I'm in awe of you."

And that's the difference between me and a God. He's in awe, I'd be stewing in pettiness.

Death gives me a most wicked grin that makes my toes

curl. "I think I'll let my Shadow Self sleep, but I have to tell you…I'm not so tired anymore."

He puts his hand around my neck and pulls me to him.

CHAPTER TWENTY

HANNA

"THE HALL OF SKULLS"

The first time I realized I was different, I must have been two years old. It's probably one of my earliest memories. Scientists say that it's nearly impossible for anyone to remember being that young because of how the brain develops, and that if they do remember something it was probably influenced by someone else. If you tell someone a specific event happened at a young age, painting it out, chances are that person will go on believing it happened, eventually seeing it happen in their minds like a memory.

Maybe that's the case with me. I suppose it doesn't matter in the end.

I was sitting in a stroller while my mother pushed me around a grocery store. I remember the lights were bright, the ceiling was low, the people in the narrow aisles were pale and stern-faced. I'd thought them all mad at the time but later I realized they were just Finnish.

My mother had left me alone for a moment to go back and get something. I was in the produce aisle, next to a tower of cabbages. Finns love their cabbages. My mother not so much, but my father loved his cabbage soup. Funny how I remember that. That even though she hated it, she still made it for him. She must have really loved him.

Anyway, I remember staring at them, their purple shapes, and thinking I wanted to see them all topple to the ground, bounce around the store like bowling balls. There was no one around and yet one rolled off the top and onto the floor.

I smiled. A distinct feeling of a smile. Like someone had done that just for me, though I couldn't be sure who. But I wanted more. I wasn't satisfied with the one.

So another toppled, hitting the linoleum floor with a splat. Then another one.

Soon all of them were rolling off the shelf and onto the floor.

By then, this had attracted attention so everyone had gathered around. I remember them looking bewildered.

Then my mother came and saw it and assumed I did it.

Of course, I kind of did. I was sitting in the low stroller, there's no way that I could have reached up and knocked them off, but it didn't matter because she knew.

She yelled at me, told me I was bad, that I was a wicked child and that if I ever did that again, she would drop me off at the church for good, a place, she had assured me, that my father would never step into. At the time I didn't understand the concept of church so all I knew was it was a place that I would never see my father again.

I'm thinking of this now because I'm trying desperately to marry together my two realities. Me, as just your basic bitch posting selfies on Instagram from Venice Beach, and me as your not-so basic bitch Goddess, currently the Queen of Tuonela.

It's been two weeks since I found out my mother is a Goddess, since I saw Vipunen without my mask, since I had a threesome with Death and his Shadow Self (which I guess isn't technically a threesome if it's two of the same person, but I still had two dicks in me, so I don't know what you'd call that).

I've been busy continuing my training.

Death has been busy, planning for war.

Everyone—meaning myself, Kalma, Sarvi, and Death—feel that time is running out. In a land where time feels infinite, there is this definitive feeling of things happening sooner rather than later.

But since we don't want an uprising and aren't about to instigate a war, our job is to hold fort. Death is currently interrogating his ranks, going through his Deadhands to see who is fit for battle, who is on our side. I don't know how he figures it out, but he says he has a way of filtering through the loyal ones. He thinks by holding a few more Bone Matches, we can recruit even more members of the army, those that are strong and can be generals and pledge allegiance to him and so on.

I'm excited for my first Bone Match. I want to see Tuonen again, get a feel for my stepson, as weird as that is to say. I want to see what Inmost looks like. I want to enter the City of Death and get a tour of the afterlife, the Golden Mean and Amaranthus. I want people to look at me like I'm their queen. Because I am. But we're still a few weeks off from the first match.

"Hanna," Death calls to me from his Hall of Skulls.

That's right. The Hall of Skulls. At first, I was surprised at the small size of Death's closet because of how well-dressed he always is, you know, in that leather-clad medieval rockstar Viking way he has. Then I discovered the Hall of Skulls, which is just an extension of his closet, a long creepy-as-fuck corridor lined with skull masks. I thought I had a lot of shoes back home, his collection of masks put me to shame.

I walk over to the hall and peer inside. I try to spend as little time in it as possible. There's nothing like the feeling of dozens upon dozens of empty eyes in horrific faces staring at you.

Death is standing in the middle of the room, a mask in each hand.

"Which one for the meeting?" he asks me.

He lifts up one, which is like a silver boar's face with obsidian tusks and horns, mouth curved up in a ghoulish smile. Then he lifts up the other one, a white skull with a downturned smile. Reminds me of the sad clown, Pagliacci. Both creepy as hell, of course.

"The clown one," I tell him. He looks surprised and stares down at it.

Then he puts it back in the display case, choosing the boar instead.

I roll my eyes. What was the point of asking?

"The boar is sexier," he tells me, slipping it on over his face.

I laugh. "Says you! No one wants to have sex with a pig."

"Oink."

I laugh again. "Okay fine, since we're at the stage of our relationship where we're asking each other's opinions now, what do you think of this dress?"

I twirl around with him, the gauzy white layers flowing as I do, reminding me of the star jasmine that lined our neighborhood in North Hollywood.

As usual, the pang of nostalgia hits me for what was. But I can't let myself dwell on it, not now, not when I can't do a damn thing about it. First, I have to train, figure out the prophecy, end an uprising, and find out who my mother is. Then I can take a moment to think about my old life—and whether or not I'll even want to return to it. Seems the longer I'm in Tuonela, the more I feel my old life slipping away, like it was just a dream and my real life has always been here.

"You're going to get wet," he says. There's nothing carnal in his voice, so I'm not sure what he's saying. "We're going underwater," he clarifies.

"Underwater?" I repeat. "What are you talking about?"

Even though I can't see his eyes through the mask at this distance, I know he's rolling them. He takes a wide stance and folds his arms across his chest.

"I told you. Ahto is hosting the meeting."

"Yeah and?"

"He's the God of Oceans."

"And?"

"He lives under the sea, Hanna," he says with a patient sigh.

"Okay, I get that. But I figured he would still hold the meeting on land. His wife, lady God, Goddess, Vellamo, she was on land when I saw her. Or at least above water."

"That doesn't matter."

"It should matter, unless you have scuba gear I can use."

"You're half Goddess," he reminds me.

"And as far as I know, I do not possess the ability to breathe underwater!"

He just grunts and walks down the hall toward me. "Well, we will find out, won't we?"

I grab onto his glove, stopping him. "Are you serious? Is this a toss Hanna into the sea and see if she'll drown, similar to toss Hanna into—"

"I know what you're going to say, you don't have to say it."

"—into the oubliette?"

"Listen," he says, leaning into me, his breath tickling my ear, "wear whatever you want. But if you're going to wear white, I might have to kill my brothers and cousins if they even so much look at you."

Then he walks off.

I look down at my dress and sigh. As beautiful and flowy as it is, it will turn see-through the moment it hits water. Back to the drawing board.

In the end, I choose a black dress. This one is more slinky than anything else, almost like a slip dress, but with some boning around the waist that pushes my boobs up to new heights, and the skirt falls to my feet, with a high slit in the front. In the world I knew this is not meeting material, but in the world of the Gods, in the Land of the Dead, where I am a Goddess and a Queen, I think it'll freaking do.

The meeting has been a few days in the making. While we've both been busy with our own things, Death has also been trying to figure out who my mother is. Asking around has gotten us nowhere, and Vipunen has totally turned into a vault, so Death decided to call a meeting of the Gods and Goddesses. After all, one of them has to be my mother, right?

I'm nervous as hell. I'd be nervous if it were just a normal meeting with the Gods, you know, but one called to figure out who my mom is? Talk about pressure. Don't get me wrong, I have a ton of questions that need answers, but I'm not looking forward to a bunch of grumbling Gods gathering at the bottom of the sea together all because of me. I mean, the Gods I have seen all seem to be pretty grumpy. I can't imagine the weather here puts you in the best mood.

For some reason, we have to wait until dusk to get a move on. Raila comes to my bedchamber to escort me down to the dungeon area.

You look beautiful, my queen, Raila says to me from beneath her black veil. That dress is very becoming on you.

"Good," I say. Because I'm hoping Death will be coming all over it, I think, smiling to myself, then realize with horror that Raila probably heard that.

We walk down the many levels until we start heading underground. I immediately get the creeps, having flashbacks to the wedding and everything that happened afterward. "I don't understand why we're going by boat," I tell her. "Why sail when you have a Sarvi?"

I don't know, my queen, Raila says. But I assume it's the safest way.

She brings me toward the dock where Death is waiting for me.

Now I am totally having a Phantom of the Opera moment here. There is Tuoni, God of Death, standing by a boat in a dark cloak, wearing the silver boar mask—the tusks glinting in the flickering torches that line the waterway. If he starts to sing "Music of the Night" I'm going to lose it.

He holds his arm out for me and I immediately get butterflies in my chest. Okay, I'm losing it over something as simple as that. It's like he's my prom date. This is already a million times more romantic than the wedding.

"Are you ready?" he asks me, pulling me toward the waiting boat.

I nod. I have my selenite knife attached to my inner thigh. Just in case, though I'm sure that's not what he meant.

"Is this dress better?" I ask him, arching my back slightly so my breasts are pushed out.

His eyes drop to my chest, nostrils flaring. He looks at me like it's his birthday and I'm both his cake and the present.

"Not sure this is much better," he says in a low, gruff voice. "But it's too late to change."

I grin at him. "Yup. Too late."

He can tell when I'm wet and ready, and I can tell when he's hard. It's easy. I just glance down. His cloak doesn't hide everything.

I get whisked into the boat at that and we push off, leaving Raila at the dock. I wave goodbye to her and she raises a hand to do the same.

The boat heads toward the opposite direction of the Crystal Caves, against the small waves that are coming in.

I try to steady myself with the rocking of the boat and look around. The vessel isn't too dissimilar from the one that Lovia and Tuonen use to ferry the dead, except this one is higher off the water and seems to have quarters below deck.

I settle on a seat beside Death near the bow. At the back of the boat there are a dozen Deadhands who are rowing us forward through the underground tunnels. It's nearly pitch black here save for the torches lit along the side, illuminating the water in swaths of orange.

"Can I ask a question?" I say.

He shrugs. "You're going to ask it anyway," he says, his attention on the rowing Deadhands.

"Why are we taking a boat? Faster to use Sarvi, no?"

"Sarvi is staying here at the castle. With my Shadow Self. We must keep the illusion that I'm here. As soon as we come out of the waterways and into the open sea, we will retreat below deck."

He puts his hand on my thigh so I don't get the wrong impression of what we'll be doing when we retreat below.

"All anyone who is watching me will see are the Deadhands paddling out into the open sea," he continues, "which they have been doing a lot of lately when I've had them training. Business as usual."

I put my hand on top of his, feeling a thrill run through

me.

He glances down at me. "What?"

"I don't know," I say, realizing I'm grinning at him. "I guess I just find this all so exciting."

"War isn't exciting, little bird," he warns. But he rubs his thumb along my hand, his way of holding it. "We need to take all precautions. I won't lose my role, I won't lose this kingdom of mine. I'm not just doing it for myself, it's for the greater good of all the worlds. I have been tasked with providing an afterlife for the dead. If that's taken away, if Hell is all there is, then…I've failed more than anyone ever has."

He sounds so grave, almost sad, but the last thing he wants is for me to coddle him. "You won't fail. You haven't yet." I pause, swallowing thickly. "There's always a way to get a leg up, right now. You know what we have to do," I add, my heart starting to thunder in my chest at even the thought of it.

He tilts his head toward me, and I can barely see his gray eyes beneath the mask. "I don't want to risk it."

I don't even have to explain what I'm talking about. He knows. We both know that we could put all our questions about the prophecy to rest if he just took off a glove and touched me. It would change the game in a second.

But neither of us want to change the game that fast. Who knows, maybe when push comes to shove, when Death grows tired of fucking me, or tired of losing the war, he'll take off the glove and grab me by the throat and watch me disintegrate under his bare fingers. Then we'll both have the answers we're looking for.

"One day you'll have to," I tell him softly. "You know you

will."

He gives a subtle shake of his head. "Maybe not. Maybe the war never comes. Maybe it comes and we win. Maybe Louhi is defeated, the uprising is squashed, and we can just go on as we are. Maybe in the end, the prophecy won't matter at all."

I appreciate him saying that, saying he doesn't want to risk killing me. It's the little things. Honestly, even though we're married and screwing each other every chance we get, I always, always, keep in mind that he is the God of Death and could do away with me if he wanted. The things that Vipunen said, about how in the end I can't rely on Tuoni to protect me, that stayed with me and I think about it often.

He will become my king, but I will never be his queen.

I clear my throat, wanting to switch the subject.

"So, if Sarvi is staying here, why isn't Lovia coming with us?" I ask. "Shouldn't she be at a meeting of the Gods? She is one."

Death shakes his head. "You know I love my daughter, but she can't be trusted."

My eyes go wide. What does that mean?

He shrugs, having read the look on my face. "Her mother is Louhi. This meeting isn't just about you, Hanna, it's about the war. Louhi, Rasmus, Salainen. The uprising. It's all of it. I don't like putting my daughter in a position where she has to turn against her mother."

"Yeah but…"

He grunts. "No buts. I know you're new to this game, but it's always been this way. I love her, you know I do, but she still loves her mother."

"No way." I shake my head. "Not her. I've seen her mother." I shudder, remembering Louhi's cruel demon eyes, the way her tongue felt as it tried to choke me to death.

"Family is complicated," he says with a tired sigh. "Love doesn't go away just because you find out your mother isn't who you thought she was." I feel his eyes latch on me. "Does it?"

I open my mouth to speak, then clamp it shut. I want to argue, but then I realize how foolish that is. For one, he's right, I'm new to the game, I don't know what the family dynamic is like, how it's evolved over centuries instead of the months I've seen it. And for two, well…I did love the mother who raised me, even if she never loved me back. It's a messy complicated kind of love, which always made me stay off social media on Mother's Day because of all the adoring posts from everyone else, posts that made me feel like there was something wrong with me for not having that relationship. But it's still love, and it hasn't turned off since I found out she's not my birth mother.

I guess I can relate to Lovia in that way. I just assumed because she was here living with her father, doing the proper duties of the Gods, that she was on his side, not Louhi's. But maybe it's not about picking sides at all. Maybe that's what makes it so complicated.

"Bars up!" Death commands and I twist around to see the entrance to the caverns. Between us and the open, roaring sea is an iron gate that sinks into the surf. Slowly it comes up, lifted out of the water by gears, and the boat glides beneath it. I recall Bell telling me that Death had put those bars in so that she wouldn't escape when she was kept in the waterways, back when she was a full-sized mermaid.

Man, that is fucked up. I can't help but study him, even though he's wearing the mask and I can't get a read on him. How is this the same person who turned a mermaid into something the size of a Barbie? How lonely do you have to be to keep someone else as a pet?

I don't bring this up now, of course. I have the rest of my marriage to figure him out. Right now, I need to concentrate on the meeting of the Gods.

Death gets to his feet and grabs my arms, hauling me to my feet.

"Time to go under," he says, double-entendre in his words, leading me toward the cabins below deck.

CHAPTER TWENTY-ONE

HANNA

"THE GROTTO"

"You're still seasick?" Death questions me.

I'm sitting across from him at the galley table below deck as the sea hurls waves at our ship, trying to hold myself together. I am freaking green.

"Gods don't get seasick," he mutters, sliding another cup of tea toward me.

"No?" I manage to say. "Then I probably can't breathe underwater either."

He looks disappointed in me. No, wait, it's not that. He looks out of his league, like he's just been put in charge of something he has no idea how to take care of. A sick mortal? How very alien.

I didn't think I got seasick either, until we went below deck to hide out from prying eyes. We were in various stages of making out and undressing when the waves really started picking up and slamming against the boat. Suddenly it was like I was going to vomit all over him.

I've been sitting at the table for the last few hours, wishing I had a porthole to look out of to try and find the horizon, but these old ships aren't built that way. But I can't go up top either or some spy will see us or something like that, so I'm stuck down here feeling absolutely awful.

"Aren't we far enough out in the sea?" I ask, shoving a dried piece of mountain rye bread in my mouth, the only food on the ship. Pretty sure it's old as hell too, but I can't be picky right now. Luckily, I have some hot tea to wash it down with, though that tastes odd, too.

"We are," he says carefully. "But we don't want to risk it if we don't have to, because we will have to when the moment comes. Shouldn't be much longer now."

Vellamo and Ahto normally reside at the bottom of the Great Inland Sea, but to make things easier, they arranged for us to meet them at some undersea grotto close to Shadow's End. Because yeah, it's really making things easier.

Finally, the rowing up above comes to a stop. Death gets up, stooping over as he goes, his frame too big for the boat, and carefully pokes his masked head above the deck. After a while he nods for me to come over.

"We're here," he announces.

I stagger over to him, dying to get fresh air, and hurry up the ladder as fast as I can go. The fresh sea air feels like heaven and I immediately feel my vertigo lessening.

"We have to be quick, get right in," Death says, gesturing to the water.

It's night, so aside from the candles on the boat, I can't see anything except what little light the moon affords us. As far as I can see, we're in the middle of nowhere with the dark sea stretching out into infinity. No land, no nothing. The only landmark is a piece of rock that sticks straight up, waves crashing against it, and a couple of skeletal seagulls perched on top, eyeing us warily.

I glance behind me at the Deadhands. They're all holding in position, one tossing an anchor overboard. I assume they'll be here when we come back up.

The seas are still rough though, and Death has to steady me as he leads me to the side of the ship. He shucks off his cloak, boots and shirt until he's just in his pants, gauntlets, and mask. I do the same to my shoes. Then he grabs hold of my hand and gives it a squeeze.

"Are you ready?"

I shake my head, feeling nauseous again, this time due to panic. "No, not even a little."

"You'll be fine," he says quickly.

"I can't breathe underwater!"

"We're going to find out," he says.

Then he jumps.

I'm pulled overboard with him.

I scream then hit the cold water with a splash, sinking far deeper than I thought I would, like a fucking stone. I want to scream again but I keep my mouth shut and instinctively I'm trying for the surface.

Death is still holding onto me, pulling me down. He's the reason why I can't break free, can't get to the surface, can't breathe. He's going to drown me, this asshole.

Panic bubbles up inside me, closing my lungs. I need air. I have to breathe. I stare up at the dim gray light of the surface, watching as it gets smaller and smaller and smaller. Every part of me yearns to live, to survive, to fight for the surface, to gulp for that breath of air.

We keep going down.

Down.

Down.

Down.

Sinking like a stone.

Until I realize Death isn't sinking. He's swimming. Powerful strokes going into the deep, dragging me along with him. He moves through the water like a shark, like it's second nature to him.

Below us, the darkness of the sea starts to fade, a blue light coming through. By now I'm fascinated, staring as we descend, getting closer and closer. I don't even realize that my mouth is open and that…

I'm breathing.

Somehow, I'm able to breathe without sucking in water through my mouth and choking on it.

Holy hell, was Death right? Either he was right or I'm dead.

I try again, breathing in and out, and while I don't quite feel air in my lungs like I do on land, I'm not drowning and I'm not suffocating either.

Wow. Guess I have more Goddess in me than I thought.

It's not long before I start to see shapes moving in the

light; a kelp forest, one that seems to keep going down to an unseen sea floor.

Death pulls me through it, the kelp sliding past me in various colors—teal, purple, green—like a field of flowing ribbons.

Below us, a grotto appears in the middle of the kelp forest, resembling a small amphitheatre carved into a mix of volcanic rock and coral. It's lit up by a few of those creepy-ass angler fish that live in the deep. They're half bone and half scales, as if they'd been the meal of someone who got full too early, and they're harnessed to the rocks with twine. The blue light that dangles at the end of their antennae thing illuminates the whole area, including the Gods, who are standing in the middle of the grotto, looking up at us.

At the feel of their godly, inhuman eyes, I immediately panic, wanting to go back to the surface, but there's no way Death is letting go of my hand now.

He swims until we're right above them, circling the Gods like a school of fish.

One God with bright aqua eyes, tanned skin, and a wide, clean-shaven jaw reaches up and hands Death something. Death takes it and then twists around to hand it over to me, placing it in my hand.

It's a small black disc with a strange symbol carved on it, resembling a gothic sand dollar of sorts. The moment it hits my palm, I start to sink like someone's tied rocks to my ankles, until my feet are flat on the grotto floor.

"That will keep you down here," Death says, standing beside me with ease. I can't see his mouth under the mask but it seems like he's talking like normal, not telepathically. A stream of bubbles rise from him, disappearing into the darkness above us.

Then he puts his hand at my elbow, taking on a most commanding posture, and turns me to face his brethren.

"Gods, Goddesses, Brothers and Sisters of the Underworld," he says in a booming voice, the voice he uses when he feels like being king, "may I introduce to you my wife, Hanna, Queen of Tuonela and the Goddess of Death."

I swallow uneasily, looking at all the eerily beautiful faces staring at me.

Thankfully, I recognize two of them. One of them is a pale girl about my age, maybe younger (looks-wise, anyway) dressed in a dark green dress that flows around her like seaweed. Her hair is vibrant red with tiny antlers poking out of the top of her head. This is Tellervo, Goddess of the Forest, who helped me in the Hiisi Forest back when Rasmus took off in the night, right before I was traded for Death.

I give her a quick smile and she nods. Her eyes are friendly but from the stiff way she stands, I guess she has to keep up the formalities.

Then there is Vellamo, Goddess of the Sea. She's just as amazing as I remember. Her otherworldly beauty is complimented by the most intricate outfit, half-gown, half-armor comprised of fishbones, shells, octopus legs and pearls. On her head is a bishop-like hat made of scales with crab claws on top.

She eyes me coolly and raises her strong chin in recognition. Guess that's the most I'm going to get. I want to ask her about Bell, if she's with her, or if any of the mermaids are, but I have a feeling that isn't on the agenda.

"Nice to finally meet you, Hanna," the square-jawed God says. Now that I have a better chance to look at him, I notice he's bare chested, like Death, but his pants are made from shells and fish scales. In his hand he has a tall staff made of bone and starfish. I know who he is even before he says. "I am Ahto. God of the Oceans and Seas. Tuoni's brother, husband of Vellamo. I have heard a lot about you from her. My brother hasn't said much."

He glances at Death, who doesn't move.

"You know you can take your mask off, Tuoni," Ahto says with a smirk. "We all know what your hideous face looks like."

A few of the Gods chuckle. I burst out laughing. Guess all my nervous energy needs a place to go.

Death reluctantly reaches up and removes the boar mask, appraising his brother with a discerning look, his eyes appearing a shimmering silver in these depths.

Ahto grins at him. "There's that ugly God I know so well." He looks to me. "I don't know what you see in him, Hanna."

"Stop," Vellamo says, in that low, hypnotic voice of hers. "We can heckle Tuoni later. We have an agenda we need to keep to."

Okay there's no question who the organized God is here in this group. Death had said that Ahto had called the meeting, but clearly it's Vellamo who is in charge of everything. And even though we have more Gods to get through, I'm really enjoying seeing this side of Tuoni, seeing his family with him.

Especially a family that isn't afraid to poke fun at him.

We continue with the introductions.

After Ahto, Vellamo is quickly introduced, though we've already met. Even though she makes me feel mortal and insignificant, I still really like the Goddess of the Sea. I wish I could become a cool, judicious kind of ruler like her, but I'm not sure that's in the cards for me. Then again, I'm only twenty-four years old. Maybe in a few centuries I'll mature to her level.

Then there is Tapio, God of the Forest, with his long gray beard, rams horns, and stoic demeanor.

The next God introduced is Tapio's wife, Mielikki. Like her daughter, Tellervo, Mielikki also has horns coming out of her head, though hers are much larger, elk antlers peppered with wildflowers. She's dressed in a modest brown dress patterned with a bear-paw print, with small animal bones adorning the neckline, and she has the kindest smile that reaches her emerald eyes. She even gives a little curtsey.

"Pleasure to have you in our realm," Mielikki says to me, her voice airy and gentle. "Tuoni has chosen well for his new queen."

After Mielikki, I meet Tellervo again.

Then there's Tuoni's sister, which I haven't heard much about. Her name is Ilmatar, Goddess of the Air. She's very quiet, impassive, and vaguely translucent, dressed in a long sky-blue gown, white hair pulled back into a braid. When you're looking at her head-on she's completely solid but when you see her out of the corner of your eye she kind of disappears. A trick of the eye? Maybe, maybe not.

Everyone now is chatting with each other, and I find myself stepping back and observing, not having much to add to the conversation at the moment. It seems it's been an awful long time since all the Gods were in the same room together, or in this case, the same grotto under the sea.

"So, how is it that you're breathing underwater?" Ahto asks me.

"Because she's not a mere mortal," Vellamo interjects, fixing her eyes on me. "Are you?"

Death clears his throat. "That's true. She's technically not. That's one reason why I called you all here today. But I, uh, may have slipped her some magic when she wasn't looking."

My mouth falls open. "What magic?"

"The tea," he says simply. "In the event that you couldn't breathe underwater, I didn't want to chance it."

"You drugged me!"

He shrugs with one shoulder, not looking the slightest bit remorseful.

"Oh, Hanna," Vellamo says with a mirthless laugh. "You know this isn't your first rodeo with Tuoni."

I ignore her and narrow my eyes at him. Dick.

He avoids my eyes, addresses the group. "As you may know, Hanna has been training with Vipunen, just as the rest of my family has."

"Big fucking mistake with that one," Tapio grumbles. I'm caught off-guard by his swearing. He seems too quiet and old-fashioned for that. "By making Vipunen train Louhi, you only gave her evil extra power."

"Tapio," Vellamo admonishes him with a sigh. "You know

Louhi would have been pulled to the dark side on her own."

I nearly snicker at dark side, but decide that no one here, aside from Death, has probably seen Star Wars.

"Please go on, Tuoni," Vellamo says firmly.

He nods. "Hanna was training and Vipunen told her something I'd always suspected. That her mother in the Upper World isn't her actual mother. And that her mother is a Goddess. From here."

Everyone looks at each other. Everyone looks surprised.

Could it be that one of the Goddesses here is my mother? I'm examining all of them and I can't be sure, they honestly all look shocked. Maybe they're acting—Gods are known to be the greatest tricksters.

"Are you sure?" Ahto asks, adjusting his grip on his staff.

Death nods. "Vipunen does not lie." He pauses and gives me a small but proud smile. "If you need further proof that my queen is special, she was able to look at him without the mask on."

My queen. Swoon.

But, of course, no one cares about the hint of intimacy Death just afforded me. Everyone is gasping over the news of the giant, all eyes staring at me in a mix of awe, disbelief and envy.

"You saw Vipunen in his true form?" Vellamo asks, hand at her chest.

I nod. "He made me do it, actually. Told me to take off my mask and look at him. Then he told me my mother was a Goddess, but said he couldn't tell me who. Said I would find out in time, when it would save my life."

"Typical," Ahto mutters.

"What does he look like?" Tellervo asks with big eyes. "Was he a giant?"

I'm not sure I'm supposed to be telling the world what the legendary giant looks like, but I guess he picked me for a reason. I try to explain exactly what he saw, though I think most of the Gods are disappointed. I know, I too kind of wanted to see some Fee-Fi-Fo-Fum type of action instead of a blob of light.

"Well, well, well," Vellamo says to herself. "I think we all have to assume that the light is his natural form, but that he can multiply and become solid when it comes to things like training."

"I'd heard that Shaman Väinämöinen once tricked Vipunen, stabbing him as he was buried underground so that he would give up his spells," Tellervo says. "Back in the days of the Old Gods."

From the stern looks around us, I gather they don't talk about the Old Gods often. But Death uses it as a segue and says, "Speaking of the Old Gods, while figuring out Hanna's mother is of importance to us, we also must discuss the impending uprising. I have reason to believe it will happen soon. My spies have heard the chatter in Inmost is increasing. They are all waiting for a signal or sign of some sort."

"They have been waiting for a while," Tapio says gruffly. "This is old news."

"I would be inclined to agree," Death says. "However, now that Louhi has Rasmus, I feel she will hasten her response." He eyes everyone, and when they remain impassive, he says,

"I assume that you all know what happened, in that Louhi took Rasmus, the shaman. News travels fast. What you may not know, however, is that Rasmus is both Hanna's brother and Louhi's son."

There are audible gasps and murmurs again.

"Louhi has another son?" Vellamo says in a booming voice.

"It's not Ilmarinen's?" asks Tapio.

Death shakes his head and proceeds to fill them all in on everything. It's a lot. He ends with the Prophecy of Three.

"I haven't heard of there being two other prophecies," Vellamo says. Everyone else murmurs in agreement.

Except for Ilmatar, who has been watching us in silence this whole time, barely saying anything. Her eyes are the palest blue, matching her dress, and in the depths of the sea they shift to white and green, like a moonstone.

"Sister," Tuoni says to her. "Did you know about the three?"

She gives the slightest of nods, her pale eyes staring straight ahead, not looking at anyone.

Tuoni lets out a frustrated grumble. "And you didn't think to share with me?"

A subtle shake of her head. "I see all," she says. Her voice is so soft, I have to strain to hear her. "When you see all, there's too much."

"All as in you're psychic?" I ask.

Everyone looks at me like I'm an idiot.

Ilmatar avoids looking at me, which is probably for the best because I think if she held eye contact with me I'd probably be hypnotized or something. "I am not a psychic," she says, as if it's a strange word. "I am the Goddess of the Air. I see all below me. There is a Prophecy of Three, but not all prophecies come true. Remember the one of how the great Väinämöinen was to be resurrected and return to our world? That never happened."

"Yet," Vellamo says sharply with a raise of her chin. I have a feeling there's some tension between the two Goddesses, sisters by law only. "Until time comes to an end, there's always a chance for a prophecy to come through."

"Fine," Death says with a raise of his palm. "So Ilmatar knew about the prophecy, but her brain is too full of air to make any sense of it." Ouch. Guess there's some tension between brother and sister, too. "The question is, what are we going to do about it?"

"We can't do much," Tapio says, running his hands through his long beard. I'm just noticing all the moss and twigs stuck in it. Woodsy Gandalf. "Not until we know who is which." He gives me a steady look, though his eyes aren't unkind. "Hanna, you are no doubt part of this. Everyone wants to believe you are the one to touch Death and unite the land. But there's also the chance that you might fall into the other categories."

"A chance, yes," Vellamo says, regarding me. "But I don't think that's Hanna."

"I don't think so either," Ilmatar says softly, still not looking at me. "Her spirit is good. She doesn't come from a dark place."

"Doesn't mean she won't go to a dark place," Ahto says,

giving me a somewhat apologetic look before looking at Vellamo. "As you've said, dear wife, there is always time for prophecies to come true and for people to turn. Those who we trust the most are often the ones we underestimate."

"For what it's worth, I have no intention or desire to raise any Old Gods," I tell them. "Their followers, the Sect of the Undead, are creepy as fuck and if they're that bad, then I'd hate to see who they worship." I glance at Death, who is watching me intently. "As for my husband, even though we may seem at odds with each other, I don't wish to destroy him."

"You're a newlywed," Ahto says with a snort. "Give it time."

"Be that as it may," Tapio says, "Hanna, you're asking us all to trust you."

"No," Death says, his voice low and commanding. "I'm asking you all to trust her. And so you will. She is my wife and my queen. She will be the one to unite the land."

My heart warms at his sudden faith in me.

"And if she isn't?" Tapio asks.

"Then I can promise you she won't be able to destroy me," Death says gravely.

Yep. Because I would be totally dead.

"What I'm going to need from you all," he goes on, looking each and every one of them in the eye, "is for you to keep your eyes open and ears to the ground. In the sea. In the air. Wherever. We must find out the role of Rasmus, we must know what Louhi is doing with him, and more than that, we must find out who Salainen is." He eyes Ilmatar. "Goddess of the Air, in the event that you have information about this one born from shadows, do you care to share it with us?"

Ilmatar shakes her head. "I have not seen Salainen but if she is with Louhi in the Star Swamp, then I am unable to. I will let you know, dear brother, if I come across her."

That seems to signal the end of the meeting. Small chats start up again amongst the Gods.

While everyone talks, I sit back with Tellervo on the coral benches that line the back of the grotto. I feel like we're at the kids table at a family reunion while the adults yammer away. Tiny bonefish have gathered around Tellervo's antlers, nibbling at them and she giggles, swatting them away, her red hair flowing.

"Hey," I hear a small voice speak up from behind me say, "What up, mortal?"

I freeze at the familiarity and twist around to see a little mermaid poking her head out from the corner of the grotto.

"Bell!" I exclaim.

She puts a finger to her mouth.

I look around. Neither Death nor any of the other Gods are paying any attention to me. Tellervo is for a moment, but she doesn't seem all that interested, more fascinated by her new bonefish friends.

"Come here," Bell says, beckoning me to come over as she hides herself behind a piece of kelp. I get up off the coral bench and crouch down beside her.

"Nice rack," she says as she floats. I guess my boobs are kind of in her face. She gives me a salacious grin. "So. How does it feel being the wife of Death?"

I laugh. "It feels…fitting, oddly enough. I can't believe you're here. I was hoping I would see you again, I just didn't know when."

She brushes her hair behind her ears. Her hair used to be white, so did her tail. Now her tail is iridescent seafoam and purple, her hair streaked with pink and lavender. I guess being in that fish tank for so long caused her to lose some of her pigment. I feel a little flare of anger at Death again for keeping her captive, but I'm glad she's looking healthy now.

"I thought about coming to pay you a visit," she says. "But then Vellamo told us that you were coming to the grotto, so I figured it was a good chance to see you. The rest of the mermaids are here too," she says, jerking her thumb behind her. I squint until I see dark shapes moving through the water just beyond the angler's lights. "We never pass up a chance to come out to the open seas. Lots of good eating out here."

"So you never leave without Vellamo?" I ask.

"She protects us. You'd be surprised at how many people and creatures want to either fuck or eat mermaids. I mean, I guess you're not surprised at the fucking part."

She almost conjures an image of Death fucking her in my head but luckily I'm able to push it away. "I didn't think you'd still be so small," I admit.

She shrugs. "I don't mind it," she says. "Keeps men away from me."

"With Death here maybe he could reverse the spell?"

She shakes her adamantly. "Hell no. Even with you as queen, he'll probably want me back in that tank. You know how he is. Wants what he has under lock and key. Possessive alphahole."

I laugh at her use of alphahole.

"Anyway," she goes on, her Barbie-doll aquamarine eyes twinkling with excitement, "I've been listening to your meeting. Congratulations on being part Goddess."

"Thanks. It's been a trip, I can tell you that much. I just wish we'd devoted a little more time to figuring out who my mother is. I mean, she has to be here, right?"

Even with all the talk of the war and prophecies and everything, I still spent that entire meeting wondering if any of them gave birth to me.

"Not necessarily. There are a few deities missing."

I look around. "Who?"

"Not that he's a Goddess, but Nyyrikki, Tellervo's brother," she says quietly. "God of the Hunt. He's a bit like Death's son though, kind of does his own thing. Then there's Kuutar, as you know, Goddess of the Moon, and her sister Päivätär, Goddess of the Sun. There's Auringotar, Goddess of Fire. All of those Goddesses can't get down here into the sea. They rarely leave their lands, if ever. There's also Ved-Ava, who is the Goddess of Water. She looks like a mermaid and is bound to rivers and lakes. I've never seen her in the sea. In fact, I'm not even sure she exists anymore."

"Some gods just cease to exist?"

"Or they're killed. Gods can kill other Gods. The politics of the all-mighty can be like a soap opera but I don't always hear all the gossip down where I am."

"Ilmatar is a strange one," I comment, keeping my voice low. "Maybe she's my mother."

Bell snorts. "I don't think so. She's the virgin. That's like her whole thing."

I guess she does have a virginal air about her. Like purity but turned up to the max. "Weird that she doesn't look at anyone."

"She can't," Bell explains. "I mean, she does but she can only see you out of her peripheral vision. And when she's in our peripheral she all but disappears." She suddenly swims downward toward the base of the kelp and then brings out a small mesh pouch, that looks garbage bag sized in her hands. "Here, I brought you some things."

The pouch seems heavy to carry so I pluck it from her. I open it and take out a small round crystal.

"That's a sunmoonstone sphere," she says to me. I've never actually had a good look at one before, so I take my time inspecting it. The sphere is a rust red, glittering with a million sparkles. On the top and bottom of the sphere are iridescent white patches that resemble polar ice caps. When I move the sphere, there's a shift in the white, the shimmery glow of moonstone. "You know how these work, right?"

I nod, wanting to demonstrate, but I'm afraid the light will draw attention to us. "How did you know I wanted one?"

"Just a hunch," she says with a shrug, and nods to the pouch.

I take out the other item, another sphere. This one sparkles as clear as a diamond with a tinge of pale gold and yellow.

"And that is portal glass," she says.

"Portal glass?" I repeat, turning it in my fingers. There are a few imperfections that catch the light and produce a ton of tiny rainbows.

"It's a crystal from the sun," she says. "Kuutar gave it to me, it came from her sister. You can use it to peer into the lives of those you love the most. I haven't tried it out because, well…I don't have anyone to love." She looks a little crestfallen, then shakes it off. "Yet. So I thought I would give it to you. You can see your father inside."

"What!?" I exclaim, loud enough for Tellervo to look over at us. "What?" I say again, whispering. I hold the sphere to my eyes, but I don't see anything except the image of Bell reversed. "I don't see him."

"You have to spin it," she says. "And you have to be alone, in the dark. Try it tonight and you'll see. I think you can only see him for a few seconds at a time but I mean, that's better than nothing."

Tears spring to my eyes, an odd feeling since I'm already underwater. I clutch the two stones to my chest. "Thank you so much, Bell. You have no idea what this means to me."

She gives me a soft smile. "I have some idea." Then a grave expression straightens her brow. "You know, I can get you out of here," she says, her voice barely audible.

I frown. "You mean out of the meeting?"

"Out of Tuonela. There's an actual portal at the bottom of the Great Inland Sea. If you could arrange to get to the sea somehow, I could show you the way."

Tempting. So tempting. To be able to leave the land of the dead and go back home, where my father is, where there is no impending war, no prophecy, no forced marriage to a God.

And yet…and yet…

I shake my head. "I'm not ready to go yet," I tell her. "I know it seems silly, but I need answers and I don't think I'll find them back home."

"Even with your father there?" she asks.

I think that over. I know if I had the chance to talk to my father again he would tell me everything. But what use are the answers if I can't get back to Tuonela? Because make no mistake about it, if I leave there is absolutely no way I can come back. Death would not let me. He would not have me. He would probably kill me, and if he couldn't bring himself to do that, then I really would rot in that oubliette.

The answers I now seek only help me if I'm still the queen. There's no way in hell I could function as a normal human back in reality with all the knowledge I would have.

"I can't," I tell her. "I want to see my father, but I have a duty now, whether I like it or not. I am bound in law to Death, and maybe the law doesn't stretch into the Upper World but it's important to me." I just had no idea how important until I said it out loud.

"Wow."

I frown. "Wow what?"

She gives me a small smile. "You've really fallen in love with him."

"I'm not in love with him," I protest quickly. I'm not, I know I'm not. "But I care about him. And I care about Tuonela. What happens here affects all the worlds, not just this one. I can't abandon it now."

"You've probably made the right choice, fairy girl," she says to me. "You're already sounding like a queen. Guess I need to start bowing in front of you, huh?"

She does a little bow just as Death's voice booms across the grotto. "Hanna! What are you doing?"

Bell's eyes widen and, in a flash of iridescent scales, she disappears into the kelp.

Bye, Little Mermaid, I say inside my head, quickly stuffing the pouch into my bodice. I straighten up and give Death a smile as he comes toward me.

"I was just looking at the kelp," I say to him. I notice Tellervo gives me an inquisitive look and I tense, but she doesn't say anything.

"You don't have kelp in California?" he asks. He grabs me by the elbow, but his touch is gentle. "We need to head back up to the surface. I don't know how much longer that tea will help you breathe underwater."

He doesn't know? Okay, now I'm feeling a little panicked.

We say goodbye to the Gods and Goddesses and I give my black sand dollar back to Ahto before Death starts swimming up toward the surface, pulling me along.

CHAPTER TWENTY-TWO

DEATH

"THE CALM"

The sea is as calm as glass. I don't linger on deck for too long, in case I am spotted by someone, perhaps a pelican under Louhi's command. But it's enough to take in the brisk air, the glint of sun on the horizon as it rises. I know the weather will turn, but at the moment I welcome the sun. I feel one with it, like it's been away from my realm for too long and I need to welcome its return, and maybe then everything will be whole again.

But then the clouds lower and the dawn is sucked away into the steel-gray sea. I let out a low breath and look over at the Deadhands. They are all rowing steadily, the ship slicing through the water like a sharp blade. We have a few hours until we reach Shadow's End.

I go back below deck and over to the captain's quarters. I once had large, tall-ships that used to anchor in the water off Evernight Point, but over time the sea consumed them. I still have some grand ships up further north, one located in a tiny cove off of the Hiisi Forest where it resembles a tropical island. Mortals would call that paradise, with the lush flowers and jungle and warm, clear waters, but my paradise is dark and cold and sharp.

Yet, part of me wants to take Hanna there. Even if the ship has deteriorated, we could make a home on the white sand beaches. She would love the place, it would make her feel at home, and I would be happy because she's happy.

I would be happy because she's happy.

The feeling catches me by surprise.

That is not how a king thinks. Not how a God works.

I give my head a shake and push it away. I think back to the tall ships.

In those tall ships, everything was stately and grand, gleaming with obsidian and leather. On this ship, the captain's quarters at the aft are barely big enough for me to fit in. But the bed is comfortable and, when I go inside the small cabin, I see Hanna is fast asleep.

Naked, of course. We had to get off our wet clothes. I had to fuck her until she pretty much passed out. I was so impressed with the way she handled herself today at the meeting, with all my kin, and I could tell they were impressed with her. Made me feel very lucky to have her as my queen. When I was with Louhi, I was in awe of the wickedness of her mind, the way she indulged her powers. With Hanna, my wonderment and pride come from watching her bloom into the Goddess she's yet to become. I'm not sure she sees the changes herself. She is too young and too focused on the changes of her body and appearance, which are growing stronger and more beautiful every day. She doesn't know yet that the greatest, most crucial changes are the ones happening inside her.

She is exhausted, though. From her training, from being underwater, from the residue from the magic. Fuck, I think she's still tired from the way my Shadow Self and I shared her the other week. The sea is finally calm, so I don't want to wake her. She needs this rest.

I sit down next to her on the bed, the mattress dipping in from my weight. Her body is a work of art. It's the work of long days training that have made her thighs sleek and muscular, her ass firm and powerful, her arms strong and tight. And yet the rest of her is so soft. The natural curve of her belly, her full breasts, the sweet flesh of her inner thighs. I need her to see that who she is on the outside is matching who she is on the inside: powerful, vulnerable, strong, and soft.

Sometimes I wonder if Vipunen is the real God just rolling the dice, guessing the future. If not him, the Creator, someone, anyone, just trying to see where things will land. It's so easy to think how Hanna might have turned out. Had I not rescued her from Louhi at the Star Swamp, would she have lived? Would Louhi have taken her in? Is that where she could have become Salainen, the one to destroy me, or the one to raise the Old Gods? If we go back further than that, if Louhi or the Bone Stragglers had gotten their hands on Hanna when she first came to Tuonela in search of her father, could she have been turned then?

Is it luck or happenstance or destiny that I took Hanna for my own and in the end turned her into a queen?

Of course, I can't help dwelling over Tapio's words, that there was always time for Hanna to change and become what we fear. It's one reason why I wish my trust in Vipunen was one hundred percent. She's training with him alone…what is he shaping her to be? I have no doubt now that Hanna can defend herself, she has shown me some of her acquired moves, plus she had fighting skills to begin with. Vipunen doesn't need to turn her into a warrior. If he does, then that's a problem.

Could a warrior Hanna, turned to darkness, turned against me, become this Salainen? Is the Salainen that exists already her but from a different timeline, a different future?

Get a fucking grip, I scold myself. *You're thinking like a hapless mortal now, not a God. Hanna is your queen and she will unite the land, end of story.*

I pinch the bridge of my nose and exhale heavily. Despite the all the sex, tension has a way of creeping back in.

It is at the sound of my breathing that Hanna makes a small noise and turns over in her sheets. It would be pitch black down here save for the sunmoonstone sphere that's giving off low moonlight. Funny, I don't remember bringing one along, but there must have been one on the ship.

"Tuoni?" she whispers, her eyes fluttering open.

My chest tightens. I've always hated the sound of my real name—except when she says it. Then I just want to hear it more.

"You've been sleeping," I tell her, placing a hand on her

calf. "It's dawn. We're close to Shadow's End. The seas are still calm."

"Do you have coffee on board?" she asks in a husky, drowsy voice that makes me hard.

"I can check," I tell her. "The beans might be spoiled, it's so damp here. I might have decaf, but I choose death before decaf."

"So do I," she says, giving me a small smile. "I can wait." She slides her palm over the empty space beside her. "Why don't you lie down? I'm guessing you haven't slept at all."

I shake my head, a jerk to the left. I can't sleep in a situation like this. I can't show any weakness. Even when I was screwing her, I was still paying attention to the sounds outside the boat, part of me always ready to attack or defend if it came to it. I think I've mastered it for good now, having been able to do so with my Shadow Self. At the moment he is sleeping too, but soon he will rise and I will have to split into two different bodies. Ever since we united in the library with Hanna, it's been fairly seamless.

"Then lie down," she says. "Please."

"You know I love it when you beg," I tell her.

And I oblige. I lie down next to her, feeling both large and powerful next to her tiny body, yet strangely vulnerable as well.

She rolls over on her side, her breasts so perfect, and reaches forward, pressing her fingertip on my nose. She smiles to herself, as if pleased.

I frown. "What are you doing?"

"I just booped you."

"You *booped* me? Is that mortal slang for fucking? Because if it is, I prefer the word fuck."

She lets out an airy laugh. "No, silly God. You boop someone when you touch their nose. Like this." She does it again. "Boop!"

I can't help but chuckle. "I suppose I told you to never stop surprising me. You really are something else, Hanna."

She *boops* me again and this time I try to bite her finger. She retracts it just in time, holding it coyly against her chest. The raw, overwhelming need to dominate her comes over me and my dick stiffens. How can she be so sexual and adorable and lovely all at the same time?

I cover her body with mine, my hands coasting over her body, her hands tangled in my hair. She's already wet, I slide right in. A tight fit as usual, I drive myself in deep until I'm pressed up against her and grinding.

She moans, music to my ears.

I want a lifetime of those moans.

I go slowly. We both move with calm urgency, mirroring the seas outside. I take my time feeling, licking, tasting every inch of her. Things feel different somehow in this cabin now, like the closeness of the quarters is making me feel like I'm in her skin and she's in mine.

You're losing it, Tuoni, I tell myself. *You're losing yourself in her. Do not let that happen.*

But the words fall away and I don't listen to them, not at this moment. I don't listen to much except her quick, shallow breaths as the heat inside her builds, the wet sound of me sliding in and out of her, the creak of the boat as it glides through the waves.

"You're mine for eternity," I whisper to her, running my hands through her hair, wishing I could feel her strands between my fingers. "Tell me you know that."

She gives me a look of faint surprise before my hips pump against hers again and she's gasping, mouth open, eyes rolled back.

"Tell me you're mine," I go on, determination and release chasing me at the same time. "I need to hear it."

"I am yours," she says softly. "I am yours, you are mine."

Then she cries out as her body tenses, pulse quickening, and I push her over the edge.

"Look at you little bird," I whisper to her as her back arches and her body shakes, her orgasm rolling through her. Cheeks flush, lips pink, eyes full of wild tenderness. "Look at you fly."

She comes and comes and then I explode inside her. I move roughly into her body, grabbing her hair, grinding my teeth as thoughts escape me, a low growl coming from my chest.

Fuck.

Another thread unraveled.

I pull out, muscles shaking, which is strange since my body is never pushed to the limit, and I roll over beside her, trying to breathe, feel like myself again. My heart is a drum inside my skull.

I can't stop thinking about her. About this. About us.

Her breath is deepening and she's almost asleep again when I find myself saying:

"What do you want, Hanna?"

She stirs. "What do you mean?"

"I mean, what do you want?" I repeat. "What do you really want? Right now. Everyone wants something, Hanna. What is it that you desire the most?"

"At this moment? In the whole wide world?"

"In all the worlds."

I hear her swallow. She rolls over on her back, licks her lips. A lengthy pause as she tries to gather her thoughts. I'd say I caught her off-guard, but the truth is, so many mortals don't ever really stop to figure out what they want from life, let alone what they want in that very moment.

"I want to make sure my father is alright," she says in a quiet voice.

It's as I thought she'd say. Loyal to the end. "Is that really it? Is that really all you want?" I take in a deep breath, wondering if I'll regret the words I'm about to say. "If I let you go, would you go, right now? Would you just up and leave me?"

She rolls her head to the side to eye me, frowning. "Why are you asking me this?" she asks cautiously.

"I'm curious. I have been for some time."

She swallows and then nods. "If I was allowed to come back, I would go. Just to make sure he's alright. I would come back."

"Would you?"

"Yes. I would."

"So then, what do you want? If your father is taken care of and safe for the rest of his life, then what do you want? Would you want him to come back with you here?"

I'm trying not to promise anything, but her eyes already glint with hope. "Yes. If he could come back here…I would have everything I want."

I study her ethereal face, knowing she has the blood of a Goddess flowing through her. "Would you though? Aside from him, what do you need? What are you after? What are you hoping to gain during your time here in your position?"

I expect her to hesitate, and it takes me by surprise when she says:

"Power. I want power."

My heart beats with pride. "I can respect that."

"I want to be someone to be reckoned with," she says, gnawing on her bottom lip for a second. "I want to live up to my potential, and I want to find out what my potential is. Test the limits. I want security and safety and I want it to come, not because I'm married to you, but because no one can cross me, no one can mess with me. I want to know what that feels like."

I sit up, careful not to hit my head on the low ceiling. There's a fire in her that I've seen before, but never like this. I want to fan the flames.

"You're on the verge of that, don't you feel it?" I tell her.

"I don't know." She shakes her head. "I'm on the verge but…it's just out of reach. I'm not sure if I'll be worthy of it."

"Feeling worthy of something and being powerful are two very different things. Perhaps true power is knowing your worth."

She cracks a grin. "Okay there, Dr. Phil."

"I can't be expected to know all your tedious pop culture references."

She rolls her eyes and then sits up beside me. For a moment I'm afraid she might boop me again. "So, what do you want? The same? Power?"

"I have power, little bird," I tell her. "I always have. For better or for worse. The problem with having power, as I'm sure you'll find out, is that you have to learn to hold onto it. You can't be at the top forever, even as a God or a leader, your power will wane and ebb and flow throughout the years. I am in the valley at the moment, doing all I can to make sure it rises again."

"So what you want is to keep power."

"That sounds so simple when you say it like that. Besides, I am not one-dimensional. I want more than one thing."

"And what's the other thing?"

I swallow thickly. "You."

"But you have me."

"Do I?" I raise my brow.

"We're married. You just fucked my brains out. We're lying naked in bed together. How can you think otherwise?"

"There are different ways of having someone, Hanna, some are easier than others. What I want is what I don't have, and that is your heart and your soul." She may have said things I wanted to hear when we were in the Crystal Caves, but hearing and feeling are two different things.

She stares at me for a moment, her brows drawing together in a delicate frown.

"You told me you'd never love me," she says quietly.

I nod. "I know I did."

"That you'd pity me if I loved you."

"Then perhaps I want to pity you." Perhaps I want to know what it fucking feels like for once in my damned life.

To be loved.

But I've said too much already.

We fall silent, the air feeling heavy, the tension thick. This boat could use a hatch back here, anything to let in the sea air. As if the air could sweep away everything I just told her.

I've let myself become too vulnerable for my comfort.

Only one way to fix this.

I take my finger, lean over, and press it on her nose.

"Boop."

She explodes into laughter, the sound filling the cabin, and all the awkwardness of the moments before disappears in a second.

"Oh jeez," she says through giggles. "I just got booped by Death."

TWENTY-THREE

DEATH

"THE PRE-GAME"

The snowbird chirps at me from the corner of the solar room, mocking me. It's perched on the tarnished metal tip of one of my globes located on the highest shelf. So high that I can't actually reach up there on my own.

I made the mistake of opening the cage. I thought that since the snowbird had been here long enough, that I was talking to it, feeding it, that it wouldn't leave me.

I was foolish.

I let it out and it immediately flew to the highest part of the room, just out of reach. Now it's perched there, staring down at me with red lizard eyes, preening feathers of distrust, and there's a fucking lesson in here for me, I know it.

I've been too lax with Hanna. Too open. Too much like a husband, less like a king or a God. I feel like a big softie. I need to throw her down the oubliette again. Maybe send a few

Deadhands to Oblivion. Anything to make myself harden a little more. Now is not the time to be stewing in my feelings for her; now is not the time to be having feelings at all. The only feelings I need to have are ruthlessness, determination, persistence. There is a war coming and I need to be as prepared as possible. There shouldn't be a single moment of my day where I'm not entirely focused on that.

There's a knock at my door.

Speak of the devil.

I know it's Hanna before I even hear her. I smell her, I feel her, like sunshine.

Shit.

"Come in," I say, keeping my eyes on the snowbird. It opens its mouth, displaying a row of tiny needle-like teeth, then takes flight, gliding over my head and right over to Hanna.

I twist around, trying to catch it to no avail, and Hanna's eyes widen as the bird approaches, beak open, wings out. She's silently screaming as the bird lands on her shoulder and then it has the nerve to give me the stink eye. It squawks now, then starts running its beak through Hanna's hair, as if asserting its property.

"So I take it you let it out of its cage," Hanna says uneasily, eyes glued to the flying lizard thing.

"A big mistake in hindsight," I admit, coming over to her. "But I think it likes you."

"I hope so," she says. "Because there's a literal flying dinosaur on my shoulder. I read Jurassic Park. I know the little ones cause the most trouble."

Seeing that she's still uncomfortable, even though the bird dinosaur absolutely loves her and is trying to build a nest in her hair, I make a move for it. The bird opens its razor beak and hisses at me viciously, snapping at my gloves.

"Foolish little thing," I tell it, grabbing it by its long neck.

"Oh, don't kill it," Hanna pleads, pressing her hands together in prayer.

"Is that how you see me?" I say, giving her a disappointed look as I bring the snowbird over to the cage, careful not to choke it.

"You are the God of Death," she points out.

"I am discerning," I mutter, placing the snowbird back in and quickly slamming the door shut before it can escape. It cries out, pecking at the bars. I grab the animal pelt and throw it over the cage to end the incessant squawking. It doesn't work.

I glance at Hanna properly for the first time. She's wearing a long red velvet and satin dress, making her waist small and putting her breasts on display. Her hair is curled and loose around her shoulders, though some of it is tangled because of the snowbird.

She takes my breath away, a kind of pain that only she brings me.

"How do I look?" she asks, holding out the sides of her dress in show.

"Like a queen," I tell her.

"Good enough for your people?"

"Good enough to fucking eat," I say with a curl of my lip. "And they're your people too, my dear."

She gives me a nervous grin, her fingers twitching.

"You need wine and food," I tell her, walking over to her. I grab her hand and hold it in mine. "Perhaps a good fuck."

"No," she says sharply, then laughs. "You are not messing up any of this. Do you know how long it took for Raila to get me this pretty?"

"She didn't even need a minute," I tell her, slipping my arm around the small of her waist and pulling her up against me. I push myself against her hips, hard as iron.

"No," she says again and swats my grip away. "I need to prepare for tonight instead of you making me forget my name."

"It's Hanna," I murmur, pulling her back to me and kissing her on the neck. She tastes so sweet, like honey and sunshine. "Also known as little bird and fairy girl. Goddess, wife and queen."

"I'll be a disheveled blubbering mess with cum in my hair when you're done with me." She presses her hands against my chest and it makes me even harder, this whole predator and prey thing, but in the end I let her loose because she's got a point.

Tonight I'm having a feast. We often have one here right before a Bone Match, an excuse to celebrate with family and friends. The matches sometimes last hours—it can take time for the opponents to die, the second death coming much harder—which means we get hungry, and other than the booze we bring into Inmost for the occasion, you do not want to have the food down there.

Because Tuonen is the referee for the match, he is here

at Shadow's End tonight, along with Sarvi, Kalma, Tapio, Mielikki, Tellervo, and Tapio's righthand man, Vaki. Lovia would be, but someone has to ferry the dead.

"Is Tuonen here yet?" Hanna asks, retreating out of the office. I guess I should get changed, too. I think I spent far too long trying to get the bird back in the cage.

"He should be," I tell her. "He doesn't miss a meal. He often eats and leaves, saving his energy for the match, but he'll be here."

She nods and I take her arm as we go down the stairs to our floor, her dress gathered in her hands. "Too bad Lovia has to work."

"It is," I admit. "She's never seen a match."

"Maybe…" she begins, then trails off.

I glance at her. "What?"

"Maybe you should think about, I don't know, hiring someone else to take on the responsibility."

I bring her to a stop at the bottom of the stairs.

"Responsibility?" I say with a shake of my head. "I know in the Upper World you have jobs that you can choose and get paid to do them, but it doesn't work like that here."

She raises her chin and meets my eye. Oh, she's going to be a handful tonight. Fuck, I'm getting hard all over again.

"Why not?" she counters. "You're a fucking God, Tuoni. You can do whatever you want."

She's not getting it. Mortals and their ideas.

"That's not how it works."

"Why not?"

"Because it's not."

"But why?"

I let out a growl of frustration. "Mortal woman. Listen to me. Things are a certain way because to knock them out of balance would destroy the natural order of things."

She crosses her arms and cocks a brow. "Uh huh. And who told you that? Antero Vipunen?"

"Yes," I say reluctantly.

"And the natural order of things, does that include your ex-wife demoness plotting your demise along with the Old Gods and the underground uprising? Is that part of the natural order of Tuonela?"

I open my mouth to counter her. Close it. Decide I have nothing intelligent to say. Damn, she's constantly besting me.

"Why do you care what Lovia and Tuonen do?"

"Because…" She says the word like she's been holding it in for too long, "Lovia is miserable."

I'm taken aback. "Lovia?" Every time I think of my daughter, she's always this flighty, smiling, girl. Yes, she has that wicked side, but she enjoys that, too. She doesn't strike me as miserable in the slightest.

Alright. Perhaps now that I've thought about it for a minute, she does complain about ferrying the dead a lot.

"Yes," Hanna says adamantly. "She hates her job. She wants to do…other things. She wants to quit."

I bark out a laugh. "You don't get to quit being a God." Kids these days, always trying to shirk out of their responsibilities.

"It's not about her quitting that, she knows she's a Goddess of the Dead, through and through. But she has her own ambitions and they don't revolve around the dead."

I frown in concentration, trying to think about what her interests could possibly be. She's always there when I'm watching a vintage movie from the Upper World. She likes to read any and all of the books I have lying around. She's got a strange obsession with fashion. Her slang is all procured from the Upper World…

"I don't understand. What are her own ambitions?"

"She likes to…travel."

"Travel where?"

She chews on her lip for a moment, her eyes cagey as if she's debating what she's going to say next. "The Upper World."

"Has she even been there?" I ask. Not that it's impossible for her to get access, I just don't know when she would have done so. She's never said anything to me about it.

"Please don't tell her I told you that," she says, eyes huge. "She wanted me to talk to you about it. She just wants some time and space to figure herself out. She hoped that you could find someone else to take over her position."

"Someone else? Doesn't she realize the importance of her role? The reverence of it all, to be the one to meet the dead and bring them to the afterlife?"

"Then you do it."

I narrow my eyes at her. "That's not amusing."

"See? You don't want to do the job."

"It's not my job to do, Hanna."

"Well, Lovia thinks someone else should do it. Think about it this way. Back in the Upper World, if I checked into a hotel that I was unsure of and the front desk clerk was a real bitch, it would sour my opinion of the whole hotel, maybe even the whole trip. That's what people who arrive here are going to think. They've just fucking died, the one thing they've feared their whole entire short little lives. I don't care that you're the God of Death, you obviously have no idea how scary the idea of death is for a mortal. They live their whole lives around the concept, without ever knowing what really happens to them. So, they die, maybe there's a white light, then they see a boat coming across the river, coming to take them to the afterlife which they know nothing about, and guess what? The person steering the boat doesn't want to be there. She hates it. She'd rather be in France, eating brie and drinking two-euro bottles of wine underneath the Eiffel tower. No doubt the people on the boat are going to wish for the same thing."

Hanna is out of breath by the time she finishes talking.

"Nice speech. Are you done?"

"Tuoni," she says in a warning voice. That's not a good sign. That's the first time she's used my name in that tone before. "She's your daughter. Let her live a little. Same goes for your son. Let him live a little, too. Wouldn't he be a better addition here in Shadow's End, working at your side as confidante and advisor, than out there on the boat?"

I almost laugh, but I remember Tuonen is in the castle and the last thing I want is to show him disrespect. "He doesn't have the experience."

"Then give him a chance to get it, in a few eons he will. Look, I wouldn't be talking to you about this if she hadn't confided in me, hadn't asked me to talk to you. Maybe you can ask one of the other lesser Gods to do it. Or Goddesses.

Or spirits. Someone like whatever the hell Kalma is. Someone who will want to do the job with the reverence it deserves."

Hanna is so impassioned, her big brown eyes pleading with me, that I can't help but be touched by her devotion to my daughter.

"You care about her greatly, don't you?" I ask.

She nods. "I do. And I don't want to overstep any boundaries or step on any toes. I know she's not my daughter at all. But I care for her all the same. Just tell me you'll think about it. Please."

I give her a half-smile. "You know I like it when you say please."

"There you are," Tuonen's voice calls out, preventing me from getting carried away with my wife.

I look over the railing and see my son coming up the stairs. He's wearing black head-to-toe, lots of leather straps and iron accents. Like father, like son. The last time I saw him was when he was ferrying the almost nude women to the City of Death.

He stops at the steps below us and looks at Hanna.

"And now we meet again," Tuonen says, bowing slightly. "A queen this time." He looks at me under his mask of obsidian vipers. "Do I have to call her stepmom?"

"Please no," Hanna says with a laugh. "Just Hanna is fine."

"Okay, Just Hanna," he says as he adjusts his bowtie, which is the only piece of color on his body: red. If I wear red we can match as a family, which wouldn't be a bad move. I have no idea if any of the members of the uprising will be there at the Bone Match, lurking in the shadows, but it can't hurt to look like a united front.

"I came up to tell you that dinner is almost ready," he says to me, and it's then that I can catch a whiff of Pyry's cooking wafting up through the castle. He takes his mask off for a moment, pushing his black hair off his forehead.

I eye Hanna, watching her closely. I'm quite aware that she's closer in age, comparatively speaking, to my son than she is to me, and I have to say that Tuonen is pretty handsome. Obviously. He's got all of my genes, aside from the horns. And the tail. But I'm not allowed to talk about the tail.

But while Hanna seems to be taking him in appreciatively, finally seeing him without his mask, she's not fawning over him. Still, I put my arm around her for good measure.

"I have to go get changed, I was chasing a flying dinosaur around," I tell him. He frowns at that and slips the mask back on. "But come with me, Tuonen. Hanna had a really interesting idea she just sprung on me."

The three of us walk down the corridor toward my chambers and I tell Tuonen all about her idea, about getting another lesser God to take over the role to give him and Lovia some space. It's not like me to do this. Usually I stew over something for months, even years, before I come to a decision.

"Another ferryman?" Tuonen says as I grab suitable clothes from the closet. "I wouldn't be opposed to that." He's trying to sound blasé, but I can hear the excitement in his voice, which makes me realize that perhaps this is something my children really need. I know they're immortal and have been around for eons, but perhaps they deserve to hold on to their youth a little longer.

It's what she said about Vipunen that really has me reconsidering things. Vipunen is the one who is constantly reminding me of my place, of not upsetting the balance of the land, of keeping the natural order of things. I've had that drilled in my head since I woke up naked on the floor of his caves, just a fucking child about to become a God.

But if the almighty giant is so determined to keep me in line, how come he isn't keeping anyone else in line? I don't know. Maybe it's because I'm the only one he has access to, but then sometimes I wonder why that is. Why doesn't my brother Ahto have to deal with Vipunen? Or my sister Ilmatar? Even our parents, Ukko and Akka—Old Gods that are far more powerful than we are—keep out of the way. They don't interfere.

"It's just an idea," I tell him. "I'll ask around, see if it's possible."

He lifts his mask up enough to grin at me.

Shit. I've given him hope.

I look at Hanna. She's grinning too. It's like they've both won already.

"Careful," I warn them. "If you push my generous mood too much, I might toss the both of you into the oubliette."

"Ideal threats," Tuonen says.

I ignore him. I get changed behind the divider, then go into the Hall of Skulls to select my mask for the match. Since I haven't made a public appearance in the City of Death in a very long time, I have to be particular, choosing one that makes me look the most fearsome.

In keeping with the color theme, I choose a red one made

from the dyed bones of the northern crocodiles. There's a pair of iron spikes for horns, a reptilian ridge over the brow bones, scales etched under the cheekbones, and fangs protruding from a maniacal grin.

I slip it on and look at Tuonen and Hanna for approval.

Tuonen grins, charmed by it.

Hanna looks repulsed.

Perfect.

I grab my hooded cloak and we start toward the stairs when Hanna suddenly remembers something. She runs into the bedroom and then comes out moments later adjusting her dress.

I give her an inquisitive look.

"Sorry," she says. "I forgot my knife and sunmoonstone."

"Where did you put them?" Tuonen asks, looking her over.

She smiles proudly and is about to lift up the layers of her skirt, but I reach out and grab her wrist. Not necessary, I tell her silently.

"She has a holster on her leg," I say to him. Even with his face covered he still looks disappointed that he didn't get a peep show of my wife. "Selenite knife for protection and a sunmoonstone for light."

"Did Vipunen give you the knife?" Tuonen asks. "I tried the selenite, but it doesn't cut for me."

She shakes her head. "No. Actually, your father did. If it were up to Vipunen, I'd be dragging a sword to the Bone Match for protection. I keep feeling like I'm going to need it."

I squeeze her hand in mine as we go down the stairs to

the main floor. "Nothing to be nervous about, my dear."

"Who said I was nervous?" she asks, but it's written all over her face.

Everyone has gathered in the formal dining room and the Deadhand guards stationed outside part to let us in.

At the long table everyone is already seated and the banquet table is filled with food, Pyry and the other Deadmaidens coming in and out of the kitchen with trays of glorious food in their hands.

The doors close behind us and my son and I take off our masks, able to be ourselves around the present company.

I have my seat at one end of the table but as this is Hanna's first time sitting at a formal dinner, I lead her over to her chair at the opposite end. She sits down on the iron throne and then looks up at me with anxious eyes. I give her shoulder a reassuring pat and then head down to my end.

Tuonen takes his seat beside me, then there's Tapio on the other side, then Mielikki, Tellervo, Vati, and Kalma. Sarvi is closest to Hanna. Obviously, the unicorn doesn't have a seat but it stands there all the same. Tellervo keeps on staring at the unicorn with child-like glee and I realize she's never been to dinner here before. It usually takes a bit for new guests to get used to an equine dining at the table with them.

Winc is poured in the goblets and Tuonen gets to his feet, holding out his glass.

"I know my father is usually the one making these speeches, but I thought I would beat him to it," he says, looking at everyone. "I wanted to say a special welcome to our new queen, Hanna, since this is her first big dinner as queen, and definitely her first Bone Match as one. It's an important night and I'm very happy she's here to share it with us."

Hmmm. Tuonen's speech was rather touching. I've never heard him be sentimental before. I have a feeling he's sucking up to me because Hanna put the idea of getting another ferryman in his head.

I clap, along with everyone else and we all toast to Hanna, who smiles demurely at the opposite end of the table. Her pale cheeks flush with embarrassment which makes my dick twitch. Fuck. I should have taken her while I had the chance; I'm going to be uncomfortably turned-on all night if she's going to continue to look so ravishing.

The food comes out and everyone tucks in. It tastes especially good tonight. There are plates of gold melon cooked in fried moose strips, roast chestnut stew with ice pumpkins and baby apples, an oven-baked snow pheasant stuffed with mountain rye, cliff turnips and flowers from the garden. Chestnut ale and juniper lager are flowing, along with the sweetvine wines and shots of cardamom liquor as a palette-cleanser. There's even a side dish of rice that I had one of my helpers smuggle from the Upper World. Try as they might, the Deadmaidens still haven't figured out how to properly grow rice in Tuonela.

"What is this?" Tellervo asks, staring in disgust at the bowl of rice as Tuonen passes it to Hanna. "Maggots?"

"It's called rice," Hanna says, trying not to laugh. "It's from my world. We eat it with everything there, from seaweed and fish to cinnamon and sugar. It's very good. Try it."

Tellervo wrinkles her nose. "No thanks."

"Tapio," I say to Tellervo's father, the God of the Forest. With his ram horns and gray beard peppered with moss, twigs and leaves, Tapio looks out of place at the table, surrounded by so much metal and darkness. "Your son," I point my fork at him, "Nyyrikki. He wasn't at the meeting and he's not here. What does he do all day?"

A displeased look comes across his old face. "Nothing, as far as I know."

"He hunts," Mielikki says, though she doesn't seem happy about that either. "All day. Kills precious animals. As you know, I am the protector of them, so it's like he's trying to rebel or something to that effect. He likens himself to the God of the Hunt. Says there's already a God of the Forest."

"Afraid to follow in his father's footsteps," Tapio grumbles.

"Not really your footsteps if you never plan to be out of the picture," I point out. "Would he be interested in another role? Part-time. An honorary God of Death?"

Out of the corner of my eye I see Tuonen and Hanna exchange a look of surprise. Bet they thought I'd never even consider it. It feels rather good to catch them off-guard.

"Doing what?" Tapio asks, but he looks intrigued. So does his wife.

"Being a ferryman," I tell him. "Sometimes Lovia and Tuonen are busy doing other things, helping me, and so forth. It would be a very prestigious position in the realm." I'm not exaggerating either. Everyone has the highest respect for my children because they transport the dead to the afterlife. This world would not function without them.

"Well, I know we would be honored if you gave him that

role," Mielikki says, pressing her hands into the table with emphasis.

Tellervo snorts. "If you can convince him."

"Hey," Tuonen says sharply. "It's an esteemed job. And you get to meet a lot of interesting people." There's a twinkle in his eye as he says that, and I know he's thinking about the half-naked variety.

"I will talk to him about it," Tapio says. "If there are extra privileges involved, he may take it. I know he does want a name for himself."

"We can talk more about it another day," I say, raising my glass of wine.

Everyone lapses into small talk, eating away, but I have to do a test. I close my eyes in the event that something looks amiss and I go searching inside my head, looking for my Shadow Self. I find him where I left him, up in the eastern wing of the library, lying down on the floor.

I open his eyes.

I am seeing through them.

Staring at the ceiling and the celestial designs etched above, star systems from worlds that don't have names yet.

But while I am staring at the ceiling, I am also at the dinner. I can hear everyone's conversation—Tuonen is talking about tonight's match and the money he has riding on it, even though money is useless and he's not supposed to do that as a referee—and when I open my eyes for a moment I can see Hanna at the end of the table, watching me with concern. She knows what I'm doing.

I also see the ceiling.

I see her and I see the library. The images aren't superimposed on top of each other, rather they are happening side by side and all at once.

I am two different places at the same time, but my thoughts are as one.

I smile to myself, sitting at the dinner table, but the Shadow Self's face remains impassive. Ever since I was inside myself, the union between my mind and the body's has been perfected.

Tonight, though, I will put us to the test.

I will take Hanna to the Bone Match.

But my Shadow Self isn't remaining behind here at Shadow's End.

He's coming with me.

CHAPTER TWENTY-FOUR

HANNA

"THE BONE MATCH"

I saw my father last night.

While Death was in the library, doing some sort of bonding exercises with his Shadow Self, I took advantage of the dark to look for my father.

I took the portal glass from the jar of salt I keep beside my bedside (I've been in the library too, learning about portal glass and how to keep it), and I put it on the floor, the best place to spin it. I got on my hands and knees, and I watched it go.

I wanted to try it before, but when darkness falls on Shadow's End, I'm never alone. Last night, however, I was sure that Death was preoccupied (probably giving himself a blow job for all I know).

The sphere spun and spun, though I could barely see it in the dark. Then it started to glow. It wasn't like the light from a sunmoonstone sphere, rather it was like the glass was becoming visible, illuminated from within.

And in the spinning yellow glass of shimmering rainbows, I saw my father.

Like Bell had warned me, it was only for a few seconds. But those few seconds were enough, for now.

I saw my father's face. He was talking to someone, but I couldn't see who. There was green grass in the background, which was confusing because I thought it was winter back in Finland, but who knows how time is behaving now that I've been in this world.

My father didn't look upset. He wasn't mad. He was in deep conversation and he seemed deeply concerned. That was all I got of him until the sphere stopped spinning. I tried again immediately, got another glimpse of him before the spinning stopped. On my third attempt I couldn't get an image of him at all.

Still, I fell asleep last night feeling heart-warmed. Not just from seeing my father's face again, knowing that he's still alive and well enough, but I thought back to what Death had told me while we laid in the ship's cabin. He had tossed out the idea of having my father live here with us. Now, I'm not sure if that's what he meant or not, but if it was…

It nearly made me cry. I never thought Death would consider it. It was never part of our bargain. But the more time I spend with him, the more our lives start to intertwine for good, I'm starting to think—to hope—that the bargain might not matter anymore.

Maybe *I'm* what's starting to matter.

Naturally, I don't want to get ahead of myself. I know we've gone about everything ass backwards. I was forced to marry a God to fulfil a contract, love was never part of the picture. We didn't even like each other much. And even though love isn't in the picture yet, we've grown closer. Even this morning when I was lying beside him, I felt something strong in my chest, beating against me like wings, trying to get out. It was immense and hot and scary. It was a feeling I'd never had before, not for him, nor for anyone.

Is that what love is? Is it a bird in your chest, trying to break free?

"You ready, Hanna?" the God of Death calls to me from the stairs. More and more he's calling me Hanna. He says my name sometimes like it's a sacred prayer, a spell to be invoked. When we're in the throes of passion, when he's deep inside me, he says it like he's asking me to ascend into the skies to live forever.

"I think so," I tell him. We finished our dinner twenty minutes ago and the guests are feeling pretty good with all the cardamom liquor that's been going around. I've been standing in the main hall with everyone, talking with Tellervo about her absent brother, the hunter, Nyyrikki. That shocked the hell out of me when Tuoni announced that he'd actually consider him to take over the ferryman duties. Judging by the look on Tuonen's face, he'd shocked his son too.

Death appears on the stairs, with his Shadow Self behind him, dressed identically.

"*Vittu Perkele*," Tapio swears from behind me, staring up at the two Deaths. "What is going on here?"

"Magic," Death says, and even though he has his mask on I can hear his arrogant smile. He gestures to himself who then gestures right back to him. If I wasn't so used to seeing them (*feeling them*) together, it would be a total headfuck. "Everyone, may I introduce you to my Shadow Self. He'll be accompanying me to the Bone Match tonight."

Are you sure that's a good idea? Sarvi asks, anxiously swishing its tail.

"Father," Tuonen says in a low voice, "the last time you brought him out, things got a little weird. Are you sure you want to do this?"

"When was the last time he brought him out?" I ask Tuonen.

"It's a long story," Tuonen says tiredly, giving me a dismissive wave like it's a "you had to be there" kind of story. Oh, I'll be getting that one from my husband.

"It's much better this time around," Death says to him, coming over to me. "I found out a way to perfect him. Something I didn't do last time. A magic trick."

I give him a warning look, like *oh my god, please don't tell your guests that your magic trick was that you had to fuck yourself*.

His eyes glitter darkly at me from under the sockets of his mask but he doesn't say anything. He turns to everyone else. "The journey to the city will be fast when we take the passage. Hanna and I will ride at the front on Sarvi. My Shadow Self will be with the rest of you in the carriage. Tuonen will bring up the rear."

I raise my hand slightly. "I have questions. Why am I not in the carriage? Seems like a comfortable, protected place to be."

"You're safest with me," he says gravely. "The wards that guard the passage have never failed us, but I'm not taking any chances. If anything were to happen, if we were to be attacked, everyone in the carriage would be sitting ducks." He looks at the guests. "No offense."

"Oh, none taken," Tapio says through a derisive scoff.

"And why are you taking your double?" Tuonen asks.

Death glances at Kalma, though I can't see his expression. "I need an extra pair of eyes. I have reason to suspect the leaders of the uprising will be at the Bone Match. Your mother might even make an appearance."

I shudder. Oh hell no! Louhi might be there?

"But he's dressed the same as you, people will wonder why there are two of you," Tapio says, pointing at the Shadow Self like he's vermin.

"There are other clothes in the carriages. Just trust me, old man. I know what I'm doing."

At that, we head to the stables. There is a large black carriage pulled by big black horses, Friesians maybe, with long black manes and white eyes. The Forest Gods, Kalma, and the Shadow Self climb inside. Death climbs aboard Sarvi and pulls me up so I'm wedged between his crotch and Sarvi's neck. He's right in this does make me feel safe, but after I fell off Alku and all that shit went down, I'm still a little nervous.

We take off for the passage. Sarvi walks half the time, flies half the time. Between Shadow's End and the Mountains of Vipunen, Sarvi does loops above the convoy, flying high and then back down. Death is silent for most of it, and I know he and Sarvi are scanning the land, but everything seems fine. I don't think we'd be attacked here and now, but I guess being out in the open is different than being inside Shadow's End.

Even if Rasmus did make parts of the castle crumble. If he had that power back then, I can't imagine the kind of power he has right now.

If he's even alive, I remind myself as Sarvi lands and we resume our walk in front of the horses and carriage. Even though he's my brother, I have no way of knowing if he's alive or not, no sixth sense telling me he's out there. Maybe that means he's already been corrupted, no longer the person I knew.

If he's not dead, then he's been taken over by Louhi. I'm starting to understand Death's paranoia now. It's been so quiet these past weeks, with me focused on training, like we're just waiting for the first shoe to drop.

Something tells me it could drop tonight.

"My queen, you're nervous," Death says, his lips at my neck. "I can feel your heart beating."

"I was already nervous," I admit. "Before you told me you were bringing your Shadow Self, before you mentioned that we might be attacked, before you said that *Louhi* might be there. Now I'm petrified."

"There's nothing to be worried about," he says, taking the rim of my ear between his teeth. He runs his hands down across my thighs and starts gathering up the voluminous skirt of my dress.

Not everything can be whisked away through sex, I think.

I beg your pardon? Sarvi asks.

Oh hell.

"I'm just thinking," I tell Sarvi. "Please turn that part of your brain off."

Very well, Sarvi says, sounding relieved.

"I need to know your plan," I say to him, my voice turning husky as his gloved hands find my bare thighs, the cold wind off the mountains giving me gooseflesh.

"I need you to trust me," he says. I hiss in a breath as his fingers slide along me. "Your body does. Always so drenched."

"Trust you?" I ask through a stiff jaw, trying to maintain my composure. We're not in our bedroom, we're on top of a freaking unicorn for goodness sake. "You don't even trust *me*."

"Little by little," he says, gliding his finger inside me until my breath hitches. "One doesn't rush into trust. They earn it, slowly."

I pant. "Seems the only way I can earn your trust is by spreading my legs."

Death chuckles against my skin. Sarvi snorts. Of course, he can hear us when we're talking out loud.

"Fine," Death says, retreating his hand, making me ache for him. "Tell me how I can assuage your fears."

"I wanna know your plan. What will you do if Louhi is there?"

"You have your dagger, right?"

I twist around to stare at him, past the mask and into his eyes. "That's my defense?"

"Vipunen has been training you for a reason," he says. "In your hands, a selenite knife can hurt Louhi. If it came down to it, you could defend yourself again." When I still look shocked, his tone softens. "My dear, I will always be by your side. I won't let anything happen to you. We go in, you're introduced, we watch the match, we leave. Our appearance, together as King and Queen, will hopefully make people think we've united the land."

Sounds a little too easy, but I don't tell him that.

I'm distracted anyway. We've come to Death's Passage, a narrow chasm that cuts through the Mountains of Vipunen, heading straight to the City of Death. The chasm is about thirty feet wide and thousands of feet high. I stare up at the top as we ride through until I feel immense vertigo. Along the top I see tiny dots, which Sarvi informs me are our soldiers. Vipunen has his wards up to give Death and crew safe passage, but it's a failsafe.

I can see why, too. If attackers had overtaken the soldiers at the top and broken through the wards, it would be easy to swoop in and get us. I also understand now why I'm on Sarvi with Death. Sarvi isn't just a mode of transportation that can fly, unlike the horses and carriage. Sarvi is also a weapon in itself. Even though it didn't serve Alku all that well, the unicorn was able to fight with its horn.

It feels like it takes forever through the passage. The wind howls through it, making it sound like crying and wailing. Death says that it's probably coming up from the souls trapped in Inmost, which makes me feel *really* good considering that's where we're going.

When we're finally through the passage—breathing out a huge sigh of relief that nothing happened—the City of Death looms above us. One moment it seems far away and in the next it's stretching up into the sky, disappearing into the cloud cover. Miles wide, the tower reflects the weather, making it look sometimes like it's not there at all. It reminds me of Ilmatar and how she seems to disappear from view.

We ride along an iron path that leads us to the giant gates that glint with silver. I expected it to be a little more gothic, then I remember that every dead person passes through these gates. They'll be pearly to some, flaming to others.

There is a man standing in front of the gate holding a deck of cards.

The Magician.

He is the only one here. The rest of the tower continues along, like a wall that goes on forever, completely devoid of sound or people. For some reason I expected to see a bunch of Bone Stragglers around, causing a ruckus, but there is only desert sand.

The man is covered by a cloak, doesn't say a word.

He steps to the side and the gates open.

I look back at him as we ride past.

His face is the night sky. I see universes in it.

I stare in a mix of awe and horror.

Then he takes the deck of cards he's holding and flashes me the one from the top.

It's the Death card from a Tarot deck.

I hear him laugh, then toss the card behind him. He picks up another card, it's the Death card again. He does this until I can't see him anymore.

We continue inside the gates.

"Uh, that was the Magician, right?" I ask warily.

Death nods. "Yes."

"He flashed me the Death card."

Silence.

"Impossible. He only doles out three cards: Amaranthus, The Golden Mean, and Inmost. And we're going to Inmost."

I go inside my head. *Did you see that, Sarvi? He flashed me the Death card.*

I'm afraid I didn't, Sarvi says. *But Magicians are known for their tricks, aren't they?*

And I am the Goddess of Death. Maybe that was just a way of honoring us.

I try to shake the creepy feeling away. Unfortunately, it only gets worse. Once we're through the gates, we're in a dark, narrow tunnel. There are torches lit along the walls, walls that are made of stone and look scorched, like a fire once raged through here, burning everything.

Well, I am going to Hell. Literally.

And down we go. The tunnel continues to slope, curving slightly until I realize we've been spiraling downwards. My ears pop, something they haven't done since I got to Tuonela, and the smell of garbage and burning hair fills my nose. It's all sorts of awful and I'm glad I ate beforehand because I have zero appetite now.

Finally, Sarvi slows and the tunnel opens up until it looks like we're standing on the top of a huge coliseum, the kind where gladiators fight. And, like those coliseums, the stands are absolutely packed with the world's most wretched human beings. They're all gathered in their seats, the sounds of their excited and depraved voices filling the air.

"Here it is in all its glory," Death says as he gets off Sarvi. He hoists me down, my feet landing in soft goo. I don't even want to know what I stepped in. Save for the torches, this whole place is smelly, dark, slimy, and…*ew*. Ew. I swear I see someone's entrails a couple of feet ahead.

"You'll be fine," Death says to me, putting his arm around my waist to steady me. Yeah. Totally gonna faint, totally don't want to faceplant in guts. "It's a lot to get used to, I'm sure."

"Now what?" I ask, looking around. The Forest Gods come out of the carriage, but the Shadow Self doesn't. Tuonen is already walking away and through an iron door.

"We introduce you to the crowd, we watch the match."

He takes me to a section that overlooks the whole arena. Because this is all underground, it's both a grand sight and claustrophobic, knowing that the blackness above is in fact a ceiling.

I want to sit down on the iron chairs stationed here, still woozy, but Death keeps me up.

"Ladies and Gentlemen," Tuonen's voice booms.

I look down at the ring and see him standing in the middle of it, skeletons holding torches all around him, a vintage looking microphone in his hands. "This is a very special Bone Match we're holding tonight, in that not only are we holding multiple matches, from which the fighters will go on to better lives as Deadhands or Deadmaidens, but that we also get to introduce your new queen." He swings his arm in dramatic flair, gesturing up to me. "Please welcome our new queen, Hanna, the new Goddess of Death."

Ever had thousands and thousands of the worst people

and creatures in the universe look at you all at once? It's quite the feeling. My mouth goes dry, my blood runs cold. I'm scared as hell.

"Am I supposed to say something?" I ask Death out of the side of my mouth. "Should I do the queen wave?"

I put my hand up halfway and wave my wrist, smiling blankly in my Queen Elizabeth impersonation attempt.

"What are you doing?" Death snipes, reaching out and holding my hand. "Say nothing, do nothing. Do not provoke them."

"Gee," I say, trying to keep my face motionless, "you could have told me that before."

Luckily, the Inmost dwellers don't seem all that concerned that I'm here. I mean, they definitely don't love me, but I could think of worse things that could happen, like having body parts thrown in my face like rotten tomatoes.

"Let's get ready to kill!" Tuonen whoops into the microphone in his deep announcer voice. Quite the twist on the usual intro to a fighting match.

But everyone cheers, the whole crowd erupting in a frenzy. I already see people starting to attack each other and they're not even in the ring.

"What the hell is wrong with these people?" I find myself saying.

Death snorts. "Hell *is* what's wrong with them."

Then he reaches inside his cloak and hands me an iron flask. "Frostberry liquor," he says. "You'll probably need it to get through this."

I couldn't be more grateful. Grinning at him, I take the

flask and tip it back into my mouth. It burns, but it promises relief from the guts and gore.

Which is now in full swing. There isn't much to a Bone Match. Being a fighter myself and having had a passing interest in MMA, I assumed that there would be some kind of skill in these fights.

NOPE.

Two awful dead people go into the massive ring, and it's all about fighting to the death. And in this case, if you're an Inmost dweller, who is technically already dead, you can take a beating before you're sucked into Oblivion. Fighters are ripping each other's head off, chopping off limbs, punching holes through skulls, popping out eyeballs, yanking guts out through throats, sawing off penises. It's the most disgusting thing I think I'll ever see. God, I hope I never see anything worse.

Death leaves me for a moment and then comes back with what looks like a bucket of popcorn. He hands it to me.

"Popcorn?" I ask, staring down at it, refusing to take it. I mean, it looks like the movie theatre kind but… "Like fuck I'm going to eat popcorn from this place. It's probably baby bird brains or something."

Now Death looks disgusted, staring down at it with a raised brow. "Thanks for that image. I brought this from Shadow's End, it was in the carriage."

He ends up tossing the bucket over his shoulder. In seconds the ground behind us is filled with the sound of skittering bodies, like giant insects I never want to see.

I shudder and lean into Death, wanting to leave but

not wanting to be a wimp about all this. I'm the Goddess of Death, but I don't think time in Hell is meant for me.

I sigh, putting my head on his shoulder.

He stiffens.

Rude. Are we supposed to keep up some kind of decorum? In *this* place?

I straighten up and look at Death.

But it's not him at all.

CROWN OF CRIMSON

CHAPTER TWENTY-FIVE

HANNA

"THE SHOWDOWN"

I stare at him, mouth open.

"You're not him," I say.

He doesn't say anything for a moment. "Of course I am."

"No, you're not," I say. "You're the Shadow Self."

"Which is still me."

"How long have you been this way? When did you switch?"

"When you weren't looking."

I glance around. Some people are looking at us and whispering to each other, but for appearances sake, he looks no different. No one would know it's his Shadow Self. Except for me, of course. Now that I'm clued into it, I can tell. He smells different. No sea spray and cozy fire. No, now he smells a bit herbal and sulphurous. It's not a bad smell, but it's not my Tuoni.

"Why did you switch?" I ask.

He slowly takes off a glove before putting it back on. "I thought we would give them a show."

My brows go up. "You're going to fake the prophecy?"

"That's right. Politics is all smoke and mirrors, little bird. After this round, we'll stand up, Tuonen will call attention to us, and we'll put on a show. I'll touch you with my bare hands, you won't die, and they will all know that the uprising, Louhi, and the Old Gods won't win. Game over for them."

It feels so disingenuous but at the same time…*genius*.

"Was this your plan all along?" I ask, a little in awe of his thinking.

"Part of it," he says. Then he turns his attention back to the match just in time to see someone's arm get chopped off. The opponent then picks up the arm and uses it as a weapon.

I watch the gruesome yet comical scene for a few moments, then I look back to the Shadow Self.

"Tuoni," I say in a low voice. "Where are you right now?"

"Here."

"And where else?"

"I'm in the dungeon."

I frown. "Why are you in the dungeon? The dungeon where? In Inmost?"

"Yes," he says, his voice sounding faint. "There is a dungeon underneath the ring. It's where the opponents wait before they go up to the ring to fight, and where they go when they come out of the ring."

"Why are you there?"

"I want to see who is worthy of joining my army."

Makes sense. He did say that was part of the bigger picture.

"I also want to hear what they're talking about. If anyone is part of the uprising."

"Don't they recognize you?"

"They can't. I've cloaked myself."

"You have an invisibility cloak?" No way!

"No. That's just what it's called. Cloaking. I can use magic to prevent others from seeing me."

"Would it work on me?"

"I haven't a clue. You're part Goddess, so maybe not. Why? Are you getting ideas?"

I bite my lip. "Maybe."

He falls silent. I expect him to laugh at that or come up with some kind of sexual comment. Even grunt. But he doesn't say anything, doesn't move, doesn't breathe.

"Tuoni?" I ask. I lean over to peer at him closely. His eyes are completely white. I know they do that sometimes when he's trying to access both bodies at once but, even so, it's giving me the creeps. My scalp prickles. "Death?" I repeat.

"We need to leave," he says.

Fuck.

"Now?"

He nods, getting to his feet and pulling me up with him. I look around for Kalma and Sarvi, so they can follow us, but I don't see them anywhere. Below us the Forest Gods are intently watching the match, and Tuonen is still down in the arena.

Death pulls me along, the crowd parting for us, chattering to each other in awe and scorn.

"Where are we going?" I hiss at him. "Aren't we going to show them the prophecy thing?"

He doesn't say anything, but his grip grows stronger. Tighter. To the point where it feels like my bones are being crushed.

"Ow," I whisper harshly to him, trying to pull out of his grasp to no avail. "You're *hurting* me."

I know my husband likes things rough and I'm usually game for that too, but if I ever tell him to stop, he stops. He's not a monster, at least not to me (ignoring the oubliette thing, which I will be reminding him of for the rest of eternity), and he does respect me more than he probably cares to admit.

So when his Shadow Self doesn't let up, even when I tell him once again that he's hurting me, that's when my skin crawls, pins and needles washing over my entire body, my gut twisting with panic.

Something is fucking *wrong*.

The Shadow Self brings me around a corner, away from the crowd. There is nothing but a dark hallway cut into the earth. A lone torch is on the wall further down, giving off little light, enough to illuminate the creature propped up against the wall. It's like if a person and a spider had a horrible love child, and it's hunched over with its hairy back to me, a row of black eyeballs down the spine. It's eating something that whines like a baby, tearing into it with wet snapping sounds and savagery, and I think I see what looks like a tiny human foot fall from its mouth to the ground with a splatter.

The sight is so gruesome, so horrific, that I nearly forget what's happening.

I reach for my knife, cursing myself for having to wear such a voluminous dress, and pull it out of the holster just as Death's Shadow Self spins me around, pressing me up against the slimy wall.

He grabs my wrists with one hand, pinning them above me, forcing me to drop the knife where it clatters to the stone ground. I hold my breath, knowing how fragile the crystal is when it's not in my possession, but it doesn't break.

The Shadow Self lets out a triumphant grunt and starts undoing his pants.

But this isn't him, this isn't him.

He is no longer in control of his Shadow Self.

I don't know who this is.

"Who are you?" I manage to say. "What do you want?"

His eyes glitter menacingly beneath the mask. "I want you, Hanna dear," he says smoothly. "So precious. So pure." His voice turns ugly, mocking. "Such a rare jewel you are, pale and fragile and untainted by the horrors of this land. You think you're better than us. You think you're better than me."

It's Death's voice, and yet it's not.

It would take someone with great power to take over his Shadow Self, because to do so they'd have to get past Death himself.

Who—or what—did he find in the dungeon?

"What did you do to him?" I whisper, horror running through me. "What did you do to Death?"

"Same thing I'm going to do to you, you insignificant

human," he says, voice dripping with acid. "But first I'm going to show you what true humiliation is. If Tuoni wasn't already Dead, he'd never want to touch you again, you worthless, tainted whore."

He takes his cock out from his pants, starts lifting up my skirts.

Oh Jesus. Oh no.

No.

I have to break free. I have to get my knife.

"Struggle all you want, bitch," he hisses at me. "I prefer it when you bleed."

Tuoni says a lot of dirty stuff, but he would never call me a bitch.

"When I'm done making you ugly, I'm going to take that pathetic knife of yours and fuck you with it, push it so far inside you that it comes out your throat. Slice off your tongue. See how you like it for a change."

I gasp internally, my eyes shocked wide.

Louhi!

This is fucking *Louhi*!

My heart drops out of my chest, freefalling.

I am so fucking screwed.

I'm dead.

And, apparently, so is my husband.

She murdered my Tuoni.

Rage rises inside me, pushing aside the pity for myself, the sadness, the defeat.

She's not going to fucking win.

I won't let her.

She's trying to rape me first, but I won't even let her get that far.

I've been caught in this position before in many of my classes, and I've learned when and how to get away.

I start to haul my knees up, hoping to get them to my chest so I can push out. Usually when a male opponent has you in a lock, your first move is to get them in the groin, which is difficult because every male instinctively protects himself there.

But a female hasn't learned the hardship of being kneed in the groin.

In the Shadow Self's body, Louhi barely moves—I doubt she'd move even if she were in her own body—and she doesn't know how Tuoni's body operates.

I get her in the dick. *Hard.*

In the back of my head there is a faint satisfaction of getting payback for the oubliette thing, but then I'm focusing on the now and springing into action.

Louhi yelps in agony and lets go of me, distracted by pain for just a second, but it's enough time for me to roll out of the way, pick up the knife, and get into the *ginga* pose, moving back and forth, crouched low, figuring how to strike. I'm also still aware there's a deformed spider person behind me eating a baby, but hell, I think at the moment I'd rather be fighting it than Louhi.

Don't say that, I think to myself. *You want to fight her. You want to defeat her again.*

"You bitch," she snarls at me in Death's voice. She reaches up and rips the mask off her face and I flinch, because it might be the last time I look at my husband's face. How fucking beautiful he is, even when it's not him inside.

She comes for me, fast.

Fuck! She knew it would distract me if she took off the mask.

She tackles me against the wall and the impact makes bricks fall, and the torch topples to the stones, lighting the ground on fire as if it's been doused in gasoline. The wind is knocked out of me and I can't get a single breath in.

"You whore," she says, Death's hand going over my throat and squeezing hard, the other hand pressing my wrist against the wall. The fire is now racing toward us, and I have to wonder why everything is so flammable, but then I realize—*hahahaha*—I'm in *Hell*.

And I'm going to die here too if I don't do something.

Problem is my neck is about to be snapped in two, I can't breathe, my vision is going fuzzy, and there's not a fucking thing I can do about. The selenite knife is still in my hand, to the point where it feels fused to my skin, but there is no way I can stab her from here.

The fire is now licking at our feet. I always wear boots under my dresses because apparently I'll never be a real lady, and I believe that true queens wear shitkicker boots, but even so I have a few seconds before the leather starts to melt.

So I do what I can.

Using some waiting energy from my core, something I've accessed before, I put my training to use and envision what needs to be done.

Then I do it.

Pick up the sword and try again.

I flick my wrist with all my strength and watch as the dagger goes soaring through the air toward the opposite wall.

Right before it collides with the stone, it flips around like a boomerang on steroids and comes sailing right back to me.

Or, should I say, sailing right into Louhi's back.

Even though Death's Shadow Self was wearing the same outfit as Death, including a type of suit and heavy leather cloak, the selenite knife pierces through the material with ease, sinking through into his muscles.

He roars and it sounds more like Louhi's high-pitched ghoulish scream than anything. I drop to the ground, jump out of the way of the flames, then twirl around, doing a dance that unfortunately puts me right back into the flames again.

I pluck the knife from the Shadow Self's back and Louhi screams again.

Then I stab her in the side, under the ribs.

Then the back of her head.

Then the base of the spine, severing the spinal cord.

The whole time I feel like a madwoman because I really have to go to another place in order to get this done. I have to make sure she's dead as can be before I try to find where Death really is. But each time the knife cuts into him, I think I'm giving myself trauma that I'll be unpacking for a really long time.

I'm stabbing the love of my life to death.

The realization, the big one, the deep one—*love*—makes me want to cry.

But there's no time for tears. The fire is climbing my body

now, my dress going up in flames, but for some reason isn't burning my skin. I can't dwell on it; anything goes at this point.

Death's Shadow Self finally collapses to the ground, Louhi letting out a haunting scream. It finally catches the interest of the spider person, who is now perched on the wall to avoid the fire, bony spider-leg hands and feet stuck in the cracks. It starts moving fast toward the body, sideways on the wall, in a way that's so disturbingly familiar, like I've seen it recently but I can't place it.

I get out of the way, the spider person more interested in eating the Shadow Self's body than mine. Death turns his head to look at me with pleading eyes.

"How could you do this to me? Hanna?"

The anguish and sincerity in his voice nearly makes me fall to the ground.

His eyes twinkle, beautiful gray, as the life is drained from him.

The life I took.

But no, no, it's not him.

It's still Louhi. She's somewhere else though, somewhere safe, controlling him from there. His eyes close and he goes still, black blood spilling out around him, making the flames leap even higher. Death isn't inside the body anymore. Neither is Louhi.

I turn and run.

My dress is half-burned off and my shoes melted away, but because the spider person is still staring at the body, debating if it should take a bite, and I know fire can't hurt me,

I run in the opposite direction we came from. I need to find the dungeon.

I keep running, bare feet slapping the dirty ground, passing by rooms that hold sights I wish I could scrub from my brain—humans and creatures in all levels of deformity, depravity, and anguish. No wonder they want to be Deadhands so badly, anything to escape Inmost.

I keep going, the passageway starting to slope down, so I know I'm on the right track. Or possibly going to an even worse place. When you're in Hell, the last thing you want to do is go down.

Finally, the passageway starts to fill with the sound of voices, cheering and booing, and I know I must be close to the ring.

Hope leaps in my heart. Maybe Death got knocked out somehow, maybe his cloaking magic got him in trouble, maybe it made it hard to maintain connection in his Shadow Self's body.

Maybe he's alive.

He's the God of Death, King of the Underworld. He can't die.

But he can, I remind myself. Another God can do it.

Louhi probably reached him first.

I try not to think about it, running along still, going past jail cells full of Inmost dwellers chained up, past holding rooms where they practice fighting. They all look at me when I pass but I don't want to ask them where Death is. Even though they're all trying to become his soldiers, I know they all want Death out of the picture. They're the ones in Hell, who don't believe *they* belong here. They want to punish the God that put them here, even though they did this to themselves.

And by default, they hate me too. I'm a Goddess and their queen.

Fuck. I probably shouldn't be here or I'm going to get thrown in the ring too.

But that fear doesn't stop me from going forward, trying to find my husband.

I'm near the last cell, one where the iron door is open just a crack, when suddenly I feel a burst of energy at my back. It makes me freeze, total and complete terror taking over every cell in my body.

"Stop," a voice says behind me.

The most familiar voice in the world.

A female voice.

My voice.

Oh *shit*.

No. No. NO.

I try to swallow.

Can't.

Try to breathe.

Can't.

The only thing that seems to be working is my heart, which is going to punch a hole through my chest.

"Turn around," the voice says.

And I find myself moving even though I don't want to, even though it feels like it will break my bones.

I turn around to face myself.

I'm standing ten feet away.

Wearing a dress that looks similar to the one I had on, the one that hangs in tatters on my body.

Everything is the same.

It's my twin.

She doesn't smile.

But I'm not smiling either.

I grip the selenite knife in my hand.

Oh, now she looks a little amused.

"We finally meet," she says, staying where she is, her posture mimicking mine. "I've been waiting a very long time for this. Twenty-four years."

I can finally swallow. It's painful, feeling bruised from where Louhi choked me.

"What is your name?" I ask her, sounding raw.

"Salainen," she says simply, tossing her hair over her shoulder. It's then that I notice we're not *exactly* the same. My eyes are lush brown. Hers are black, and when she speaks I see that her incisors are little too sharp. She has a scarf around her neck, and I get the feeling she's covering something up.

"I've been waiting to meet you, too," I say.

Oh god, please have courage.

She lets out an acidic laugh. "No. You haven't. You've only heard about me recently, only been in this land for a short while. Me? I've been here since the day our father discarded me."

It kicks me in the gut because I have a feeling it's true.

"I don't know what my father did but—" I start to say, but suddenly she's behind me, so fast that she has her arms around me, holding my back against her chest, her hand over my mouth, immovable.

"*Our* father," she snipes through a raspy breath right into my ear. Underneath her voice is another layer, like it's the *real* her, and it's utterly inhuman. "He is *our* father. Not just yours. And he betrayed me. He created me out of nothing just to fool that woman you called your mother."

I try to speak. Try to tell her I don't understand. But I can't.

She goes on, voice deepening, her grip on me growing harder. "Do you know what it felt like to be abandoned the way that I was? To be created for the sake of being tossed aside to the wolves, left for literally dead? He got your Goddess mother pregnant and didn't know what to do about the baby. He knew about the prophecy, and she thought it would be safest if the baby was raised in the Upper World, with him and his then wife. Yes, our father was involved with a Goddess while married. What a man. Not to mention already being with Louhi, having Rasmus. So, our father, decided the only way to raise you and not lose his marriage was to get his wife pregnant and switch the babies out at birth."

I swallow hard. The things that Tuoni told me about what he saw in my book are starting to make sense, but I can't believe it at the same time. How could my father do that to my mother?

"He got her pregnant using Shadow Magic. He conjured me using parts of himself, wishing for me to be identical to you. I grew in your *mother's* belly, I remember all of it, being trapped in there, waiting to be free. You grew in the Goddess' belly. We were both taken away at birth. Our father took you from Tuonela and brought you to the Upper World. Then he took me from the Upper World and left me in Tuonela. Just rang the ferryman's bell and left. I'll always be grateful that it was Loviatar that found me, brought me to Louhi. The discarded child of Torben. Louhi gave me a home. Now she's given Rasmus a home. We are the prophecy."

I'm having a hard time understanding any of this, but it doesn't matter right now. She could be telling the truth, she could be lying. All that I know is that she's the Kaaos bringer and she views Louhi as her mother and that's enough for me to know that I've got to destroy her.

I flick my knife, feeling power surge through me.

The knife goes flying in the air, then heads back toward me.

But instead of stabbing Salainen, it pauses, as if confused.

By the time it figures it out, Salainen has moved out of the way, taking me with her as we topple to the ground, and the knife goes into the wall, stuck there.

I reach out, waving my hand around, trying to conjure the energy back. The knife starts to shake but, before I can get it to come to me, Salainen is picking me up and throwing me in a cell.

I go flying through the air, landing on the cold damp ground with a thud that makes me think I've broken a few bones.

"Fuck," I groan through the pain, feeling a strange wash of embarrassment. How was I able to fight off Louhi in Death's body and yet, when fighting my own fucking self, she's tossing me around like a sack of potatoes?

Black magic *bullshit*.

I growl at my father for creating such a beast and then I'm trying to get to my feet and go after Salainen who is at the door, watching me with those frozen black eyes.

It's then that I notice I'm not alone in the cell.

Don't look, I tell myself. *Don't look. Get up and fight. Pick up the sword and try again. Don't look, don't look.*

But then I smell ocean salt and bonfires on the beach and I practically disintegrate.

Death.

I look behind me and see him there.

The real him.

Lying on his back, not moving.

I start to shake. I don't know what to do. Do I go to him? Do I fight my shadow twin?

I choose him. Crawl over to his body, needing him to be alive and yet not seeing a single breath come from him, not a pulse from his heart. Even his energy is cold, like it's been turned off. It's vacant. Gone.

"No," I whisper. I pick up his gloved hand in mine. "No."

It's all over.

"Welcome to your new existence, Hanna Heikkinen," Salainen says to me coolly. "You may have come from a Goddess, but you were discarded and unwanted as much as I was. At least here, in the bowels of Inmost where you belong, you can still be with your king. Me, however, I will be out there with the new king. No one will know the difference, except maybe his family and advisors, but they should all be in Oblivion by now anyway. Rasmus won't leave anything to chance."

She pauses. "The moment I shut this door is the moment that Kaaos will reign. The afterlife will never be the same again."

"You won't win!" I yell at her, fury flowing through me. "You won't! They won't listen to you alone, believe me they won't, and Death's Shadow Self is dead. A spider thing has probably eaten him by now. You, Louhi, Rasmus, you won't be able to use the body, you can't impersonate him."

"That's what you think. Shows how foolish you are." She finally smiles, showing those fangs. My heart sinks. Silly of me to assume a body made from spells and shadows, conjured from nothing, could be easily destroyed.

"Enjoy an eternity with your dead God," she says. "He was especially fun to kill."

CHAPTER TWENTY-SIX

HANNA

"THE DEATH"

Salainen slams the iron door in my face, the sound of multiple locks, no doubt bound by dark magic, sealing it shut. The sound is finite and cold in this dark place, and I have no energy to run for the door and pound on it for help, demanding that my shadow twin release us.

Because there is no hope.

Not for me.

Not for Death.

Because Death is dead.

The thought hits me so hard that I can't even take a breath, my lungs seizing. All the adrenaline has left my body, now plunging me into a despair that I'm not sure I can crawl out of.

I twist around to face him, even though I can't see him in the pitch black, my hand gripping his gloved hand tightly, so tight that if he were alive I know I'd be causing him pain with my newfound strength.

I wish there was even a speck of light in here, but when you're miles underground, it's not easy to come by. And to think this might be where I'll spend eternity. In literal Hell.

What will become of me down here? Will Salainen ever come back, perhaps with Louhi in tow? Will the two of them torture me for the rest of time? Or will I be left here to rot alongside Death, until I finally die of thirst or starvation or madness? Will the tunnels of Inmost be where I end up, or will it be Oblivion?

Where is Death now? Could he somehow be alive? I wish I could see his face, just one last time. The last time I saw it, that didn't count. I know his energy usually speaks to mine, our atoms collide with lightning when we're mere inches away, but now, in pure death, there is nothing at all. Just this emptiness, like he never existed at all. I'm holding onto him and, with each passing second, I fear that he'll turn to sand between my fingers.

I want to see him before he goes. I need to see him. One more time, one more time. Then I remember the sunmoonstone sphere. I had put it in my thigh holster with my dagger. My dagger might be gone, but perhaps the sphere isn't.

I reach down and feel for the edge of my dress, hiking up the ruined rags and run my hands to my inner thigh. My holster is gone. It must have snapped off when I was thrown in the cell.

I get on my knees and start crawling around on the floor

of the cell, the damp dirt and rocks cutting into my shins. I know I could be reaching blindly for horrible insects and other creatures that thrive in this hellscape, pinchers and claws and slimy legs waiting for a taste of my hand. The thought makes me want to be sick but I keep going until my fingers curl around the familiar feel of leather.

I snatch it toward me, fumbling over the sheath where my knife was, and then, with a burst of relief, feel the hard round shape inside. I push the sphere out of the leather until I feel its cool weight in my hand and immediately make a fist over it, holding it tighter and tighter until the crystal begins to warm.

Like magic, because it is magic, light starts to seep through my fingers, slowly illuminating my hand, my arm, the space, with the softest, ethereal glow.

I turn around to see Death.

I gasp, nearly dropping the stone.

He's still lying there on his back, looking like he's asleep, but it's the absolute stillness that accompanies him that makes my heart feel like it's being ripped to shreds. Despite being the God of Death, Tuoni has always felt filled with life, like he's bursting at the seams with it. It's in his eyes, it's in what he says, the way he laughs, the way he fucks, the way he sees the world. He's just so undeniably a fucking *God*, that it has seemed impossible that anyone could take that away from him.

And yet here he is, lying before me, eyes closed, his dark hair spilled around his shoulders, his skull mask knocked off somewhere. I don't know what Salainen did to him, but whatever it is, it appears to have worked.

The third part of the Prophecy of Three.

The one to defeat Death.

And I never found out my own role in it. I was supposed to be the one that Death could touch, the one to help unite the realm, but Death and I were too scared to put it to the test, to find out the truth. If I had let him touch me earlier with his bare hands, all of this could have been avoided.

Yeah, if you were the one he could touch. If you were wrong, you'd be in Oblivion. It was a risk you didn't want to take.

I stare down at Death and feel the hot press of tears behind my eyes. What fucking difference does it make now? In the end, the risk was too great, because I am here but he's not.

"Where are you?" I whisper to him, my voice sounding like a child in the dark cold depths of the cell. I place the stone on the ground beside me, then put my palm against his cheek, the angles of his face harsh in the shadows.

He's not cold yet, but he's no longer warm.

There is no life beneath my fingertips.

Nothing at all.

Tears fall from my eyes, landing on him like rain. I brush my fingers over his face, tracing his features—his firm brows that seem to frown even in death, his broad forehead, his sharp cheekbones, his strong nose, those impossibly soft and full lips, lips that know my body better than I do.

I wish more than anything I could go back in time. How funny that death repeats. When I thought my father had died, all I wanted was a time machine to see him again, to step back into the past and grab hold and spend every moment appreciating him and soaking him in.

Now I want to do the same with Tuoni. I want to go back to this morning, when we were in bed together and though the future seemed scary and uncertain, he was alive. He was alive and I didn't appreciate it because I was too scared of what I felt for him. I want to go back to the moments when I was lying with him under the sheets, and I wish I could have just turned off my brain for a moment, ignored the fear, and told him how I really felt.

That I loved him.

That I *love* him.

My husband.

My king.

I should have said it, but I didn't even know it this morning because I didn't allow myself to feel it. I always felt that I could negotiate this new life, that I could rise above what I've been thrust into, so long as I didn't let my feelings and emotions come into play. I could do the role of the Goddess of Death, I could be married to Death, as long as I knew I was pretending, that I was staying strong and true on the inside. I wanted so badly to be made of stone that I really believed I was.

But I wasn't. I'm not.

It was just a lie that I told myself.

I am in love with Death.

My husband.

My God.

An immortal God who should have never been able to die.

Fuck.

A raw sob escapes me and the tears now pour like a waterfall. I collapse onto his body, pressing my ear against his chest, hoping I can hear a heartbeat, even if faint, but there's nothing, nothing at all. Each moment that passes contains the singular realization that he's never coming back.

"No," I cry out. My fingers wrap around his leather vest, the shirt underneath, and I'm pulling it off, undressing him until I see his skin, feel it beneath my touch. He's growing colder.

I press my lips to his collarbone, his chest, tasting his skin and then I pull back to look him over. He's a fully bronzed color, like he's spent all his life under the sun instead of the exact opposite. There's not a single line of silver on him. No more runes, no more traces of the dead that have gone before him.

No sign at all that he was a God.

I sit back and stare, having never seen him like this.

He almost looks human.

Mortal.

Is this what he is now? A fallen God becomes a fallen mortal?

"I love you," I whisper to him, barely able to speak. My throat feels like it's closing up, choking on tears. "I should have told you that I loved you, but I didn't know. I didn't want to know. I was so afraid. Afraid what loving you would mean. I shouldn't have been afraid, Tuoni. I don't want to be afraid anymore. Fear is…" I close my eyes, trying to breathe through the pain, "Fear is the real death. It's what keeps us from living. I should have been fully alive with you."

Despite the urgency in my words, the love in them, the honesty, the room remains quiet. I don't even hear the rest of the Inmost. It's like we're the only two people left in Hell. I have to wonder if that's true. If Salainen and Death's Shadow Self go on to impersonate me and Death, then they could turn this City on its head. They could imprison those in Amaranthus down here, they could let the Inmost dwellers have control of the Golden Mean. They could raise the Old Gods, cut open a hole to Kaaos, and let all of Tuonela destroy itself.

I feel like I'm in the last scene of a horror movie, when all the world outside is crumbling, monsters running amok, and I'm one of the last sane people alive, locked away in an asylum. God, I hope that's not happening out there.

But then again, what does it matter if I'm going to die?

It matters because of your father, a voice inside my head says. *It matters because when he dies, he won't have Death to guide him to where he belongs. He will be in Hell along with everyone else.*

"And what the fuck am I supposed to do about it?" I growl. I'm trapped here, with my dead husband. If the God of Death can die, there is no hope for me, no hope for anyone.

And yet...and yet...

I find myself reaching down for Death's hand, sheathed in leather. I grip his mid-forearm, just where the glove ends, and hold his hand up. It's heavy as a log and limp in my grasp.

I reach for the tips of his fingers and then gather the leather in-between mine, slowly pulling the glove off until his hand is bare.

I stare at it, gawking, his bare hand in the soft glow of the sunmoonstone. How large and strong and beautiful it is. How bare it is without the crisscrossing runes.

If he is dead, then he no longer has the touch of death.

And if I am wrong, I will find out soon.

Oblivion might be a better Hell than this.

I bring his hand toward me, still holding him by his forearm.

A single tear rolls down my cheek.

I suck in my breath.

Before I lose my nerve, I press his bare palm against my cheek, placing my other hand over it to hold him in place.

Nothing happens.

There's no sensation but cold.

I press his palm harder against my cheek, feeling how terribly soft his skin is, wishing upon wishing that I could have done this while he was alive.

And still, there is nothing.

He does not stir and I am still here.

My eyes flutter closed and I cry. Just holding him, holding on. I don't know what I thought would happen, and I still don't know if I'm able to touch him like this because he's dead or because I'm the prophesized one, but I hold him close just the same.

I don't know how long I must sit there crying, letting my tears spill over his fingers as I hold his hand to my face, but it feels like the room is getting brighter somehow.

I open my eyes, surprised to see the sphere glowing brighter and brighter, the light still soft and glowing, but with growing intensity. Soon the brightness eclipses the sphere, so that it's no longer visible, and the dirt floor turns from black to white. Rays of golden light start spreading across the cell, eradicating everything until the only things visible are me and Death.

I keep his hand pressed to my face and look around us. It's like we're no longer in a room at all, just a place of light that stretches on forever. And yet there's nothing scary about this place. It's comforting. It feels…like home.

I'm dead. I must be dead. But this can't be Oblivion…

Death's fingertips suddenly press into my skin.

I gasp and gape down at him.

His eyelids are fluttering.

Oh my god!

"This can't be real," I whisper.

"You're telling me," he says, his eyes focused on his bare hand, the way he's touching my skin. "How am I able to do this?"

I shake my head. "I don't know. Are we dead?"

He gives me a soft smile. "Does it matter?"

I smile back. It honestly doesn't. If this is death, if it's us together in a peaceful light, then I don't know what there's ever been to fear. Maybe this is the true death, one that lies beyond the city and the stars. Maybe this is the death for Gods.

"You're alive," I say, a tear spilling down my cheek. A tear of happiness, of relief.

"Maybe," he says. "I don't remember much, I was just not here and….now here I am." He frowns, trying to recall. "But I know what happened to me."

"I'm so sorry," I tell him. "I failed. I wasn't able to stop—"

"Shhh," he says, placing a gloved finger against my lips. Then he frowns and rips the glove off, tossing it away until it disappears into the light. He runs his bare thumb over my lips, his eyes glittering with satisfaction. "Always wanted to do that."

"You can do more than that," I tell him. I climb on top of him, straddling him, pulling the burnt dress off until I'm naked. He doesn't ask questions about why it's burnt; in fact, he doesn't say much at all. I think now, in this existence, there isn't much to say anymore.

We only have to *be*.

And we want to be with each other.

Like someone kept in the dark who sees the light for the first time, Tuoni runs his bare hands all over my body. Slowly, tenderly, soaking in every inch of me. He does this like he's memorizing each section of skin so he can recall it later.

"This is more than Amaranthus," he whispers to me, voice low and full of awe. "This is something I never thought was possible. The greatest gift."

"But are we really dead?" I ask again as he runs his hands over my breasts, focusing now on giving me pleasure.

"Does it really matter?" he repeats, giving me a wicked grin before sliding his fingers between my thighs. "Fuck me, Hanna," he says gently. "My wife."

He doesn't have to ask me twice. Even though we're lying in this white glowing space of nothing, I undo his pants, finding him hard, and glide him inside me.

I moan, gasp, move my hips on top of him, finding a slow

and gentle rhythm.

"I love you," I say quietly, the words feeling like raindrops in the desert. "I know we might be dead, but I had to tell you that I love you."

He doesn't say anything for a moment, but I don't care. He doesn't love easily. I have to earn it. I didn't get a chance to while I was alive, but he earned my love. And love is love. As long as it's there, that's all that matters. Sometimes I think it's a miracle that we're even given a chance to love at all.

"I heard you, before," he says eventually.

I laugh as he thrusts up into me, his beautiful bare hands holding onto my hips. "You could have woken up sooner."

"I was waiting," he says. "To see what you would become."

"What do you mean?" I glance down at him through my hair that's fallen over on my face. "Were you not dead?"

"I was dead. You brought me back to life."

His grip on my hip tightens, moving me back and forth.

"Fuck me," he says again. "Let yourself feel, little bird. Spread your wings."

I close my eyes to the encompassing light and throw my head back, letting myself feel everything as I grind down onto him, moving together in synchrony. It feels like we are one, that we are melding into each other, fusing into each other's skin, and I honestly can't say where we are separate.

And in all the shallow breaths, in our hearts which I know are beating in sync, in this melding of the bodies, of the souls, there's a heat inside me that's building. It's not the sexual heat—that's been simmering for a while—but it's something else. Something pure and bright and powerful. I felt it before, though I can't place when, and when I try to pinpoint it, it shifts.

It moves from my stomach to my chest, then to my back where my shoulder blades are. And while this heat is coursing through me, Death is pistoning up into me and I'm riding him and I'm lost to the reality of us together again, even if it's not much of a reality at all.

"Tuoni," I say through a shaking breath. My eyes are still closed and yet they feel open at the same time, like the light from outside is coming through my eyelids and this, *this*, is my real sight.

I come, both soft and hard, swept away in an undertow before being thrown into the sky. And while I'm crying out, crying for my God, my husband, my love, I feel wings sprout from my back. Golden wings that propel me through the heavens, right onto the surface of the sun.

"Hanna," Death says in fervent awe, coming slowly. "Hanna, look at yourself."

I open my eyes.

Everything is brighter.

I'm brighter.

Just as it was when I saw Vipunen, I am shining like I've swallowed the sun and the rays are shining through me.

"What?" I manage to say. "What's happening?"

"You've grown your wings, little bird." His expression is both dazed and triumphant.

I curl my back forward and a giant pair of gold wings curve over me, sparkling in the incessant light.

I stare at the tips, watching as Tuoni reaches up and tugs

on the ends of the shiny metallic feathers.

I gasp.

I felt that.

It was as if he were tugging on my arm.

What the fuck?

"I don't understand," I say, shaking my head, staring at them. I can move them up and down, back and forth. "I don't understand. Why do I have fucking wings?"

I pause, looking down at him. "Am I an angel?"

I don't mean to sound horrified, but I do.

He laughs. "No. You're definitely no angel, fairy girl."

And then the light that we're currently in starts to fade, slowly, like someone taking down a dimmer switch. It fades and fades until the darkness starts to infiltrate and I can see where we are.

Back in the cell in the dungeons of Inmost.

Lit only by a sunmoonstone sphere.

My wings are gone.

I guess they retreated or faded the same time the light did. One minute they were here, glinting and glorious, and the next they disappeared back inside my shoulders, along with that heat I had inside me.

Reality comes crashing down.

We didn't die.

And Tuoni is alive.

But the golden peace is gone and we are stuck in Hell.

I stare down at him. His hand is still on my thigh.

I have not died.

He can still touch me.

"I am the prophecy," I whisper. "I am the one to unite the land with you."

"You know who else you are?" he says to me.

"Who?" I ask, leaning forward on him. He reaches up, running his fingers over my face, making my eyelids flutter.

"You're Hanna Heikkinen," he says. "Fairy girl, little bird. And Daughter of the Sun."

Daughter of the Sun.

THE END...ISH

Hanna and Death's story will continue in Underworld Gods Book #3, coming 2022.
Please visit me on Instagram for updates (@authorhalle)

EXCERPT FROM THE NOVELLA GOD OF DEATH

GOD OF DEATH
An Underworld Gods Novella (#0.5)

Death:
The Grim Reaper.
The Destructor.
Darkness personified.

There are countless phrases and words to describe Death, but none matter much to Tuoni, God of Death and Tuonela, the Underworld. He's got his hands full, trying to keep his errant family in line while lording over the unruly dead in a dark and fantastical land.

But even all-powerful Gods have enemies, and Death will have to rely on his quick wits and merciless drive to reclaim his throne as life's ultimate villain, even if it means sacrificing those closest to him.

God of Death is a prequel to River of Shadows, an adult dark fantasy romance based on Finnish Mythology. Though it is set before River of Shadows, it can be read before or after the book as added insight into the Underworld and the character of Death.

PROLOGUE
AGES AGO

The boy awoke in immense pain. Every carved pewter line on his body felt like it had been laced with burning acid, as if the rune tattoos themselves were trying to poison him through his skin. Though the boy had never feared death, this was the first time he felt the totality of raw fear. What if the pain didn't stop?

With his eyes still shut, he wailed, his voice echoing in the cave, and rolled over on his side. The ground was hard and cold and smelled like iron. Perhaps blood. He wanted to rip his skin right off and his hands were shaking, as if possessed by a mind of their own.

The burning was too much to take. The boy dug his sharp nails into his skin, shredding through flesh and spilling black blood, using more pain, controlled pain, in an attempt to stop the agony. But still the runes burned and he could only scream, his skin hanging in tatters from his nails.

"Ukko!" he cried out helplessly. "Akka!"

But his father and mother were nowhere to be found. It was just him, Tuoni, the young God of Death, wishing for once that he could die.

His eyes opened to the black void in front of him. Was he in Oblivion? Was this his fate for eternity?

But his sight adjusted and through the darkness he could make out a faint sickly green light in the distance that slowly showcased the slick and grimy rock walls, and with another stab of fear, Tuoni realized what had happened to him.

It was his God's Day today, a milestone for the day he was born. He had always known that at some point in time, during the stage of his life where he wasn't quite a boy anymore and not yet a man, that he would be sent to Tuonela, the Realm of the Dead, where he would fulfill his destiny as the God of Death. Tuonela had always existed, ever since the Creator made the worlds, since the dead needed a place to go, but it was a land of chaos, with more and more dead added each and every year, and suffering ensued. The Creator didn't want his creations to suffer, especially as some of them lived good and honest lives, so they told Ukka that one of his children would be born as the God of Death to watch over the land and keep order in the afterlife.

Ukka, a great and powerful God (though no one would ever be as great and powerful as the Creator), and his Goddess wife Akka, had two children—Ahto, God of the Sea, Ilmatar, Goddess of the Sky—before the youngest, Tuoni, was born.

He made quite the arrival.

The first person that Tuoni had contact with, the Birthmaiden that delivered him, died instantly the moment she touched him. He was screaming, flailing at the horror of being born in the dead woman's arms, as his parents looked over the body in shock. Ukko quickly wrapped the writhing Tuoni in a reindeer pelt, careful not to touch his newborn son's skin, while his mother held her arms out, begging to hold the child that she wouldn't be allowed to.

Eventually, his parents discovered that it was only Tuoni's hands that could kill, not the rest of him—but if his bare fingers did touch you, it was a fate worse than death. You weren't sent to Tuonela, instead you were sent to Oblivion, to live forever floating through black space until you went mad. Even Gods weren't immune to this fate.

Because of that, Tuoni's deathly hands had to be sheathed in gloves at all times. But even with that protection, as the years passed his brother and sister kept their distance. His mother was kind but wary. His father always busy. And so Tuoni grew up knowing he was different, and that he'd never stop feeling alone, and that it would serve him well when he became the God of Death.

And that day was today. His last memory was going to sleep the night before in his bed in his father's castle, feeling a little drunk on the frostmint liquor he stole from the kitchen, and that was it. He expected to wake up and have there be a celebration like there always was for a God's Day, perhaps a feast in the castle with his siblings, or maybe even a parade through the streets, where mortals would stare at him in fear and awe, at the one who could kill you with a touch of his finger.

Instead, he was here. A place that both seemed nowhere and everywhere. A place that was dark, dank and reeked of death, a smell he would become well accustomed to.

He was in the Caves of Vipunen, which meant he was no longer with his family in the Realm of Lintukoto. No, he was waking up in Tuonela, and he knew at once that his time as a God had officially started.

"Are you afraid?" a voice sounded from where the green light was seeping through, a voice so deep and ancient that it shook the ground and rumbled through the marrow of his bones.

"No," Tuoni managed to say. No matter what, he had to be brave. He wasn't a boy anymore. Fear belonged in the past.

"But you are in pain," the voice continued. "Your runes, they are hurting you."

"They aren't," Tuoni said, his voice sounding so small and pathetic in the dark fathoms of the yawning cavern, and he immediately was hit with another burst of pain, stinging him from the inside out.

"You will learn to live with the pain," the voice said and though it hadn't changed in volume, Tuoni had the impression that it was getting closer. "This pain is what the Creator has bestowed upon you, to remind you of your role."

"Are you the Creator?" Tuoni asked, hopeful. He wanted to meet the Creator so that he could give them a piece of his mind, ask them why he was born like he was, never to touch anyone with his hands, never to have love, even love of family, to be fated to a future he never agreed to.

"You know I am not," the voice said. "I am Antero Vipunen. And I have been waiting a long time for you to come home."

Vipunen. The name itself caused a shiver to run through Tuoni, momentarily distracting him from the pain of the burning runes. His father had told him that one day he would meet Vipunen, who possessed all the world's knowledge and magic, but that the meeting would come at a price. When he was younger, Ahto teased Tuoni that Vipunen was a giant that lived in the Caves of the Dead and that if he found you, he would swallow you whole. His sister, Ilmatar, trying to outdo her brother, told him that Vipunen was a monster that would suck the life force from you until you were shriveled and gray, and then cut you into tiny pieces, scattered like food on the surface of the underground lakes, for the giant pikes to eat.

Tuoni wasn't sure what version of this legend he was about to meet.

"Stand up," the voice commanded from the recesses. "Come into the light."

Tuoni didn't want to admit it, but he was scared to the bone. The fear would have been immobilizing, if it weren't for the fact that he thought moving might help the pain.

He got up, surprised to find himself naked, and in the dim chartreuse light, his body looked like a horror show. Not only was there torn skin and black blood from where he tore at his own flesh, but the pewter-colored runes that were tattooed on his body were pulsating, flashing and gleaming like the pewter was alive and flowing over him.

"Come closer," Vipunen said. "So that you may see what you are."

Tuoni staggered forward a few feet and then stopped cold. For a moment he had forgotten about the pain. All he could focus on was a pair of eyes in the darkness. They were lingering in the shadows beyond the arches of the cave. The eyes were at least the same size as Tuoni and Tuoni was extremely tall for his age. They were narrow, shaped like an upside down half-moon and glowed red, forty feet in the air.

Whether giant, or monster, Vipunen was impossibly large.

"You will not see me," Vipunen said. "Though I see you. But do not be afraid of me, for I am here to help, not harm you. I live in the darkness, as do you now. Whenever you need council, I will give it to you. Whenever your job requires knowledge of this world, it is my knowledge that you will seek. Whenever you need magic, I will provide the elements."

"What's happening to me?" Tuoni asked, trying to keep from scratching up his skin again as the pain pulsed beneath his tattoos.

"You are feeling the pain of every being that has died," Vipunen said from the darkness. "Going forward, every time someone dies, your runes will pulse with pain and light. It is the price you are to bear for being the God of Death. It is a reminder from the Creator of how important your role is, that it is something to be respected and revered. In time, you will learn to live with the pain and ignore it, but for now it is part of your awakening."

"This isn't going to stop?" Tuoni cried out, panic seizing his chest like a vice. He couldn't imagine a world where this pain never ended. He didn't want to live in one if that was the case. "I can't take this anymore!"

"It will stop in time," Vipunen said. "For now, you must endure. Everyone experiences pain, some more physical, some the pain of the soul. You are not exempt because you are a God. You must feel pain as well."

"I know pain!" Tuoni screamed, his hands going to his black hair, pulling sharply at the ends of it in total anguish. "I know pain of the soul! I can't touch anyone without killing them, to a fate worse than death!"

His words rang across the cave like a bell.

"We all must endure the lives we have been given," Vipunen said after a moment, his voice lowering. "The only way we can escape is through change. To change oneself is one of the bravest things one can do, and even Gods aren't born perfect. One day, perhaps, your freedom from this pain will come, if only you're brave enough, wise enough, vulnerable enough to take that risk. Until then, Tuoni, you are the God of Death, and you will wear your pain like armor."

Tuoni shook his head. All his life he was told he was a God. He was told that when he was ready, he would be the King of the Underworld, the Lord of the Dead. That it would be his responsibility to create order out of chaos, to provide an afterlife more suitable for the deceased, perhaps one that allowed for nuances and levels depending on how beings lived their lives. He did what he could to prepare himself for this role and yet now that his time had come, it terrified him. He didn't know what he was doing, no one had ever trained him. He was lost, in pain, and scared.

Perhaps he was still just a boy in the end.

"I want to see Ukko," Tuoni said, his voice a whisper.

"You will, in time," Vipunen responded. "But he has his duties as a God, and you have yours. He cannot help you here."

"Then I want to go home."

Vipunen chuckled, the sound making the cave walls shake and a few errant rocks to come loose. In the distance stalactites that hung from an unseen ceiling fell to the ground and shattered.

"You are home," Vipunen said. "Look deep within yourself and you'll feel it in your bones. You've never belonged anywhere but here. Here, in the land of the dead, where you'll revel in the shadows and befriend the monsters and become one with everything cold, frightening, and caliginous."

Tuoni looked down at his arms, at the torn flesh, at the shimmering pewter runes that snaked across him in agony. Then he closed his eyes and tried to make space for the pain, so that it wouldn't overwhelm him or control him. He imagined a dark, fathomless realm inside him, one much like the cave. He pictured the darkness spreading inside, starting at his heart and flowing into his organs and limbs, sweeping the pain to the side, filling him with strength.

"That's it," Vipunen said encouragingly. "Open yourself up. Welcome it. Take it."

Tuoni kept his eyes closed, his brow furrowed in the kind of concentration that made his muscles shake. The blackness he imagined inside him multiplied like a million shadows, until he was struck with the terrifying thought that perhaps he wasn't imagining things at all.

That's when he opened his eyes.

For a moment everything looked normal, but then the green glow grew stronger and that's when he noticed the movement on the walls of the cave, and the yellow-white eyes glowing all around him. He stared in horror as the movement took shape, and the eyes belonged to bodies. There were creatures, each four or five feet long, that looked like a combination of a human and an insect, made of flickering antennae and rattling bones, sharpened claws and those awful yellow-white eyes.

Tuoni didn't have time to speak, nor to scream.

The creatures moved faster than a blink of his eyes and in a split-second they scurried down the walls, their claws creating this ghastly screeching sound as they scampered, and then they were upon him.

Vipunen's words echoed throughout the cavern.

"Now you are darkness personified." He paused as Tuoni's scream filled the dank air. "Now you are Death."

ACKNOWLEDGEMENTS

Since my brother and father passed on within a couple of months of each other, writing for me has been very painful and very slow. I'm sure if you've read the two books I have written since then, Nightwolf and River of Shadows (oh, I do hope you read River of Shadows before this book!), then you know the story.

This book, I am happy to say, came a lot easier to me. Not at first. At first I couldn't write it. I was exhausted after River of Shadows and my muse had left me so I could focus on my self-care and mental health. I get it now. Grief is a mother. It will consume you and its okay to be consumed by it, because grief is love. So I stopped beating myself up about being "slow" and focused on just feeling my feelings and doing whatever I needed to do to be okay.

It was frustrating at first because it meant I had to push this book's release back a month. I thought, foolishly, that I could just write it fast and be done but I don't work that way anymore. The speed didn't come, the muse didn't come.

I stepped back and said, what do I need to do to make this book fun for me to write? What do I need to do to enjoy the art and process of it? These are things that you forget to focus on when you're written 70 novels over 11 years.

The answer was to take my time. Remove the deadline. I discovered I could no longer create with pressure, it wasn't letting my creativity be free. And this is the type of story where you want your brain and creative soul to be as free as possible.

Moment I did that, it came together.

And I fell in love with this book.

I hope you did too. It's enough that going forward, I'm not announcing any release dates ever again until the book is done. That way I'm writing purely on mood. No pressure, just freedom to create.

Unfortunately that will apply to Underworld Gods #3, but I know it will come this year and I'll announce more once I have it mostly written (plus a title, cover, etc). So make sure you're following me on Instagram for that!

Okay, shameless plug for my social media aside, I have a lot of people I want to thank and I know I will miss some. Laura Helseth for editing and also plotting that threesome with me while we stood in line for the Peter Pan ride at Disneyland. Chanpreet Singh for always being there, you're solid gold! Sandra, Kathleen, Anna, Kelly, Rachel, Ali, Jay, anyone who reached out to me with love for my mental health and belief in my writing.

OH, of course the gorgeous Renee Carlino for being such a fabulous cover model (and amazing person and author all around).

Hang Le for more of her special magic.

My Finnish mother for not disowning the way I've portrayed her Gods (actually they're even worse—check out Finnish mythology to get an eyeful), and for still being in my life and believing in me.

Always my biggest thanks goes to Scott and Bruce. Said it 70 times before, I'll say it 70 more, but I couldn't do this without my husband.

And even though my father Sven and my brother Kris are no longer with me, eternal thanks goes to them. I am grieving you both so much but I know that's only because I still have so much love in me to give.

ABOUT THE AUTHOR

Karina Halle, a former screenwriter, travel writer and music journalist, is the *New York Times*, *Wall Street Journal*, and *USA Today* bestselling author of *The Pact*, *A Nordic King*, and *Sins & Needles*, as well as over fifty other wild and romantic reads. She, her husband, and their adopted pit bull live in a rain forest on an island off British Columbia. In the winter, you can often find them in their condo in Los Angeles, or on their beloved island of Kauai, soaking up as much sun (and getting as much inspiration) as possible. For more information, visit

www.authorkarinahalle.com

BOOKS BY KARINA HALLE

Contemporary Romances
Love, in English
Love, in Spanish
Where Sea Meets Sky (from Atria Books)
Racing the Sun (from Atria Books)
The Pact
The Offer
The Play
Winter Wishes
The Lie
The Debt
Smut
Heat Wave
Before I Ever Met You
After All
Rocked Up
Wild Card (North Ridge #1)
Maverick (North Ridge #2)
Hot Shot (North Ridge #3)
Bad at Love
The Swedish Prince
The Wild Heir
A Nordic King
Nothing Personal
My Life in Shambles
Discretion

Disarm
Disavow
The Royal Rogue
The Forbidden Man
Lovewrecked
One Hot Italian Summer
The One That Got Away
All the Love in the World (Anthology)
Bright Midnight
The Royals Next Door

Romantic Suspense Novels by Karina Halle
Sins and Needles (The Artists Trilogy #1)
On Every Street (An Artists Trilogy Novella #0.5)
Shooting Scars (The Artists Trilogy #2)
Bold Tricks (The Artists Trilogy #3)
Dirty Angels (Dirty Angels #1)
Dirty Deeds (Dirty Angels #2)
Dirty Promises (Dirty Angels #3)
Black Hearts (Sins Duet #1)
Dirty Souls (Sins Duet #2)

Horror Romance
Darkhouse (EIT #1)
Red Fox (EIT #2)
The Benson (EIT #2.5)
Dead Sky Morning (EIT #3)
Lying Season (EIT #4)
On Demon Wings (EIT #5)

Old Blood (EIT #5.5)
The Dex-Files (EIT #5.7)
Into the Hollow (EIT #6)
And With Madness Comes the Light (EIT #6.5)
Come Alive (EIT #7)
Ashes to Ashes (EIT #8)
Dust to Dust (EIT #9)
Ghosted (EIT #9.5)
Came Back Haunted (EIT #10)
In the Fade (EIT #11)
The Devil's Duology
Donners of the Dead
Veiled (Ada Palomino #1)
Song For the Dead (Ada Palomino #2)
Black Sunshine (Dark Eyes Duet #1)
The Blood is Love (Dark Eyes Duet #2)
Nightwolf
River of Shadows (Underworld Gods #1)
God of Death (Underworld Gods #0.5)
Crown of Crimson (Underworld Gods #2)

Printed in Great Britain
by Amazon